UNWRITTEN

Alicia J. Novo

EQUINOPSYS
PUBLISHING

Equinopsys Publishing
978-1-7371791-0-8 Hardcover
978-1-7371791-1-5 Paperback
978-1-7371791-2-2 ebook
Unwritten
Copyright © 2021 Alicia J. Novo
www.alicianovo.com

Cover design by Micaela Alcaino
Interior design by Fatima Murphy Pupparo

www.equinopsys.com

To Aunt Vivi, who always believed.
May the words reach you and make you smile.
I miss you.

"That is part of the beauty of all literature. You discover that your longings are universal longings, that you're not lonely and isolated from anyone. You belong."

—F. Scott Fitzgerald

Part One

PANGEA

1

WHISPERS

The books lied to Beatrix that morning. Their whispers failed to reveal the end. Instead of warning her, when she stepped into her home library, they greeted her with commonplace chatter.

Through the paneled windows, the morning light fused the spines lining the walls into a multicolored tapestry.

"I need something for Grandpa," Beatrix told the books. Her voice soared, stretching the way it always did in this room. In response, the whispers broke into an animated debate, their voices hushed but brimming with excitement.

Their conversation surrounded her in an embrace more solid than any she'd received from her father. Not that she cared about his signs of affection anymore. But she had, years back.

Grandpa had been the only person to hug her. Less often since she'd grown up, and he'd been forced into a nursing home. Her body tensed up at the thought, the temperature in her blood rising. If she'd been eighteen—not even two full years older—she might have been able to prevent Grandpa's move. As it was, the decision had fallen to her father. The unfairness of it made her ball her hands. She had tried everything short of legal action. But she'd been prevented from taking responsibility for her grandfather. Even if she knew better than anyone how to care for him, when his meds were due, and how to calm him when he got agitated. Beatrix slid her hands in the pockets of her jeans—the feeling that she'd failed Grandpa, a weight that made everything else twice as hard. He had always been there when she'd needed him. The worst night of her life, he'd come to help. But once their roles reversed, and it became her job to look out for him, she hadn't managed to keep him home.

And last week Grandpa had been lost, his old light all but gone.

"Make it special," Beatrix told the room. "A fun story. We all need a laugh."

The library was small and sparse. Aside from an armchair weathered from hours of sitting and a red-gold rug infused with paper must, there was nothing else except for books. No paneling or drywall peeked through. From the baseboard to the twelve-foot ceiling, walls of spines. Thick, thin, gilded, and plain, they gleamed in the sun, cutting off this room from the rest of the house and opening Beatrix's life to a million worlds. Because Beatrix had learned that books made inadequate boundaries. In her library, she sat in the middle of infinity.

Her eyes fixed on the center shelf, she tapped her foot on the wooden floor. "Come on. Show me, guys."

With a swish and a rustle, followed by the rubbing of leather on wood, the books began to shift. She smiled, a bit of the old joy seeping in, as if she were still a kid and her mother had just shown her this trick. *La guitarra encantada de Sevilla* had been the first tale chosen, and even to this day, Beatrix remembered the story of the musician whose tunes traveled through Spain to the girl meant to save him. It was so long ago that Mom's presence felt discolored and insubstantial. But in the library, the nine years since her death shortened, her mother's voice growing more vivid and the memories brighter.

Around Beatrix, the light changed, the sun coalescing into a shaft of orange that highlighted a title halfway down the north shelf. With the reverence of an acolyte, she grabbed the book, its warmth transferring to her fingers, up her palm and arm. The power inside her tingled with recognition, and her skin crackled, turning yellowed and porous like paper.

Her vision blurred, the result of a shift in the invisible cloak that shielded her magic from everyone's eyes. It lasted a moment. When she opened the volume, both her magic and her skin were once again settled, the spell obscuring her power now back in place.

Beatrix scrunched her forehead. It was happening more and more—random blips in Grandfather's cloaking spell. So far, nobody had caught her during one of those lapses. The thought of her magic exposed was unbearable.

At another time, she'd have gone to him for answers. But he wasn't capable anymore. It had been a couple of years since she'd had to figure things out on her own. She'd done okay. And she would manage this as well. Who knew? He might have a good day, and they might talk about the cloak. He had moments when, for the glimpse of a few sentences, he returned to his previous self.

One more reason to visit him today.

Beatrix had just needed the perfect book for him.

She looked at the title she held. *The Importance of Being Earnest.* The hint of a smile curved her mouth. In her appreciation for stories, she was equal opportunity, but the voices of old books had a mellowness that crispy new ones could never imitate.

Old books loved her best.

They were the most stubborn too. It was a chorus of them who refused to leave her, even when their books of origin were nowhere in sight. They'd become the soundtrack of her life, those old stories, her elevator music, offering advice, wise quotes, the odd joke, and on rare occasions, a warning.

Now, as Beatrix stroked the fabric cover of the book she'd pulled out, the tale winked at her, promising a reality better than her life.

"I've never seen you before." She shook her head, hair tendrils slipping out of her hastily made bun, as she accepted the mystery that no matter how often she scanned the shelves, new stories appeared when the need arose.

"Thank you," she told the books. "Another one for my to-read list."

"Who the hell are you talking to?"

Beatrix turned, dropping the book, which hit the hardwood with an echo. Martin, her father, stood by the doorway. He never crossed the threshold, yet from the other side, his presence threatened. She picked up the story and straightened her back. The warmth this room had called forth evaporated. "What do you want?"

"*Tan loca como ella,*" Martin said, his top lip curling. "Your mother was just as crazy. Spoke to the windows, the mirrors, the paintings on the walls. *Una chiflada,* totally out of her mind. You have her eyes. I'd worry if I were you."

Inside Beatrix, the Furie stirred. Its anger, foreign and familiar, coated her mouth with rust. "Don't talk about her like that."

Martin laughed. "Or what?"

From the molten core where it lived, the monster clawed up the walls of her chest. Rage welled, a creature with its own will. Which was why

Beatrix called her magic "the monster." Grandpa, in his optimism, had dubbed it a gift. "Anger can fuel courage if you wield it. We'll name it a Furie. A bit of training, and you'll be the best of allies."

Grandpa wasn't often wrong. He had been mistaken about that.

"Like I thought." Martin sneered. "You got nothing. As worthless as ever."

Beatrix sucked in a breath. Held it. Counted down, imagining blues and soft light and lapping waves. And the droning of her grandfather's teachings calmed her. But she had to get out. Before she broke her ten-year-disaster-free streak. "Let me pass," she hissed, pushing toward the door. "I'm off to Grandpa."

This time, Martin guffawed. "Another wacko. *Dios los crea y ellos se juntan.*" He stepped aside to let Beatrix through. She snatched her phone and the car keys from a porcelain tray. Her forearms ached from the effort to rein the monster in, to avoid giving in to the desire to destroy. That impulse was the most natural and the one she struggled the most to contain. Sometimes Beatrix wondered if she fought a doomed battle. After all, how long could this rage remain caged inside a body before it broke the dam and exploded? Before she burned it all?

She grazed her father's work jacket on her way out, a pop of static electricity the perfect metaphor for their relationship.

And his words trailed after her. "Yes, run away. That's all you're good at."

Without looking back, Beatrix raced to the garage and slid into her Jeep. Arms shaking with unspent power, she folded her head over the wheel and gulped several breaths.

After a bit, she straightened and attempted to conjure the Taming Sphere, the cage for the Furie Grandpa had spent a decade teaching her to construct. But like every other time, her effort disintegrated in a spray of shimmering dust.

Beatrix took the fastest way to the nursing home in the next midsize town. No facility for her grandfather's condition existed in her hometown, a tired Midwest place named after a city halfway across the world that would be appalled rather than flattered by the association.

Three miles later and a lot calmer, she rolled the window down. The smells of the back roads wafted in. Summer had decided to crash spring's party, and the heat drew lacy shapes above the pavement ahead. The old water tower, with the inscription "Go Panthers" for the high school football team, gleamed white against the earliest sprouts of soybeans and corn. There was no mistaking the season around here. Or who planted what. Beatrix knew who owned the land, and who was on the verge of losing the farm too. And as the daughter of a respected agronomy engineer, everyone recognized her, which explained why as she drove down Main Street, heads turned in her direction and then away.

For the millionth time, she wondered why. Why did they dislike her?

It wasn't the Furie. The night he'd arrived in her life, Grandpa had cast the cloaking spell, which produced an amnesiac effect in anyone who caught her using her power—something she seldom did, other than to practice daily control exercises in the backyard.

Was it her appearance that fueled the town's despise?

In elementary school, she'd agonized over the why. Was it her "nest" of hair, like Julie had called it then in between hooting and chirping sounds? The fact that Beatrix had to hunt down "Short" jeans in the store? Or maybe her eyes—freaky, too large for her face, changeable, and anime-like?

It could be the books—not their whispers, of which people were unaware—but the tales that had been grafted onto her soul, so that story friends trailed after her in an invisible entourage.

Mrs. Elliot, the math teacher, had taken Beatrix aside once. "You don't have to show them. Hide the books. Don't make yourself a target."

By now Beatrix had stopped caring about the reasons. All she wanted was to be left alone.

Two more years. Not even that—less than seven hundred days, and she could get out of this place for good.

And go far.

Far, far away.

All her choices for colleges took her halfway across the country. One, halfway across the world. She could thank Grandpa for that too. Without the school fund he'd grown for her over the years, she might have been stuck in this town for life.

A stutter came from underneath the hood. The carburetor again. It needed work. The thought tightened her throat. Before, her grandfather would have made a game out of fixing it. The orange Jeep had been his project all along. It sounded like him too: raspy, rusted, in need of an oil change.

"You have to love things, Beatrix," he used to say. "And you have to name the things you love. See, this is Jude. She's my torque wrench, and this is Bertha, my favorite screwdriver. Next time you help me with the car, and I ask for Jude, you'll know who to get."

The ringtone from her cell jolted Beatrix back from her thoughts. She fumbled in her purse to retrieve the phone and hit Accept. Metallic and distorted, the voice of the nurse came down like Thor's hammer, and before the woman finished, Beatrix knew. Tears erupted.

The whispers hadn't warned her Grandpa would die today.

"He's not here!" Grandpa's favorite nurse intercepted Beatrix in the nursing home's lobby. "Your father ordered his body taken to the funeral home."

The words left Beatrix reeling. Her father had known. While he'd stood outside the library insulting her, insulting Mom, insulting Grandpa—all along—he'd known.

She swayed, tears pooling in her eyes. A sob escaped her. She'd been aware it would happen. That one day he'd be gone. In her bed in the dark, with the stars of the Orion belt shining through the window, she'd even acknowledged it might happen soon. His recent frailty. The reduced frequency of his episodes of rationality. He'd become quieter too. He, of the grand gestures and the dramatic proclamations, had turned inward, as if back to a cocoon.

The nurse took Beatrix's hands and drew her into a hug, and Beatrix sank into it, drenching the woman's iodine-smelling scrubs.

"Which one?" Beatrix asked, wiping her eyes and stepping back. "Where did they take him?"

"I'm not sure." The nurse shook her head. "And *they* won't tell you." With a subtlety that would have made a pickpocket proud, she signaled toward the nurses' station where several staff members pretended to be engrossed in a chart. "Privacy regulations. All I know is your father ordered an immediate cremation and for the funeral home to dispose of his ashes."

"He can't. I want to spread them. I'm his family!" Outrage made Beatrix shake, and from habit, she tightened her hold on the monster. The Furie kept quiet though, subdued as never before.

Still, her eyes burned.

There was pressure in her chest.

Pain everywhere.

"I'm sorry," the nurse said. She lifted her hands in helplessness. "I can give you a few minutes in his room if you want."

Half-dazed, Beatrix nodded and followed her to suite twenty-nine.

She was unprepared for the shock of the barren room. They had cleaned up. No coat in the rack, no slippers in the basket she'd painted for him, no books on the shelves. The bed was remade, all tight corners and starchy pillows, with a quilt folded at the foot.

"Where's everything?" Beatrix's voice came out strangled.

"Your father told us to burn it all."

Of course. Beatrix could see Martin—because she'd long ago grown out of the habit of calling him Dad—grimacing while saying it too, his mouth crooked with a disgust he'd reserved for his father-in-law.

"You didn't. Burn it, I mean."

"No. But management disposed of it. I'll give you some time alone."

Beatrix stepped into the room that had been Grandpa's for over a year. The AC rattled as always, and a whiff of his old-fashioned aftershave lingered, expanding his absence until it consumed all air.

He was gone.

And everything of his, lost too.

The closet door stood open, sanitized shelves gleaming. Even the corkboard Beatrix had set up hung plundered. The pictures of the yard, the beach, his favorite tools, and assorted art had been taken down, a few tacks clinging to the corners of torn images. She spotted several peeking out of the mesh wastebasket. Beatrix dropped to her knees, tears streaming. She rummaged in the bin to rescue a photograph of them together, and the yellowed image of a poppy that could pass for a field guide sprite.

A glimmer under the bed caught her eye. She crawled toward it, flattening herself for a better look.

Something remained after all.

Two things.

Grandpa's Tirolese hat lay atop a chest the size of a shoebox. Beatrix pulled both items out and set them on the bed, then caressed the hat's plaid weave and the feather adorning it. He had been wearing it the day she'd met him. Nine years ago, almost to the day.

And for a moment her story folded onto itself, taking her back inside the skin of her seven-year-old self. Like an enemy never vanquished, fear gripped her again. Same as that night when the monster had awoken. Worse, perhaps.

She'd been wearing colorful pajamas with Disney characters. Beatrix could still name each one, the heroes who'd kept her company at night. Like she could close her eyes and feel the million pinpricks stabbing her while she'd sat in bed, wracked in spasms. Or the throbbing in her veins, her eyes melting in their sockets.

The monster had erupted out of her hands, a discharge like a whip of nine tails, each made of lightning. White-hot and crackling, the currents arced, exploding whatever they touched, until outside her window they illuminated the night and ended a life. While it lasted, the violence of the Furie held her up, and when it was over, she'd collapsed. Crumpled by the window, she'd wailed for her mom—knowing the dead couldn't respond, and she wouldn't come. In her place, Grandpa had shown up.

He was an old man in weird clothes and a weird hat.

"Are you real?" she'd asked, because he looked like an escapee from *Heidi.*

He'd grabbed his hat and sat it on Beatrix's head. "As real as you are, little one. I'm your grandfather."

Her young brain didn't wonder where he'd come from. Instead, she told herself she'd never fear again with him around.

Whisking the memory away, Beatrix stuffed Grandpa's cap into her purse and focused on the box, her throat so knotted she struggled to breathe. She didn't recognize the chest, but it was solid cherry wood, covered in floral carvings, and waxed to show off the grain—all the signatures of her grandfather's work. Hinges suggested a lid, although the top didn't release.

"Beatrix," the nurse called from the door, and Beatrix knew she'd outstayed her welcome. She tucked the box under her arm.

"Thank you," she said on her way out. "For everything. For being there for him in the end."

"We'll miss him." The nurse's eyes shone too. "He was one of a kind. A character, for sure. But we all loved him. Those are the ones we don't forget."

Outside the nursing home, the brightness of the afternoon hit Beatrix. The world hadn't stopped; it shone sunny and hot with complete disregard for the dead. She loaded the Jeep, setting the box on the passenger seat next to the book Grandpa would never read. Then she laid his hat atop the chest, and for the short drive back, he was almost there with her.

2

MONSTER

By the time Beatrix arrived home, she'd rehearsed the exact way in which she would unload on Martin. She would get the name of the funeral home and, though too late to insist on a burial, she'd force him to allow her to scatter the ashes. Maybe she'd confront him about his hiding Grandpa's death.

But Martin wasn't there, and deprived of a target, Beatrix's rage circled her in a toxic cloud.

Anger followed her into her bedroom upstairs, and when she dropped her load on her desk, it threatened to buckle. Not because the chest was heavy—a pencil too many would have toppled that desk. She needed a new one. More like a new bedroom set. The décor was juvenile and worn, but it had been her mother who'd picked everything, and for that reason, Beatrix hesitated to change it.

Her gaze flitted to the characters Mom had painted on the walls. The blond girl sat atop her usual pile of books, the gnome tended to the same blue flower, and the toad, crown on head, stretched midhop as always. And still, somehow, they seemed at a loss too.

A truck's roar reached her from outside, and after she walked to the window to check—a neighbor, no sign of Martin—her eyes were drawn again to the chest. Five minutes of turning it this way and that, and she heard the click. The lid's mechanism hid in between a rose and a leaf. She knew Grandpa too well to be fooled by a trick like that.

The contents left her dumbfounded.

Grandpa had wrapped the interior with French-blue satin, and the coolness of the fabric breezed against her skin when she dug in. First, she pulled out a hand mirror that she recognized as the twin of her mother's silver brush. Mom had been the one person capable of taming Beatrix's curls, of helping her hate them less.

Beatrix set both the mirror and her melancholy thoughts aside and searched the box again. This time she retrieved a dull pocket watch. The lid sprang open with a clank to reveal a design of curves, astronomical signs, and a smiling moon and sun. It did not sport a single number, and neither an hour nor a minute hand. Maybe not a watch after all.

Next, she pulled out a thimble. She didn't remember ever seeing one in real life, just in movies and books. It was a dull brass, decorated with intricate loops and swirls that ended in a thistle. The bottom edge looked shaved off.

Despite the strain of the day, she smiled. Typical Grandpa. Boxes and trinkets and gadgets missing parts.

Beatrix smoothed the lining of the chest and, not expecting anything else, flinched when her fingertips caught in a pocket in the fabric. Wedged inside lay a letter.

A letter for her.

Her fingers trembled at the sight of the initials on top. She recognized them from the stamps that marked every book in her library. Dizziness gripped her. Beatrix had been seven when her mother died. The fragments of memories were a washed-out sepia. And now this.

A letter.

From Mom.

Written on cream-colored paper with a plastic texture, the letter was folded to double as an envelope, sealed with wax where the edges met.

"A message for Beatrix," read the cursive calligraphy on the front, "to be opened only after your eighteenth birthday." And next to that, in pencil, "Forbidden Lines: 3X May the words."

Although the seal was torn, Beatrix hesitated. She'd barely just turned sixteen a few weeks ago. *Close enough,* she guessed and opened it.

Inside, she could read a single line. Her mother had ended with, "Giving you all my love, always." And if Beatrix hoped for proof of her caring, she'd have to make do with that. Because above that signature line was a collection of symbols that tore her heart open with disappointment. She sucked in a breath to keep her anguish at bay and studied the letter further. Toward the bottom, it contained a hand-drawn map with no place names—only a circular symbol, atop a hill.

Her tears stained the satin of Grandpa's chest, and the letter plummeted to the desk, while the monster spiraled up.

A letter full of gibberish. That was what Mom had left her. And Grandpa had kept it from her. Beatrix felt the betrayal like ice at the back of her neck.

Numb with hurt, she began to stuff the contents back into the chest, and as she did so, the mirror glinted. Beatrix lifted it. She almost dropped it again.

Because what greeted her wasn't her familiar reflection.

Her heart fluttered, and the shaking of her hands made the image wobble while she struggled to breathe.

Who was that?

It wasn't Beatrix.

Or was it? Her eyes seemed the same, but her hair draped long and white; her face had become wrinkled and her lips thinned out. High cheekbones poked through translucent skin. Was it herself? Mom? Someone who resembled them both?

Beatrix leaned closer with a mix of fascination and dread. The lines on her face were hypnotic, and her hands were aged too, mottled and frail, with blue veins that popped. Cold fear slunk down her spine, wrapping around her chest and her stomach. She'd wanted to be older, true. Had hoped and wished for it. For Grandpa's sake—and to be able to run away. But this...

As she stared into her reflection, the sense of being cheated of her future heated Beatrix, calling the monster up. She must be seventy, eighty even. She couldn't stay like this. She had too much to do. Too many plans.

Wait.

Beatrix dropped the mirror and snatched the letter from the desk. *To be opened only after your eighteenth birthday.*

A weird calm settled on her.

She seemed old enough now, didn't she?

This time, when she unfolded the message, she tasted the rust of magic. And in a flutter of silver-blue, the symbols on the paper reorganized themselves. They twisted and danced and curled—and when they stopped, a few sentences in English stood out amidst the unintelligible writing.

Beloved Beatrix,

Before you is a riddle only you can solve.
Look to see truth where others won't.
What's denied holds power, and you wield it all.
Take Mary Brandt to the Eisid Naraid,
and we will reunite.

giving you my love, always,

Mom

A shiver went through Beatrix, and she collapsed onto her chair. When she checked her hands, they were wrinkle-free. Her body must have returned to normal. Relief mixed with awe—and confusion. She'd never experienced magic like this.

And the message nagged at her with its cryptic wording. A riddle only she could solve. Beatrix wondered how. Other than her Furie, she kept no secrets and didn't feel she held power—barely control over the monster. Of course, what struck her most was the ending. "Take Mary Brandt to the Eisid Naraid, and we will reunite."

Reunite... Reunite. With Mom...

Her chest spasmed. She wished she could work it out with Grandpa, make sense of the inexplicable as they'd done once upon a time. Before his illness.

Beatrix heard the sway of her father's voice in her mind. Telling her she was crazy too. But no, she'd seen the words transform.

Their truth resonated marrow-deep.

This letter—and its message—were real.

Beatrix held on to the paper, knuckles white.

She'd lost Grandpa. But there was a chance she could get Mom back.

The next day, still puzzled by the letter, Beatrix walked toward Franklin High School slower than usual. The red-bricked building loomed ahead, too large and too stately, the legacy of a mayor who'd overestimated the growth of this town nestled in cornfields. The school was flanked by a parking lot of pickup trucks and an occasional John Deere tractor.

Beatrix wiped the sweat from her hairline with her cuff. The heatwave hadn't budged, but the electric pulses that clawed at her scalp and cooked her body had nothing to do with the weather.

This heat came from within.

Since last night, the monster had been overexcited, and after hours researching the map and the symbols from the letter with no success, her frustration hadn't helped quiet it. The only thing she'd gleaned was that the message must contain a spell. *3X May the Words.* The phrase with the three times repetition was typical. Even Beatrix knew that. And the setup on the page reminded her of the instructions Grandpa used for charm-casting. She just had to figure out how the spell worked. And its purpose.

"Hey, freak!" yelled someone. "Heard a loser died and got excited it might be you."

Julie. Of all people.

Beatrix kept walking.

Just a few more feet to the entrance...

Too late.

It happened in fast-forward. First Julie laughed, a cackle that fired up Beatrix's chest. She spun around, sliding the letter toward her pocket at the same time—but not fast enough. Julie snatched it.

Beatrix snarled as she grabbed for the paper, the monster swirling. She almost tore it from Julie. Almost.

"What's this?" Julie stepped forward, the letter clutched in her manicured hands. "Did you get your papers? Not illegal anymore?"

I was born here, Beatrix could have blurted out. Again. But there was no point trying to reason. Instead, she charged. With honed reflexes, two guys held her back. They were Julie's usual minions: both tall, both athletic, both in her thrall.

"Give it back," Beatrix growled, shaking from rage. "Now!"

Julie ignored her and unfolded the letter. "Listen to this crap, guys. Beloved Beatrix..." She looked up, her lips in a sneer. "Really? Who says that? You couldn't be any more pathetic if you tried."

Her audience tittered, and Julie quieted them with a wave as she continued to read the letter aloud. By the time she got to the forbidden words, Beatrix had bargained with the devil for the chance to choke her.

"Awww," Julie mocked. "I get it. A love letter from your mom from the crazy house. I thought she'd killed herself so she didn't have to look at you."

Beatrix stepped on one of her captor's feet. She elbowed the other in the side. A third guy, a big lineman, dug into her forearms to imprison her. She fought him off, and in his zeal, he tore her backpack strap. The bag plummeted, spilling books.

Julie laughed, turned the letter around. "What's 'May the words'?"

"Shut up!" Beatrix said, freeing herself with a well-placed knee. There was a reason some words were forbidden. "Stop!" She might not understand the spell in the letter, but one did not mess with unknown magic.

"What? This? May the words? What does 'May the words' mean? More crazy crap. You're so embarrassing."

This time when Beatrix lunged, the lineman pushed her hard. She staggered back, fighting for balance. It was the rush of power that kept her upright, a current, foreign and dark, that shot her rage up to new heights. In a frenzy, the monster squirmed, and Beatrix shook from the need to stop Julie. Silence her. Push the words back into her mouth—and down her throat.

Beatrix could. If she wanted to.

But she shouldn't.

She didn't.

She moved not at all. She stood so still time held its breath.

"I'd tell you to go back to your people, but not even the Latino club would have you." Julie laughed, the chorus of her friends echoing her. "Just like you, your grandfather was a waste of space." She said it as if bored, with the most dismissive flick of a hand, and Beatrix's control cracked.

The Furie rose, flaming her throat and burning her pupils on its way out. Power blurred the scene away. Her skin rippled and her hair sizzled. And when the lineman tried to push her again, he released her with a yelp.

Then came a flash.

A few screams.

The patter of their feet as they ran away.

And a glimpse or two of blood.

When everything righted itself, Beatrix found herself on her back, concrete underneath her, bright sky above. She sat up and took in the scene. Franklin High's front staircase lay in ruins, split in at least three places. And she was alone. Julie and her gang had scurried away, with foggy memories and a few minutes of their lives erased. But mostly unscathed.

Beatrix bent her head back against the cement and closed her eyes.

Damn it. She hadn't even made it to first period.

Grandpa would've been disappointed.

She knew she should leave—before the cloak hiding her magic wore off. It hadn't failed. Or else Julie and her friends would have brought an army of teachers to inspect the destroyed front entrance. Instead, they'd swear the stairs were fine when they left. That was the brilliance of Grandpa's cloak. Not only could people not detect her magic, but for a short time after, they couldn't even see the results of it. They would in time. By then Beatrix would be far away, and everyone would scratch their heads wondering when and who had taken a sledgehammer to the stairs.

Beatrix scrambled to her feet and began to gather her things. They were scattered among the rubble like trash, pops of color against the grey stone.

Anger still rushed through her, a pulsating ember. Why the hell couldn't they let her be? She didn't expect to be friends. Was too old to wish on stars to have any. All she asked was to be ignored. But no. They had to push and push. Today she hadn't been able to stop herself.

When she caught sight of the letter, crumpled in a bed of petunias, she struggled not to let go again. Her rage tasted bitter, the monster at its worst.

She stuffed it in her pocket, then closed her eyes, waiting to calm down again.

Her head tilted up, she kept her lids shut, the sun on her face too warm and her cotton shirt clinging to her shoulder blades.

"Are you all right?"

Beatrix jumped back. An older boy she'd never seen before stood in front of her, a worried look on his face. She watched every detail of his expression, searching for outrage, for the obvious dismay he should be feeling if he understood the demolition around them.

She found only concern.

"I'm not sure what happened," he said with a furrowed brow. "Are you hurt?"

Beatrix released her shoulders with relief. So far, the cloak's blips had been haphazard and sporadic. It was a miracle it hadn't failed this time.

"I'm fine." Surveying the scene, she attempted to observe it through his eyes, wondering what he saw, and what he believed had happened. Not reality. At least not yet. For now, all he might notice were her belongings strewn around. But she had to get out of here fast—before truth began to pour through the magical shield as it invariably did. It was a temporary spell after all.

"All's good." She bent to collect more of her things, shoving them in the mauled backpack.

"Don't miss this one," he said, holding out a paperback. He had a playful smile, more of a half smile, as if he were reserving part of the fun for himself.

Beatrix glanced at the book he offered her, a childhood favorite she'd been rereading the previous night, and the moment she touched the cover, the whispers exploded. Usually, the choir of book-voices was gentle, offering encouragement or a bouquet of pretty words—measured even in their warnings. But now they screamed. They begged. They railed and screeched.

And the stranger noticed something. His grip firm on the book, a few expressions flickered across his face. Shock? Confusion? Curiosity? He settled on amusement and relinquished the volume, his smile widening to a grin.

"I'm William," he said. "And you are?"

"Would you call me Anne with an *e*?" As soon as the response snuck out, she froze. Why would she ever say that? How old was she? Ten? And where did it come from? She knew where. The stupid book and the wretched whispers. She wished to disappear. *Way to make a fool of yourself.*

William didn't mock, although his lips stretched so far she could have counted all his teeth. His black hair was tousled just so, in a never-heard-of-a-bad-hair-day style. "Anne of Green Gables, huh? Interesting choice. Does that mean if I poke fun at you, you'll break something over my head?"

"And I won't talk to you again." Beatrix's throat squeezed shut. *Stop it.* She was half ashamed, half impressed. Ashamed she'd made such a silly reference. Impressed that he would pick up on it. Which guy in this century would know that book?

But then, something about him seemed atypical. She could have focused on that; instead, like it did most of the time, shame won out. It brought forth disgust because, once again, she couldn't act normal. No. She had to make a childish comment in front of this guy and then double down on it. She couldn't even blame the whispers. They might put ideas in her head. Murmur suggestions. But the choice on what to heed was hers.

William bent his head left, assessing her. "Never talk to me again? I don't know about that." He spoke with a strange cadence, a foreign note so subtle you found yourself wanting to hear more, so you could catch it. "I bet you can't hold a grudge."

"Try me."

"No need. I'd rather be friends. You still haven't told me your true name." He leaned in while he said it, and not for the first time, she regretted she hadn't been called anything cool.

"It's Beatrix. Most people here use Bea, which is even worse."

"I prefer Beatrix too. Fits you better."

The bell rang.

"See you around, Beatrix."

The whispers shrieked again, insisting she call after him, but too stunned or too uneasy, she didn't react in time. She was left staring at his back, wondering if she'd get a do-over.

With a sigh, Beatrix grabbed her ruined backpack and headed to the school. But she hadn't started navigating the cracked stairs when a voice called for her.

"Wait, Beatrix!"

Beatrix pivoted to find William again. With two strides he was back at her side. This time he surveyed her with narrowed eyes, as if trying to x-ray her.

"What is it?" she asked when he kept staring at her.

William scowled—and a perfect eyebrow shot up. She'd always wished to do that. Characters in books always could, but Beatrix's eyebrows moved in concert.

"No, you didn't cast the hex," he said. "You couldn't have."

She flinched. "A hex?"

Did he mean magic? A million possibilities swirled in her mind while she studied him, searching for signs of the supernatural. Not that she was an expert. Other than her own power and the basic spells Grandpa performed, she'd never encountered other magic. William seemed a little out of place, but she picked up no telltale signs of power. Regular people didn't assume they'd been hexed, though. "Who exactly are you?"

"We were nudged," William said as if that clarified things. He ran his hand through his hair, which remained as perfect as ever after the fact. "Pushed to act recklessly. I was, at least. I said I wouldn't get close to you." A thunderhead obscured his features for less than a second. "I won't risk the curse. Must be why he hexed me." His gaze, which had kept surveying the ground around them, settled at the base of a nearby tree. "There."

"What are you talking about? Who hexed us? What for?"

But he'd already crossed the distance to the evergreen and picked something up. He returned in seconds and showed her a brittle roll of parchment.

Its heavy scent reached her. The acrid tang that lingered in the nostrils. "Magic."

"I don't know about you, but I hate being pushed." He bent his head in a semibow. "I apologize. It was nice meeting you."

So fast she didn't get to form her next question—like who he was and where he came from—William pulled a lighter from his pocket and popped it open. A green flame jumped to grab hold of the paper.

Beatrix gasped when the magic released, and as the fire licked the parchment, a shrill scream pierced the scene.

For a moment, time stopped, suspended. Then it coiled and lurched backward, on a frenzied rewind. It reversed until she found herself on her back in front of the destroyed entrance to Franklin High. Concrete underneath her, bright sky above. Power prickled on her fingertips, and the scorching pavement seared her legs through her pants. With a wince, she stood up and began gathering her belongings. Her broken backpack, all her books and her notes were scattered around—pops of color against the grey stone. But Julie and her crowd were gone, and guilt was fresh on her mind.

"Hey! You, there!"

Beatrix turned around to find an older boy she'd never met. He had the most perfect hair. And the fiercest of scowls.

"This one tripped me." The stranger held out a paperback, a childhood favorite she'd been rereading the previous night. And before Beatrix had the chance to thank him, he threw it her way.

She scrambled to catch it.

"Keep track of your stuff," he said, glaring, and walked away.

Beatrix and the Furie both agreed. What a jerk.

3

EMMA

Beatrix never made it to first period. She ended up running straight to her next class. Nobody asked questions, so she pretended nothing was wrong. Even when a lot of things were.

Now, while the physics lesson flowed over her, she played with her old Tiffany's bracelet, flipped the little heart back and forth with her finger, searching for calm. The bracelet had been Mom's. One of the few things Beatrix had inherited, and she seldom took it off. Julie had mocked it too at some point. That reminded her. Anger simmering, Beatrix retrieved the balled-up letter from her pocket and flattened it.

She felt violated. As if by yelling them, Julie had stolen the words away from her.

But like every other time, Beatrix hadn't known how to stop Julie and her friends. She didn't want to hurt them. But she didn't want to be hurt either. And between those two hid the balance she never got right.

Of course, she could have killed them. She'd wanted to. But she refused to be that. A monster. Even if inside her the violence churned, begging to be allowed out. It was red and hot and blinding, and sometimes it made Beatrix forget everything except for the rush of letting go. The rest of the time, the real her could see the Furie for what it was: a foreign, aggressive power with a hunger to destroy.

She caressed the battered letter, studying the writing in pencil again. *3X May the words.* An odd choice of phrase. Incomplete. Part of a sentence that begged for an ending. What could her mother have meant by it?

Even in Beatrix's mind, the words produced a lingering disquiet.

And things didn't improve.

For the rest of the day, no matter what she tried, Beatrix couldn't shake the uneasiness of that morning's confrontation. It lingered like a sticky residue and mixed with the drained feeling of the after-magic.

A sense of undefined dread settled within her, and however much she tried to convince herself otherwise, it wouldn't let go of her.

It all fell into place when she unlocked the door to her house after school. The air vibrated with electric tension that ran icy fingers along her spine. Up the stairs, the smell of rust wafted like incense, sickening and acrid. She rushed to her bedroom on high alert.

Only the room she entered looked nothing like the one she knew.

A tropical jungle bathed in green fog had sprouted in its stead. The floor had grown leaves, branches, and roots, while weeds the size of elephant trunks nailed the windows shut.

The silhouettes of her furniture were unrecognizable. Her desk had been struck in half by a treetop protruding from the corner wall, the night table lay sideways, suffocated under vines with black thorns, and her bedpost was warped and covered in moss. Jade fumes—blended with the wetness of decay—floated to her nose, an odor almost pungent enough to obscure the other, more familiar one. The scent of magic.

Because that much she could tell: complex, powerful sorcery lurked behind this.

"Who's there?" Beatrix said, standing at the threshold. "Show yourself."

She waited. An artificial echo made her words resonate, deforming them into the rustling of leaves. When it became clear there'd be no response, she took a step. Then another.

Toward the opposite side of the room, her comforter spilled onto the rug like a mercurial river. Waves of fog slithered across the hardwood, giving her the impression of stepping on sea-foam.

Bracing herself, she padded forward. The temperature dropped the farther she advanced, and her teeth chattered. The room breathed around her, puffs of smoke and rancid sighs, and when her foot touched the floor again—as if she'd trod on a snake pit—tendrils of green shot up and curled around her. Beatrix let out a yelp while they tightened on her shoulders and elbows, crawled up her legs and ankles, rooting her to the middle of the room. Desperate, she fought against the ties, only to feel them dig deeper, cutting the circulation at her wrists.

Her breathing escaped in gasps, while pain strangled any possible screams. A scrap of a story tickled her mind then, the whispers dropping a hint in her ears. At their urging, Beatrix eased up, relaxing her stance, and in response the bounds got slack. Another step forward and again a sharp stabbing shot through her. It released her when she stood still.

A flash reminiscent of a firebolt stunned her, and phosphorescent bars crisscrossed the room from top to bottom, shaping a giant cage. And as the walls curved in, one by one the characters her mother had chosen to decorate her bedroom transformed, leaving the walls they'd occupied throughout her child-hood. First, the doves and the swallows broke free, extending their wings and turning three-dimensional. Then the toad, the blond-haired girl, the owl, and the gnome plumped up and jumped out. In the half-light, they appeared hellish.

A scream froze the scene, a cry desperate enough to hold the rotation of the earth. Beatrix's blood sped up and her body tensed. The sound came from above, and in perfect coordination, the creatures stared upward. The fastest to reach the ceiling were the doves, which began circling, batting and shriek-ing, their pupils a nightmarish red. By the time the owl joined them, they were pecking at a suspended boot that soon after dropped next to Beatrix.

"No! You're hurting me. No more!" someone yelled.

Through the top bars, a dangling foot, dark and dainty, kicked back and forth.

"Please!" the owner of the foot begged while the doves threatened to tear the toes with their beaks. "Please, leave me be!"

For a moment, Beatrix hesitated. Semiforgotten warnings poked at the edges of her brain. For all his fun-loving ways, Grandpa had been repeti-tive about intruders and the power one gave someone by letting them in. But the crying wrenched at her heart. She couldn't bear how the birds were mangling that foot. She'd deal if there were consequences.

"Enough!" Beatrix said, pulling against the bindings that cemented her to the floorboards. "Stop it now!"

The Furie triggered. Abrupt and violent, her power rushed in. Beatrix released it without regret, and the tongues of her magic shot out, flashing in the mist like lightning. They landed in an explosion of red: crashing, cracking, breaking, and tearing, the way her Furie loved best.

"Are you quite well?"

Beatrix shook her head to dislodge the paint chips in her hair. She lay facedown on a rug, the ruins of her dresser splattered around her bedroom. Using her palm to push up, she sat and blinked several times. Drywall dust snowed across her eyelashes and clouded her vision. A figure swam before her, and it took Beatrix a moment to identify her as a young girl.

"You're not a boy," the newcomer said in a curious British accent. "He insisted you'd be a boy."

"What?" Beatrix glanced around and shrank as she took in the mess. Pieces of glass and wood littered the floor, books had fallen off the shelves, her telescope poked from underneath the bed, and the walls showed several telling scorch marks. The decorative characters, who had returned to their two-dimensional selves and proper places, seemed innocent at first sight, though a second look revealed they were worse for wear. The gnome had lost the tip of his hat, and a conspicuous hole besmirched the blond girl's apron. Only the doves shone pristine, hovering over her nightstand where a lamp dangled, hanging from its cord.

There was something new, though. Beside the window and looking ready to spring, a painted puma crouched behind two Philodendron leaves, its coat velvety black and its eyes fluorescent green. The rune from the letter marked its flank—the one from the map. A snake eating its tail. So the memory of the jungle was here to stay, and it had to do with the message. Something about the symbol niggled at her. But now was not the time to delve into that.

"Who are you?" Beatrix asked the girl instead, deeming the rune, the decorative puma, and the clutter less pressing than the new arrival. "Where did you come from?"

"A magician. You were supposed to be a magician. How can it be? Farisad tracked your magic-print."

"Who's Farisad?" Standing up, Beatrix inspected the visitor. Out of the million questions falling over each other to reach her mouth, a single one mattered. Was the stranger dangerous?

Beatrix didn't know much about protection magic. Even though Grandfather had spoken of untold peril, he'd always failed to give details, so she hadn't taken him seriously. Now she wished she'd paid more attention.

This girl didn't appear threatening. She stood, her chin tucked in, while she removed the debris from her clothes, using the tips of her fingers like tweezers to pinch the wood shavings one by one.

Every so often she assessed herself in the standing mirror, which had escaped the worst of the destruction and stood lopsided. She wore an old-fashioned dress buttoned up to her neck, with frills and ruffles and a white petticoat peeking under her maroon skirt—an outfit that would have fit in a story with brass gadgetry and zeppelins. No older than eleven or twelve, she was at least two heads shorter than Beatrix, and so light she appeared elf-like. Her hair glowed blue, short and spiked.

"Who are you?" Beatrix asked again. "Did you come because of the letter?"

Losing patience with her task, the girl patted her clothing down. "You ruined the wordhole. I can't go back now."

Beatrix decided she couldn't fear a child. "I'm Beatrix. Is your name Mary Brandt?"

The visitor gawked at her. "Never heard of such a person." She looked around. "The place's quite a wreck. You should call service to tidy it up."

Beatrix scanned the room once more, dismay catching up with her. What believable excuse could she offer for this? Martin would strangle her. Then expect her to pay for repairs. One-handed, she undid her half-falling bun and massaged her scalp.

"I'm Emma," the girl said. "I suppose I should thank you."

"No big deal. Glad I could help."

"Glad?" Emma's skin bloomed red; her arms flailed. "I wouldn't go as far as being glad! You made a hash of everything. All you had to do was tell your wards to pull back. So simple. Instead, you go and destroy my hope of returning."

"Wards?"

"Those." Emma pointed with a slim index finger to the wall. "Nasty piece of work, those doves. And don't remind me of the toad. Took you a while, but thanks for deactivating them." Her perky nose up, she studied Beatrix with a judgmental eye. When finished, she sighed, pranced toward a broken chair, and sat, folding her hands in a ladylike manner. "You're not at all what I expected. Not a very good magician for starters, exploding your Furie without restraint. If I were you, I'd revisit Altrana's first class. You didn't follow a single magic rule."

The rules of magic…

That's what it was. Beatrix glanced at the puma on the wall. She recognized the symbol on its flank now. Not because it appeared on the letter's map, but because Grandpa had used it once—when reinforcing her cloak. So her suspicions had been correct. The letter contained an enchantment. Maybe she could dig through her old notes, see if the symbol showed up somewhere. Where had the girl said she'd come from?

"Did you even try to control it?" Emma was saying while shaking her head. "Sad show if you did."

That was when the rest of the girl's statement pierced through. Inside Beatrix, the Furie rose. The visitor remembered. She'd witnessed the Furie and hadn't forgotten it. Only Grandpa could do that. Her protective cloak must have blipped again—this time in front of someone. Beatrix winced, a ball of dread making her stomach contract. Two explosions in a day. Damn it. She was undoing almost a decade of restraint and probably stretching the cloak to its breaking point.

"Pretty decent aim, I suppose," Emma went on. "So there's hope…"

Beatrix had always wanted a little sister. Now she reconsidered. "Hold on," she interrupted. "Start at the beginning. Tell me who you are. If not about the letter, why are you here?"

"You're so odd." Emma's forehead furrowed. "But that's all right. It's what I love most about books. They are about people who are different. Nobody changed the world by being like everyone else." She turned thoughtful, wistfulness oozing from her. "I'm a taelimn, of course. I hail from the Zweeshen. Where else?"

"I've never heard of this Zweeshen. What's a taelimn?"

"I'm so far from home." Emma shook her head. "Now I'll never go back. What am I going to do? What will become of me?" Her voice turned high-pitched, her hair drooped, and hiding her face in her arms, she burst into tears.

Unsure how to console her, Beatrix grabbed a tissue box from her desk. "Hey, don't cry. I'm sure it'll be okay."

"No, it won't be." Emma's sobs broke down into hiccups. "Nothing will be okay."

Beatrix waited, searching for the right words and finding nothing. Emma's weeping increased in volume, her chest heaving, and Beatrix's heart scrunched. "Come on, Emma. Whatever it is, we can fix it."

The girl looked up with eyes as pitiful as a puppy's. "You mean it? Do you promise to help me find my author?"

Beatrix hesitated. What did she mean? But Emma was sobbing once more.

"I'll try," Beatrix told her. How hard could it be to find an author in the age of the intrusive, no-privacy internet?

"Promise?" the girl insisted in between sniffs.

"I promise."

Emma let out a sigh. Huge tears streamed down her chin, spotting her blouse.

"Would you like some water?" Beatrix offered, because that's Grandpa would have done.

Emma sniffed one last time, wiping the sadness off as if the tissue were a magic eraser. "My writer insists there's nothing a cup of tea cannot make better. If you ring the bell, I'll pour."

4

EVENZAAR

"What kind of civilized household doesn't have proper teacups?" Emma wrinkled her nose, eyeing the cat-shaped mug in her hand.

Beatrix was about to tell her to count herself happy any tea existed in the house, when the cup backflipped and crashed against the wall. All three panes of the bow window burst as a tree-sized funnel swept through the bedroom, thrusting Beatrix to a corner along with a rope of twisted clothes from the closet.

"What the hell!" Beatrix screamed as her head bumped the wall.

Once again, pictures and books fell. Drywall dust swirled, and her shoebox of memories toppled, pouring old family photographs, two opaque paperweights that had belonged to Mom, her great-grandmother's mantilla, and a white feather from a bird Beatrix had tried to bury in the yard.

The turning accelerated and the room tilted, until, as if someone had pressed Stop on a remote, the rotating column of air died down. At once, all floating objects collapsed, and the quiet revealed a robed figure with a four-foot-long beard and a headdress that tempted gravity. It resembled a spiraling tower ending in a red tassel.

"Good evening, Evenzaar," Emma said with such poise that even the Queen of England would have been impressed. She moved forward with care, treading over the new wreckage without crushing anything breakable.

Beatrix straightened up. In the back of her mind, forgotten alerts began flashing. The whispers went berserk with warnings.

Things were getting alarming. First the girl and now this odd figure. It was as if her bedroom had been opened up to one and all. That stopped her short, and she shot a look at the characters on her walls. *Thank you for deactivating the wards,* Emma had said. This was a problem. If Beatrix had undone some kind of protection, she'd need to restore it. Grandpa had never mentioned it, and the pictures had been there before he'd arrived. Which meant...

"Good evening," the robed man said.

Beatrix focused on him. "Who are you? Why are you here?"

Stepping over the toppled curtain rod, he steepled his fingers. "I'm Evenzaar, the Librarian and ruler of the Zweeshen. I've been eager to make your acquaintance, Beatrix. As for the why, it's obvious, isn't it? I've come to help. Messy little room you have here, ladies." He stood the lamp on the nightstand and lifted a paper clip. "Mind if I keep this? I imagine myself a bit of a collector. Own the biggest odd-object assortment in the whole Zweeshen." Something slimy dragged after his words, showing in the way he took note of everything, cataloging each item as if for use later on.

"What's the Zweeshen?" Beatrix surveyed him, from the black robe adorned with purple threads to the long beard and the elaborate hat. She hadn't missed that he'd known her name—which was creepy. Having read enough fantasy books, she knew magical didn't always mean good.

Oh, no! He'd just taken an object of hers too. She could beat herself for that. Wasn't there some rule about it? He might now have power over her or something. "You still haven't explained what you're doing in my bedroom."

Evenzaar gave her a dismissive wave. "Yes, yes. This is nice and all. Great to meet, blah, blah, blah. We all love the intro part. I'm afraid there's little time for chitchat now. We'll get to know each other once you're safe."

"But I haven't found my author yet." Emma's mouth puckered into a pout.

"A sad business, that," the Librarian said. "It cannot be helped."

"That's not fair!" Emma shouted. "I came here to find my artisan, and I will not leave before I do. I won't. I won't," she ended in a tone that suggested she'd stomp her foot next.

"Oh, dear," the Librarian said. "Such an unfortunate penchant for melodrama."

Beatrix observed from one to the other while the whispers' warnings resounded inside her head. "Hold it. Both of you! Tell me why you're here. And about this place you come from. This, this Zweeesshen." Either they clarified things, or she was going to have to take measures. Extreme ones. The monster inside her jumped, excited at the idea.

Evenzaar aimed his gaunt face at Beatrix, narrowing his eyes. "We need to go. That's all that matters. You should have been guilded and bound years ago. Your Inaechar, your very lifeblood, is running out. I can see it from here. A shame we couldn't find you until now. Danger grows the longer you spend away from your book."

The headache that had been gnawing at the edges pushed down on Beatrix with full force. "What kind of danger? Which book?"

"Your story, naturally. Your biblioworld." He paused, his chin quivering. "Why, didn't Emma tell you? You're a taelimn, Beatrix. It's time to go home." The Librarian clucked. "Dear, dear, I've always wanted to say that. So classic."

Beatrix refused to be sidetracked. This was too important to let it go. "I'm already home. What's a taelimn?"

"What's a taelimn? Oh, my! Such ignorance stabs the soul!" The Librarian wiped his brow and, faking a summons of patience through a theatrical sigh, recited his answer in a rehearsed way that betrayed the many times he'd done it before. "Taelimns are a miracle. Taelimns are a mystery. We're the ones who teach humankind how to live. How to see through eyes not their own and learn from fates so foreign they touch their souls. We're the truth of what's told, and sung, and remembered. Some call us storyfolk, or paper-souls, the inked, or the carved. We're born of the word and are the stuff of legend, of fairy tales and adventures, of stories laced with love and horror. We are none other than the Written. And you, Beatrix, you're one of us.

"Didn't you ever wonder why stories have such a hold on you? Why you miss the people in them after the last page? Did you ask yourself why some books feel so close? Why you mourn and cry and laugh as if what happened in them were real? More real than the rest of life itself? It's because it is. We are."

Beatrix watched him with a wrinkled brow. "Taelimns are characters?"

The Librarian drew in a breath. "A bit pedestrian, don't you think? To boil down my beautiful explanation to that?"

"You can call us characters if you must," Emma said with a shrug. "But many taelimns consider that name an insult. They believe it steals the 'richness and nuance' from our reality. And wordsfolk are proud. I wouldn't go around upsetting them."

"How can I be a character and—?" Beatrix began.

"Not now," the Librarian said. "We can't delay. You will be dead soon if we don't take you away. In your state, the Zweeshen is the best place for you."

"I still don't understand why—"

Evenzaar didn't let Beatrix finish before an ornate staff materialized in his grasp. He mumbled, tapping on the floor. By the area where her window used to be, a whirling wind appeared again. This time, it wasn't a regular tornado, rather an eight-foot-tall cyclone of pages that rotated around an invisible axis, accordion-like, as if the covers of a book had been pressed together, the arched pages left to revolve untethered.

"Step closer to the pageturner," the Librarian said. "Both of you." When he marched to stand before the revolving pages, the breeze from their flapping messed with his beard and hat. He pulled an object from his robe. As the light hit the gem, it flashed red.

The pages ceased to swirl and settled on one. It was blank but for a circle of intertwined vines printed halfway up. The Librarian held out the gem to the vines, and the inky branches grew out of the paper to capture it. Like organic fingers, they gripped the jewel and receded back with it to the heart of the page. The gem blinked, and the ring of vines began to shift, expanding to shape an oval opening with a center of ochre fog.

"There we are," the Librarian said. "Go on, Emma. You know you have no choice."

With a sigh, Emma approached the pageturner. "See you soon, Beatrix," the girl said, her shoulders slumped, before stepping through and into the fog.

"You're next." Evenzaar waved, urging Beatrix forward. "Come along."

Beatrix pulled away from him. He had to be kidding. Did he really expect her to just follow him? Without knowing where, for what, and whether she would get to come back? Granted, the idea of a world of stories tempted her to her toes, the thought pumping excitement through her. The whispers—the regulars who always followed her—were joined by the many other book-voices in the room. They spoke all at the same time, in such a cacophony only their elation came through. A world of stories. It was tempting. But also unsettling. A thread of unease mingled with the curiosity and the desire to ignore caution and go for it. "I'd like to know—"

From the shadows, a voice shot out, each vowel a poisonous dart. "Where do you think you're going, Evenzaar?"

The Librarian spun around, his hat rocking from the sudden movement. A figure stood in the opposite corner, enveloped in shadows.

"It has been a while, Threshborne," Evenzaar said. "This is none of your business."

"On the contrary. Her family called on me. I've made an oath." Walking out of the dark, the newcomer pointed to Beatrix. "She'll come with me."

"You!" Beatrix recognized the jerk who'd flung her book at her that morning.

"I'm William Threshborne." With his full attention on her, his stare unsettled her, as if he were able to pull her skin back and look at her innards.

The Furie stirred, and Beatrix's irritation grew. Ember-red anger crawled along her arms. This was all monster. All frustration and raw power. The events of the day weighed on her, but instead of dragging her down, they ignited her. This guy's presence was one weird occurrence too many. "I don't care about your name. I want to know why all of you are here. Are there more people coming?"

"Young lady," Evenzaar said, "time ticks away. Let's go."

Beatrix took a step in Evenzaar's direction. "Before I consider going anywhere, I have to know—"

William grabbed her arm. "Don't even think about it." His tone overflowed with anger. "You can't follow this fool without putting up a fight. Weren't you taught to distrust strangers?"

"And what are you?"

With a wince that had him releasing her arm, William mumbled a curse. He squished his shoulders back. "I shouldn't have undone that hex," he muttered, then addressed the Librarian. "What are your plans for her?"

What hex? Beatrix wondered. Too many questions were accumulating, and the Librarian's avoidance of all of them annoyed beyond measure. When had she lost control of her *own* bedroom? These two kept on talking as if she weren't there.

"My plan is to save her," Evenzaar said. Lowering his staff, the older man rocked forward. He seemed ancient, leaning on his cane to prop himself up. His skin had become crumpled and yellowed, and his lips sloped down.

"We're taking her where she belongs. To the Zweeshen. It's distressing she's been kept hidden all this time. Council policy requires we rescue her."

William's lips shaped a sneer. "How considerate of you. A bit below your station, wouldn't you agree? I wonder if you're taking this much care with every lost taelimn. Are you certain there isn't another reason?"

Around the handle of his staff, the Librarian's knuckles whitened. "I don't need to explain myself. We're leaving now."

"You have no right to push her to cross."

"I haven't agreed to go anywhere," Beatrix said with emphasis. She refused to let some strangers discuss her and decide on her behalf.

The Librarian shrugged. "The Zweeshen is your only hope, Beatrix. You won't last here." He turned to William. "I can facilitate her passage to the Eisid Naraid. Can you do that for her?"

The name jolted Beatrix. The place from Mom's letter. "What do you know about the Eisid Naraid?"

"That he can't take you there." Evenzaar wore a satisfied sneer.

William growled. "You prefer to risk her when there is a safer choice. I won't let you. She'll come with me."

"Stop that," Beatrix burst out. "I'm right here. And I make my own choices. I haven't agreed to go with either of you."

The Librarian waved his arms in concession. "Very well. Choose. You cannot stay here. You may follow him, to some unknown destination where your Inaechar will stabilize but never recover. Or you may come with me, to the realm you're a part of. The land of stories. And, once you've recovered enough, travel farther to your mother's original world, the Eisid Naraid."

Beatrix gasped. Mom's world. So that was what the Eisid Naraid meant. She tested the name on her tongue. It tasted of secrets. *Take Mary Brandt to the Eisid Naraid, and we will reunite*, her mother had written in the letter. Was this it then? If this Zweeshen place gave her a chance to go to her mother... *Reunite. We will reunite.*

She'd only half believed it could happen. Kept a skeptical toe out of the pool rather than plunging in and hoping with a full heart. Disappointment worked that way. A bit like fire. Tended to make one too wary to risk believing. But it was tempting. Mom, of the chestnut hair and the multiple read-aloud voices, the one who'd untangled her curls and sang while cleaning, always off-key. Reunite with her?

"Do you know Mary Brandt?" Beatrix asked the Librarian. "Can you take me to her?"

The Librarian's eyes glinted. "I'm not acquainted with that person. However, the Zweeshen keeps track of every taelimn who's ever existed. If whom you search is one of us, there's no better place to find her."

"Don't," William said. "You can't trust *him*. Things aren't as straight-forward as he makes them sound. Even getting you across into the Eisid Naraid won't—"

"Let her choose!" The Librarian thumped his staff on the floor, and the room rumbled. "Your options have been spelled out. Make your decision."

Beatrix didn't take more than a couple of seconds. If there existed even a remote chance to see Mom again, if she could find this Mary, like her mother wanted, then the path was obvious. No choice at all. "I'll go with you," she told the Librarian. And the words floated and stretched.

William seemed about to protest but stopped himself. Maybe it was her face, the way her eyebrows rose and her pupils burned, or it could have been the Furie as it sprang up, curling around her arms and zinging the air, but he nodded. "If that's what you want." He addressed the Librarian. "She won't go alone."

A hint of glee snuck into Evenzaar's expression that could be mischievous or evil. "I won't guarantee your safe passage."

"I never expected you would." Striding closer, William bent down and retrieved a jacket off the back of Beatrix's overturned desk chair. "Put this on."

"Stop telling me what to do." The belligerence of the Furie tainted her words. Her fingers tingled with power.

"I only suggested it because you're shivering," William said.

And she was. But not from cold. The whispers. The monster. Her own cautioning words. Everything resounded in her brain at maximum volume. Her resolve eroded. Goosebumps rose on her skin.

"Beatrix, if you need more time—" William began, when she gave in and put the jacket on.

But she wasn't sure time would help. And she had made a choice. She picked up her backpack and stashed Grandpa's chest inside. "Let's go."

William signaled toward a path now visible through the pageturner, a winding, bluish trail that beckoned. "After you."

For a fraction of a second, the walls threatened to curve, a greenish haze leaking through the baseboards. The monster prowled, and her skin prickled. Magic, both unknown and familiar, hovered about them.

Beatrix stared the Librarian down. "Wait. How did you find me? You knew my name."

The Librarian shook his head. "You're being ignorant. Reckless. Do you suffer from migraines? Unexplained cramping? Does your skin crinkle sometimes, or turn porous and pale?"

She didn't need to respond; he read her answer on her face. "You're wasting away. We cannot linger." Evenzaar pivoted and headed for the path. "If you want to die, remain here. But it would be such a pity. You've got Goddess-touched eyes like her."

"You knew my mom?"

"Once I thought I did. No time for exposition now." With a twirl of his robe, the Librarian stepped through the pageturner and disappeared.

Beatrix hesitated no more. She breathed in, took a few steps, and plunged into the abyss.

5

AESTER

Beatrix fell, and falling was exhilarating. She gained speed as she dropped, so she had no time to fear. Her body should have broken the water below with a splash. Instead, Beatrix decelerated and stopped ten feet above, hovering over an ocean of deep turquoise.

A boulder rose up to meet her soles, water sloshing around its edges in waterfalls, but as soon as she connected with solid rock, the world turned dark. When she could see again, a foggy hallway opened before her. It smelled of leather and old books and a touch of wax.

Then a bellow rattled the scene. "This is the Test of Character. Those who wish to enter the Zweeshen must abide by its result. You have one chance. Only the worthy may pass. The rest will be fed to the Fogges."

Beatrix flinched at the last words. Even if she didn't know what the Fogges might be, serving as prey for anything sounded ominous. Evenzaar hadn't mentioned anything like this. How dangerous was this test really?

She stood alone, in a hallway that stretched into nothing. "What's the test about?"

"Everyone must pass the Test of Character," the voice said.

"Yeah, I got that. But what am I supposed to do? What is this test? And where is Emma, and the Librarian, and the other guy, William?"

"This is your test, not theirs. The Test of Character preserves the balance of the Zweeshen. Always has and always will. It will prove what motivates you and whether you're strong enough to cross through. Now, move. If you stand still, you'll never grow."

Beatrix gritted her teeth. She could see nothing ahead. Only darkness and mist. A hoot resounded in the distance, and the air grew cold—and wet. The whispers buzzed, their speech farther away than usual. "*Caminante no hay camino...*" *Hiker, there is no path. You make your way as you walk...*

They were right. Beatrix inhaled. She'd come this far, and if she needed to complete this test to get to Mom's world, then she would. With the monster grumbling inside her, she stepped forward.

The fog dispersed a bit as she walked, and around her, the air changed, the closed-up smells replaced with the fresh and cool scent of summer shade. The hallway was so narrow she could touch both walls if she stretched her arms, and her shoes scraped against the uneven stone of the floor. A dim haze pooled in intervals, pouring in from countless windows on either side.

Beatrix reached the first window and peered in, surprised at the rush of joy when she recognized the scenes unfolding on the other side of the glass. She took turns moving from one to the other, a smile taking over her face as she alternated to peek left and right. All fear was forgotten. Every concern dispelled by wonder.

Real. They were real. They were here. Clear and crisp, each vignette offered an invitation. People talked and paced, joked and cried, going about their business unaware of her watching them.

Enthralled, she stared through each of the windows, identifying most books without the need for a second glance. She knew the characters and settings too well. These were some of her favorite stories. Heroes she'd relied on. Loyal companions when everyone else turned away at the lack of coolness of a girl whose first love was Gilbert Blythe. They had given her advice, offering answers when nothing made sense, opening a world where her otherness was shared. And here they were, a mere hairbreadth away, the flimsiest of barriers between them, and with all her soul, Beatrix itched to crack the crystal and join them. Wasn't that every reader's dream? To leave their own reality behind and become part of the story world instead?

"These are windows. What you seek are doors" came the voice from beyond, far ahead where darkness reigned. "To pass, you have to choose. Once you do, you can't go back to what was."

"Do you mean return home?" Beatrix almost laughed. The idea was not only ridiculous. Here in front of her favorite books, it seemed obscene.

"Home isn't a place. Neither is what was. Death might await you on the other side, but nothing worth anything comes without a cost. Choose now—the known or beyond."

Go back? When she might have the chance to see Mom again? No way. The Librarian had insisted the answers she needed awaited in the Zweeshen. A place that lay forward, not behind her. She would discover nothing by staying home.

Whatever came, Beatrix would brave it.

She took a breath. In books, heroines lifted their chins, so she did that too. "I'll keep going."

"Then pick a story and meet your fate. Consider that what you take away, you keep for yourself. So choose wisely."

"What do you mean?"

"You can always change a story. You may decide to intervene. To make things better or worse. Every action has a cost, and it is yours to pay. Choose a tale."

Beatrix considered the stories she'd spied behind the windows in a different light. She retraced her steps, looking inside with care. The scenes had transformed, the tales in them progressing.

She stopped in front of a particular favorite. And when she pressed her hand on the glass, she was there. In the moors. The smell of heather and brine in her nose. The sharp wind on her cheeks. Both her hair and the long skirts of a day dress fluttering. The cliffs a few feet ahead.

Then she saw her.

"No, don't!" Beatrix shouted to the figure on the edge. "It's all a lie. Don't believe it." Tears glimmered on the woman's cheeks, her gaze lost and her hands on her stomach. She didn't turn. No surprise registered.

She can't hear me, Beatrix realized, feeling the solid glass under her palm. Like a lit fuse, a rectangular shape drew itself around her. A glimpse of sun showed through the jamb, and Beatrix knew the window had turned into a door—hers to cross. Now she understood what the voice meant. She could save the woman. Change the ending. If she stepped through the door and talked to her.

She almost did. Almost. At this stage in the story, Beatrix had ranted, wished for a different outcome, and yet... She thought of what had to come later but wouldn't if this weren't allowed to pass. Was stopping it her right? Would Beatrix want someone to interfere with her own story like that? Another figure appeared and the woman of the moors turned to the man. The door flickered away.

"Not Truth. Not Control," the disembodied voice from earlier said, returning Beatrix to the hallway. The window had darkened, and she felt the trace of water on her skin. She dried her face with the back of her hand. So that's how it worked. No, control wasn't her motivation; that much was certain. Truth? She wished for it. But she had too many secrets for truth to be her guiding force.

The next story was tougher. When the sultry beauty smiled at the detective, Beatrix struggled not to warn him about her future betrayal. She was all glamour and jeweled charm; he, all shadows and jaded humor. His office stank of alcohol and stale cigarette smoke. One hung from his lips, his sardonic smile a poor cover to hide all the hurt inside him. But he needed this.

"Not Cunning. Not Sacrifice," said the voice, and it startled Beatrix back to the test and the windows.

Other choices were easier. The young magician tempted by the secrets of darkness and the spells that rose the dead. His hunger made the Furie thrum but frightened her at the same time. She didn't struggle as much allowing him his mistakes, and when the door faded, she felt no regret.

"Not Power. Not Ambition."

There was a story she would have loved to share in. Not to change, but to snatch the handsome protagonist for herself. What would that mean to the heroine, though? And would the guy be faithless enough to transfer his affections? Beatrix doubted she'd want someone who would.

Some were heartbreaking, and she set one foot past the threshold before stopping herself, undecided. Especially when a single hit from her Furie would have decimated a killer that had gone on a rampage. Or a well-placed insult would have brought down a bully after a kid twice his size.

"Not Self-interest. Not Strength."

"Not Independence."

"Not Justice."

At some point, it all began to blur—the decisions, overwhelming.

"Not Passion. Not Adventure," the voice droned.

"What? Wait, that one moved too fast." But Beatrix already faced the next window.

"Not Beauty. Not Perfection."

"Not Recognition."

"Not Status."

By now, her mind floated and her body swirled with emotions, with shared experience and too much adrenaline. How could she choose one story when they all meant so much? She no longer knew what was right. What felt real. What belonged to her and what she could live with. *What you take, you keep.*

The next book she couldn't identify, and she stepped forward, eager for a closer look. The glass was smeared and dirty, so Beatrix wiped it with her cuff. It remained stubbornly opaque, and even with her eyes pressed to it, she distinguished but a blurred silhouette. Then from the other side, a hand matched hers against the glass. "Help me."

"Help me." The request resonated in Beatrix's blood, reminding her of the times she'd hoped for aid herself. She wasn't spooked. Not even startled. The fingers of whoever was on the other side matched her own.

"Help you with what? What can I do?"

"I need a story," the other said.

Like before, the door drew itself around Beatrix, and she realized she hadn't liked the idea of changing a tale. This was different. Exploring, searching, even creating felt right. A bit safer and a lot more exciting. Part determined, part compelled by the mystery, she crossed through.

But she found no one there.

Behind her, the lights from the windows died out, and a sparkling road unrolled to create a runway in front of her. The passage gone, she was outdoors again, and a darkness imbued with the smell of the woods surrounded her.

The night sky was starless, the moon hidden behind clouds tinged Prussian blue, and ahead, against a backdrop of dewy trees, she spotted a white figure.

The same gauzy fog from earlier surrounded it, and when she approached, Beatrix recognized a horse. Not exactly a horse, but a horselike creature with strange green eyes, a pewter coat crisscrossed by scars, and a tail more fit for a lion.

"I'm glad you picked me," the creature said. "While you could have traveled faster with a different choice, nothing and no one can take you further. The test unveiled your motivations, and I represent curiosity and empathy. Together they may—perhaps—lead you to wisdom." He spoke in a deep baritone, with a built-in echo that gave it a narrator's feel.

"Does that mean the test is over?" Beatrix asked, noticing a faraway note in her voice. Tiredness gripped her as an otherworldly stupor clung to her, and she struggled to detangle from it as if from a cobweb.

"Not quite. I'm Aestrer. Remember my name and use it to call me when your need is true. From today on, I'll serve as your guide."

Beatrix ran her hand through her hair and finished dismantling her messy bun. A guide. She smiled. This felt just like a book. Who hadn't wished for a mentor like heroes got all the time? "What kind of guide?"

Aestrer moved nearer, his hooves making no sound on the spongy forest floor. "A guide helps you see what you don't. And walks by your side when you're lost. Beware though—in this realm, I have a voice. In the next, you must listen with your soul. Now, cup your hands."

She did, awe and excitement bubbling up as an iridescent spiral appeared on her palm. It twirled and grew larger, gaining substance.

"My gift to you," Aestrer said. "This hollowed horn is an Alicorn. Precious and rare. It will warn you in the presence of danger. A shaving is enough to heal many ailments, and if you drink from it, your eyes will be opened to magic. Go ahead. Try it."

Aestrer led her to a spring, where Beatrix filled the horn with an oddly dense water. The liquid tasted heavy and sweet; it lingered on Beatrix's tongue. And the world became new with her borrowed sight.

It wasn't foreign. Rather, it was as if her focus had been adjusted and everything recolored with a brand-new palette. She scanned her surroundings, astounded at how many details she'd missed, and when Beatrix turned to Aestrer, she gasped. No longer a battered warhorse, he stood in majestic beauty, white mane flowing and horn shining. A unicorn. A mythical beast whose body gleamed from the inside, light pouring through his coat.

"You're a unicorn!"

"I'm a unicorn this once and just for you," Aestrer said. "I, too, am surprised by the shape you decided upon."

Beatrix walked to him. The air burst with wildlife around them, and unconsciously imitating a tapestry she'd admired once, she touched his neck. In the moonlight, her skin shimmered pale and blue. Beatrix jerked. She gaped at her hands, held them up to examine both sides, and rolled her jacket sleeves to check her forearms. Twisting lines marked them like a webbed tattoo. They curled up her arms, over her wrists, and through her fingers in a lacy filigree.

She pushed down her collar. The spirals coiled around her shoulders and neck. "I'm covered in tattoos!"

"That's the language of your world. Words that are your essence. When they shine through like this, we call them morphlines."

"That means— Is it true? Am I really a character?"

"You are half taelimn. But that's a taelimn, nonetheless." Despite his gentleness, the statement slammed into her like a jail sentence.

A character...

"Do I have this writing on my face too?"

"Morphlines show on your body alone," the unicorn said. "Your face is yours, the reflection of your choices. Only taelimns will see these, and only under a blue moon. They are infrequent and random, but we're blessed with one tonight. Are you able to make out the words?"

Beatrix studied the intertwining lines on her skin. "Not really."

"When you learn to read, you will understand yourself better. Know that some secrets you seek hide in the Zweeshen. You must uncover them before moving on. It doesn't do to run so fast we leave the answers behind."

"You know about the letter! Can you help me figure out the riddle? Is that what a guide does?"

"I'm not all-seeing and can't interfere with your path. I will help as I may. Watch for me in the dark. Now we must go. Climb up."

Aestrer knelt and, still shell-shocked, Beatrix swung her right leg over and settled on the unicorn's back. She was disappointed when instead of flying or performing another fantastical action, Aestrer galloped through the woods, carrying her to a beach.

"The Singular Door," the unicorn said, letting her dismount in front of a colossal gate flanked by two gnarled columns. "So called because the one is always many."

Beatrix understood when, on closer inspection, she found that the gigantic gate consisted of a dozen doors. Each stood behind the other, several feet apart and in a perfect line, so that from the front, they appeared as one.

But they were all different, some intricate, some plain, one made of black glass. Each had a distinctive knocker. None of them had knobs.

"This is the last part of the test," Aestrer said. "Unlike what came before, it's no longer an evaluation of your character. Step forward to be recognized by your kin."

Kin. The word alone made her warm with anticipation. Beatrix marched to the first door and knocked. On a round tablet toward the top, a carved symbol glowed for an instant before it darkened. The metal entrance disintegrated, and the entire row of domino-stacked doors slid forward until she stood in front of the next.

"Try again," Aestrer urged.

Sweat dripped down Beatrix's face as one by one the gates rejected her. Her gaze met the unicorn's before her knuckles hit the last.

This door was softwood, purple and pink. The carved circle illuminated and shone bright yellow. Beatrix smiled. Then it flickered. And went out.

"Step back!"

She had seconds to jump out of the way before a swirling funnel materialized where the doors had been.

"Welcome to the Zweeshen," the Librarian said from inside the vortex. "Took you long enough."

Part Two

NAVARSING

6

UNWRITTEN

The Zweeshen was an office. A square room, shadowed everywhere but in the center, where a set of two hard-plastic chairs stood next to each other.

"This can't be the Zweeshen." Disappointment slumped Beatrix's shoulders as she took in her drab surroundings.

"Of course not." Emma pulled on a strand of hair and stared at it as if checking for split ends. When she released it, it curled up like a blue spring. "We're behind the protective shield. Once you're approved to stay, the dust cover will lift."

Beatrix dropped her jacket on a mauve chair and sat. "I'm so glad to see you, Emma. I just hope we won't have to hang out here for long." Evenzaar had guided her through the swirling vortex and delivered her to this room with bad lighting, blurry beige walls, and spotted linoleum designed to hide the dirt. The place struck her as anticlimactic after everything else. As far from the romantic idea of books as a dentist's practice. Like bringing your long-awaited son to life and getting, instead of Pinocchio, Frankenstein.

And yet...

I'm in the land of stories, came the thought, and the whispers exploded in chatter.

She was here. In the realm of tales and characters, of magic and possibilities. A place that shouldn't exist. And there was a chance—a much bigger one than it had seemed at first—that Beatrix would see Mom again. Her heart couldn't decide whether the pressure it felt came from happiness or fear.

But something wasn't right. "Why am I in a waiting room? I thought I'd go to the Zweeshen straight away."

"Oh, they're stumped by you." Emma snickered. "The council's deciding on lodgings. Since you didn't pass the guild test, you can't be housed in their buildings."

"Wait, I didn't pass?" Beatrix's windpipe squeezed shut while the insults she fought daily to keep at bay pierced through. Her father's voice screamed the loudest, and she had to avert her eyes from the memories. They'd rejected her. She didn't belong. Not even here. She had failed...

"You didn't fail, fail. You just didn't get picked by a guild." Emma yawned, covering her mouth with a slim-fingered hand.

Beatrix lifted her head with a start. "How did you do that? I heard you in my head. Do you read minds?"

Emma had the decency to blush. "Well..." She blinked. "You heard *me?*"

"Loud and clear," Beatrix said.

"I'm not a true thought-reader. I can overhear shallow musings, like when you bite your tongue rather than speak, but I can't dig deeper unless you want to share." Emma switched to regular speech. "Did it work?"

"Yes," Beatrix said, giving the girl a smile of appreciation. "Reading thoughts, even superficial ones, is way better than a Furie."

Emma clapped her hands together. "This is marvelous. I have been hoping someone would hear me. Other than Farisad. And you can." Her face turned thoughtful. "I'd be grateful if you didn't spread it around. The guilds would insist on testing me." She wrinkled her nose in disgust.

And there came the reminder—the guilds. Beatrix had failed their test. "I won't mention it. Tell me everything about the Zweeshen. How big is it? How do we visit other books? Is *every* single character from *every* story alive?" she rattled on. Anything not to face the reality of her failure.

Emma tilted her head, inspecting Beatrix. "You're sad. You feel like me, like a book's loose leaf. It's better to accept it, I've learned. The truth hurts less than the avoidance of it."

"I'm just tired." Beatrix surveyed the place. For a moment, she thought the walls rippled, like when a stone hits water, and beyond, she recognized the silhouette of a bed. Was she so exhausted that her brain tricked her with mirages? "I'm fine."

"I am not. Not fine at all." Emma sighed. "I missed my best chance of finding my writer. Now all is lost." Her tone wasn't whiny. She appeared resigned as she paced around the room. From time to time, she played with her cameo, flipping it and stroking it, then readjusting a shoulder bag she wore across her chest. In the quiet, a clock they couldn't see ticked away.

Emma dropped her arms to her sides in a gesture that yelled defeat. "The truth is I'm not a real taelimn. Only a Draft. If my artisan never finishes my story, I will fade away... I should be grateful. It's weird enough I'm here at all. Drafts don't make it into the Zweeshen. And it has been an enjoyable time."

She sighed again, her whole body slouching.

Beatrix shifted in place. Maybe if she'd had a little sister, she'd know what to say. She stroked her bracelet, looking for the right words. They didn't come. "I'm sorry, Emma."

"Don't be. That's why I understand you. You aren't a regular taelimn either."

"I'm not sure I believe I'm a taelimn." Beatrix struggled to accept this place even existed. The sense of unreality that had accompanied her since Emma's crash in her bedroom wouldn't ebb. What did it mean anyway, to be a character?

Sitting by her side, Emma squeezed Beatrix's hand. "It will be all right. There's room for you in the Zweeshen. Evenzaar told us that while your dad is human, your mother was a taelimn."

Mom.

Mom, who'd left behind the only place in the world where Beatrix had ever felt safe: a room full of stories. The home library that still clung to her mother's scent.

It made sense.

Yet the idea that her mother might be alive was dizzying. It grabbed Beatrix with such force she couldn't let go of it. But if Mom had been in the Eisid Naraid all these years, if her death hadn't been real, then something monumental must have happened. Big enough to force her to leave. To prevent her from returning to Beatrix. Perhaps Martin had lied all along. Maybe he knew.

The questions were unending, a spiral that networked out into a web. Inside Beatrix, longing grew wings. Maybe Mom would help her understand the mysteries of her life. Why her father hated her, for instance. Or rather, as Grandpa said, "Can't find his way to his caring for you." Grandfather had always been too generous.

"You're lucky you were found," Emma said, pulling Beatrix from her thoughts. Several wisps of blue hair lay flat against Emma's forehead, and she thumbed her cameo again. "Taelimns can't live outside of their books for too long. They get sick. True free-roamers like you don't survive past ten years."

"I'm over six beyond that," Beatrix said.

"Bewildering, isn't it? Could be cause you're an Unwritten."

"What's an Unwritten?"

"Until now, a theory." Emma giggled. "An Unwritten is a taelimn without an artisan, a writer, that is. Something experts insisted couldn't exist. You're the first Unwritten ever."

The thought floated and settled on top of Beatrix, pushing down on her like Sisyphus's stone. Unwritten. Was that good or bad?

"All arranged," the Librarian announced, entering the room. "The council has approved your stay at this guesthouse."

With a turn of his wrist, the beige walls disappeared to reveal a welcoming bedroom ruled by a four-poster bed with embroidered silk coverings.

Offering a grimace, which Beatrix guessed was his attempt at a smile, Evenzaar instructed her to make herself at home. He clicked his staff, and a happy fire awoke in the fireplace. Then, robes dragging, he strode across the room to light a candle near the window.

"Rest well," he said and turned to leave.

"Wait! I have some questions," Beatrix called out. But the door clicked closed, the sound as frustrating as nails on a chalkboard. She looked toward Emma. "Rest well? How am I supposed to fall asleep now?" When she'd just arrived in the world of stories. Were they deranged?

"You should. After spending over a day on the island, I fail to understand how you aren't exhausted."

Over a day? It hadn't seemed quite that long. "I *am* tired." The minute Beatrix acknowledged it, the hours collapsed on her, as if being able to measure time made it heavier. "I'm dying to know more about the Zweeshen. I can't believe this place is real." Maybe learning more would dispel this dreamlike state where she alternated between surprise and the instinct to take the most bizarre of events in stride.

Emma watched her with the expression of a mother humoring a child. "There's time to figure it all out. The Zweeshen won't go anywhere. I, for my part, would like to retire now."

And when the girl yawned again, Beatrix saw the signs of weariness. Poor kid.

"You're right," she said, stashing away the multitude of questions that brimmed in her head.

Emma stood on tiptoes to kiss Beatrix good night before heading out, her feet dragging.

And Beatrix was left alone—slumber the furthest thing from her mind. Her blood ran fast, and excitement kept her jittery. She wished she could set out to explore right away. But it was nighttime, so instead, she studied the room, becoming familiar with the plush furnishings that, although old-fashioned, appeared comfortable and well-used. She opened a heavy wardrobe with an apple tree's carving and discovered a robe of Japanese design. Good enough to sleep in until she got something better. She also found a desk with writing supplies, the ornate letterhead worthy of a royal tale. There was no bookcase—surprising, that—and other than the orphaned whispers that were her constant companions, she heard no books.

A wry smile curved her mouth. Books tended to be omnipresent. Ever since she'd begun hearing their voices when she was six, their comments phased in and out as she entered classrooms and offices, clinics and grocery stores. Wherever people lived, there were stories. Printed words. And Beatrix heard them all.

The mystery was why some whispers had stayed for good, regardless of the distance to their books of origin.

It had simply happened.

One day, an old lady with an eye for the absurd had stuck around, accompanying Beatrix to school and back—long after she'd returned the paperback to the library. Soon, another joined. And over time, Beatrix's head had become crowded with the chatter of those stories that persisted when their volumes were out of sight.

Their commentary was mostly one-sided, like a Roman chorus of sorts.

Books were bad at proper conversation. They reminded Beatrix of a toddler—ignoring entreaties, responding to questions at whim, drawing impossible-to-follow connections, and spouting information whether relevant or not.

And now she was expected to believe she was one of them? A character herself.

The idea felt too extreme to fit inside her brain.

She walked to the window. It was dark, and the scene outside, indistinguishable, but the bluish moon reflected on the ocean not too far away, its light bouncing off the waves like glittering shards of glass.

Her drowsiness surprised her, and Beatrix recognized the truth. She didn't want to sleep for fear of waking. She couldn't handle the disappointment if she opened her eyes to find herself curled up in her armchair, a fallen book on her lap.

Her mind whirled, and when a little later she gave up and burrowed under the covers, she was still trying to grapple with the impossible: that she was a character and that she belonged in the land of stories.

The first thing Beatrix noticed when she opened her eyes the next day was the silkiness of the sheets. She owned nothing this soft back home. The mattresses—there were three stacked, and she'd needed a short set of steps to climb them—were so supple she wouldn't have felt a pea if it'd been the size of an avocado pit. The curtains of the canopied bed filtered the sun, so a gentle orange light coddled her awake.

Let yesterday be real, she wished, before her mind focused, and she located Emma sitting at the end of the bed.

"Morning!" the girl said. "Well, not truly. You missed breakfast and lunch. If we sneak into the kitchen, they might give us snacks. There's much to do."

"Mooorning." Her mouth chalky, Beatrix blinked a few times, working to shake the padded feeling of sleep.

It was not gone. It wasn't a dream.

And yet, the sense of unreality hadn't cleared away with daybreak. Despite a full night of sleep, it clung to her, the feeling that she was in an impossible place.

Willing the haze to recede, she rubbed her eyes and trained her gaze on Emma. "What did you do to your hair?"

Emma patted her pointy-ended pixie-cut. "Do you approve? I don't get to pick anyway. Since my artisan never finished my story and couldn't settle on my appearance, my hair chooses for itself. Pink hair days seem to be naughtier. You must inspire my wild side."

Beatrix's lips curled up. "I like it."

"Well, hurry up," Emma urged. "You were eager to discover the Zweeshen, weren't you?

She was.

She couldn't wait.

Beatrix kicked the blankets aside and jumped out. "Give me five minutes, and I'll be ready to conquer the Zweeshen." Maybe seeing the place would help her believe and lose this fog-like incredulity. Excitement rose in her. And with the clarity of day, other ideas pushed to the forefront. She might struggle to trust the existence of this place, but she didn't doubt Mom's letter. She couldn't waste any time before beginning to decipher it.

"Do you know where I could find the Librarian?" she said on her way to gather the clothes she'd set aside the night before. "He promised to help me find someone." Beatrix's mind kept going back to Mary. She had to be the key. After all, once found, Mary could help with the rest. Yesterday, with the shock and the novelty, Beatrix hadn't considered it; now it seemed obvious.

Emma hopped off the bed and followed her. "I think the Librarian plans to check on you. He's left instructions. I'll show you around the Navarsing University campus a bit. If you ever finish dillydallying, that is. We have an appointment."

Beatrix walked to the bathroom to remake her ponytail and wash her face. Without toiletries, she couldn't do much more. "How come this never happens in books?" she asked. "People keep on going and going without deodorant or a toothbrush, forever. One would think I'd get those same perks. What does it mean anyway, to be a taelimn?"

But Emma ignored the questions. "Are you finished?" She had reached her impatience melting point and headed for the door. "You might want to take your jacket."

Right. Judging by Emma's fur-lined coat, the heat wave hadn't followed Beatrix from home. And as soon as she put on her jacket, the weight in the pocket reminded her she still carried the Alicorn.

She shook her head at the improbability that she had a guide. A unicorn of all things. "I wonder where Aestrer went."

"Guides don't cross dimensions." Emma laid her hand on the doorknob. "I'm a Draft, didn't get a test, so I can't share any more."

And with that, Beatrix remembered an idea that had snuck up last night as her eyes were closing. "Emma, I forgot something. I need a few more minutes."

Emma sighed as if the burden of the world had settled on her dainty shoulders. "Very well. I'll wait for you in the parlor downstairs. At least they serve a lovely tea."

As soon as Emma left, Beatrix pulled the hollowed horn from her jacket. Then the letter.

The Alicorn will open your eyes to magic, Aestrer had said. And maybe, just maybe, it would work on the enchantment that kept the message hidden.

There were no water jars or bottles anywhere, so she opened the bathroom faucet straight into the horn. She grimaced, unable to imagine a less romantic solution. Real life intruded even here.

But the Alicorn worked regardless. After she'd drunk but two sips, the scene around her gained color and texture. Beatrix's gaze settled on the letter. For a second, she thought it had worked. The writing shifted. A slight blurring. Then it went back to its normal gibberish of symbols.

She tried to clear her eyes and looked again. Just underneath the verse in English she'd revealed in her bedroom, there was a set of symbols that looked different now. A faint shadow peeked from behind them as if there was writing underneath looking to poke out. Was that a *C*? An *l* maybe. And that might be a *t* in the next line.

Beatrix's heart sped up. She raced to the window, setting the letter against the glass to see better. There they were again. Fleeting characters in the softest of grey, hiding in between a few lines of unintelligible symbols.

Careful not move the message, she grabbed the complimentary paper and pen from her desk and began to write down every character. It was slow and painstaking, but after several passes, she had a readable paragraph on the sheet emblazoned with the elaborate seal of the Zweeshen:

> *Com to me dau ter; let me b your gu de.*
> *Th sta s h de the sec ets to op n the sk .*
> *Wh le dea h is chas ng your ev ry step,*
> *the cho ce is you s but not T e End.*

She wanted to laugh from both joy and surprise.

A new verse. Or most pieces of one. Beatrix filled in the likely options for the missing letters and assessed the results.

Come to me, daughter; let me be your guide.
The stars hide the secrets to open the sky.
While death is chasing your every step,
the choice is yours but not The End.

Awe and delight sped up her heart. She'd tried the Alicorn on a whim, not expecting it to work, but even though the letter itself hadn't changed, she had a new piece of the puzzle.

On the mantel, a weird hourglass gave a strident call and exploded, sending fragments of crystal and sand flying in every direction. Agape, Beatrix watched it reassemble itself a few seconds later. It underscored the realization about where she was. In a place full of magic. The world of stories. That thought expanded the smile on her lips. The Zweeshen awaited out there for her to discover it—and Emma was probably going insane at the delay.

Beatrix stashed the letter and the paper in her jacket pocket.

She left the room in high spirits. The door sealed itself behind her with a satisfying snap, her name appearing on the wood in pale green lettering.

Herein resides Beatrix Alba.

Her lips stretched farther into a grin.

Downstairs, she found Emma in the foyer, tapping her foot and raring to go. "All done," Beatrix said. "We can leave now."

Not yet, it seemed, because after two steps, they were intercepted.

Emma huffed. "We will never be off!"

William Threshborne, all good looks and fiery scowl, walked through the doorway. "Good. I hoped to catch you before you left for the Bounding. Here." With a brusque motion, he pushed a brown bundle into Beatrix's hands.

"My backpack!" Relief flooded Beatrix. She'd been avoiding the impulse to mourn Grandpa's things. "I thought it was gone."

William's mouth started to curve, but he strangled the gesture with a frown—as if he'd caught himself in a forbidden act. "I managed to grab it when it was flung up during your jump."

"Thank you," Beatrix said in her kindest tone. He might have been rude at school, but everyone had bad days, right?

His glower deepened. "Yeah. Anyway. You should have this too." When he held out a leather pouch, Beatrix grabbed it by reflex. He'd already turned to walk away by the time she untied the knot. It was her turn to frown. The pouch brimmed with gold coins reminiscent of Spanish doubloons.

Emma's grin shone sun on her face. "My, my. We'll be able to buy anything we want."

"Wait!" Beatrix said. "Come back. I won't take your money!"

William pivoted and lifted an eyebrow. "Why not?"

Did he mean apart from the obvious issues with accepting funds from a stranger and becoming in his debt? Plus, this was the world of stories. How could she be certain there wasn't a monkey-paw type of cost attached to it?

"Thank you, but no." Beatrix stepped forward and pressed the pouch back into his hands. At the slightest touch of her skin, William recoiled.

"You don't understand," he said. "The guilds won't pay for your Bounding."

"Then I won't get bound, whatever that is. No big deal."

The growl he sent her way could never pass for friendly. Maybe some people had more bad days than others. Or maybe her first impression held, and he was a jerk.

"You *have* to be bound," he said. "It's a legal requirement."

"Not just that," Emma said, warming to the subject. "If you aren't bound, you won't get access to the facilities to find this person you seek, or public transport, or passes to the cafeteria."

"Exactly," William said. "There are permits and paperwork required to survive in the Zweeshen. It all costs money." He again lifted one eyebrow. "Would you risk not accomplishing what you want because of pride?"

"It's not pride," Beatrix said. "I appreciate the offer, but—"

"Ugh! You're both impossible." Emma snatched the pouch and waved it in front of Beatrix's face. "You're not in a position to say no. We need the money. The guilds didn't leave you a welcome bag with shampoo and conditioner. What makes you think they'll spring for your legal costs? And how do you expect to dress without cash? You're begging for a makeover." To prove her point, she wrinkled her nose while taking in the dried-up mud in Beatrix's jeans and the mystery stains on her shirt. "You didn't pack clothes for this trip, did you?"

"I'll figure something out. Maybe—"

"It is not mine," William said. "If that's what worries you. It's from your uncle. You can consider it an advance on your inheritance."

"I don't have any uncles."

"You can't be sure of that, can you?" Emma said.

"If my uncle's giving me money, why is it you delivering it?" Beatrix pinned William with her stare. "Why are you even involved with my stuff?"

"I told you," William said. "I made an oath. So you'd better get used to having me around. Whether I like it or not." He followed that with a look of disgust that would have seemed arrogant if not for the squeezing of his shoulders that followed it. "But don't worry, I have to keep my distance, so I'll avoid you as much as possible."

Beatrix decided that, no, it wasn't a matter of mood. William really was an ass. And she had no interest in having him ruin her excitement of the Zweeshen.

"Don't exert yourself on my behalf. Oath or not. I'll be fine on my own."

"Not without funds," he said with a glance toward the coin bag.

"Beatrix, for goodness' sake," Emma said. "Just take it. Please." Her voice grew pitiful. "Drafts are quite poor. Accept it. If for nothing else, so that you can share."

And under the girl's pleading, Beatrix's resolve crumbled like a matchsticks model. She didn't know anything about his world after all, so it made sense to follow their advice. Even if she'd never admit that to William. "Fine. But I'll pay it back."

William inclined his head in a nod-bow and walked away so fast one might have thought Beatrix was infectious.

"Wonderful." Emma slipped her satchel's strap across her chest, grinning. "I don't have your scruples. I'll be delighted to spend your money for you."

7

JANE

Navarsing University consisted of three dozen buildings attached to each other by covered galleries and skybridges. With an abundance of turrets and spires, it spread, multiarmed and medieval-inspired, over grounds that faded into woods to the north and the ocean to the south and west.

"What's to the east?" Beatrix asked.

Leaving the guesthouse behind, Emma led them along a gravel path that circled a pond, past a grove of dogwood trees and a pergola where a head-scratching variety of flowers bloomed in midwinter.

"To the east is the Yellow Road," Emma said. "Everything of note lies along it. Right now we're heading to the Market Square in the center of campus. And before you begin barraging me with questions, we're on our way to meet people whose job's to answer everything."

"Sounds great," Beatrix said, stifling a laugh. "People I can torture with questions." After taking off her jacket, she draped it over her arm. Not cold enough to crystallize the humidity, the air had a muggy quality. "I have so many things to ask. I mean, look at this place."

"First things first." Emma strode into a walled rose garden full of roaming sculptures that were "stretching their legs," as Emma put it, and would return to their immobile work after their break. They murmured "excuse me" when they bumped Beatrix by accident, their walking clumsy from disuse.

"The priority is to get you bound. The rest can wait," Emma said as they reached the farthest edge of the extensive garden. "As of right now, you're quite vulnerable, so the sooner we get that done, the better. This way—shortcut."

Emma sounded like Grandpa with his vague warnings. "Vulnerable to what?"

The young girl lowered her voice. "Don't call evil by naming it. It's out there. No need to be anxious, though. The guilds have special means to protect their members. That's the main reason for the Bounding. On top of keeping track of taelimns and where they belong."

Beatrix thought something about that concept seemed wrong. But she kept the assessment to herself. She focused on observing everything around them, trying to take it all in. To convince herself that, indeed, she wasn't in a dream.

They sneaked through a door hidden behind wisteria and poured out onto another path, this one with purple gravel. The gardens spread out around them, terraced in picture-worthy perfection except for a few black vines that crept in between wrought-iron benches.

"To get you bound," Emma said, "we'll need Prologs." She pinched her skirt to lift the hem and skipped a couple of times. "That's where we're heading now. Prologs are the source of all wisdom around here. They will answer all your inquiries. That's their main role—to be experts who help new taelimns understand the rules." Emma sighed in a self-important way. "I didn't get Prologs. Or any kind of welcome. So I'm excited to live vicariously through you."

Beatrix laughed. Emma's joy was contagious. It reminded Beatrix of Grandpa. And if Prologs truly were that knowledgeable, they could prove a boon for her quest to decipher the letter. They might know what May the Words meant, what the map was, even how to find Mary.

Wearing a smile at that thought, Beatrix bit into a pastry from the stash they'd received in the kitchen before setting out. "These are amazing! Here. You need to try one."

Emma shook her head. "I only eat at a table."

"Come on, you can't miss this." Beatrix offered a phyllo braid with sparkling jam, holding her hand out until Emma softened and accepted the treat.

When the girl nibbled off a corner, a puff of powdered sugar scattered in the air. Her expression grew mellow. "That's why! Enchanted fare. We've got a variety of Souvenesses. They taste like your favorite memories. This one is A Lazy Summer Afternoon with a Book."

"They're beyond good." Beatrix's teeth sank into a chocolate-covered wafer

"That one's a Rhodosheart. The Pride of Your First Success. I'm so glad the Fantasy Guild has the kitchen rotation this semester!"

"Fantasy Guild? Ay!" Beatrix tripped on one of the weird vines that had slithered onto the path. Up close, they glowed like hematite, and at their touch, a thrumming woke up the monster and brought rust to her mouth. She narrowed her eyes, noticing how their tendrils stretched along paths, clawed up the sides of buildings, and twisted around the arms of statues and lanterns.

"Like I was saying," Emma continued, "there are twelve genre guilds and many subgenres. You'll have to ask the Prologs for a full listing. I pity their job with you." She grimaced but ruined the effect with a smirk.

"So everyone around is a char—taelimn," Beatrix said more to herself than to Emma.

She surveyed the scene around her. They must be. She'd spotted people in outlandish fashions, a few from bygone eras, and several with nonhuman appearance. Emma had greeted a blue-skinned woman with extra arms for legs and a man with catlike ears. There was a centaur chatting with a Narnian-sized badger, and an albino cyborg flirting with a fairy, but almost everyone ambling through the streets looked ordinary enough. Scratch that. Perhaps not the Aztec with the feathered headdress and the T-shirt that read: "Don't mess with me. I am a God."

"Everyone's a taelimn," Emma said. "Either a student, a worker, or a short-term tourist. You can't stay in the Zweeshen otherwise. One can tell which guild they belong to by their wristbands."

Now that Emma pointed it out, Beatrix noticed the thick band everyone wore around their right wrist. In several materials, colors, and styles, all they had in common were the badges that adorned them. She identified at least eight variations, although she couldn't see details from the distance. William had one too, she realized. Thick black leather. In her bedroom, she had thought it an odd adornment.

"You'll get one too," Emma said. "Once you're bound and connect to your book."

Beatrix wondered what style she'd receive, and a sunny excitement ran through her at the idea of being part of this world. Bound to her book, to all the taelimns that came before her, as Emma had explained. *It can't be. I can't be a taelimn. This is unreal.* The now-familiar mantra rang in her head, punctuating her thoughts like a metronome.

"It *is* real," Emma said, reading her mind. "You should just accept it. The wristbands are a sign of your Bounding guild. Even I have one." Emma lifted her arm to show off a thin band with a shining dragon-like design. "It's paper, mind you. Temporary. Because I'm only a Draft. But at least I'm legal." She shuddered. "If they hadn't bound me within twenty-four hours of arriving, I would have been forced to leave. And since my world isn't finished..." She drew some runes in the air before mouthing, "Devoured by the Fogges."

Beatrix's brow furrowed. It was the third time she'd heard the term. "What are the Fogges?"

"No, no." Emma shook her pink-haired head. "I will not do the Prologs' job for them. You better add that question to your list for them."

"Fair enough," Beatrix said, laughter in her voice.

Soon they reached the heart of campus, where larger buildings loomed, the crowds grew thicker, and the gravel turned into cobblestone. But even though the hedges, mature trees, and geometrical flower beds were left behind, the strange vines continued into the busy streets. The more Beatrix watched for them, the more she noticed them. Sometimes thick as branches, sometimes spider-vein thin, they curved around street signs, the legs of benches and restaurant chairs, and the Moorish arches of the clock tower, as if their black threads were knitting together the landscape. "Emma, what are those weeds?"

"Beg your pardon," someone said, and Beatrix stepped aside to let an old gentleman pass.

She was jolted as recognition struck, even though she had never seen him before. "Was that—?"

Chewing on her last bite of pastry, Emma nodded. "Yes, the incomparable Mr. Scrooge. He must have come ahead of the Monsters Ball in a few weeks. Lots of tourists around the Zweeshen this time of year for that reason. He's a huge philanthropist, organizes the Out of Print Benefit Gala every year."

Beatrix couldn't help but laugh. The thought was effervescent: she'd met her first true character. No. That wasn't right. The first one she'd read about. The experience was both more exhilarating and less life-changing than expected. Like growing up.

"He didn't look like the usual depictions." Doughier and older, in fact. How had Beatrix known him?

Emma read her mind. "If you've encountered a taelimn in a book, your souls have touched, and you'll recognize them. Did you notice the girl who gave us the Souvenesses in the kitchen? She's a famous taelimn too, a third parlor maid in *Wuthering Heights*, no less."

"I did think she looked familiar," Beatrix said.

"Oh, wonderful!" Emma picked up her pace. "We're here. See that park across the street? The Prologs will meet us beyond it."

With determined strides, they set out toward the park, Beatrix's mind spinning with the possibilities of meeting characters in real life. Halfway through the green space, she froze. A few feet to her left, under a gazebo surrounded by orange trees, a girl was pointing in her direction.

"Come on," Emma said.

But Beatrix didn't move. She stood, her cheeks pulsating with heat.

"It's her," the girl said in a tone that didn't bother to be discreet. Six friends dressed in puffy 50s swing dresses gathered around her, next to a bench that kept expanding as more people sat on it.

"Illegal trash," the girl shot with a disgust Beatrix had seen repeated on dozens of other faces. One of the girl's friends bent to mutter, and the leader dropped her head back and let out a glittering laugh.

Inside Beatrix, the Furie leapt, its tongues of fire lapping. The whispers surged in indignation.

Another group huddled to her right, staring and murmuring. The snippets of their conversation whizzed in a language she couldn't understand. Their spite was universal.

"Go back where you came from." This voice carried more vitriol and originated behind her. It belonged to an ancient man who stood by a billboard with a "You are here" arrow. "Leave! You don't deserve to be here."

"Emma, what's—?" Beatrix's question died off as someone interrupted her again.

This time, she spun around fast enough to catch an eight-foot, fox-faced woman in maroon pants spit sideways. "You shouldn't have come," she muttered before veering off to the opposite side of the street.

Even the monster yelped now, while a cannonball of memories opened a hole in Beatrix's chest. She inhaled, trying to repress a shudder.

Please, not again. Not here too.

She was scarred from the overexposure to insults like these, that weren't deadly and yet, sharp like needles, left tiny splinters under the skin that never healed. She didn't know if her exhaustion or her dismay was worse.

"*Bloody kitchen busybodies!*" Emma murmured mind to mind. "*They must have told you're an Unwritten. Up, chin up, ignore them.*" She lunged forward, and the brightly dressed girls shrank as she stuck her tongue out and mock-punched her hand. Emma scanned the scene, eyes fiery, hair orange-red, baring her teeth like a wild imp. "Nobody gets away with attacking my friends."

Beatrix's surprise replaced the self-pity.

Now she had a little-sister-friend.

With a temper.

⸻

A few hundred yards later, Emma pulled on Beatrix's sleeve. "*There!*"

A trio consisting of two girls and a tall gladiator bantered by a gate with a golden crest.

"Prologs!" Emma said, and Beatrix hurried in their direction.

One of the girls turned as they approached, straightening away from the pillar against which she'd been leaning.

"Are you Beatrix Alba?" she asked.

"Yes, hi," Beatrix said, accepting the other's solid shake.

"I'm Jane." A couple of years older than Beatrix, she wore shabby leather pants paired with military boots, a cowboy hat, and a brown trench coat—an outfit that, despite being mismatched, appeared natural on her. "And you must be Emma." A twang sneaked into Jane's speech, a hint of humor on the tip of her tongue.

Emma nodded.

"We're excited to meet you, Beatrix," the gladiator next to Jane said. He was handsome in an impossible-to-ignore way and flashed her a dazzling grin as he extended a hand. His hair was sandy, his eyes a deep blue that lured one in. "I'm Trelius, and this is Neradola." He waved to include the ethereal girl to his side. "We were just talking about how best to welcome you."

Beatrix found herself smiling at the Prologs. She'd never had anyone welcome her anywhere.

"Awesome," she said. "Emma has been telling me all about Prologs. I have like a million questions."

A look passed between Jane and Trelius.

"We expected someone younger," the pale girl called Neradola said. She was a dainty figure, with white hair and semitransparent skin.

"True," Trelius said. "I suppose that rules out an excursion to Hecater's Sirens & Sylphs Amusement Park as a welcome celebration. Perhaps cloud surfing instead?"

"Oh, cloud surfing, please," Emma said.

Jane shook her head. "Not today. We have plans."

"Soon." Neradola's voice reflected the rest of her, soft and enveloping like a breeze. Her fluid coat floated, ending in arches, like the wings of a bat. Beatrix tried not to stare too hard at her transparent skin, the way the gate behind her showed through her arm.

Emma didn't have the same compunction. "You're a ghost!"

Neradola faced the young girl with a smooth turn of the head. "Part ghost, part fey."

"And a heck of a healer is what she's failing to say." Trelius grinned. "Her race's known for bringing folks from the brink of death. But Nera's especially good."

If she could have blushed, Beatrix was certain Neradola would have.

"That's impressive," Beatrix said, meaning it. Why couldn't her power be something like that?

Emma, who'd been assessing the Prologs with a critical eye, spoke then. "I'm confused. Are you Fantasy or Historical? The sham gladiator costume is throwing me."

"I told you." Jane patted the gladiator's back. "Why would anyone think gladiators wore capes? Worst clothes to fight in. You might not believe it from his ridiculous outfit, but Trelius is a sorcerer."

"More like an all-purpose magician," Trelius said. "Sorcerer's a different level."

Beatrix wondered if he was humble or truthful.

"Even more reason to drop the Halloween costume," Jane said.

"I like it." Trelius smirked, a spark in his eye. He preened, and his magnificent breastplate shone. The shoulder medallions that secured his short red cape glinted too.

"*I can't stand people who show off,*" Emma whispered mind to mind.

"*He's being friendly,*" Beatrix responded. "*And you have to recognize he's good-looking.*"

"*Bah,*" the girl said, and even inside Beatrix's brain, she sounded like a disapproving eighty-year-old dowager.

Trelius seemed immune to anyone's judgment. "I'm Jane's worst nightmare."

"Jane despises historical inaccuracies." Neradola's voice was cool and husky. As if she were miles away and not invested in her own words.

Trelius shrugged. "Nothing about me is accurate. My artisan had no clue about real gladiators." His blond hair swooped in a wave that enhanced the shape of his brow. He looked at Beatrix. "Hint, they weren't taller than five-five. But I enjoy the outfit. Next best thing to a kilt in girls' imaginations."

Jane scoffed, and Beatrix rolled her eyes.

"We thought," Jane said, "that Trelius and Nera could handle the paperwork that can be done without you, Beatrix, while we complete your Bounding. What do you think?"

Beatrix thought that she'd love to understand more about what the Bounding entailed. And what being a character meant. But there was clearly a plan, and with as little as she understood, it seemed fair to follow the experts. "Sounds good."

"Perfect." Jane grinned.

"There's one thing," Beatrix said. "I get I have to complete this Bounding before anything else, but I was hoping to speak with the Librarian. He promised to help me with something." As much as she wanted to explore the Zweeshen, she couldn't afford to get too distracted. She had a mission. And it started with looking for Mary Brandt.

"I'll add an audience request with Evenzaar to your miles of paperwork," Trelius said. "No other way to see him unless he summons you."

"That would be great." Beatrix would not let Evenzaar wiggle out of his commitment to her. She beamed at Trelius. "Is there a lot of red tape?"

"The usual," Neradola said in her soft way.

Trelius stared at the ghost as if she were mad. "There will be a pile of forms taller than you before we're done. One thing the Zweeshen doesn't lack is documentation. Everything's written somewhere. My fake Roman ancestors would be proud."

"If it's so much work, I can do it myself." Beatrix definitely didn't want to be a burden.

Jane laughed. "He's messing with you."

Trelius winked. "We're happy to help. It won't take us long."

"It will if you don't leave." Jane pushed on him. "Go away already. You have your task."

With a casual wave, he sauntered off.

Neradola lingered a few moments longer, her gaze fixed on Beatrix. "You'll find me at the Navarsing Greenhouses," she muttered before following the gladiator.

Beatrix wasn't sure if that constituted an invitation or just a piece of information. Neradola made her uneasy. Maybe because of the way her voice swooshed—as if carried by mysteries.

Jane turned to Emma and Beatrix. "We'd better be on our way." She tried to soften the message, all smiles and enticing black beauty, but the tempered steel in her tone shone through.

"How long have you been a Prolog?" Beatrix asked as they walked.

Jane's hesitation might have been infinitesimal, but Emma caught it.

"Just a moment." Emma stopped, the suspicion in her words unmistakable. "I didn't see a striped badge." She lifted Jane's coat cuff and revealed her wrist. "You aren't a Prolog!"

Beatrix looked at the exposed band. It had a plain design in gold against a cream background that she hadn't yet seen.

"No, I'm not a Prolog." Jane took off her hat and looked to Beatrix with apology. "I didn't mean to deceive you."

Beatrix scowled. Emma and she might have assumed, but Jane hadn't corrected them. Some people believed omitting information was not the same as lying. Beatrix disagreed.

"You could have told me," she said. There were enough people in Beatrix's life who played fast and loose with the truth.

Jane shifted on her feet. "I'm sorry. But I *can* assist in taking care of the official items and provide any information you need."

"Out of the question." Emma's face twisted in anger. Her muscles must be extra flexible because they warped like a contortionist's, creating grimaces impossible to ignore.

"William asked me to help," Jane added, as if that changed things.

It did.

Beatrix stiffened at the mention of his name. Butting in again. Why did he insist on getting involved? Hadn't he said he'd keep his distance? Now he was sending people to her. It was too much. The monster agreed with a flare of annoyance.

"I appreciate your offer, Jane," Beatrix said. "But I told him I don't need his help." He had left no question as to his distaste for her, and there were bound to be lots of more interesting people in the Zweeshen. Even if, for the briefest of seconds, she'd wondered about his story and had considered him intriguing enough to get to know better. He'd ruined that quick enough.

Jane played with the brim of her hat. "I'm not just here because of William. I think you deserve assistance in getting settled in. Unwritten or not."

Emma exploded. "They're not coming, are they? The welcoming Prologs. Those dirty periods. Nasty splices." She grumbled more curses while she shaped smoky symbols in the air with her finger. "Guild titterets! Their ink be clumped. Beatrix needs an expert to explain everything. She's entitled to a welcome. Every taelimn gets one."

"It's okay, Emma. Let it go." Endearing as the girl's attempt to defend her might be, Beatrix preferred she wouldn't. She'd rather not advertise all that made her different. Because, clearly, she had failed another adequacy test. However the business with the Prologs was supposed to work, it wasn't happening for her.

"Give me a chance, Emma," Jane said. "While I'm no trained expert, I was an archeologist, and I've spent quite some time traveling the Zweeshen. Bet I know a trick or two those Prologs have never heard of." With a smooth flourish, Jane folded Emma's hand into a fist, and when the girl opened it, a silvery butterfly flew away.

Emma squealed. "A magicless mirage! Teach me."

Over the young girl's head, Beatrix and Jane shared a smile. Jane had a wide mouth, and the barest curl of her lips gave her a teasing expression.

"We can practice the basics on the way back," Jane said. A shrill alarm sounded then, and she retrieved a hexagonal crystal from her trench. A foul curse escaped her when she peered at it. "Damn it. I knew they'd try something like this. They've moved up your Bounding appointment, Beatrix. By law, they cannot be rescheduled if missed. We have to run."

8

OFFICERS

Bent forward, hands on knees, Beatrix struggled to take in air through the pain in her side. Blood throbbed in her ears, and her lungs were on fire. But they'd made it.

At least Jane smiled when she checked her watch, not a drop of sweat anywhere despite the brutal combination of marching and trotting she'd subjected them to.

They'd reached the Market Square, a cobblestoned plaza around which the guild headquarters stood, each mansion-sized building competing for attention in their genre's architectural style. The fountain in the middle would have fit in… Beatrix searched her memory. Not Lilliput, the other.

"*Brobdingnag*," Emma supplied mind to mind. "*The world of the giants.*"

"Don't let up now," Jane urged, crossing the square with the speed of a gazelle while both Beatrix and Emma dragged behind her.

"Here we are." Jane pushed the double door of the tallest building, the All Guilds Zweeshen Bureau, a renaissance palazzo stolen out of a sixteenth-century play.

"The Bounding's a magical process. You'll become connected to your book, join the taelimns in your biblioworld who've been bound before you," Jane had explained on the way.

Now that they'd reached the Bureau, Beatrix felt overcome, not quite with trepidation, but with a sense of expectation tinged with it. She'd barely had time to get used to the idea that she was part character—and had no clue what "connecting" to her biblioworld meant. Everyone insisted it was important, though.

Straightening her back, Beatrix stepped through the threshold.

In full contrast to the romantic exterior, the lobby of the All Guilds Bureau had been painted in shades of grey and stripped of all historical flavor.

It was crowded. Countless name-tagged officials filled the hall, and she watched them with interest, trying to determine what they were doing with little success. Many hunkered behind heavy desks, gazing into screens and holograms. Others scratched away at stone tablets or typed on notepads, while several more read from immense books set on pedestals all around the hall.

Books. Beatrix listened, her ears perked and her mind eager. What would the books of this world have to say? But she heard nothing. The realization drenched her in cold.

She hadn't expected that. This silence was different. Eerie with the holes of what should be. Because the whispers were gone.

Not her ever-present entourage. Those remained with her. A bit quieter, subdued in their chatter and more distant, but present. But the others had disappeared. The ones she heard whenever books were around. The new voices that came in and out as she went into offices, stores, garage sales, and libraries.

In this world full of stories, Beatrix could no longer hear the voices of books. She was on her own.

The loss felt visceral. Almost too big to handle, and she stored it away to mourn in the quiet of her bedroom. Right now, she had a task to accomplish.

"Is it okay if I do the talking?" Jane asked her. "Prologs usually do that."

"Of course," Beatrix said, proud to sound normal.

Jane gave her one of her generous smiles. "Let me figure out who can help us."

And while Beatrix scanned the room, the magical and nonmagical mixing, she thought that perhaps everything would work out.

A few minutes later, she'd changed her mind. The weight of prescience slammed into her. Chin up, she told herself, repeating Emma's encouragement.

Because as soon as she noticed the segregated workstations with guild banners, the dozens of taelimns dressed in their genre's garb and badges, she knew. No surprise registered for Beatrix when Jane gesticulated and argued with the receptionist, when she asked to see a supervisor and invoked the name of the Librarian. It was to no avail.

"Let's get out of here." Beatrix felt double the embarrassment when her voice came out desperate.

"We have an appointment," Jane said, determination setting her jaw. "It's a binding contract. There, they've called our number."

Crossing the checkered floor, they approached a monitor blinking with the number 388.

Behind a rococo desk sat a woman in a pompadour wig. A neon sign flashed overhead: *Information, Taelimn Services, Rules & Regulations.*

"The receptionist has already explained," the woman began.

As Jane sank into a heated discussion, Beatrix felt tempted to join in, then decided there was no point.

"It's unnatural. An aberration. I can't possibly... Unwritten, you understand... And that world... I cannot," the powdered face was saying. "No guild, no induction. Those are the rules. You, girl," she called to Beatrix, "read it yourself." She pointed her forefinger with shimmery pink polish to the middle of the room, where a large scroll hung from the ceiling, unrolling across the floor and down a set of stairs at the back. "Page post to desk forty-four!"

An orange origami crane detached itself from the parchment and fluttered toward Beatrix with a low hum.

"Go on. I don't have all day," the official said.

Beatrix caught the bird and unfolded the paper to read. *All Boundings shall be completed by the Guild Bounding Officers of the All Guilds Zweeshen Bureau. No other authority shall be permitted to perform Boundings.*

For rules regarding taelimns of prebound and Rogue-bound books, see section 1035, article 22.

Beatrix shrugged, using every bit of practice she'd developed as Martin's daughter to hide her true feelings. "I get it. Only the guilds can bound me. So we'll skip the Bounding. I have other things to do." She released the paper, which folded itself and flew away. After all, she'd come to the Zweeshen with a purpose. And whether she could complete this legal stuff or not, she was determined to fulfill that. She'd find Mary and decipher Mom's message with or without this woman's approval. Beatrix stepped back. Wasting more time accomplished nothing. They could keep their wristband. "I really don't care to be bound."

Hands in the air, the woman gaped at her. The oversize beauty patch next to her mouth trembled. "Section two-thirty-five, article eight, addendum five," she recited. "Every taelimn *must* be bound into the Grand Codex by either transitive induction or individual induction. Taelimns who are not, or cannot, be bound shall not be allowed to remain in the Zweeshen and will be banned from traveling into other biblioworlds." She bobbed her head, and her wig rocked. "Free agents won't be tolerated. You cannot stay in the Zweeshen unless you're bound. You cannot be bound without a guild. I'll have to report you!"

"You do that," Beatrix snapped. Her Furie stirred, but she clamped it down. Next to her, Jane's until-now easygoing demeanor turned menacing.

The official shrank a bit, though her mouth pleated with dogmatic determination. "No guild, no Bounding. No Bounding, she gets deported."

For a second, Beatrix thought Jane might turn violent. Her hands tightened to fists at the sides of her hips. She must've reconsidered because, putting her hat back on, she retreated.

They were escorted out to the street.

"Unsightly ink splatters," Emma said, her expression downtrodden.

Jane did her best to hide her frustration. She pulled out a glass hexagon and blew on it, fogging it with her breath. "Give me a minute."

The Furie paced inside Beatrix, and she had to devote most of her energy to calm it. In an obvious ploy to distract her, Emma began pointing out the guild buildings. Beatrix tried to keep track, while her heart ached, and her eyes followed the black vines that tattooed each mansion, creating the illusion the structures had sprouted from the ground.

"Inkthreads," Emma explained with her usual perceptiveness. "The fingers of the Fogges. The reminder we're one step removed from a thought."

"I'm sorry, Beatrix." Jane joined them, dropping the transparent communication device back into her trench. "This is ridiculous. William will speak to the Librarian."

Beatrix shook her head. "I'd rather he didn't. This has nothing to do with him. I have several things to discuss with the Librarian anyway, so I can tell him myself. Could we just forget about the Bounding?" She'd much rather focus on locating Mary. By now, Beatrix's dejection was shifting into anger. She didn't want to try again. Or beg. She preferred to move on to what she had to do. And to leave the pit of pain inside her nice and undisturbed. She'd barely gotten here, and already she was facing the same familiar issues from Earth. Why did it have to be so hard? Why couldn't it work out the same as for everyone else just this once?

"Miss Alba?" The voice sounded metallic, like a call center recording, and Beatrix pivoted to find two boulder-sized men with military fatigues and dead eyes. "Beatrix Alba?"

"Yes…"

Before she had a chance to react, the soldiers grabbed both her arms and, using them as leverage, flipped her around. They slammed her against the Bureau's fluted column, and Beatrix's head smashed on the plaster. Warmth trailed down her right cheek, and the monster growled. Like lava, power erupted from her belly and rose up to her throat while the men recited unintelligible words. Emma screamed, and Jane assumed a battle posture. Then the blow of a cudgel exploded her forehead in pain, and Beatrix caved under the sense of vertigo, falling to her knees, hands trapped behind her back.

"You can't do this," Emma shouted, her hair a Medusa of snakes. "You have no right to arrest her."

"She's under the Librarian's protection," Jane said. "Her deportation's unlawful."

The words reached Beatrix from afar. Their figures were undefined, as if from the wrong side of a dirty glass. Her ears rang with a piercing frequency, and the Furie jumped. Metal reached her tongue, and her body pulsated, the monster's magic hovering above her skin. So when the soldier grabbed her elbow to pull her up, his hands caught fire. The man released her with a scream and a swing of his baton that met her across the stomach.

Under Beatrix, the ground gave way and she wobbled but managed to meet the officer's eyes. "Release me." Her voice came out all wrong, doubled and echoing.

"Goddess-touched eyes," his partner said in a whisper, and with the press of a button on his lapel, he vanished the ties that kept her prisoner.

By then, several Bureau officials had congregated around them; tourists stretched their necks in curiosity; students poked their heads from the guild buildings and groups of gesticulating foreign-speaking people sent Beatrix critical stares. She cringed at how much attention they'd attracted. She saw

William heading this way too, his long strides eating the distance from the Fantasy Guild tower. She winced at the sight. Why was he here, appraising her with that impenetrable gaze? She held it, refusing to back down and let him win the staring contest. But she hated how his observing made her feel. Exposed and unsettled.

Right now, he looked mad. Worried too, perhaps. Which seemed odd. And with reluctance, she wondered why. Who was he really?

Her attention was torn away as the rococo lady who had handled the Bounding appointment clicked-clacked out the door on her pink heels. Her wig teetering, she crumpled her mouth. "You! You filth! Outsider trash! How dare you! Those are officers! This is an outrage. It will be reported. It'll be escalated. You will be removed!"

Beatrix's rage rose back up, the monster attack-ready once more.

"Knock yourself out," Beatrix said, as with a tug, William pulled her away—before her Furie exploded again.

9

FOGGES

There's a superstition in the Zweeshen that runs deep in the inky blood of taelimns. A belief so stubborn no rational argument can put it to rest. Nobody knows where it came from or whether it's based on any truth at all. And yet, every day at dusk, in thousands of worlds across thousands of lands, taelimns light a candle to scare away the spirits of the Fogges.

They say that the Fogges are alive, full of hungry, unformed thoughts and discarded stories. That envious Drafts lurk in the dark, ready to steal themselves into life. Some whisper, too, that those who betray the laws of balance become vulnerable to the mists, and that at night—at the time before dawn, when the veil is thinnest—the Fogges slither onto the Zweeshen to prey on those traitors and take over their souls.

Beatrix lifted her eyes from *Tome III on the Essential Knowledge & History of the Zweeshen*, which someone had left behind in her turret room. A spiraled candle had burnt by the window when she'd returned to the guesthouse. After reading the book, she now knew it for what it was: a Fogges candle. Who had lit it for her? Not anyone with connections to the Bounding Bureau, that was for certain. Beatrix winced at the memories from earlier that afternoon.

When she touched the bandage around her head, her initial wince turned into a frown. More proof about the disappointing nature of this place. She didn't doubt its reality anymore. But whatever she would have imagined if she'd known the world of stories existed, it wouldn't have been this. To her, books were at times comforting, often exciting, always full of wonder. Filled with people one wished to meet. With adventures to partake in. But unlike the books she loved, the Zweeshen felt familiar in an all-too-human way. Flawed like the real world. With a lack of altruism or heroics, and little magic to make up for it.

As if to belie her thoughts, one of the pesky vines overhanging the window frame moved. Perhaps a trick of the light. This vine was thorny and thin, shining blue-black. And when Beatrix touched it, it shied away like an anemone. Its contact filled her with a longing so intense she swayed from vertigo. The need for more, where the more was indefinable, grabbed her. Familiar magic swirled, mixing with something else, deep and unfathomable, older than anything she knew, but that her soul recognized all the same. Her body attuned itself to a heavy power that smelled of moss and ink, rather than her Furie's rust. Without thinking, she reached out again. This time the vines wrapped around her wrist with the strength of an Amazonian liana and held on. They grew and looped around her fingers, pushing them into her fist. A sound, more song than words, reached her mind.

"Unwritten," it murmured, "may the words keep you safe." As soon as it came the singing went away; the vines fell off and slunk out the window. Her blood hummed with the same earthy power as the inkthreads and spooked Beatrix with the yearning it lodged inside her heart.

May the words... The phrase in the letter. Was that the rest of the sentence Mom had left unfinished? *May the words keep you safe.* It seemed an innocuous well-wishing, and yet... The buzz of danger in the cold room challenged that conclusion.

Her head throbbed, and she shivered despite her long-sleeved shirt.

"Are you feeling better?" Emma's voice came from the door. The girl pushed it to slip in. She went to check the hourglass on the mantel, which Beatrix had inspected earlier. It had four labyrinthine chambers through which emerald sands looped back and forth. "The time's up. You should be like new."

"I feel perfect," Beatrix said, undoing the bandage and dropping it on her desk. She watched herself in the age-spotted mirror by the wardrobe. There was no sign of the gash in her temple or the marks on her arms, and after turning left and right without pain, she assumed her broken rib had mended too. "I don't have a single bruise. That healing cream of Neradola's did wonders. Amazing magic."

As soon as they'd arrived at the guesthouse after the episode at the Bureau, William and Jane had called the ghost. Neradola had shown up with Trelius in tow and quickly gotten to work. While William scowled in the corner by the fireplace, mumbling about the excesses of the council and the guilds, the gladiator tried to distract Beatrix. She appreciated the effort but would prefer to keep quiet. Her bedroom felt too crowded, and the shock from the altercation had left her off-balance.

The second Neradola completed her exam, William had walked over to Beatrix. His frown was deeper than ever. "What were you thinking?"

Beatrix's hackles rose at the question. "I don't know what you mean. They tried to arrest me."

His voice rolled out like the growl of a beast. "The officers are allowed to kill. You don't fight them. You stay away from them. It's not as if you had Inaechar to spare that you can afford to waste magic."

"Nobody asked you. I didn't need your help. I did fine." The Furie, exhausted as it was, nevertheless made an effort to jump up. "I thought you were going to avoid me."

"I would if you stopped getting in trouble."

"What I do is my problem."

"William, Trelius," Neradola had called then. "If you would leave now. I will wrap Beatrix's cracked rib."

Now Beatrix touched the side of her forehead in amazement. Neradola's ointment had fixed all her injuries, so there remained no evidence of the confrontation with the Bureau's officers.

Her memories were a different matter. The pain when her head had hit the column. The snap of the baton against her chest. The fear while she gasped, thinking she might not breathe again. She'd never experienced anything like that. Even Julie and her friends contented themselves with cutting her things, once or twice keying her Jeep. But a bad shove was as far as they came in terms of true violence. This had been different. She wondered if she'd ever look at a uniform the same way, without seeing it come for her.

"Neradola's salve wasn't magic," Emma said. "Tissue regeneration science. I heard William got you the latest bio-tech stuff from the sci-fi labs. Who knows how, since it's close to impossible to find. Don't frown. You need all the help you can get regardless of the origin. Nera shared she and William met during their Introduction to the Zweeshen. That's the one mandatory class taelimns attend at their guild after Bounding. And Jane has known him forever. If they both like him so much, he can't be all bad."

"Maybe he's not a jerk to them. I don't get why he's even around. You heard him tell me he would keep his distance."

"Not what he said." Emma hooked a purple strand behind her ear. "He explained he *had* to keep away. It isn't the same."

Beatrix didn't see a difference. She wanted neither his assistance nor his meddling—but she struggled to explain why he bothered her so much. A skin thing, probably. Whenever she interacted with him, it took all of two minutes for her to become violently annoyed. Maybe because he seemed both absent and in the middle of everything, often aware of what was going on in advance while she still struggled to catch up. Case in point: this salve business.

Emma scanned the room and wrinkled her nose. "Smells like a grave in here. And your Fogges candle's out." She retrieved a waxed lighting stick from a dish and bent to borrow fire from the salamander that made its nest in the fireplace. The creature stretched into a joyful flame, pouring out violet and green plumes that twisted in pirouettes and shaped mythical animals before exploding into fireworks.

From across the room, Beatrix had to concede there might be an upside to the Zweeshen's overabundance of fireplaces.

"Well," Emma said after she'd lit the candle on the windowsill, "what have you been up to?" She looked in the direction of the letter that lay on the desk with unfettered interest.

Beatrix had spent hours studying it while waiting for her healing to take effect. Then she'd picked up the history tome. Gathering information about the Zweeshen seemed critical if she was to formulate a plan. Riddles didn't get solved by touring the city, getting new clothes, or shopping for "essential" artifacts—even if Emma had been delighted to go procure all those things while Beatrix recovered. Beatrix needed a systematic approach. And fast. Now that the Bounding had failed, her time in the Zweeshen might be limited—at least according to Jane—and Beatrix was determined to squeeze every moment she had here.

"My mother left a letter for me," she told Emma now. It would be good to have the opinion of someone versed in the Zweeshen. And Emma was... endearing. "There's a riddle in it, and I'm working to decipher it."

"A riddle!" Emma beamed. "How exciting. Can I be part of your quest? I didn't get one of my own, being a Draft and all, so I would love to help you."

Whatever last bits of reserve Beatrix had, melted at the eager look in Emma's eyes. Had she been like that at her age? That free to be excited? She didn't think so. "Sure."

"Excellent. Where do we start? What is your plan?"

Beatrix hated to recognize she had only the beginnings of one. Ever since she'd arrived in the Zweeshen, she'd been swept in a wave of situations not of her choosing. Distractions, all of them. It was time to focus.

"I believe there are several paths to investigate. Take a look," she said, and Emma approached, her ever-present satchel bouncing on her hip. In her journal, Beatrix had numbered the main options: Mary Brandt, the riddle and the symbols, the map, and the Eisid Naraid.

The young girl bent over the paper to read. "So exciting! To be part of a real-life mystery." She tapped her finger on her cheek. "The riddle's a bit odd. I'm not quite sure what to make of it."

"Neither am I. I couldn't match the symbols to any writing system, and the text I've revealed doesn't tell me much. But I believe I should find Mary Brandt first. That way she could assist with the rest."

"Mary should be the priority then." Emma's hair twisted, rearranging itself into a bronze braided crown. "But how to locate her?"

"I had an idea at the Bounding office," Beatrix said. "People keep obsessing that all taelimns must be bound. That everyone needs to be accounted for. If that's true, wouldn't Mary show up in the Bureau's lists?"

"Of course!" Emma's face brightened. "In the Grand Codex. That's where all Boundings are recorded. She should be there along with her biblioworld of origin."

Beatrix's insides warmed with a stirring of hope. "How do I get access to the Codex?"

"I've never heard of anyone reading it. I guess you'll have to ask the Librarian." Emma's grimace was that of someone who'd eaten a lemon. "He did agree to facilitate your search. What other leads could we chase? Oh, I sound all Mystery and Adventure, don't I?"

"Another path is the map." Beatrix eyed the drawing at the bottom of the letter. "The lack of labels doesn't help there."

"It could be anywhere." Emma squinted a bit while looking at it. "But I recognize the rune. I've seen a similar version in my story. It stands for the never-ending cycle." She looked up, pride glinting in her voice. "My book deals with a bit of alchemy, you see. The snake eating its tail is an ancient symbol."

Beatrix studied the drawing, a twisting ring made up by a serpent biting its tail, half white, half black. She, too, had seen it before. Grandfather had drawn it on a parchment. She massaged her temples, willing the memories back, so she could recall how he had used it. Maybe that would give them a hint about the nature of the spell in the letter.

Emma plucked the thought from Beatrix's mind. "Alchemists marked objects with it. They traced the symbols on their tools. Sometimes on the bits of skin they used for their incantations. It's often an empowerment rune."

"Tracing." The image of Grandfather's hand took over Beatrix's mind, as he dipped into an inkwell and followed the rune she'd seen repeated on the puma's flank. Once. Twice. Three times.

Grabbing a pen, she was about to try the same when Emma stopped her. "Use your finger. You have your own ink."

As Beatrix's index finger settled on the rune, her fingertip throbbed, and a thin thread of black floated out. She drew a smoky trail over the symbol to shape the head of the snake, then its spiraled body, creating a full circle where mouth met tail.

A first pass caused the lines in the map to darken. With the second, colors bloomed throughout, and by the third, the map's surface stretched and grew upward, the landscape lifting and dropping to shape valleys and hills. Trees and lakes. The edges of a rocky cliff. All in perfect detail, a most accurate three-dimensional model. A banner flew over it, like a standard ribbon, curling at the ends.

Beatrix almost exploded with satisfaction. Her success felt like a warmth that reached everywhere.

Emma read the title on the pennant. "The Sacred Valley of the Eisid Naraid." The girl wrinkled her nose. "As reveals go, that's kind of disappointing."

True. Beatrix laughed. But promising.

A couple of minutes later, the map receded into the rough, hand-drawn lines from before. Flat and colorless.

"Predictable but helpful regardless," Beatrix said. "Now we know where I'm supposed to go. Instead of anywhere in the Eisid Naraid, Mom is guiding me to a particular spot in her world."

Beatrix shook her head at her own words. Her pleasure at their progress mixed with wonder. It still seemed unbelievable that her mother was a taelimn. Beatrix had nine years' worth of questions for her. Not just the obvious, like where she had been and why she'd left. But others, conversations like moms had with their daughters all the time. At a coffee shop or the salon. She wanted to talk about nothing and everything. Maybe ask how her parents had met.

Beatrix had often wondered, especially after a despicable comment, how the sweet mother of her memories could have chosen Martin. Had she loved him? Was there a different side to him that Beatrix didn't know? In most ways, he was a stranger. She'd thought Mom dead for close to a decade, and Beatrix knew her better than she knew Martin. Now the desire to spend time with her mother was a knot of want. And the unveiling of the map took Beatrix a step closer. "We need a full map of the world to match this region. Do you know where I could find one?"

Emma bit her lip. "The cartographers should help. We can try tomorrow since no one's left at the faculty now."

Beatrix made a note in her journal. "I wonder if there's a map at the beginning of my book."

"Evenzaar said your book is Fantasy, so I'd think there's a good chance of that."

My book. Beatrix smiled with disbelief at this conversation. She still struggled with the concept. "I can't wait to live through the story and learn everything about my world. I know nothing about it."

"Oh, Beatrix," Emma said with such sadness the room seemed to slump with her. "You can't live through your mother's tale. It's impossible to enter a biblioworld while a tale is in progress."

"But the Librarian said I could travel."

Emma nodded with emphasis. "You can. But the bridges open only after The End. Taelimns become free from their artisans—their writers—at that point and live forever as they wish. Whoever is still alive, that is. So you cannot *live* your mom's story. You can, of course, *read* it if you wanted."

Read it. Somehow, as obvious as it should have been, Beatrix hadn't even considered that. "I have to get that book now."

Emma grinned. "We can search the Main Library. There's time before dinner."

10

SPHINX

This, Beatrix thought as they entered the Main Library, this was more like it. The paneled walls, the shelves full of books stretching into the distance. The study tables with their green lights, the stained glass, and the beautifully carved lecterns upon which the most treasured manuscripts rested, enclosed in glass. And the smell. That precise mixture of wood and wax and leather with a touch of aged paper. The sounds of pages as they turned. The motes of dust dancing in a shaft of colored light. Now, this was what one would expect of the world of stories. A library to please the most exacting of readers. To delight the most romantic of book lovers.

"Destination?" asked a short man, probably no more than three feet tall, and Beatrix realized Emma had navigated them both to the Library help desk. There was something familiar about him, with his folded ears and playful eyes, but Beatrix couldn't place him. Which book?

Instead of the whispers, Emma answered in her mind. *A pub patron from that story with the ring.*

Beatrix smiled. That made total sense. She surreptitiously looked down, in search of bear feet.

"Research, borrowing, or guild-exclusive sections?" the man asked.

"Excuse me?" Beatrix said.

"First-timer, eh?" He climbed on a stepstool to talk eye to eye. "If you tell me what you're after, I can have it pulled. The Library has eight floors, three sub-levels, and countless private storage rooms. Wandering is not advisable."

"I'd like to read a copy of my biblioworld's book," Beatrix said. It was still unbelievable to be asking for that. To think *her* book was here. Impossible.

The man nodded, his pudgy hands waving back and forth over a piece of slate. "The borrowing library is on the third floor, West Wing. If you'd lift your band, I'll forward the directions."

Beatrix frowned, confused.

"Band, please," he insisted.

"Here." Emma extended her arm to have her wristband scanned.

"You can't borrow with that one," he said. "You may read it here. Title?"

That took Beatrix aback. "I've no clue. Can you find it with the name of the world?"

The man shook his head. "I don't do searches. That's the Sphinx's purview. If she accepts your query and lets you through to the search rolls. Anything else?"

"Is there no other way to locate the book?" Beatrix asked. "A database of some kind? A search engine?" How could this be? She felt cheated.

"Try the Sphinx," the library employee said. "Any other requests?"

"How about maps? Are there any books that contain maps of Fantasy worlds?" Maybe she could check the index for the Eisid Naraid. Not efficient, but it might work.

The short man turned thoughtful.

Beatrix's patience frayed. "Do I have to ask the Sphinx for that too?"

"No, I can recommend several. *The Ultimate Guide to Fantasy Cartography* by Erasmus would be a good start." He tapped a few times on his stone tablet and then made a notch with his stylus. When he looked up, Beatrix read pity on his face. "Sorry. You can't get access with that band." He pointed to Emma. "Only full guild members."

"Use mine."

Beatrix turned to find William and groaned inside. Seriously? "Are you stalking me?"

He stared at her with clear disgust at the suggestion. "I'm making my own inquiries. I will retrieve the book you want and have it delivered."

"No need, I—"

"Yes, please," Emma said, dragging on Beatrix's sleeve.

"Emma, hold on." But William had already moved away and was disappearing down a corridor.

"He'll get you the book," the help desk employee said, probably thinking himself supportive. "Talk to the Sphinx about your other query. What was the biblioworld again?"

"The Eisid Naraid," Beatrix said.

"Yes, yes, check with the Sphinx. Main lobby, third alcove, next to the cave of Ali. And fill in the survey on the way out, if you would. Helps with my bonus."

Beatrix walked away with a mix of defeat and annoyance. "I guess we should find this alcove," she said to Emma and noticed the girl was staring into space. Like a gunshot victim, her face had hemorrhaged all color.

"You okay, Emma?" Beatrix asked.

Emma's hair had grown out into a pair of slate grey braids. Her eyes were filled with concern. "Are you sure it is *Ei*-sid Na-*raid*? That exact pronunciation?"

"My mom's world? Yeah, that's what the Librarian called it."

Emma pulled on her cameo. "I've never seen the name in writing before, so I didn't put two and two together while reading your letter. I know of the place. It's an Original. Famous. But not in a good way. It's a forbidden land, quarantined after the Rebellion War."

Her words punched Beatrix in the stomach. "What? Why?"

"Because of black magic. Horrible stuff. The world's imbalanced, so it's been sealed off." Emma lowered her voice. "The Eisid Naraid was the headquarters of the Pioneers, the rebels who opposed the council in the great war. No one's allowed to leave or enter. It's a dark place, powered by corrupting magic. You can't go there, Beatrix. Please. Even if you made it in, you'd never escape alive."

As if under the weight of a book press, Beatrix gasped for air. Shock acted like an anesthetic, rendering her speechless. One certainty got through her muddled thoughts. "It doesn't matter. Once I find Mary, I have to take her to the Eisid Naraid." Mom's letter was unequivocal. Her mother waited there. Sealed land or not, Beatrix would get to her.

Emma avoided Beatrix's eyes when she spoke again. "I'm sure the Librarian has some plan. He's got the authority to make an exception."

Beatrix thought of Evenzaar. He seemed the kind to have a scheme. The question was, for whose benefit.

"I will ask him," she said.

Emma pulled on a newly formed orange ringlet. "You'll have the chance to ask him in an hour. I know you wanted to go to dinner with Jane and Trelius, but earlier I was asked to escort you to the great hall. Let's go back to the guesthouse, so I can advise you on wardrobe. You cannot show up to a banquet in a t-shirt."

"But we can't leave. We have to check with that Sphinx about the title." Beatrix wanted to read Mom's story now more than ever.

Emma shook her head. "The Sphinx doesn't ever answer—and you won't find the story in any official Library anyway. For safety reasons, all books from sealed biblioworlds get destroyed. After all, a sealed land is a doomed world."

Even though Beatrix could never find it on her own, less than an hour later, she and Emma reached the Great Hall. A mountain of a man with a fresh gash across his face and a ring full of keys opened the wooden doors and announced their names in a stentorian voice.

Less great than large, the Great Hall was cold and damp more than anything, but the festive atmosphere and the appetizing smells managed to overpower the humidity.

Lighting was poor, all candles and torches, and Beatrix thought that the University had a distinctive medieval flavor, as if its designers came from a tale filled with swords, bloody knights, and court intrigues.

Silence fell when she crossed the enormous archway, and with the experience of a lifetime, Beatrix sensed both the eyes she saw and the ones she didn't size her up. There were at least sixty people in the room, most seated at a long, food-loaded plank table and a few chatting in small groups, sipping from goblets.

"I'm delighted you could join us." The Librarian approached Beatrix with loping strides. He held both his hands out in greeting. A shudder crawled up her back. She forced a smile, which came out misshapen, and retrieved her fingers from his grasp at the first opportunity.

"Evening," she said. "Thanks for inviting me."

The Librarian puffed up. He wore an elaborate robe in crimson and gold.

"I have a request," Beatrix went on, determined to grab her chance. "Back on Earth you agreed to help me find someone. I'd like to look at the Grand Codex after dinner and—"

The Librarian cut her off. "Goodness gracious, such impatience. Not an attractive trait. All in due time. The Codex will keep. I heard of the little—ahem—misunderstanding this afternoon. Not well done. Reckless of you. But no matter. It was a thing of a moment to scatter the protestors outside the guesthouse."

"What do you mean?"

"It's not every day an Unwritten appears. There are some who, let's say, disapprove."

Beatrix found that perplexing. Unless she misunderstood, her being an Unwritten didn't affect anyone but herself. So what, no writer had created her? She couldn't come up with any reason why others should be bothered by it.

"Why do they care about me?"

The Librarian studied his cuticles. His knuckles protruded with such sharpness they resembled teeth. "Not you. What you represent. Some worry if you were allowed to stay, the doors would open for other 'questionable' cases to petition. Your deportation could set a precedent. Now there's been a formal complaint lodged with the Criminal Court due to your behavior at the Bounding appointment. Quite the clamoring to expedite your removal. I managed to hold your arrest warrant. Never fear, a public defender will be assigned. He should prevent your being thrown to the Fogges."

"Thrown to the Fogges?" Was he serious? "I thought they were a superstition."

"The efficacy of Fogges candles is superstition. The Fogges of Unformed Thoughts surround everything and are very real. Their fingers creep into the Zweeshen. They're harmless if you're bound—most of the time... You must've noticed them around. The creeping vines? We call them ink-threads. More PR-friendly. The Bounding wristband of each guild keeps them at bay. There, there," he added at Beatrix's expression of horror. "Do not concern yourself too much. You'll probably avoid the worst fate."

Probably? The air pushed out of her lungs, asphyxiating her hopes of peace and belonging, her dreams of a place better than the one she came from.

They'd been malnourished hopes anyway.

Across the room, she spotted William. And when their eyes met, he gave her one of his old-fashioned head bows. Maybe it was his stiffness that did it, but Beatrix straightened. She clenched her jaw. Whether people liked it or not, she had a mission, and she wouldn't be derailed.

"I have to see the Codex. You promised I'd be able to search for Mary Brandt."

The Librarian looked at her through slitted eyes and caressed his beard. "Do you know why I wear this tedious facial hair, Beatrix?"

She almost growled. "Does the Codex have something to do with it?"

"The snark doesn't suit you." The Librarian sighed. "You can inspect the Codex the day after tomorrow, at the Bureau—I will make sure they expect you. A single query, mind. Use it well. And don't argue. That's the fastest that a permit can be arranged. Now, about that other matter, I've drafted an interim Bounding waiver, so you can move around the Zweeshen until your hearing." He patted his hat with a self-congratulatory smile. "You can thank me later."

Beatrix studied him with suspicion. Had he known this would happen? All these complications? The refusal to bound her? Back in her bedroom, he'd made it sound like her coming to the Zweeshen would be as much a safety measure as a homecoming. Here, it seemed everything but.

"One more thing," Evenzaar said. "You'll come in front of the high council within a couple of weeks. If you hadn't attacked an official of the Bureau, they would have seen you tomorrow. Now we have to allow the lawyers time to prepare, so for your own sake, keep that Furie of yours chained."

Beatrix's body ignited at the jibe; she struggled as the monster growled and paced. "They attacked me."

"Be that as it may—" Evenzaar dismissed her comment with a wave. "—control yourself and try to fit in. I suggest you enjoy your dinner. This banquet's in your honor and keeping taelimns hungry won't help make a good impression."

"Wait. There's something else. What is the title of my mom's book?"

Evenzaar showed teeth when he smiled, a gesture that more resembled a snarl. "Ask the Codex."

Her hands clenched, the rust of the Furie coating her throat as Evenzaar pivoted on his heels, ready to leave.

"See you later," Emma said, and Beatrix realized only then the girl hadn't left her side.

"Why aren't you staying, Emma? Come eat."

The Librarian turned around and snorted with the delicacy of a boar. "Only real taelimns are allowed to dine at the hall."

At the hurt in Emma's expression, the Furie rose higher. "That rule has changed already. I won't stay if she doesn't."

There was an intake of breath somewhere near. Beatrix searched for the origin—a skinny girl with a crown—and behind her, she caught sight of William again. He stood much closer, in conversation with a robed man with a hat that resembled a tree. William's expression was no longer distant but approving. He and the rest of the room must've heard her oppose the Librarian.

"You'll throw your lot with the likes of a Draft?" Evenzaar's upper lip curled in disgust. "You don't know what you're doing."

"She stays," Beatrix said.

"All the way to dessert," Emma added, and the old man flinched when her hair became wild, the tips glowing silver and snapping like the heads of a hydra.

"At your own risk then." Evenzaar sneered. "I sport this beard because every Librarian since Merlin Taelisin has worn one. Sometimes breaking with tradition can cost you your life." Holding onto his hat, he marched away toward the head of the table.

Beatrix glared at his back.

"*Inksmudge,*" Emma spat, mind to mind.

"*You don't have a better insult for ass?*" Beatrix could think of several.

Emma frowned. "*I'm from a middle-grade story. I don't cuss. But around him, I wish I could.*"

11

BELLE

It started around midnight.

At first, Beatrix felt feverish. Unsettled and unable to sleep, she dragged her feet to the bathroom and splashed water on her face, the freshness a welcome sensation on her skin.

She took a sip from her cupped hands and inspected her reflection in the mirror. As a defense mechanism, her mind's vision always corrected the evident flaw, the unmistakable feature that rendered her face out of whack. What she hated about herself the most. Even more than her hair.

Her eyes.

Huge and wide-pupiled, she had despised them for as long as she could claim consciousness. She abhorred the way they popped, causing everything else about her to fade into the background, dragging people in with their sheer strangeness and pushing them away equally fast.

But something else seemed amiss. In the gold-framed glass, her cheeks were flushed, while the rest of her appeared sallow.

"What's wrong with me?" she asked the image, and in answer, a searing pain shot through her stomach and bent her forward, twisting her insides as if they were being wrung out.

The hair on her forearms pulled up in goosebumps. Next, she vomited. And a blade cut up her spine and transported her across time to the terrified girl of seven she'd been when the Furie had first awakened, standing amidst the ruins of the bedroom she'd just destroyed, a kill on her conscience. Like then, her skin rippled with power, her pulse a drumroll in her ears.

Beatrix held onto the sink, hands clutching the porcelain, and when the pain passed, she slid down into a puddle, exhausted.

It must have been around ten in the morning when she ventured out. She couldn't bear her stuffy room any longer and other than the tiredness, she felt almost back to normal. She wouldn't let the weird episode distract her from her task. Beatrix had a plan for the day.

During the tedious banquet the night before, which had lasted through eight courses of professors debating academic minutiae, she'd had time to review all she knew. Beatrix had realized in her search for information she had overlooked a source. William Threshborne had mentioned an uncle. If she could get in touch with him, wouldn't it stand to reason he could aid with the letter? He had to be Mom's relative, after all, so at the very least he could reveal the title of her book. Maybe he'd know who Mary was and how to locate her. Unfortunately, that required talking to William. Beatrix twisted her mouth. He had always been brusque, but with goodwill and squinting an eye, she could interpret yesterday's smile in the Great Hall as friendly. Maybe. It was an avenue. And she would pursue them all. Even if she had to swallow her pride and ask him for something.

Beatrix crossed the lobby and left the guesthouse by way of the skybridge connecting it to the Union Commons building. She struggled after the second turn. In some ways, Navarsing University disappointed with its lack of originality. Complete with winding corridors, bare stone halls, and galleries lined with banners and coats of arms, the staircases repeated themselves and the rooms were not twins but octuplets, impossible to tell apart. Wood, brocade, and chintz decorated the living space, and robed scholars passed her by without as much as a greeting.

"Fancy finding you here." Lime-green hair flowing, Emma startled her. The young girl carried a box so big she had to crane her neck around it.

"Hi, Emma," Beatrix said, glad to see her. "I don't know how but I'm lost."

"It's not you. Things in Navarsing change constantly, and without a wristband's navigation to guide you, it's natural you have a difficult time." Emma readjusted her satchel, and the box teetered in her hold.

"Need help with that?"

"No, thank you very much. These are copies of my author's other books. They didn't make it to the Zweeshen, so I'm studying them. What were you searching for?"

"Jane, originally. I figured she'd know how to find William. By now, I'm so frustrated I just want out of the building."

Emma giggled. "Follow me."

"Is it my impression," Beatrix said after walking down three identical hallways, "or are old universities all the same? I've done a few college tours, and this place could pass for any of them. A bit underwhelming. Where's the awe and the magic?"

"Don't be fooled," Emma said. "The University has to appear circumspect to appease the majority guilds. We're probably seeing the dust jacket. Nothing's what it seems at Navarsing. Ah, there we are." Emma pushed a door like all the others and a blast of cold hit Beatrix's cheeks. "I saw Jane at the Bookends Café earlier. It's where most people your age hang out. Follow the gallery almost to the gardens and go right. Although if you're searching for William, he was at the marina just now." Emma reset her hands on the box. "I'd come along, but I've a meeting with researchers. They're helping me pro bono. Hot news about the search for my artisan." The last she sang before skipping away.

Beatrix soon found the covered gallery Emma had mentioned. It looked like the cloisters of a monastery, with a vaulted ogive ceiling that arched between columns and surrounded the Union building, connecting the inside with the outside seamlessly.

She followed it as advised, and at the edge of the gardens, took a left. If she remembered Jane's layout explanations correctly, the marina should be to the west.

Savoring the silence, she ambled through the grounds, past several playing fields, their white and yellow lines painted on the grass. The breeze that toyed with her hair smelled of salt, so she guessed the ocean must be close. A minute later she saw it: the water glimmered beyond a boardwalk that curled around the coast like a ribbon and ended in a boathouse.

She spotted William nearby. He stood against the backdrop of the marina punctuated by the dots of sailboats, his dark-haired figure balancing on the platform of a dock.

Beatrix traversed the lawn with purpose, deciding not to spend another second inspecting why, for all that he annoyed her, he also intrigued her.

The cartography book he'd promised had shown up during the banquet. But instead of stopping at that, William had sent an additional one this morning that she hadn't yet reviewed.

"Hi," Beatrix said, when she reached the dock.

Tangled in his thoughts, William didn't notice her, and she caught a glimpse of a protective amulet in his hands like the one Emma hid inside her cameo. He slid it into his pocket, intent on coiling the line.

"Hello," Beatrix said again.

His surprise showed as confusion, maybe annoyance on his face. "*Ey ti grashtrath?*"

"Excuse me?" she said. The language sounded unlike anything she'd ever heard.

His brow furrowed in a by now expected look. "I asked if you can see me. Didn't Jane get you an Inter'E?"

"Of course I can see you. What's an Inter'E?"

"An interpreting device. Most books aren't in English."

Beatrix made a mental note to ask about that. She'd begun to wonder if, on top of being too beautiful, everyone around her was also a polyglot, because she understood only a few of them as she walked around.

With a practiced movement, William threw the line into the sailboat and dried his hands on a rag. Then he pulled out the amulet he'd placed in his pocket earlier and threw it into the ocean, where it skipped five times before sinking to the depths. "Figures it'd be useless."

"What was that about?" she asked.

For an answer, he scowled. He looked out to the sea while he rerolled the sleeves of the rough-cotton shirt he wore paired with dark trousers. When he jumped back onto the boat to retrieve a waxed-canvas bag with leather straps, his shoes gleamed, smooth black, with no seams at all.

"*Belle?*" she asked. The name of his sailboat shone in gold against the blue of the water. Not a very creative choice. Except that the illustration of a beast intertwined with the lettering.

"Borrowed," he said and began to fidget with the hardware of his bag. He had long fingers, tapered and marred with light scars below the knuckles.

"So... I was hoping to learn more about this uncle of mine," Beatrix said. "Perhaps meet him if he's around."

He seemed reluctant to answer. Ran his hands through hair that for once was imperfect, windblown and messy. He waited so long she began to doubt he would speak. But after he'd secured the bag's buckle, he pivoted to her. "Not much to tell. Your uncle asked for my help. I owed him a favor, so I made the oath." Grabbing a metal bucket, he climbed the stairs at a brisk clip, but not so fast that she couldn't catch up.

"And what's this oath about?"

"Does it matter?"

"Hard to tell if I don't know what it is. I've never heard of any uncles. How can I meet him?"

William ceased his progress and faced her. "I have no idea." After that, he resumed his climb as if Beatrix should accept that paltry piece of information and move on.

They'd reached the top of the stairs, where the docks joined the boardwalk. "If he's my uncle, I don't understand why he didn't come see me here. I could use his help. Where is he?"

She sensed William's wall go up. The way he distanced himself before speaking, and when he did, his voice had a cutting edge. "I'd like to know where he is myself. He's your mother's uncle. Same series, different installment."

She could tell he held back. Everything about him seemed restrained, from the way he navigated the path to the boathouse to his not-too-loose, not-too-tight grip on the bag.

"So he's from the Eisid Naraid too. Great. Do you know how to get in touch with him? How do people communicate around here? Are there phones?"

William stopped midstep and locked eyes with her. Whatever went through his head must be painful, and Beatrix didn't envy the struggle in his stare. Maybe that's how people felt about her eyes too, like a wild, dangerous rabbit hole you feared you couldn't get out of.

He winced, readjusting his shoulders, and she caught the precise moment when the anger won and spilled over.

"Look," he said, his tone on a tightrope of spiteful. "I don't have time for this. I might have made a promise, but I've no interest in scampering across the Z searching for your uncle so you can satisfy your curiosity. If you have questions about communication devices, ask Jane. She agreed to assist you, so I wouldn't have to."

Like a caustic palm, the words slapped Beatrix, pushing the Furie up so fast she almost choked.

"It was a simple question. Nobody's asking you to do anything," she said. "I'll make it easy for you. Forget your stupid oath and stay out of my life."

12

ELİZABETH

Fighting the dark mood her encounter with William had produced, Beatrix located Jane at the Bookends Café a half hour later. An idea had blossomed in her mind, and she wouldn't let the anger William had awoken divert her from what mattered. Mom. The letter. Mary.

Just like Emma had predicted, the Bookends Café was bustling. The perfect size to be inviting without feeling too crowded, with quaint tables organized in groups, and lounging areas full of deep-cushioned sofas and plenty of space to stretch out, Beatrix could immediately understand its popularity.

Jane was in conversation with three women dressed in old-fashioned gowns, one with ruffles around the neck. They dispersed before Beatrix reached the table with a centerpiece of glittering crystal, feathers, and geometrical golden accents. In this part of the dining room, soft lighting fooled one about the time of day as a pianist in a tuxedo played jazz. A woman wearing a flapper dress and holding a long cigarillo swayed next to him. *West Egg Day*, an A-framed chalkboard had proclaimed at the entrance of the café. Made sense now.

"Hi, there," Jane said, and taking in Beatrix's dark expression added, "He isn't that bad, you know. More bark than bite."

"I don't like being barked at," Beatrix said, without needing to ask who the other girl meant.

Jane laughed. "Fair enough."

But Beatrix had no interest in discussing William. "He did mention something that got me thinking. About an interpreting device?"

Jane paled, a touch of embarrassment in her eyes. "I'm so sorry. It must have been a nightmare to communicate. How could I forget such a vital tool? Don't tell Emma—I've completely failed as a Prolog." She retrieved the hexagonal glass from her coat and breathed on it. "If you have no other plans, we can head to Læsting city now and get you properly outfitted."

"Sounds perfect," Beatrix said, both eager to get a hold of this interpreter—it would be great to understand people around her for a change—and to see this city both Emma and Jane kept mentioning. Beatrix still felt drained from the weird episode during the night, but there had been no repetition of the awful pain. Maybe it was something she'd eaten the eve before.

"I've been wondering," she began once outside the café. "Does this interpreter gadget work on writing too?" That question had brought her to Jane in the first place. "I have a letter from my mother with weird symbols. Could I read it with this Inter'E?"

Jane caressed the lapel of her battered trench coat as if it were a cat. "If it was written in her native language, that's possible. Most Inter'Es translate all Fantasy tongues."

Beatrix did not need further encouragement. "Let's go."

So ten minutes later, with the addition of Emma—who'd finished her meeting and refused to be left behind—they set out for the city.

Læsting, the capital of the Zweeshen, lay at the end of the Yellow Road, about three miles from the University campus. Perched atop a hill, it was surrounded by rolling greens and woods that softly puttered out before the land descended into the ocean, sometimes cutting the coast into fjords, sometimes shaping small beaches.

"My feet hurt," Emma complained, her hair in disarray and her shoulders hunched. She readjusted her ever-present satchel and sighed. "Why did we have to walk when there's perfectly adequate public transportation?"

"We won't get the advantage of the skyline from inside the pods," Jane said. "And it's a nice walk."

Emma pouted. "Says you. I didn't dress for a hike."

"Come on, Emma," Beatrix said. "We have to hurry a bit." In her mind, the faster they got the Inter'E, the better. She didn't want to expect too much. That it could it all be as simple as reading the letter using this device.

But if the symbols were a language... Beatrix had been studying them. They were curved and elaborate, like drawings done with a soft brush. She'd spent so much time looking at them they had lost all context, like the individual features of her face when she stared in the mirror overlong.

"Can we take a tiny break?" Emma whined.

"No!" both Jane and Beatrix said at the same time.

"How about I carry your bag?" Beatrix offered.

"No, thanks." The girl clenched her hand around her satchel's strap and said nothing more.

"We're almost there anyway," Jane said.

Sure enough, within five minutes, the road ascended at a sharp angle, and when it leveled out, the city of Læsting came into view.

"At last." Emma let out a sigh of relief. She clapped her hands together with delight. "Isn't it wondrous? Beautiful? The most amazing view you've ever seen?"

Beatrix held a hand over her forehead against the glare, and the "wow" caught in her throat. She gaped.

And had to agree with Emma.

"What do you think?" Jane asked.

Beatrix, who'd been hoping to gather her impressions in her journal, felt words had run away. Because describing Læsting seemed an impossible task.

It wasn't a city. It was more.

Much more.

It was a thousand amalgamated world heritage sites mashed into one, as if its architects had decided to steal the gems from their homelands and replicate them in a limited a few square miles of land.

Watching it felt like observing a 3D timeline of human history, like a symphony that retold the story of life, mixing elements of stone and mortar with organic spaces and glass and steel. The same capriciousness that let cascades of water plummet into aerial swimming pools had its hands in growing multicolored row houses out of shipwrecks, bending gravity to create floating skyscrapers, and bringing spiraled castles out of imagined worlds. And still the city stretched, not just out but up, a multi-level sculpture that begged one to gaze to the sky and ponder the stars.

Excitement climbed up Beatrix's legs, a charged current urging her to plunge in and explore. She patted her pocket for her phone, searching for a camera, but remembered she'd left it in her bedroom. She'd have to make do with the imperfect memory.

"This way for the best view." Jane led them up the steps of a ruined watchtower and, when they reached the top, announced with fake solemnity, "Behold, Læsting." She stretched her arms to encompass the view and with the gusto of an amateur historian pointed out the sights. "Twelve Guilds and a Thousand and One Neighborhoods," she finished, bending the tip of her hat. "That's the tagline at least."

"Where to?" Beatrix asked.

"Akos-Stellaris," Jane said without hesitation. "The most advanced Inter'Es are sold there. I hope you don't suffer from vertigo, Beatrix."

"You pull the strap down and then release," Emma said, demonstrating the mechanism of the Akos-Stellaris access lifts, which brought people up to the sci-fi neighborhood. The safety belt hovered in front of Beatrix before snapping closed into a five-point harness with a succession of clicks. The buckle tightened around her chest.

They were propelled up without warning, and Beatrix, who'd never enjoyed the g-force of roller coasters, closed her eyes and dropped her head back. It was over so fast her stomach didn't have time to complete a full somersault.

What she saw when they braked brought the bitter taste of adrenaline to her tongue. The single-person seatlift was suspended in the air, so high up that Læsting had been reduced to an anthill below. The bones in her knuckles popped white from the pressure while she held on to the security bar.

"Close your mouth, Beatrix," Emma said, unperturbed. "Hurry down. We have to zip zip."

Copying Jane, Beatrix jumped. She hit a floor she couldn't see with a light bounce, as if her shoes had been outfitted with shock absorbers. A bit flushed, she followed Jane and Emma, who already marched ahead.

The invisible walkway ended at a glass sliding door. Beyond, they strode out to an open-air memorial, stark in its clean, white lines. Art-deco buildings towered on either side, giving the expanse in between the appearance of a gigantic passage. All surfaces were shiny and scrubbed new, and the sky crowned them with Stepford-like perfection, a seamless blue.

"Because we're sitting above the clouds," Jane explained.

The buzzing of flying crafts and the puffing of air from the hovering platforms could be heard nearby. Most people, though, strolled without impatience, producing no sounds at all.

"We can't explore today," Jane said, noticing Beatrix's intrigued expression. "Not if you want to meet up with Trelius and Nera like we agreed. We'll run to the Inter'E store and leave the touring for another time."

They hurried down the street toward a narrow storefront that sported a single sign.

"What does it say?" Beatrix asked, scanning the unfamiliar script.

"It's a joke." Jane snuck her hands in her pockets with a shrug. "They sell interpreting devices. The sign reads, 'See, you need us,' in Voynich."

Inside, the store greeted them with emptiness. White and spotless, it stretched into a slim rectangle where the walls had been replaced with glass vitrines. Within each of them lay hundreds of labeled boxes with chrome lids.

A lavender-skinned humanoid figure approached them. She wore a supple tunic that swayed with her every move. "Welcome to Inter'E store fifty-nine. We have the largest selection of interpreters in the Zweeshen, and we guarantee a perfect fit."

She inched close to Beatrix and grabbed her chin, moved it left, then down. Beatrix almost pulled away, irked by her touch.

"I see," the woman said. "A single-language brain."

"I speak Spanish too," Beatrix protested.

The salesperson had already dropped her face. "Not well enough. Mono-language devices are the most expensive, require more neural programming. We'll be looking over here."

The shop assistant had moved toward the right wall, and when she pressed her palm to it, a two-foot-wide section slid forward. The glass cover retreated, exposing seven identical boxes.

"It should be Fantasy-approved," Jane said. "Originals, Dark, Lost, and Bardic. And we'll need a two-way." She added for Beatrix's sake, "That means you'll be able to both hear and speak."

Emma nodded. "Reading-capable too."

"Of course, of course." The woman tapped away four boxes, which glided back into the wall. "That leaves us with these three models. This one has the best range if you're planning a trip somewhere far, outer worlds, or premedieval. If you need obscure tongues, I recommend this option. It includes the most extensive database of rare and dead languages."

"What about that one?" Beatrix glanced at an innocuous-looking box, smaller than the other two.

"Pretty basic choice. Guild-selected languages, medium range, and three adjustable features."

"Should be good enough," Jane said.

"Try it." Emma bent to study the side of the box. "The price isn't too outrageous."

With a grimace that left no doubt the salesperson disagreed with their pick, she retrieved the larger box and set the lid aside. Beatrix peeked in but saw nothing. The purplish woman stomped with one foot, and a reclinable chair popped up from below.

"Sit down," she ordered, and when a table with a circular mirror emerged, she took a seat opposite Beatrix, behind the looking glass. It took all of two seconds for Beatrix to discover the disc wasn't a mirror at all. No sooner had she sat down than her body went stiff. Two robotic arms whirred out of the frame and immobilized her face. The chair sank and swiveled, making her stomach churn. She now lay at an incline, like an unknowing victim at the dentist.

In her belly, the Furie leapt, fear pulling her veins taut. But Emma and Jane seemed unconcerned, so she urged herself to relax.

The woman positioned the frame over Beatrix's head and reached through, the surface giving like transparent jello. "You will feel a prick. Just a moment. Bear with me." Armed with long-handled tweezers, she retrieved a piece of fishline from the box. "I'm marking the insertion area. The device itself is about a fourth of a human hair, light enough not to sag or create a wrinkle. It produces heat and pressure to match your skin, so it will become unnoticeable."

It was as painless as someone drawing on Beatrix with a ballpoint pen. Within a moment, the sensation disappeared, as did the contraption holding her still. The chair jerked back up, and she could move again. She bent forward to inspect her reflection in the now-innocent mirror. Nothing about her appeared different. No matter from what angle, the Inter'E had faded in, undetectable.

The salesperson stood up, a satisfied smile on her lips. "The only way to remove it is by pulling on the tag behind your ear."

Imitating her, Beatrix touched the spot, noticing a raised bump akin to a pimple.

"Good. It works. I'm speaking Lapineau now. If you push there, the device will release. We don't advise taking it off too often. Our systems have been designed to be worn for life. They recharge using your own energy, are fully waterproof, and new vocabulary is updated wirelessly."

With a snap of her fingers, the table dropped into the floor, and since the chair went with it, Beatrix fell. A rush of anger reddened her cheeks while she scrambled up. The Furie punched her stomach.

But she clamped it down. Beatrix had an interpreter now, and she needed to know if it worked on the letter. Under Emma's eager stare, she pulled the message from her pocket and unfolded it, hope making her hands unsteady.

Her voice wobbled after she eyed the stubborn symbols. "I still can't understand it."

Emma squeezed her hand. "It was a long shot. We'll find another way."

Jane watched them with an assessing look but didn't comment.

"May I?" the shop assistant asked. "You did go with a cheap model. Mine might work where yours failed."

Beatrix hesitated at the tone but released her hold on the paper, and the whispers went insane when the woman took it. Her oval eyes ran over the message with a covetous stare.

"I'm afraid not. No idea what it is," the shopkeeper said a few seconds later, handing the paper back. "Eighty-nine certens for your Inter'E."

"*The woman's lying.*" Beatrix heard in her mind. "*She knows something. She's thinking it's not a language.*"

Beatrix gaped at Emma and then tried to turn her expression blank. "*What, then?*"

"*A code.*"

A code. Beatrix couldn't be surprised. She'd known the letter contained a riddle. But this meant searching for the symbols was a waste of time.

"Your payment, please," the lavender woman said.

"Just a sec." Beatrix unhooked the "Bigger From The Inside" pouch from her belt. It was a small sci-fi gadget of almost unlimited capacity Jane had gifted her the previous day, and where Beatrix now carried the Alicorn. It made her feel like Mary Poppins.

Beatrix poured some of her coins on her palm to begin sorting through them. She hated to recognize that William had been right about her need for funds.

The humanoid lifted her nose. "We don't accept old money. Only guild coin."

"This one's on me." Jane stepped forward, offering her wristband to the shop assistant, who touched it with the back of her hand.

And before Beatrix could protest, a voice overhead announced, "Payment accepted. Thank you for your purchase, Jane Harriet Clifford. Have a nice day."

Unlike upon their arrival, the Akos-Stellaris lifts platform was crowded. At least fifty people were gathered around the entrance, making any progress impossible.

"What's going on?" Beatrix asked as the commotion forced them to stop.

"Not sure." Jane eyed the people loitering and elbowing their way along the invisible walkway. "That explains it," she said a minute later, as a group of leather-and-chainmail-clad figures with crossbows and swords exited the lift station. A mass of screaming fans and paparazzi chased after them, flashes blinking. "That would be the Shadow Skywarriors. Much like royalty around here, especially after the High Fantasy Guild won last year's award."

"Oh, my," Emma said. "I've never seen them before."

Beatrix gaped. "I adore that series!" Her heart fluttered, and the whispers broke into song. She must be dreaming. Here they were. The breathing, living characters she loved. Friends she'd shared adventures and sorrows with. She'd felt closer to them than family, known them so well she could recite their words by heart. And yet, in real life, they were strangers.

Fans screamed after them, offering gifts, throwing up their hands, some crying, and Beatrix's smile faltered. "Seems naïve now that I thought of them as my friends. I mean, so did a million other readers."

"Not silly," Emma said. "Readers are very special to taelimns."

"Emma's right." Jane tucked her hands in her pants with a nonchalance Beatrix wished she possessed. "Readers become part of stories themselves. Everything is connected, and without readers to inspire, stories would lose all meaning." Jane pointed at a figure in a long Regency dress. "Speaking of famous taelimns. While I don't know the Skywarriors, I could introduce you to her."

Beatrix was too speechless to respond. It didn't matter, because from farther up the line, the lady had spotted them and strode in their direction.

"My dear Jane!" she said, arms extended.

They made for an interesting contrast: the one in battered travel clothes, the other in a spotless gown and bonnet. Jane performed the introductions.

"You're exactly like I imagined," Beatrix said. "I can't believe I'm talking to you. I grew up dreaming of Pemberley."

With a laugh, the lady offered her a gloved hand. "You're very kind."

Emma curtsied and kept silent.

"You'll find Beatrix intriguing," Jane said. "What with your interest in hybrids and such. She's an Unwritten. No guild has claimed her."

"Indeed. Wonderful." The lady gave Beatrix a generous smile. Her well-modulated words sounded creamy and rich as if she packed each one with more meaning than most people. "Intricate characters are the most amusing."

Beatrix couldn't decide whether to take that as a compliment or not. Was amusing a good thing? How about intricate?

Even the Furie was happy for once. I've met her! My favorite heroine. This is crazy.

They'd almost reached the end of the line, and the buzzing of the air lifts began to overpower the scene. It became so loud Beatrix had to strain to follow the conversation. That was when the lady's demeanor changed.

"I want to know," she whispered.

"You're aware." Jane looked relieved. She took off her hat and held it by the pinch. "I didn't know if you'd heard."

"Is it true? Fitzwilliam determined to make inquiries."

"More than rumors." Jane's tone rang cautious. She held her coat closed, although it wasn't that cold. "The Librarian and the council are keeping quiet to avoid widespread panic."

"It is shocking! It cannot be concealed. Is it absolutely certain?"

Jane's face betrayed anxiety, her gestures devoid of all lightness. "It won't be kept hidden for long. The disappearances are too conspicuous. Hundreds of worlds gone."

"Good heavens!" the lady said. "How could that be?"

"There was no breach, no alarms triggered. It's a Charmancer—there's no longer a doubt. But he had inside help. This much is clear—the burnings have only started."

The sounds from belts snapping and the seatlifts whizzing echoed against the spiraled glass of Akos-Stellaris's buildings, and Jane's next sentences were muffled. Beatrix pointed her ears. "...too dangerous... warn the League..." Jane glanced at the lady's drawstring bag and an object Beatrix couldn't see changed hands.

"Tell Darcy what I've shared," Jane said. "The traitor will be found."

"He deserves to be publicly disgraced," the lady said.

"Until he is, take good care."

The lift attendant called the lady soon after, and she left them, with a swish of her petticoat and the elegance of those who never have to try. Beatrix watched her go with her mouth open.

"I've met Elizabeth. I can't believe it!"

"She's the original one too," Emma said. "About a hundred other versions around. They're nothing like her."

Jane hooked her thumbs on the waist of her cargo pants and grinned. "The fakes can't be blamed for their fate, Emma. Be generous."

Beatrix frowned. "I didn't even think of that. But wow. Just wow. Elizabeth Darcy! And you two are good friends, Jane... She's different... I guess time has passed... She's different but somehow the same. Amazing." Excitement turning her movements jittery, Beatrix fidgeted with her hair, making the strands which had escaped her bun puff up. "Up until now, I didn't really get it. But it is real. Stories are alive!"

Placing her hat back on her head, Jane let out a laugh. "I like your attitude. Don't lose it. Immortality has a way of dampening enthusiasm. Way too much solemnity around here."

Beatrix thought of the shadow that had transformed Elizabeth's face. "What were you talking about? What's a Charmancer?"

Emma's ears perked up too, her eyes eager.

"Oh, just gossip," Jane said, looking away.

"What kind of gossip?" Beatrix asked.

But Jane's features had grown unmoving. She'd say no more.

13

CODEX

The following day, Beatrix, Jane, and Emma met at the entrance to the All Guilds Bureau. Before breakfast, the Librarian had sent a permit slip to query the Codex. He'd included a note admonishing Beatrix "not to be greedy" and refrain from asking more than one question. "I will know," he had written—a comment that had made her both cringe and roll her eyes.

According to the permit, she was to appear at the East Wing, the Special Requests and Unorthodox Permits department, at 2:15 p.m. So this time, they took a right turn when they entered the Bureau's huge lobby where the whole Bounding debacle had taken place and then pushed through a side door with a knocker shaped like two crossed feathers. A lot smaller than the main hall, the Special Requests room was nevertheless cavern-like, with a vaulted ceiling covered in moving paintings and a row of customer service windows taking up almost the entire perimeter.

Despite arriving on time, the greeter, a journeyman with a wide felt hat and a knotted walking stick, instructed them to stand in line. The waiting area was cordoned off in a circular pattern and seemed to snake around the whole room. Beatrix fidgeted at the further delay. Jane shared her impatience.

"You can handle this, right, Beatrix?" she said, toying with the brim of her hat.

"Of course!" Beatrix didn't need a babysitter, and it took no genius to figure out Jane felt eager to leave. She scurried off a few minutes later, quoting the need to run some errands. Jane hadn't been the same since the encounter with Elizabeth the previous day. A fount of information about everything else, Jane had avoided all of Beatrix's probing questions regarding that cryptic interaction.

As Jane reached the exit, Beatrix saw that William waited there. His gaze hardened at the sight of her. *Whatever.* Then the door closed, and they were both gone.

"Agh, this is ridiculous," Emma said with a huff after they moved just one spot forward in the next ten minutes. "What's the point of an appointment if we still have to wait?"

Beatrix agreed wholeheartedly. After a productive morning, she wondered again why the Zweeshen bothered with queues. This felt as enthralling as a visit to the DMV.

She watched the oscillating fan turn in one corner and wiped her forehead with her sleeve. In a complete opposite to the weather outside, the inside of the Bureau was sweltering. And whose idea had it been to abstain from air conditioning?

"This heat is unhealthy!"

Beatrix pivoted to identify the person who'd voiced her thoughts. He was a tall taelimn several spots behind them in line. Even though he couldn't be over twenty, his dark hair was streaked silver. "Ought to do something about it, right?" He crouched, then turned in a controlled movement that looked part martial art, part dance. The air cooled immediately, and tiny frost stars floated, suspended close to the ceiling. Several people clapped. Others cheered. The magician bowed like a theater performer, accepting the thanks with glee.

He hadn't fully straightened when a crash reverberated as the doors to the Bureau's Special Requests department smashed open and hit the walls. Five uniformed guards burst in, followed by four men in civilian clothing from a variety of eras. The place turned silent.

The guards marched in, their booted footsteps resounding. They grabbed the sorcerer by the arms and handcuffed him. The young man didn't fight.

"T'was just a bit of fun," he said, and the guard punched him in the gut. The sorcerer caved in, folding onto himself.

"No need for that." One of the civilians pushed forward. "I'm the detective in charge." He was short and plump. Dressed in early twentieth-century clothing, he wore an outrageously ugly vest from which the chain of a watch dangled and a curved mustache that looped at the ends. "Young man, you have committed a felony. Fantasy magic is not permitted on any government grounds. If your first offense, I'll recommend lenience. Take him away."

Beatrix gasped, the shock of the scene agitating her blood. Her skin rippled with power. The rush of the Furie, the way it filled her mouth with rust, took her by surprise. It had been quiet—calm since the Bounding mess but for a brief stirring at the banquet—and she had been lulled into believing the Zweeshen might have a positive impact on her control. But now the monster jerked awake, unleashed and volatile. The scene had slashed open a raw spot, separating her from the rational part of herself.

Red rage ran through her, the desire to intervene and lash out stronger than ever. She wanted to hurt with a more virulent desire than she'd felt since the night the monster roused. A slow, insect-like crawling crept up her leg, while the Furie slithered to her throat, and for once, she didn't care about the impact, the deadly results of her magic. Whatever they got, the guards deserved it.

"*No, Beatrix,*" Emma said mind to mind. "*That's not you. Don't! Let them leave. He will get a trial and be set free. Calm down. You'll be deported if you intervene.*"

Emma touched her arm, and together with her words, the contact called forth a memory of Grandpa's face. "Breathe. You're the tamer, not the Furie. You're in control."

Beatrix exhaled. Her hands balled into fists, and she shook, every hair on her body standing while adrenaline fogged her vision. But she kept the monster in.

As the guards dragged the sorcerer out, Beatrix caught the mix of resignation and fear in his eyes. Before he reached the door, he screamed, "May the words take vengeance on you all. Long live the Pioneers!"

She gulped air. *May the words* again... "Just an old saying," Jane had said. "Used as the prefix for any number of well-wishing or bad curse phrases. Nothing special." That explanation hadn't sat well with Beatrix. She felt in her marrow the words were important. Why else would Mom mark them as forbidden?

By the door, the guard clobbered the sorcerer on the head, shutting him up, and this time, the detective did not intervene.

Beatrix's nails dug into her palms. She couldn't decide if she'd made the right choice. How often had she told herself while facing Julie and her friends that if she were on the outside, she wouldn't watch passively like so many did? That she'd do something? But she hadn't. Shame and disgust mixed with the Furie inching underneath her skin.

Her eyes strayed to the door where the sorcerer had disappeared and settled on one of the officers, whose mouth twisted into a self-satisfied sneer. The Furie became a tourniquet around her throat.

Maybe she'd get another chance to get involved.

"*Let's hope not!*" Emma murmured. "*This isn't normal. There have been detectives and spies roaming everywhere lately. But this is an outrage. It's the fear in the air—must be the Charmancer rumors.*"

Before Beatrix had the chance to ask again about this Charmancer, one of the civilian officers spoke. "Stay where you are. Do not move or talk, and this will be over soon."

The four men began weaving through the silent crowd, observing everyone. She narrowed her eyes, her jaw so tight her teeth ground against each other. They circled, calculating, surveying in a way that made everyone squirm. One of them locked stares with Beatrix—his probing, hers defiant. They dueled for less than a minute, and then he moved on.

"*I recognize them!*" Beatrix told Emma.

"*Monsieur Poirot, Sherlock, and Father Brown. That tall one watching you is a botched famous spy. But they're fakes, from adaptations or continuing stories, not the originals.*"

The men nodded to each other.

"Carry on," the Sherlock version told the crowd.

And they left.

Sound returned. Hushed murmurs and chatting, snorting and complaining—even laughing. An unnatural display that made Beatrix wince. Had she done the right thing staying quiet? A part of her, a large one, was ready to go after them even now.

"*Easy,*" Emma said.

"What the hell was that?" Beatrix burst out aloud. "Why would magic be illegal? In the universe of stories of all places!"

"You got it wrong," Emma said. "There's 'magic' everywhere. Even your Earth is full of it. Magic forces move the universe, from gravity to relativity, from rhythm to the true names to the mirror law. What you mean is Fantasy magic, the kind sorcerers and witches and magicians wield, powers like your Furie, and not all taelimns are fond of that."

Emma pulled a monogrammed handkerchief out of her satchel and wiped her brow. With the sorcerer's spell destroyed, the heat was again unrelenting. Beatrix leaned against a pillar, a strange dizziness flowing through her. Perhaps a leftover from the night's episode. Her head pounded. Then again, who could be comfortable in the kiln-worthy heat?

"I don't understand why anyone would argue against Fantasy magic. It solves tons of problems." Beatrix glanced toward the fan. "He did nothing wrong."

Emma shrugged as if she didn't care; her face told a different story. "Most books are Realistic Fiction, and purists think of Fantasy magic as a lazy, dangerous shortcut that drains Inaechar—our lifeblood and source of energy— for no good reason. Some look down on Fantasy as a guild too. Evenzaar's from Historical, but he's obsessed with Fantasy. Even he must make concessions to the nonfantastical guilds. Today was too extreme, though." Emma's forehead crumpled. "Something stinks. In general, the nonmagical guilds insist on paperwork or permits and the like. They tie us up in bureaucracy, which is tolerable if in exchange we get to have Rhodoshearts, don't you think?"

Emma sank into a dissertation on the virtues of magical flavor enhancers, and Beatrix used the chance to people-watch while the line advanced at the pace of a sloth.

Until someone said, "You're the Unwritten, aren't you?"

The question belonged to a fair girl who stood in line ahead of Beatrix and Emma. She had a gorgeous face and hair the deep red of rubies. About Beatrix's age, her blue eyes were dagger-sharp.

"Yes, I'm the Unwritten," Beatrix said, enough power left in her body for the answer to come out defiant.

"Perfect," the girl said. "I've been waiting to find out why my vision sent me here, and now I know. We'll be great friends."

She smiled, and her beauty became so luminescent it was hard to stop staring.

"You can always tell when someone is a Main rather than a Secondary taelimn," Emma murmured, mind to mind. *"They're always prettier."*

"I didn't mean to pry," the redhead said. "It's just that you're a bit of a sensation. Plastered all over the media. I just heard the juicy details during our staff meeting." She went on to cheerfully inform them she worked as a teaching assistant at Navarsing. Extending her arm, she introduced herself.

"Your name is unheeded prophetess?" Beatrix asked. Maybe some taelimns didn't get real names and were stuck with descriptors like in movie credits: waiter #1 or blond shopper.

The girl laughed with infectious mirth. "Opt out of your interpreter. It's mistranslating my name."

"Push the tab and say 'exclude name,'" Emma instructed, and Beatrix repeated after her.

She felt a slight vibration, like a phone on buzz. "So your name is..."

"Cassandra."

"All fixed. I'm Beatrix."

"I know. I would've recognized you anywhere. I *saw* you a while back. You're the unbound, Unwritten taelimn. So exciting! You have the professors squawking like chickens."

"I didn't realize I was being discussed in class." Beatrix didn't like it. Not at all. Just what she needed: people talking about her. Was there nothing more important going on?

"Are you kidding?" Cassandra said. "You're the most interesting thing to happen since the Rebellion War. Taelimns can't procreate, not unless the babies are born before The End, so this is a big break in the laws of nature. Until now, Unwrittens were a theoretical concept for a taelimn without an artisan, an impossibility. Scholars are scratching their heads, reviewing their theories. It's wonderful. I'd give anything to be half human. The possibilities... And you can live in the artisan worlds too. What's it like? I'm curious, are you immune to Roamer's?"

Before Beatrix could even ask, Emma jumped in. "We don't know yet."

Cassandra nodded with a grave expression. "Time will tell, I guess. So how can I help you?"

Beatrix watched Cassandra's expectant face. "I'm not following."

"I *saw* you, in a vision. I'm meant to help you. This stuff is never clear, so I don't know with what."

Emma and Beatrix looked at each other.

"Do you happen to be good at ciphers or codes?" Beatrix asked.

Cassandra grinned so wide a dimple appeared on her cheek. "I'm a cryptology grad."

Emma rubbed her hands. "Just what we need!"

Beatrix hesitated. *"Isn't this a bit too convenient? Too coincidental?"* she asked Emma.

Emma looked exasperated. *"This is the world of stories. There are no coincidences. She had a vision for a reason."*

"And that doesn't worry you?"

"I didn't realize how it would sound," Cassandra said, perhaps guessing at Beatrix's reluctance. "You've no reason to trust me. I never learn, do I? My visions guide me wherever I'm needed. Sometimes to prevent a bad ending, sometimes without obvious reason. I've seen us work together. I have no secret agenda."

Inside Beatrix's head, the whispers debated. Should she include another person in her search? She sensed the letter was meant to be kept, if not secret, then at least not made public. But, like Emma insisted, she could use the knowledge Cassandra offered. "I have nothing to give but my heart so full..." the whispers quoted. They'd obviously reached a consensus about Cassandra's good intentions.

"I've got a letter with a riddle," Beatrix said. "We're struggling to decode it."

Cassandra laughed. "All my wishing has been answered. Agh, no! That's my number. I have to pick up a permit for my boss, Professor Polihistor. Then I must lead a study hall. But I'm off at five-thirty tomorrow. Why don't you girls come by the University tennis courts then? We can begin analyzing your letter right away."

Swayed by Cassandra's enthusiasm, Beatrix agreed.

When it was Beatrix's turn at the customer service window, she received a gigantic key from a guy in a baseball cap who chewed gum with an open mouth and didn't bother to glance at her.

"What do I do with this?"

"Next!" he yelled, waving them away.

Beatrix inspected the key. There was a carved number on it. 12948.

"The self-serve monolith," said an old lady with a crocheted cap and a walker with tennis balls for feet. "Over there."

The monolith was a six-foot standing rectangle of shiny metal, pockmarked with hundreds of keyholes. Beatrix inserted the key in one that looked the right size, and a number appeared above it. Not the right one. "You gotta be kidding me."

Emma giggled. "The Zweeshen rejoices in complicating matters. Let's go row by row."

About twenty attempts later, the key clicked and turned. Beatrix released it, and the surface rippled, absorbing both keys and keyholes. On the now smooth metal appeared the words: *I am the Grand Codex. Whom do you search for?*

"Mary Brandt," Beatrix said. When nothing happened, she repeated it louder.

"Why isn't it working?" Emma whined, her hair a droopy grey.

Beatrix watched the bolded words blink. "Maybe it can't hear us." She stepped closer and, using her index finger, shaped Mary's name on the metal.

I'll search was the immediate response.

Beatrix tapped her foot, and as it always does, time stretched while they waited.

There is no Mary Brandt in the records of the Grand Codex, the next message read. *Thank you for visiting me. Goodbye.*

With a humming sound, a slot opened, and a folded paper the size of a birthday card slid out. Beatrix fought the desire to scream in frustration. One would think disappointment would get easier with constant practice. She pulled the card out. It was light, with the texture of plastic. Inside it, a printed message repeated the last words on the screen: the finding, date, time, and querier. But on the other side...

"Let me see." Emma pushed out her hand.

"Nothing new," Beatrix said. "Let's go back to Navarsing." She didn't want to share. Putting the paper away, she concentrated on closing her mind to prevent Emma from detecting anything. Because inside the card, the Codex had added a calligraphic note. *Leave, Unwritten*, it said. *If you stay, no story will be safe.*

14

TÆLİMNS

Beatrix had become convinced time must be broken in the Zweeshen. It followed weird patterns, stretching to pack more hours than normal into each day. The events from the previous day at the Special Requests department already felt distant in the way of memories that lose their sharpness, even disagreeable things becoming blunted.

As she waited by the playing fields late in the afternoon, time seemed made out of rubber. She watched the clocktower's minute hand tick with maddening slowness.

Where was Cassandra?

Uncomfortable, Beatrix shifted in place. After the Codex's message yesterday and today's five hours of unsuccessful research with Emma, Beatrix found herself doubting everything. All through the day, she'd wondered whether the Codex's note was a mean-spirited comment or a genuine warning. Could there be any truth in it? She couldn't imagine how her presence in the Zweeshen might endanger the future of stories.

And she'd had another horrible night, racked with pain. Beatrix had excused herself from the dinner table as soon as the pain began. Not that she'd miss Evenzaar's insidious eyes on her while she ate. He had insisted she join him and the professors in the Great Hall every eve, and she hadn't thought of an excuse quickly enough to refuse. William's intense stare had followed her as she'd raced out the Hall, and Beatrix wondered who had invited him to dine there. Not Evenzaar, she'd bet.

Now she stretched sideways, the muscles in her maltreated stomach aching, then ground her teeth, hating whatever this bug was that plagued her. It frustrated her. Because she had no time to lose. Every minute counted to find a way to Mom, and Beatrix needed to be attentive and fit.

She shivered in the cold. The weather had turned nippy, and for a moment, she dreaded the invitation had been bogus, like those birthday party setups when she was a kid, where the address ended up being an adult store in the bad part of town. And she'd come alone. Jane—who'd also spent hours with Beatrix surveying a new batch of cartography books for an Eisidian map—had left to see Elizabeth and "her contacts," whoever they were, and Emma had been summoned again regarding news from the researchers.

"Hello!" a blond girl said, plucking Beatrix out of her thoughts. "I'm Lucy. You look new."

"I am."

Lucy dazzled her with a smile worthy of a toothpaste commercial and introduced the other three friends who stood beside her with varying degrees of welcome on their expressions. They were dressed in tennis outfits and held rackets and ball tins, so it was easy to guess where they were coming from.

"So are you, like, brand-new? Freshly bounded?" asked one of the boys, an impressively good-looking guy called Matt.

"I think so." Beatrix wavered. "But my world's been around for a while, I believe."

"Which genre? Matt and I were trying to guess." This from a lanky kid with a ratty baseball cap and mellow eyes. Paul, Beatrix thought he was called. He grinned at her while he twirled his racket, trying to balance it on his finger with mixed success.

"Eh, I'm not sure. A cross between the regular world and Fantasy, maybe."

"A mix? Hybrid genre? That's different." Becca, a girl of athletic build with hair Beatrix would have given an arm for—not a curl or a bit of frizz in sight—managed to accentuate the last word to transform it into a passive-aggressive comment.

Beatrix either didn't notice or decided to ignore it. "Are you all taelimns?" she asked instead. They looked ordinary enough and about her age.

"Yep," Lucy said. She pulled out a tube of lipstick from her pocket and reapplied a coat. "Some of us are taking courses at our guild, others at the

University. My book is Teen Romance. As if I could hide it—purple eyes with golden flecks." She batted her eyelashes and giggled.

"Impressive," Beatrix said.

The girl shrugged, her delicate shoulders lifting gracefully. "I don't hold a grudge. My artisan tried her best to make me special. Becca is a zombie killer. She's amazing with a machete, the funniest thing."

Becca smirked and grew a few inches.

"Matt likes to pretend he isn't, but he comes from Teen Romance too," Paul said.

Beatrix smiled. So that explained the unnaturally perfect hair and door-wide shoulders.

"Shut up, Paul," Matt said.

"Why?" Becca's voice whizzed like a rattlesnake's. "You have to confront your origin at some time. Even if Romance is the butt of all jokes."

Matt bared his teeth, and both girls chuckled.

"What about you?" Beatrix asked in Paul's direction.

"Eh, Fiction. Realistic Fiction. Nothing wild."

"He wishes he were Mystery like Dyøt," Lucy said. "He's studying for a final today. And Cassandra comes from Historical. She loves obscure cases, so she'll be dying to talk to you."

"What mix did you say you were?" Paul asked, his racket forgotten.

"Yeah, where are you really from?" Becca added.

Ugh! That question. Beatrix had hated it on Earth. She hated it even more here.

"It's easy to figure out." Becca feigned innocence. "Just tell us which guild bounded you."

This time the jab was too obvious for Beatrix to let it go. She straightened her back. "It is not clear yet," she said, faking disinterest.

"Who cares?" Lucy twirled a strand of her hair, and something in her purple irises clued Beatrix that she was a lot smarter than she cared to show.

"But a guild had to accept you during your Test of Character," Becca insisted.

"I remember my test. I picked the motorcycle." Paul's gaze glinted with longing. "Best ride ever."

"Helicopter," Becca said. "I didn't want ground transportation or anything on water. Zombies can't fly."

"Aston Martin, red to match my outfit," Lucy said. "What did you choose, Beatrix?"

"Mmm, I didn't have those kinds of options. I got a unicorn." She hesitated to confess this. Not that she was unhappy with her guide, especially after her success with the Alicorn, but how come she hadn't been offered expensive cars or motorcycles? Was the test different for every person?

"Don't let them harass you," Cassandra swooped in, her flaming hair framing her face like a royal crown. "I ended up with a tortoise." She put an arm around Beatrix's shoulders. "So you guys have met my new friend. She's the first Unwritten ever. And she's guild-free. Isn't that amazing?"

"Guild-free!" Lucy beamed. "Why didn't you say so? Respect."

Becca narrowed her eyes. "I heard of you."

"Guildless! I wish." Matt had a deep, attractive voice that reverberated pleasantly.

"Come on, the guilds aren't that bad," Paul said. "They help us."

"There are arguments both ways." Matt drew his arm around Lucy, bringing her closer. "I agree with Cass. Guildless is not a bad thing. Look what it did for the Theolsea islands. They've built a phenomenal city, library and all, and they say their connections to the advanced artisan worlds are even better than ours."

"Huh!" Becca snorted. "Since when is that the measure for anything?"

"Don't hate cause you're jealous you were conceived on old-fashioned Pangea," Paul said.

"Let's take a look at that letter of yours over there," Cassandra told Beatrix and pointed to a stone bench next to a knotted lantern a hundred feet away. Then if you want, you can join us for dinner. We lost a bet to the boys yesterday, so it's their choice tonight." And in a gesture as surprising as it was natural, she interlocked her arm with Beatrix's. "You'll have to tell me all about you, Bea. Can I call you Bea? I know we'll be great friends. And I hope you like Mediterranean food."

"I do," Beatrix said, even though she wasn't the least bit hungry—and she didn't bother correcting Cassandra about her name. Somehow, coming from her, it didn't matter.

"We'll see you soon." Cassandra waved to the group over her shoulder, and with a few words, the others left to shower and change.

"Sorry I was late," the redhead said as they walked. "I got stuck with the task to publish grades. Then the blackboard wouldn't stop crying, and I had to redo them." She twisted her mouth. "Don't ask why. I spent a half hour reviewing career transitions with a piece of wood."

Beatrix laughed. She couldn't help but compare Jane's guardedness to Cassandra's ease.

Soon, settled on the surprisingly soft bench, Beatrix unfolded her mother's letter. Cassandra took it with the care of someone used to dealing with old manuscripts. And Beatrix realized how lucky she was to have this much help—and how rare it was.

Other than Grandpa, no one had ever cared to assist her before. For so many people to be involved in her task felt both unsettling and comforting. Strange in the way of new things. But then everything since Emma had appeared in her bedroom had been that way.

"Remarkable," Cassandra said, dragging Beatrix to the present. "Just look at this writing." She beamed. Her voice sparkled with excitement. "Bespelled every bit of it. See here, where the symbols meet? That's a magic trigger. So clever. Beautiful, in fact. Mmm. Could it be?" Cassandra lifted her head, counted aloud, tapped at the letter, and made a few notes on a floating holographic pad she'd called forth by pressing on her wristband. When she faced Beatrix, her blue eyes flashed like sapphires on a display. "You have no idea how incredible this letter is. A feat of magic cryptography. I'm in heaven."

Warmth spread through Beatrix, and she smiled. Maybe everything would work out. "So you know how to read it? What it means?"

Cassandra laughed, her crimson hair undulating with the movement. "This, my friend, is a Craxtan Riddle. The most unbreakable of codes and a method of encryption dating back to the time before the Zweeshen. Widely used by the Pioneers to send safe messages during the Rebellion War too."

"That means it can be deciphered," Beatrix said. "If they used it to communicate..."

"Sure it can. By the right person with the right artifacts. That is the most interesting part. A Craxtan is a multistep riddle. What makes it different from almost anything else is that Craxtans require several decoders." Cassandra drew on her holopad while she explained, her words creating what looked like a ladder. "Each verse in this letter is a clue to the decoder needed to unveil the next hint. They're ordinal too. They have to be decrypted in sequence. In your version, clues follow the Latin alphabet, and there are—" she looked at her pad and counted the looping steps showing on it, "—yes, there are five clues total."

"I can't believe you could tell all that by looking at the message," Beatrix said with surprise. "I've been reading and rereading that letter for days and never noticed anything."

"I'm trained to find patterns," Cassandra said, not without pride. "But Craxtans are simple to identify if you're aware of them. The alphabetical structure is telling."

"Perfect." Within Beatrix, the whispers began scheming how to leverage Cassandra's aid. "So now we know what it is, how do we solve it?"

Cassandra smiled. "The clues are bookended by the initial and last sentences, which are the setup. Because the last starts with G— 'Giving you all my love'—we can figure out the total artifacts needed. Three of the five clues are left now since you've deciphered two already. This hint, 'A letter for Beatrix,' must've led you to the object to unveil the first paragraph. Out of curiosity, what was the artifact?"

Beatrix frowned. "I'm not sure." She searched the events in her bedroom the day she'd discovered the letter. "Must've been the mirror. My grandfather left behind a box of trinkets, and there was a silver mirror in it. When I looked at myself, I appeared older on it."

"That's it!" Cassandra caressed the letter. "How ingenious to use such a simple item. What about the next one?"

Beatrix explained how she'd used the Alicorn.

Cassandra looked perplexed. "That's unlikely to be a decoder. I'm surprised it worked, so I will have to study it. I'm jealous—in a good way. You've made my day. No, my year. I have a real-life enigma, a true Craxtan in my hands."

Like Emma, Cassandra seemed unafraid to show her enjoyment, which carried Beatrix along with it. Maybe they would figure it all out. Maybe by this time next week, Beatrix would be on her way to Mom's. "I need to find the next decoder then. The mirror worked, so I think I'll test the watch and the thimble from Grandpa's box."

"My thoughts exactly," Cassandra said.

"Did you finish geeking out?" Becca approached them, the rest of the group in tow.

They both jumped up, and Beatrix stashed the letter back in the pouch. She had to untangle her feet from a few rogue vines that had crept up them while they sat.

"Quite finished and ready to eat," Cassandra said and gave Beatrix a conspiratorial look.

15

INTRUDER

Beatrix dreamt. She knew she did because she stood on the island of the Test of Character, and the air carried lilacs and wild sage.

There were doors, many more than there had been during the Test, leading to unknown worlds. William was there. He waited at the threshold, his hand extended in invitation, his eyes smoldering. But when she reached for him, Aestrer blocked her way. Surrounded in a haze of blue, the unicorn came so close she could see her reflection inside his pupils. Then he shrieked, a terrifying sound that rattled her awake.

Beatrix's eyes burst open. The bedroom was shadowed, illuminated in patches by a purple moon that seeped in through the open window.

In the next split second, a large, hooded figure lunged toward her, and by instinct, she rolled out of bed. They landed in a pile of wrestling limbs. The sheets knotted around her, she squirmed like an insect in a web while the figure tugged at the nightgown Emma had chosen for her. The cream silk ripped and gave, and Beatrix almost broke free.

But hands like tourniquets imprisoned her arms. With so much violence it all went white and black, the intruder smashed her head against the floor.

The force of the impact stole her breath.

Taking advantage, the assailant maneuvered on top of her. "We warned you to leave the Zweeshen. You should have listened. You don't belong here!"

Herculean fingers closed around her throat as she tried to wriggle out, kicking and elbowing to liberate herself. She wheezed, gasped, less and less air passing through. Darkness clouded everything, carrying her away.

"Give it up!" the intruder hissed. "Release her to me, and I'll spare you."

"I don't know what you want," she managed to say, her throat bruised and hoarse.

"We will make you." The other pressed harder on her neck, and as the light dimmed, either Beatrix's fear or her determination called it.

The Furie rose, eager and lethal, its full might prickling on her palms. Her skin pulsated. Rust touched her tongue. And something else rose too, from the dark and the night and from deep inside her. The smell of earth and moss floated, and when she let the Furie go, the monster didn't explode out. It stayed coiled and lunged only the moment she pushed on the attacker's chest. The pungency of burnt flesh filled Beatrix's nostrils.

Screaming, the figure staggered back, letting her go with a curse. Heavy liquid spilled out of an open wound, which drew a trail on the faded Persian rug as the intruder ran for the window and dove into the night.

Hours later and still shaken, Beatrix sat cross-legged on her bed, watching the dark turn to light outside. She studied the blue-black lines on her skin. They bloomed thin and twisting, marking a veinlike path from the right foot to her ankle, where they curled in a circlet reminiscent of a tribal tattoo. But they weren't art. She had seen enough inkthreads around the Zweeshen to recognize the touch of the Fogges' fingers. The meaning of it escaped her.

She must've dozed off, because when she awakened again, dawn painted the room amber, and both the reality of the attack and the marks on her skin had faded. Instead, a new sense of empowerment filled her, the certainty that she could rely on her magic and defend herself. Accomplishment. An appreciation for a power that until now she'd despised. The Furie's stirring felt welcome for once.

She smiled.

By the time she'd dressed for breakfast, Beatrix was chomping at the bit to discuss the episode with Cassandra and Emma. Who was the intruder? She couldn't fathom what the figure wanted. "Release her to me, and I'll spare you." Most of the words the intruder had muttered seemed nonsensical, but that even more so than the rest. And since the attack had failed, would they try again? She shook her head. Too many mysteries. But maybe her friends might see something she was missing.

A cramp surprised her then, and her breath caught. Last night she'd thought perhaps she'd overcome whatever ailed her; now, here came the pain again.

Beatrix fell to the bed, curled up in a ball of agony. The attack felt eternal even when it passed soon enough, and she pulled herself up, inhaling deeply to clear her mind. Her body felt battered, as if she were emerging from a boxing match—weak and sapped.

Maybe she should share this weird sickness with her new friends too. And like whenever one makes the right choice, the decision gave her serenity.

But all calm shattered as soon as she reached their usual breakfast table at the Bookends Café.

"You tricked me!" Beatrix said.

Emma's face lit up with guilt. "When I offered a marvelous breakfast, I didn't say it would be just me."

"Good morning." William's form relaxed on the velvet chair next to Emma.

Beatrix didn't sit. "I've lost my appetite." And the desire to share anything about the intruder and her strange pains. The last thing she wanted was to appear weak or in need of help in front of *him*. She turned toward the door that led to the patio sitting area.

"No! Wait, Beatrix!" William called out. "Hold on, please. I wanted to make sure you're all right." He watched her with that intense stare of his, searching for…something. Could he know about the assailant?

Beatrix dismissed the idea as it occurred to her. She lifted her chin. "Why wouldn't I be fine?"

"It's a relief you're well. I'd also like to apologize for the other day. I was an idiot." He sounded a bit sheepish as he ran his hand through his hair. "I have a peace offering." He waved toward the laden table, where a decadent array of delicacies were displayed. "A culinary journey through the Zweeshen. I didn't know what you liked, so I got a bit of everything."

She almost gave in. A part of her wanted to. The whispers were torn over it, arguing among themselves. It was the Furie that decided for her, its rusty taste reminding her of the shame she'd experienced at the marina. Beatrix was sick and tired of shame. Without a word, she pivoted and began to walk away.

"Wait. I'll leave. Don't skip breakfast on my account." William pulled out a chair for her and with a couple of strides abandoned the café through one of the arched doors that connected it to the outdoor gallery.

"You're being a brat," Emma said when Beatrix returned to the table.

The café was uncharacteristically empty. Only two other guests, dressed in the light-colored robes of first-year students, sat slouching in front of half-eaten plates, immersed in their texts. Today, following the advertised Steampunk theme, the interior had been reinvented to resemble a conservatory, with a few Victorian touches like tasseled lamps, flowered cushions, and brass gadgetry. It whirred with the sounds of robotic servers of clockwork design. Emma fit right in.

"You're acting like a spoiled child, do you hear?" Emma's hair shone a spun gold.

"He should leave me alone. He's a jerk." Following his rudeness by the sailboat, Beatrix had decided to avoid him—and she'd expected he would do the same. She'd seen him only from afar during the last few days, and they hadn't talked. So why the change now? The feast in front of her did look appealing; she had to give him that.

"Considering he's forced to protect you or die," Emma said, "I'd allow for some moodiness."

Beatrix flinched. "Is that what the oath's about?"

"Picked it off his brain the other day. Not sure about the exact rules. Why don't you ask him? When you decide to act smart, that is."

"I told him I release him from the oath. He can return to whatever it is he does." Knowing nothing about him, she had no inkling as to what that might be.

"There are rumors he's a Conjure." Emma dropped her voice in a conspiratorial tone. "A powerful one. They say he refuses to use magic, something about a curse."

"Who knew you were such a gossip, Emma." Beatrix forced her eyes to remain on the prosciutto with melon she was transferring onto her plate, unwilling to show interest. She almost convinced herself that she didn't care.

"I'm making a case for William here," Emma said. "We can use his help. Especially since you can't be rid of him any less than he can be done with you." Emma spooned some clotted cream onto a scone. "I believe you misunderstand the nature of oaths in the Zweeshen. Do you remember the guy who let us into the Great Hall for the banquet, the keeper of the keys at Navarsing?"

"The old guy with the beret?"

"And the cable cardigan and the heavy key ring. Yes. That one. Did you notice the bleeding gash across his face and arm?"

"I thought he'd had an accident the day I saw him."

"He had an accident. Some centuries ago. He broke an oath. A little one, like a pinky promise. Nothing of the caliber of the oath William made. If he renounces his, there'll be no mercy."

"I get it." Beatrix bit on her toast. "But I didn't make him swear. I told him he's free."

"You are incapable of freeing him," Emma said. "No one can. He must fulfill his task."

"Which is?"

"I suggest you ask him."

Beatrix poured herself some hot chocolate. "How well do you know him?"

"Not at all. I met him while you were going through your test. I'm a good judge of character, though. You should let him be a friend."

"Not a chance." Even the Furie rebelled at the thought and let Beatrix know with a mouthful of rust. "Never."

Emma shook her blond braids. "Bad idea to use that word. A challenge to the gods if there ever was one." She angled her knife, spreading a dollop of marmalade onto a crumpet.

After taking a sip of bubbling persimmon juice, Beatrix reached into her new backpack, an Adventure prop with a hundred pockets at least, and pulled out her journal. "I wonder where Cassandra and Lucy are. They promised to join us at ten to test the watch and the thimble."

"Someone called us?"

With a twin pair of smiles, Cassandra and Lucy sauntered in. They both surveyed the table with appreciation.

"Nice spread," Lucy said.

"From William." Emma bent her head with a suggestive expression.

"Really?" Cassandra shot Beatrix a questioning look.

Beatrix rolled her eyes. "He wanted something. Doesn't change he's an ass."

"With good taste," Cassandra said, admiring the intricate design stamped with gold leaf on one of the desserts. "There are weird rumors about him."

Rather than succumbing to the temptation to ask, Beatrix bit her lip. She searched for a different subject. "Do you want anything to eat? Tons left."

They both refused, but ten minutes later, they were all snacking while they chatted about the latest campus news.

"We should probably start," Beatrix said. After all, they'd agreed to meet here to test the artifacts and plan their next steps. Cassandra had insisted Lucy, who studied philology and old languages, would be a great addition, so Beatrix had shown her the letter too.

Cassandra moved a few empty plates aside to make room while Beatrix retrieved Grandpa's chest from her backpack and laid out the contents next to it: the silver mirror, the thimble, and the watch.

"We should be careful as we examine the artifacts," Cassandra said in her most studious tone. "Spells are sensitive. They don't allow for deviation. Not if you want them to work as intended."

Beatrix did. She had to get this right if she wanted to see Mom. Increasingly, she realized it was more than that. This task. She had to accomplish it for her own sake too. There were answers she had to get. About Mom. About Martin. Even about herself.

"These *have* to be decoders," Lucy said, a gleam in her eye while she inspected the watch. "It seems obvious, yes, but most tales are."

Beatrix spread the letter on the table.

"Which object do we test first?" Emma asked.

"Let me read the whole thing again," Beatrix said. "We know the mirror uncovered the *B* clue, and the Alicorn semi-revealed the *C*. Maybe we can glean the mechanism of the riddle if we also look at those verses."

Everyone agreed, so Beatrix recited the words she knew by heart.

Before you is a riddle only you can solve.
Look to see truth where others won't.
What's denied holds power, and you wield it all.
Take Mary Brandt to the Eisid Naraid,
and we will reunite.

Come to me, daughter; let me be your guide.
The stars hide the secrets to open the sky.
While death is chasing your every step,
the choice is yours but not The End.

They went line by line, but after thirty minutes of dissecting the verses, they were no further.

Emma twirled her newborn Goldilocks-worthy ringlets. "Be your guide... That just makes me think of your unicorn, Beatrix."

"But I already tried the horn—and it didn't work completely. Can a decoder be reused?"

Lucy appeared unconvinced. "Seems unlikely."

"On top of that," Cassandra said, "decoders tend to be artifacts tied to the code creator's world. Things imbued in their Inaechar. The horn meets none of those requirements. I'm still shocked it worked at all."

Beatrix surveyed the stuff on the table. "Let's focus on the *C* clue then. I guess a moon and sun fit in the theme of stars. So maybe the watch?"

Lifting it, she turned the object in her hands. The casing was scratched, and a few links of a snapped chain hung off it. She popped the lid open, revealing the astronomical markings inside. They, too, seemed dulled by age. "It's a bit odd for a watch." Beatrix twisted her lips in doubt. "It has no hands."

Cassandra glanced at it. "An astrolabe."

"Is that what it is?" Beatrix asked.

"Yes, it measures the position of celestial objects," Cassandra said. "A remarkable piece. Too old to be from Pangea. Let's try it."

Careful not to close it, Beatrix positioned the astrolabe on the letter. When nothing happened, she looked up. "Now what?"

Lucy caressed the metal of the lid. "No carvings."

"From everything I could find on Craxtans," Cassandra said, "the decoder needs to interact with the text in some way."

Beatrix nodded. "So maybe it isn't enough to set it on the letter."

"We know how the Alicorn worked, but how did you decipher the first clue with the mirror?" Emma asked.

"I'm not sure." Beatrix strained to recall. "I remember looking at myself in the mirror and then lifting the letter."

"Did the writing reflect on it perhaps?" Cassandra asked.

"It happened so fast." Beatrix rubbed her temples in frustration.

Next to her, Emma grabbed the astrolabe and flipped it around. Brought it close to her eye. Then she shook it. "We could take it apart," she said, staring at the little screws in one corner.

Beatrix snatched it from her hands with horror.

"Let's go for a less intrusive method," Lucy said.

For the next hour, they tried everything. Placing the astrolabe opened. Closed. Wrapping it with the letter. Peering through it, taking the lid off. Reflecting it on the mirror. Copying the signs and shaping them over the letter. Tracing the symbols with a stylus.

Nothing worked. The letter remained dead, unwilling to give up its secrets.

"I don't understand," Emma said, her now ash-brown hair dull and tangled.

"I was sure it must be a decoder," Beatrix said.

"It has to be." Cassandra ran her fingers across the astrolabe's face. "Your grandfather wouldn't have left you these things if they didn't mean anything. Plus, the mirror worked." Instead of her usual perfect posture, Cassandra was slumped in her chair.

Lucy traced the writing on the letter with her glittery fingernail. "What are we missing? I wonder what was different that day."

Good question, Beatrix thought. In her mind, she went back to her discovery of the first clue, retracing not only her immediate steps but further back. Before she even picked up the mirror. Before she unfolded the letter. The memory of her anger at Martin spilled again like fresh blood. The shock of Grandpa's death and the tang of the Furie's power in her mouth, its magic pricking at the tip of her fingers.

"That must be it!" Emma said, following her thoughts. "The *B* hint says, 'What's denied holds power and you wield it all.'"

The others were fast to catch on.

"So you have to be using your power for it to work," Lucy said.

"That would be a brilliant failsafe," Cassandra said, her tone one of awestruck respect, "so the wrong person couldn't decipher the riddle."

"Call it, Beatrix," Lucy said, her eyes aglow. "Call your Furie and try again."

The Furie.

Could it be the key to the riddle? After the intruder, the idea was less preposterous than it might have been a week ago. If Beatrix could decipher the Craxtan with its help…

Hope flourished, expectancy filling her, as if she were on the brink of something. A monumental discovery.

Even without the help of the Taming Sphere, which was meant to stabilize it, the monster had been more docile of late, so bringing the Furie forth was the work of a second; it lingered that close to the surface.

With its power crackling, Beatrix got hold of the astrolabe again, and this time when she popped the lid open, the drawings on its face lifted like a 3D projection. The moon, the sun, and the astronomical symbols turned like the planets in a tiny solar system model. She grinned, waiting for something to happen. When a few minutes had passed and nothing did, she began to worry. Her fingertips had gone numb with pins and needles, the power seeking to overflow her control. *This is why I need that stupid Taming Sphere.* And why she had to redouble her exercises. She thought she was getting a bit better. A tiny bit.

"I'm going to have to stop," Beatrix warned her friends a few seconds later. She still couldn't get used to being this open about magic. To the people around her accepting it as a matter of course. Grandpa's cloak wouldn't work on taelimns, Jane had explained, so she wouldn't have been able to hide the Furie even if she'd wanted to.

"Hold it just a bit longer," Cassandra said. "Something's changing."

Beatrix looked closer. On her palm, the astrolabe glowed still, but now, as the sun and the moon shifted across the little sky, shiny dots began to rise from the edges. Everyone gasped, wonder, a shared emotion.

Emma clapped her hands. "Stars! You're doing it."

"Should I set it on the letter?" Beatrix asked Cassandra, who was the most versed in the mechanisms of Craxtans. By now, Beatrix was shaking from the effort to hold the Furie in control. The fear of the monster releasing and hurting everyone around her felt like a living thing.

"On the paper, yes, quickly," Cassandra said.

But when Beatrix placed the astrolabe on the letter, the rotating sky faded away. Sweat dripping, she held the Furie at bay for another couple of seconds and then, using every trick Grandpa had taught her, shut it down. She could almost hear its growl as she slammed the doors inside her that kept it caged.

"Damn it," she said. "So close." Defeat swirled around the table, sad like the half-eaten rest of their feast. She lifted the astrolabe, warm to the touch but dead once more.

Or maybe…not quite. "Stars," Beatrix whispered, running her finger along the bezel, now dotted with the carvings of tiny luminaries.

"We're almost there. Try again," Emma said.

Cassandra shook her head. "Enough testing for today. We should leave it be for now before we ruin something. I have to head to work anyway."

Beatrix met Cassandra's gaze, thankful that her friend understood how exhausted she was—and how close she'd come to losing control.

"But the thimble," Emma insisted. Lucy must have given her a look, because Emma closed her mouth midprotest.

"Are you still planning to visit the Quills later?" Lucy asked, probably sensing a change of subject might be for the best. "I'd love to come along."

It was Emma who answered. "We are. We're planning to cover the bookshop mile. Someone has to remember the title of the book."

Beatrix nodded. "Even after I cornered the Librarian yesterday at dinner, he refused to let me ask the Codex again. He says he's unfamiliar with the title himself." Beatrix had spent the whole conversation gritting her teeth. The Librarian's dismissive and superior attitude made her want to punch him. Especially because she suspected he *did* know the title. He'd been acquainted with Beatrix's mom after all.

"Discovering the title would simplify the search for a copy tremendously," Lucy said. "And who knows? Mary might even be mentioned in the story."

"I'm surprised it is this hard to figure out the book's name." Beatrix began to return Grandpa's things to the chest. The astrolabe was still lukewarm. "It's not like the Eisid is an obscure place. It was the headquarters of the rebels. Wouldn't that make the book infamous?"

"Good point!" Cassandra said. "I'll ask our friend Dyøt. I don't know why it didn't occur to me earlier. He wrote his master's thesis on the Rebellion War, so he should know about the Eisid Naraid, including the titles in the series." Cassandra gave Beatrix a severe look. "Put that away. You should leave that astrolabe alone for the rest of the day. This is magic we're messing with. Who can tell what we're stirring?"

Beatrix dropped the astrolabe into the chest with reluctance—because she felt tired and also annoyed. And later, her frustration mixed with unease when she discovered the black spiderweb of veins on her forearms. They took over seven hours to fade.

16

UNCLE

Soon, just as the sun began sinking past its midpoint, Beatrix, Lucy, and Emma headed for the city to visit the Quills.

Beatrix's second view of Læsting was less overwhelming, if not any less bizarre. Its wacky, hodgepodge landscape surprised her at every turn, winning her over before she could notice. The place had an undeniable charm that she guessed was borrowed from the tales from which everything had been transplanted.

The pods got them to their destination with smooth efficiency, and Beatrix had to recognize some Zweeshen technology made up for its other letdowns.

"The Quills." Emma, who had an unquenchable enthusiasm for shopping, had spent the journey sharing the neighborhood's particularities. "They call it the bookstore mile. You won't encounter more stories for sale anywhere in the worlds."

"The perfect place to find your mom's book," Lucy said, with her typical optimism.

Beatrix smiled, wanting to believe.

They started on a hopeful note.

"I remember that name, Leyna Yoru," said an old woman with a flute stuck in her hair at the second store they entered when they mentioned Beatrix's Mom. "A good story. I haven't seen it for years."

"Do you recall the title?" Beatrix asked. "It would help our search. Or perhaps the author?"

The woman thought hard, caressing a catlike creature with two tails coiled around her neck beneath her needlepoint shawl. "Something about the stars. No, that's not right, maybe the moon..." She looked up, regret on her face. "Sorry, my memory isn't what it used to be. I've been feeding it to my baby." She stroked the cat. "He loves stories as treats and what's a mommy to do."

They left convinced someone else would remember. But their early luck proved a fluke, and after scouring every store, from dingy one-room affairs to outdoor stands, quaint fairy-tale cottages to a sleek loft overlooking the river, Beatrix was ready to scream.

"I'm so sorry, Bea," Lucy said, tiredness straining even her features.

They tried two more places, including one that Trelius had recommended, but Beatrix had a hard time concentrating.

"It's no fun if you obsess about the letter and miss everything else that's special about the city," Emma said. "Lucy and I still have shopping to do. Gotta get new gloves at Sartre's dress shop and pick up the sound-cancelling boots I ordered for you. You might as well return to check the Main Library at Navarsing and try the Sphinx. Who knows, you might get an answer. And don't believe her boasts. She won't eat you."

Beatrix never got to face the Sphinx. William ambushed her at the exit of the pods at Navarsing University station. She suspected he'd been waiting for a while.

"I was hoping to catch you."

She stared at him, trying to decide whether to be nice or let his charming smile go to waste. Seriously. They should have rules for artisans. She'd begun to develop an inferiority complex, surrounded by people who'd been designed to look perfect. Didn't writers know better? Add a crooked nose, a limp, give the girls some cellulite, for God's sake.

"I'm sorry I surprised you at breakfast," he said, his voice a tad too impatient to be contrite. "I realize it wasn't the best choice."

She felt tempted to give in. Then thought better of it. "Like what you're doing now is much different?"

"I need you to tell me if anything happened yesterday night. It's important. Do you remember any incidents?"

The intensity of his tone forced her to do a double take. Did he know about the intruder? How could he? She almost asked. No. She wouldn't give him the satisfaction of engaging. For once, her curiosity wouldn't get the better of her. "I have no clue what you mean. Go away."

William nodded. As if he'd expected her refusal and it didn't bother him. "You don't forgive easily, do you?"

"Not if I did nothing to deserve the bad treatment."

They'd reached the station's entrance, and when he stood in silence, blocking it, she had no choice but to meet his eyes. "Do you mind? I have stuff to do."

He stepped aside and opened the door for her.

What he didn't do was leave. He walked in lockstep while she crossed Navarsing's sunken gardens and followed one of the myriad gravel paths.

Beatrix huffed.

"How was your shopping?" he asked, as if they'd been making small talk all along.

"Great."

"Why are you back so soon then?"

"I didn't feel like shopping."

He grinned.

"What's so funny?"

"It's unexpected."

"Because I'm a girl? I should've guessed you'd be into stereotypes."

"I'm not. You always have new clothes on, so I figured—" He studied her for a moment. "Emma buys them, doesn't she?"

Beatrix continued looking ahead.

"I'm sorry I was so rude by the boat," he said. "You didn't deserve it. Can I make it up to you? Maybe we can make a deal. Emma said you're searching for some information. I might be able to help."

She glowered. "I need to have a word with that traitor."

"Please, don't. Emma meant well. This is my fault. I thought keeping my distance was safest. Now I'm almost certain it isn't."

"What are you talking about?"

William looked down for a moment, then at her. "Just that I was trying to be chivalrous, and I made a mess. I'd like to start over. So how about this—I'll guess what you're after, and if I give you the answer, you agree to a truce."

"I didn't start the war."

His lip curved the smallest bit. "More of a skirmish, actually."

"It's only getting started."

"I'm sure I can handle it." His voice teetered on teasing, and it annoyed her.

What was different now? He hadn't wanted anything to do with her a few days ago. Why did he insist on talking to her today?

Maybe because something *had* changed. It was in the way he looked at her, as if his armor were gone, and she saw him for the first time. And as she stared at him, trying to figure him out, the air grew taut, like the string of a violin, stretched but unreleased. Beatrix felt the tightness on her skin and deep in her belly, together with a crackling that was not magical but that she refused to investigate. Even when it pulled her forth to him.

He felt it too, whatever it was that swirled around them—she recognized it in his eyes that both darkened and warmed.

"We started on the wrong foot," he said, looking down. "But I'd like to be friends."

She almost snorted at that. "I think that ship sailed."

"Only if you can't accept an apology."

When anger flashed through her, Beatrix was relieved and freed from the weird thing floating between them. Insulted, the Furie stirred, and she could tell he sensed the energy because his skin rose in static bumps. The muscles in his arm tensed.

She still had to ask. "What changed?"

He shrugged. "I believed I was doing the right thing. I realized I wasn't. So from now on, no more invisibility amulets or shading spells to hide from you. And no rude answers."

He'd been hiding? This became stranger by the minute. It made no sense at all. "Why were you hiding?"

"Because I was an utter idiot." His eyes glimmered with mischief. "Where I'm from, knights perform a difficult feat when asking for forgiveness." He bowed. "I'm putting my fate in your hands. My apologies, fair lady. What token would you have me produce?" William straightened. "Perhaps some information you seek?"

"You're ridiculous."

"So, deal?" he asked with a smile.

It made no sense that it kept getting harder to stay angry. "What if Emma ratted me out and told you what I'm after?"

His expression showed a mix of shock and mortification. "I have honor."

She rolled her eyes. "Whatever. Fine. Guess away." She sucked at holding a grudge for long anyway. Did that make her weak? A sucker?

"All right. Here goes. You want your book's title. Your mother's story is part of the Eisid Naraid series by Kitte Istrehagan. The first volume is called the *Inninsagur: The Priestess of the Evermoon*. Am I warm?"

How did he...? "Do you share Emma's power?" Horror of horrors if he did.

"Nothing as interesting. I've been trained to read people and to predict." Beatrix spun around in the direction of the marketplace and the center of campus.

"Wait! Where are you going now?"

"You should be able to predict it."

"Touché," he said, half his lip up. "Thanks for shrinking my head back to size."

With determined strides, Beatrix began to cross the street. "Emma said that while Libraries won't carry my story, bookstores should. I'm going to Beatty's Ol' Books. Somewhere on Main. They're supposed to have the biggest Fantasy selection."

"It's on Third." A flash of pain contorted his features, and he scrunched his shoulder blades. "Hold on. I'll show you the way."

"How come you knew the title when nobody else does?" A note of suspicion must have snuck in her tone because he turned with an affronted look.

"I've been friends with your uncle Worth for years," he said. "Of course I'm familiar with his whole series."

As it turned out, Beatty's bookstore did not carry her mother's series and had no inventory search capabilities for other locations.

"Not even old-fashioned catalog cards?"

The woman behind the counter glared as if Beatrix had suggested she gave up her firstborn. "I ken nothing about that book."

"Come on." William guided Beatrix out of the store. "I'll ask Jane and Trelius to check their sources. There has to be a record of copies somewhere. Originals are easy to find most of the time."

"Originals?"

His mouth twitched. "I keep forgetting you're new around here. Originals are stories from before the creation of the Zweeshen."

"And that is what the Eisid Naraid is?"

He nodded, then turned thoughtful. "Bookstores carry most Originals. Except—"

"Yes?" she asked, her impatience fraying her tone.

"Unless it's banned. But there's no easy way to figure out if it was."

"What, no lists?"

He shook his head.

Beatrix considered this new information. "Would it be banned because the land was sealed?"

His right eyebrow drew a pointed arch. "You heard about that?"

"And I read about it." Beatrix had finished the first tome of the history book already. "I haven't found much about sealed worlds yet."

William studied her with intensity, searching for something—what, she didn't know—but she straightened her back under his scrutiny.

"There are no set rules around sealed worlds," he said after a few moments. "And it's all top secret."

Beatrix grimaced. *Of course.* "I still don't get why the Eisid Naraid was sealed in the first place," she said. "I learned a bit about the Rebellion, but their reasons weren't too clear. Who were they?"

His face grew calculating, as if he were making conscious choices on how much to share. "The Rebellion was a bloody war. A group of dissidents called the Pioneers tried to take over the council."

"That I know. But what did they want?"

"What they didn't want was the Bounding. And all its perks." His sarcasm showed, but Beatrix didn't understand why.

"Like?"

"Like immortality."

Immortality. Now that she thought of it, Jane and Emma had alluded to that. A shiver ran through her. The idea of remaining sixteen forever sent her heart into turmoil. "Are you immortal?" Then, what she really was curious about. "Am I?

William pinned her with his ever-penetrating gaze, as if trying to extract all her secret thoughts. "I'm bound. Same as everyone." He lifted his arm and exposed the wristband there. A thick leather band with a sword and the dragonesque badge across it. High Fantasy. With an added subgenre she didn't recognize. "So yes, I'm almost immortal. Which is not to say I can't be killed. As for you… Hard to be certain. Maybe you'll stop aging once you connect to your book."

Beatrix stopped walking, the effort to process that too much. Immortality in the abstract, in exciting stories and adventurous tales, was one thing. Here in the harsh light of day, quite a different proposition. Would she remain like this forever? The idea gave her both claustrophobia and vertigo. Then another thought occurred to her. "How old are you?"

He took a moment before answering. "I'd turned nineteen when my story ended. We don't age after The End. So it's impossible to tell."

A flurry of thought fragments rearranged themselves like a mosaic in Beatrix's head. "Emma told me time doesn't flow in the Zweeshen as on Earth. Just like it doesn't in the fairy realms of the legends. I guess I didn't realize what it meant. How weird. I can't imagine not knowing my own age."

"You already don't," he said, and from the suppressed glee on his face, she questioned whether he enjoyed shocking her. "In the Zweeshen, time is relative. Like in books, it lengthens and shortens and can skip altogether, so that a minute here can translate to anywhere between a second, a century, or millennia on Pangea."

She gasped. "How long have I been here then?"

"Two days, six months, maybe a year—or three. In any case, you're no longer sixteen." He watched her pupils widen and added, "Don't worry. You'll be able to return to the same time you came, give or take a week."

"A week!" Beatrix imagined the police cars and the flashing lights in front of her house. She swallowed hard. She saw Martin. Disheveled and gaunt, his face concerned. Would he be? Concerned? Would he care? Maybe he wouldn't bother to report her missing at all. *Buen viaje and good riddance.* Beatrix had often thought he'd rather she wasn't there. Or never had been born. But her disappearing altogether... Perhaps it was the distance the Zweeshen allowed, but she didn't think he'd be happy with that. As nasty as Martin could be, there were glimpses. Like the time she'd gotten into that accident with the Jeep. There had been something in his eyes, not caring exactly but—

"You'll get back home," William said, either misunderstanding her expression or more perceptive than she'd given him credit for.

She wasn't certain why she said it. The thought snuck out before she could strangle it. "I'm not sure where home is."

He slid his hands in his pockets and stared away. His voice turned soft. "My teacher used to tell me 'home' doesn't have to be where you were born. You can create yours wherever you choose. He's convinced the people you love are what counts. A bit of a romantic." William angled back to her, searching her expression.

"What about you?" she asked.

"If I'm a romantic?"

"If you believe that about home."

"I'm proof of it. My adoptive land's more my home than my world of origin ever was."

"I'm hoping the Eisid might be mine," Beatrix said.

His forehead wrinkled. "The Eisid Naraid is a dangerous place. I wouldn't count on that. You need to be careful when you ask about it too. Don't mention the Rebellion."

Even if he'd tried to hide it, the edge of an order glinted off his last words, and sharp like Excalibur, it killed whatever amiability had dared breathe between them.

Beatrix hadn't been planning to inquire about the Rebellion, but now, as if the command were a purposeful taunt, the Furie sprang alive. "Stop telling me what to do. It's already annoying I can't access my mom's book, and that the Librarian and the ridiculous council get to decide whether I stay or I go. I will ask whatever I want. What's it to you?"

William faced her, a hard line to his already angular jaw. "You cannot be that oblivious. Or that irresponsible. The Pioneers are dangerous. I won't let you kill yourself."

"I'm not planning to. Not that it's your concern."

"Your safety is."

"No, it isn't," Beatrix said through her teeth. "If you want to help, then enable my Bounding, so I can stay in the Zweeshen legally."

"That won't happen. The council's playing politics. Bounding is out of the question after guild rejection."

"Thanks for reminding me that no guild wants me!"

"That's not what I meant." Like the rest of his tall figure, William's words were strained.

"You're not good at saying what you mean then."

In the pause that followed, Beatrix saw him inhale, and when he spoke again, his manner was careful. "Look, you and I are on the same side. We both want to get you to your biblioworld as soon as possible. We cannot guess how much Inaechar you have left, and you'll need a reserve to connect to your book."

She lifted her chin. "I will travel to Mom's after I finish what I need to do here. I will stay however long that takes." And not even the council would stop her.

William's eyes flashed. "The one thing you don't have, Beatrix, is time. I'm not convinced you realize that."

"Again, you don't get to decide. Why are you involved anyway?"

"I told you. I've made a vow to your uncle."

"Yes, Worth." Beatrix tilted her face. "Where is he, by the way? Do you want to be useful? Help me find him. Help me discover more about my family. And about the Eisid Naraid. I have a letter from my mother with a complex riddle in it. Help me with that."

William didn't respond.

"Then I won't listen to you."

They hiked in angry silence. In the early dusk, the campus buildings already beckoned, limestone aglow under the yellow lanterns, when a piercing ache stabbed her head. Beatrix pressed her eyes closed and inside her fists, her nails dug into her palms. Again? The pain was worse than on any previous occasions, and when a mossy smell enveloped her, she felt it: the anger, the desire to do something reckless, to let go and just be. Magic and pain mixed and churned inside her.

"I can walk alone from here," she said, her words wheezing out in a trickle. She moved away from William, unsteady, and turned into the strip of woods flanking this part of the gardens.

When she tripped a few hundred feet later, he caught her, but she barely realized it while her body convulsed, semiaware of how William lowered her to the ground, cradling her head until the assault passed. It ended in less than a minute, and Beatrix sat up, pushing him away.

"How long has this been happening?" William asked in a growl.

"It's nothing." But the protest tumbled out, feeble. She felt so drained that lifting her hands required full concentration.

"This is what I feared. Why you can't stay around the Zweeshen as if you were on vacation. You won't recover until we take you to your world. You need a healer. Come with me."

"Leave me be!"

William dropped to his knees at her side; he bent his head forward. His intake of breath was deep and slow. "Please. I'm not telling you what to do. I'm trying to help you. I don't like this role either. This plot was written for us, and my life is at stake too. Let us be partners, please. These attacks. You're spilling magic. We need to conserve your Inaechar until you get synched. If you don't…"

Her frustration had grown its own voice. "Stop trying to scare me. I'm an Unwritten, remember? Nobody writes my story. So what if I don't listen to you? What terrible thing will happen?"

"This is Roamer's, Beatrix. If you don't get synched to your biblioworld soon, you'll die."

Part Three

LÆSTING

17

APOTHECARY

Beatrix had been wrong.

At first, she tried to hide from that truth. She wished to run away and curl up in a ball in the corner of a cave where nobody could laugh at her idiocy.

"You're making it worse. Let me help you," William had shouted after her the previous evening.

"Stop trying to scare me!" she'd screamed back and stormed off, allowing the Furie to explode a few branches into splinters on her way to the guesthouse. Just to prove she didn't care about his warnings. The outburst had fired up her blood with excitement. It had felt freeing and good. Which it probably shouldn't.

"Damn him," she'd muttered to herself. He brought out her most childish and stubborn reactions. She seemed incapable of keeping her cool around him.

But she'd been wrong. And like Grandpa had taught her, Beatrix took responsibility. Thinking of Grandfather brought forth the ever-present ache. Even when her memories of him were tarnished by the knowledge of what he'd hidden from her. By now, she'd become familiar enough with the rules of the Zweeshen to surmise he must've been a character too. Probably from the same book as Mom. He hadn't told her about this place. Instead, he had lied. Hidden things. Like the fact that Mom was even now in the Eisid Naraid. That she hadn't died. Beatrix wished she could ask him why, and rail at him, but as mad as all that made her, it was his smile that came to mind when she thought of him.

She sighed. She couldn't let nostalgia take over; her energy was best spent figuring out the letter.

Armed with the book's title, Beatrix, Cassandra, and Emma had redoubled the search for a copy of the book. So far, it had borne no fruits. No matter. They had a long list of ideas to try.

But first things first. Beatrix had her pride and a few of her own words to swallow.

"How do ladies in your world apologize?" she asked William now. She'd found him by the sailboats again. He had the appearance of someone who'd been in a brawl. "Did you get in a fight?"

He gave her a tired smile. "Is it that bad?"

"Yes. Did you?"

"No. I mean... I might have attempted to overthrow the guards that protect the Librarian to get a word with him."

She flinched. "Why would you do that?"

"Maybe I wanted to get punched? You should've seen the expression on the old man's face. Worth it."

Beatrix laughed.

"Happy I can amuse you," he said without bitterness.

She sat down on a dock step, facing the ocean. The water was choppy today. White crowns of foam highlighted the waves. It wasn't just time. The seasons in the Zweeshen must follow different patterns from Earth as well because, after the previous days' chill, it had turned warm and sunny. The temperature surprised everyone, lulling them into a sense of early spring, full of promise and possibilities.

Beatrix relaxed back, letting the sun warm her face. Delaying didn't help what needed to be done.

"You were right," she said, hoping he wouldn't gloat or say I told you so.

He didn't. He simply stared at her, then nodded.

Despite her complaints the day before, William had sent a note with directions to the apothecary. She'd discovered a folded paper on her rosewood dresser. Against the cream-colored paper with the seal of the Fantasy Guild, William's curious handwriting stood out. Simple and short, his words—more the way they were shaped than the writing itself—reminded Beatrix of treasure maps, old calling cards, and royal edicts.

At least find out what you're dealing with.
-W

She had located the strange shop early that morning, in an area of campus—east of the Yellow Road—that she'd never visited during her previous excursions. There, the buildings were plain and ordinary-looking, without any of the fairy-tale enchantment of the Market Square and the surrounding alleys.

When she'd entered the apothecary, Beatrix guessed she'd stepped inside the trunk of a tree. The round room smelled earthy, Tarzan-worthy vines hung from a ceiling too black to be seen, and mushrooms grew in multiple nooks. Countless shelves buckled under the weight of glass jars, cork-stoppered bottles, and lacquered boxes. A few specimens floated in clear and amber liquid bowls, organic shapes she didn't care to inspect any closer.

"I'm trying to find out about Roamer's," she told the hairy creature behind the counter.

Without a glance at her, he slapped a heavy book on a nearby table. "No creasing the pages."

The Encyclopedia of Personage Ailments was bound in a brown, leafy material that creaked when she opened it. It contained no index, and the entries weren't in alphabetical order.

As Beatrix scanned the book, pictures of horrifying diseases and gruesome operations flickered at her.

"Ach! Move aside." The shopkeeper hobbled next to her. "You'll be here all day if I let you. They're not even taught basic searching anymore. What passes for a taelimn today." He mumbled on, shaking his head while he tapped the cover with his long-nailed pinky. The pages flipped to the appropriate section. "Back in the times of the True King... Here. Roamer's."

Beatrix read.

Roamer's disease, or Traveler's pest, attacks taelimns who have spent too long outside of their native biblioworlds, causing their Inaechar to drop below safe levels.

Roamer's can take several forms, including convulsions, seizures, and coma.

A subset of patients has been known to develop secondary symptoms referred to as Chronic Roams. Those affected experience confusion, memory lapses, cognitive decline, and dementia.

Without appropriate treatment, Roamer's disease is fatal. Physical synching by visiting the biblioworld of origin is the only known cure. There is no cure for the chronic version of Roamer's.

Now, sitting at the marina, the briny air flowing over her, Beatrix wondered if perhaps Grandpa had suffered from Roamer's.

"We should expedite the trip to the Eisid Naraid," William said while he knotted the line into an intricate pattern.

"I understand the consequences," she said. "But I can't leave now. I have things to do here first."

"Nothing's more important than your life."

"To me, this is. I can't go yet."

William cursed, something about his knot not to his liking. "Fine. You've got a bit of time. But as soon as the council hearing's over and your passage approved, you have to travel. You can come back if you want. Once you've synched and replenished your Inaechar."

Beatrix bit her lip. She wasn't going to argue again.

With the help of Cassandra, Lucy and Emma, she was making progress with the riddle, and they'd gathered some new ideas to find Mary. Beatrix worried about reaching Mom's world without having fulfilled the tasks in the letter. *Take Mary Brandt to the Eisid Naraid, and we will reunite.* No ambiguity there. So what would happen if Beatrix was forced to travel before she accomplished it?

"I will appeal the council's decision if I have to," she said. "I will do whatever I can to stay as long as I need. I won't leave until I'm ready."

William's face tightened in a configuration of angles and sharp edges. "Pushing too hard could backfire. Public opinion is divided over you. You could be deported."

That hadn't occurred to her. "I would end up back on Earth, even farther from the Eisid." And from seeing Mom.

"I won't let it happen," he said with such violence Beatrix was startled. "You wouldn't survive even a day on Pangea. Being here has changed things. It takes Inaechar to live in the Zweeshen, and by now your levels wouldn't allow you to manage on Earth. You can't use your magic at all. You realize that, right?"

"I don't use the Furie much. I—" Beatrix stopped herself, because she had been calling on her power more often than normal since arriving in the Zweeshen. "What about my practice exercises? I do them every day." She didn't tell him how frustrating those were. How she continued to fail after years of trying. That the Taming Sphere necessary to control her Furie remained beyond her capabilities. But those exercises were as much a part of her routine as brushing her teeth. Their mere repetition, a comfort. What if, without them, she regressed? During the episode with the intruder, she'd felt so much more secure in the Furie than, well, ever. She didn't want to lose whatever progress she'd accomplished through daily training.

William pinned her with a furious gaze. "No practice. No magic use at all."

Beatrix bucked at the sight of his clenched jaw and the anger contained even in the way he stood. He had a talent for making her bristle. But then his face softened, and a shy smile curled half his lips.

"You really hate to be told what to do, don't you?"

"How about you?"

He laughed. "I doubt that would stop you."

"So we're agreed then. I'm safe to stay in the Zweeshen."

He shook his head, but resignation was clear on his face. "Not indefinitely. Too long, and this place will kill you too. You have to get to the Eisid Naraid, Beatrix. The faster, the better. Another week at most. But you were right yesterday too. I should help, with that letter and whatever you need to do here."

She hesitated for a moment, unsure about how much she'd be willing to share after the way he'd reacted in the past.

His smile was barely there. "You don't have to like me all of a sudden. I can try to assist regardless." He snuck his hands in his coat and looked to the ocean. When he stared back at her, a new weariness had been edged around his eyes. "About the other thing. You know Neradola's a great healer. Let her examine you. There are remedies against Roamer's."

"I read about the potions. They're all useless." Beatrix's voice sounded more desperate than she'd intended. "They don't stop the leak, and I'm not feeling that bad."

"Would you at least give Nera a chance?"

"I'll meet with her but won't discuss Roamer's."

He opened his mouth to argue and abandoned the plan. "You just need to synch to the Eisid."

"How does synching work?"

"When you physically travel to your story, you will reconnect with it and replenish your Inaechar, your taelimn lifeblood."

"How fast?" Beatrix was already planning her return if she had to leave before completing her task. Oh, how she'd hate that.

William answered in a flat tone. "Synching should take anywhere between a few days and two weeks. The longest I've heard is two months."

Two months! No, Beatrix decided; she had to get everything done before leaving.

William finished attaching the line and secured the folded sails.

She stood up.

Somehow, her annoyance with him had dispersed, wafted away like early mist over the sea, and the Furie slept inside her, quiet and meek. "Thank you."

He watched her with an expression she couldn't decipher. "What?"

"Nothing. I just— Nothing. Are you hungry?"

She wasn't, but the food in the Zweeshen was the only thing so far that lived up to expectations.

"I could eat," she said.

18

EXILE

That day, the Bookends Café boasted a French Proust theme. Waiters, their large napkins draped over their forearms, balanced trays around tiny round tables. Bistro chairs and Chanson music spilled onto the sidewalk, where women in sundresses and men in shorts talked and laughed in the sunshine.

"Do you want to sit outside?" William asked, following her eyes.

"That'd be nice." Her voice came out small. She felt self-conscious without good reason.

They sat, and each focused on browsing the offerings.

"We mostly come for breakfast," Beatrix said. "What's good from the lunch menu?"

"How hungry are you?"

"Actually, more in the mood for dessert."

"So you have a sweet tooth?"

"A bit." She paused, giving up. "A lot. I have a weakness for chocolate and dulce de leche."

"Crêpe Waterloo then. You won't regret it."

"I don't ever regret chocolate."

William laughed, a hearty, open sound that matched the bright table setting and the sun. A first as far as she remembered.

"There are a couple of biblioworlds dedicated to just chocolate," he said. "Popular vacation spots."

"Now you tell me? Forget the Eisid. I need to travel there."

He laughed again, but this time his stare dug deep, pulling away all the covers until she was exposed to her core.

"What's your life on Pangea like?" he asked, as soon as the singing waiter left with their orders. ("Opera taelimns," William had explained. "They can't help themselves.")

"My life's boring. School mostly. Why do they call it Pangea?"

"To differentiate it from the other Earths. The name means hope. Do you like your town?"

"It's all right. Uneventful. Too small. How about yours?"

"Nice deflection." He played with his water, tracing circles with his fingers on the condensation on the glass. "My home's cold. So you live with your dad."

"Yep."

"No other relatives?"

"You tell me. You seemed to know of an uncle I don't."

"Who taught you about the Furie?"

"My grandfather. He called it a talent but never explained where it came from, said some people were born with it. He worked hard to teach me to control it and to master the Taming Sphere."

"Did he have any Fantasy magic?"

"Am I in an interrogation?"

"Maybe." He flashed a charming smile not any less effective for her knowledge of what he was up to. "But I'm bribing you with chocolate."

It was easy to confide in him, even without the encouragement. Beatrix couldn't explain why. Perhaps the secret lay in the way he paid attention to her answers, or how he weaved in new questions so she kept forgetting her own.

She ended up telling him about Grandpa, how he'd shown up on the worst night of her life and somehow made her feel...

"I don't know. Normal?" A shy shard of glass dislodged inside her when she accepted this out loud. But nothing in the air changed between them. William's eyes stayed warm. "Or maybe he was so odd I seemed normal by comparison." She chuckled, a nervous sound squeezing out.

"Normal's overrated. Who can tell what normal is anyway?"

Beatrix's face ironed out in seriousness. "People can. They say we're all unique snowflakes. It isn't true. Some people are more different than others, and everyone else notices."

"Is it that bad?"

"What?"

"To be unique."

A weirdo more like it, she thought, but held back. "I never found an upside."

"Seems like your grandfather did."

That drew out a smile. Yeah. Grandpa had mastered that particular art. And before she realized it, Beatrix was telling William more about him. About their sun-soaked adventures when she was a kid, and the shreds of memories stuck to her brain as if stapled. About his death, the empty, hollowed-out feeling, and the struggle to keep the Furie at bay when she got upset.

"You have a lot of discipline. I've seen it," William said, and she wondered how he could have.

The waiter came and went, taking away their empty plates, refilling their sparkling water and coffee. They barely noticed.

"Your grandfather never told you about the Zweeshen?"

She shrank a little at the sting.

William must have read something on her face. "I'm sure he had his reasons not to share."

"I'll never get it. Before Emma, I had no idea that taelimns existed."

When the conversation turned to Martin, Beatrix skimmed over the subject, but the tendons in William's temples showed he guessed the truth in the holes she left.

They talked about books, how stories could both change and save a life, how they connected people across time and space, and she wondered if that was true of the two of them. If at some point, she back home, he somewhere far away, they had already met, reading the exact same page.

She didn't recognize many of the titles he mentioned. He, for his part, hadn't been exposed to some of her favorites.

"It's unacceptable you haven't read that series," William said of an epic story he was partial to. "We need to fix that."

"You have to promise to commit to Isaac's full works then. A fair trade."

He extended his hand. "Deal."

His skin was warm and inviting. "Did you read Naindiur's *Forgotten Citadel Series*? That one you can't miss."

On many titles, they agreed. They debated and argued over some.

"It doesn't matter what you think. He's one of the best heroes of all time," Beatrix said.

"If you're into overbearing and controlling."

"You don't get him. He's dreamy."

William laughed again, enough times to make her forget it wasn't his natural way.

In the end, Beatrix even spoke of her mother, of missing someone you hardly knew, of her Jeep, and the whispers of stories in her library at night. She liked the way William listened, with intensity, as if hers were the most enthralling tale in the world, as if in the whole land of stories there weren't a life that compared.

"...then Grandpa died, and I discovered the message, and Emma came."

"Interesting timing. Can I see the letter?"

Beatrix fished the piece of paper out of her pouch.

His face closed up when he touched the marking on the map.

"I know it's a Craxtan," she said, "and I've deciphered two clues. Oh, and the map is the Sacred Valley in the Eisid."

"That's why you wanted that cartography book," he said, inspecting the edges of the letter.

"Yeah, thanks for getting it. And for the other books you sent after. We were hoping one contained a full world map."

"Did any of them?"

"No."

"I will borrow others." William ran his fingertips over the symbols. "Any idea what alphabet this is?"

"No alphabet. It's all a code."

His brow furrowed at that. "A double encoding. What about the verses in English, were they there all along?"

"Only the first clue, 'A letter for Beatrix' showed. The seal was torn already, so I suspect Grandpa opened it. I'm curious about the sentence on the side. It was visible from the start too, over there, in pencil."

"'Forbidden lines: 3X May the words.' I've heard the saying, as an intro to something else. It could be a Seal in this context, an activation phrase. You're familiar with the repetition of three to close a spell, I'm sure. Did you try it?"

"I thought the same thing. And yes, a classmate did try it." Beatrix thought of Julie's triumphant face that morning when she'd stolen the letter and screamed the forbidden words. The old rage rose, fermented rather than diluted. "She shouted them a few times. Nothing happened."

"That's a pity. Who's Mary Brandt?"

"No idea. This is why I need to find out more about the Eisid Naraid. We think the other decoders might be mentioned in my mom's book."

He seemed to consider that. "Could be. How did you decipher the first clue?"

"I looked at myself in the mirror. We—Cass, Lucy, Emma, and I— believe my magic was active."

"Would you show me the objects?" William asked.

Beatrix pulled out the mirror, the thimble, and the astrolabe.

"You have used the mirror already." Instead, William inspected the thimble's decorative carvings and then turned to the astrolabe. He clicked the lid open. "A moon and sun on an astrolabe's a bit strange. What does the clue say about stars again?"

She finished chewing on her madeleine before answering. "'The stars hide the secrets to open the sky.' We actually got those little stars to appear, but it didn't help uncover any more verses."

William ran his fingers over the face of the astrolabe. Tilted it against the bright light. "There seem to be notches where each star shows."

They both bent over it.

Beatrix squinted. "Tiny ones. Like clock markings."

"Or measurements," William said and at the same time twisted the outer bezel. As he did, the stars started to blink. The astrolabe came to life. The sun, the moon, all the symbols, and now the stars too lifted in a three-dimensional arrangement akin to a planetarium model.

"Or coordinates," Beatrix said, an idea beginning to shape in her mind. "Keep twisting. Maybe they have to reach a certain configuration."

But after several more turns yielded no results, William handed her the astrolabe back. "I suspect you have to do this."

His guess proved correct, because as soon as she repeated the motion, the objects began to rearrange themselves. Her Furie coursing, Beatrix gave the bezel a twist. Another. With each one, the elements shifted in a spiraled dance. At the third try, a clank reverberated with the note of a tuning fork. A line drew itself between the sun, the moon, and each of the stars.

"A constellation," she said.

William watched, as fascinated as she was. "I don't recognize it."

Then everything blinked once more before the symbols retreated to the bezel, where they became etchings shimmering dark red. The now empty glass of the astrolabe lifted, opening like the petaled lens of a camera.

A laugh burst out of Beatrix. "We did it."

"Place it on the letter," William said.

They did. But the verse revealed itself only after Beatrix looked through the astrolabe as if through a magnifying glass.

The new clue read:

> *Dare to turn your needle to lance.*
> *The fight that's pure is what counts.*
> *You hold the key to save us all*
> *if you don't doubt or fear the fall.*

Beatrix and William both looked up, beaming at their shared success.

"I can't believe we didn't think of twisting it," she said. "My friends and I tried about everything else."

William gave her a smile worthy of preservation. "I twisted it left because the astronomical symbols looked wrong, mirrored."

The excitement at their progress made her giddy. "Now we have to figure out what this means. There's only the thimble left, so that has to be the next decoder. And it speaks of a needle, so it's kind of on subject."

"Let's try it," he said.

But no matter what they attempted, the thimble didn't work.

"I guess I was getting too greedy," Beatrix said after another unsuccessful idea. "Maybe there's a maximum of one clue a day." She settled the thimble on her finger. Such an odd object. So old-fashioned. "There has to be a trick to it."

"Beatrix." William paused until she looked up. "You look exhausted. You've been using too much magic as is. I know there's no point in telling you to let the issue be. You need to decipher this, and you wouldn't listen anyway. Just—rest for today."

Beatrix was about to fight him, but the sight of the crackled skin of her hands stopped her. "Okay." She began putting the decoders away.

William watched her every move. "One more thing. Be careful to whom you show this letter. I speak from experience."

"What? Why?"

He didn't answer.

"That's not fair! It doesn't work like that. I shared a lot about myself. I have a question too. You didn't tell me much about you. Where you come from. Why you're part of this whole thing. How did you know my uncle? How did you get to Earth when it's forbidden?"

"That's more than one question."

"It's your fault they've accumulated. You got to ask me."

"You're much more intriguing." He tried smiling.

She didn't budge. "Did you know Grandpa? My mom?"

"I never met your grandfather. Like I told you, your uncle asked me to protect you. We met a long time ago in my world."

Beatrix's eyes lit up. "Does that mean we're all from the same story?"

"No. My father liked to wage war for the fun of it. The greatest warriors from everywhere came to join him. Your uncle Worth's a mercenary. That's how he and I became friends."

The way he said *father* gave her the impression they had something in common in that arena.

"So it's just Worth who's from my book."

"He was a secondary taelimn in a different book of the Eisid Naraid series. And you're not in any one story because you weren't written."

Beatrix grimaced. "I swear. The Zweeshen's so complicated."

"Is that a surprise? It's the creation of a bunch of self-involved thinkers who were given free rein." There was a cynical sharpness to his words, as if he disapproved of them, whoever they were, who had come up with the rules.

"I'd love to meet Worth. But you made it clear you had no interest in helping with that."

"Worth lied to me. I have no clue where he is."

"Lied about what?"

"It doesn't matter."

Beatrix was about to argue but decided against it. She'd get no further by pushing. "Is that why you're so annoying and always messing with my life? Because of my uncle?"

"I promised to keep you safe. I don't break oaths."

William was no longer smiling, and her irritation bubbled up, taking over her tongue. She didn't need a babysitter.

"Safe from what? I'm doing fine by myself. Why'd you even promise? You despise the task."

"Great point," he said, not a tense muscle in his body.

Like a popped balloon, her temper deflated at his admission.

William put his cup down with a clinking of china and looked toward the street. "My assignment was to deliver you to a safe place. Not sure what dangers Worth feared."

"And you didn't ask?"

For a second, his features darkened. "I owed him a favor."

"That would not work for me! I'd never commit without knowing what I'm signing up for."

"Very wise. Look what I got myself into. I was supposed to keep you veiled for a day."

When her eyes expressed confusion, he explained, "I have a...particularity. My magic-print cannot be followed. Neither can yours if you're with me. Worth thought someone might track you. As far as I know, that's how Evenzaar found you."

"Is that your Fantasy power?"

He shifted his shoulders and reached for a sip of coffee. She thought he was gearing up to deflect. "It's because I reneged on my world and exiled myself. And before you ask, yes, it's traitorous and illegal."

"Why did you do it?"

"A long story." Beatrix could tell the exact moment when he closed up.

In protest, her Furie growled, the sound so loud it escaped through her lips. "I told you everything about me."

But the spell of the spring day had died away. Clouds obscured the sun, and when she glanced around, Beatrix saw the café had emptied, and the waitstaff hurried, performing their cleanup duties.

It had gotten colder too. When a snappy breeze made her shiver, William handed her his jacket without a word. Because of the balmy weather, she'd never thought to bring hers. Beatrix didn't want to take it. She wasn't that delicate. Besides, how cliché. But he held it out until she grabbed it anyway. It smelled of soap and wood.

"We'd better go," he said in a distant voice.

And all of a sudden, despite the chocolate, her mouth tasted bitter.

19

CHARMANCER

The next evening, Cassandra invited Beatrix to dine along with her friends once again.

"We're going for supper to a popular pub," she'd said. "Dyøt promised to come, so you can meet him and ask about the Eisid. Plus, we can discuss options for the next decoder."

"I'd love to," Beatrix said.

So together, she and Cassandra headed to the Union Commons building, where they found their group in front of the large entrance. Lucy and Matt were involved in a private conversation, but Paul's face brightened at the sight of Beatrix.

Becca eyed her with suspicion. "They do wristband checks at the pub."

"We've got you covered," Matt said with an intimate smile at Lucy. He slapped a fabric band with a castle design on Beatrix's arm. "Won't pass muster up close but should be good enough to wave in front of the doorman."

A few minutes later, they set out for the pub, which was located in Olde Town, a part of Læsting Beatrix hadn't yet seen.

"We'll take the pods into the city," Lucy said to Beatrix's delight. Jane seemed to be the only person who preferred to go the three miles on foot.

Once in Læsting, the group followed a cobbled avenue flanked by jacarandas and marched across one of the many bridges lit up in soft orange that hung over the serpentine river.

The alley they entered stretched so narrow they had to walk in a single line, and when the slimy rock grazed her jacket, Beatrix grew suspicious. It opened onto a shadowy cul-de-sac which, incongruously, smelled of gingerbread. She spotted a dumpster, a broken-down fridge, several empty beer cans, and a battered armchair upholstered in one of the most hideous fabrics ever woven. The dirty green and brown paisley torn, the stuffing poked out in several places, and the cushion had caved in.

"You first, Cass," Matt said.

Becca growled at him. "Why? It's your choice of venue."

"I'll go." Lucy backed up a little and darted forward at an impressive speed despite her heels. She leapt onto the chair, sinking into it as if the pavement beneath had eaten her. Then she bounced up.

"Not even close!" Becca said.

Lucy jumped higher and higher until she vanished.

"She's in," Cassandra said. "It'll be a minute now."

Her head reappeared midair, and Lucy dropped a knotted ladder Beatrix would swear was made of braided hair. She wondered what the beer cans did.

"Come on. We won't get a table if we don't hurry," Paul said.

They scaled one by one, the ladder swinging, and Beatrix's stomach lurched a couple of times as she lost her footing. When she reached the top rung, Matt offered a hand, and she climbed out of a manhole with a breath of relief.

After the unorthodox entrance, the street above seemed unremarkable and deserted, lined with a variety of restaurants and shops, some of which were boarded up. So it was for no reason whatsoever that rust filled her mouth, the tangy taste of iron playing on her tongue. *Quiet,* she urged the monster, and a helpful whisper took over to hum a lullaby.

The pub stood in the light of three antique lamps, which illuminated a sign rocking on rusted hinges. The Elephant & Castle it announced, next to the image of an elephant on a spider web.

The façade had been painted red with black and gold accents, and paneled windows curved outward, giving them the appearance of bottle bottoms.

"I'm starving," Lucy said, pushing the door open.

Inside, it was dark and musty, the fermented smell of beer and used frying oil hanging like a cloud above the bar. Scarred tables with rough benches crowded the dining room, while a few booths sectioned the back wall.

"Oh, no! We've missed the happy hour. No mythical burgers for us." Paul's disappointment dripped onto a floor stained by a million spills.

The patrons looked interesting, to say the least. Beatrix saw winged creatures sitting next to military-dressed brutes, oversized talking rats, and women in can-can outfits. A little girl with a paper dress swept the floor, and two boys tested a toy cannon that shot puffs of pink cotton candy across the room. A hunchback danced awkwardly on a side stage, and some kind of space-age meeting was happening in a separate room, half-visible through sheer curtains. From behind the bar, an old gypsy with an eye patch shook a sequined pouch in Beatrix's direction, then spat.

Cassandra's laughter sounded like clinking crystal. "I don't care much for this place. Even if it's one of the most popular in Olde Town."

"I kind of like it," Beatrix said.

"Oh, no. You've been infected." Cassandra faked dismay, and as if she had jinxed her, a wave of nausea threatened to turn Beatrix's stomach. The monster stirred, uneasy. The Roamer's cramps were getting more frequent.

The group settled in a booth under some weird animal heads, around a table that past guests had defaced with hundreds of doodles. A few other people joined them, several coming and going, so that soon Beatrix struggled to keep the names and guilds and who studied what straight.

"Don't stress," Cassandra said. "They won't notice."

When the waiters brought the food, the group became even bigger and more boisterous, and Beatrix was pulled into several conversations. It seemed they were mostly university and guild students.

"The music's starting," Matt said shortly after. "Coming, Lucy?"

The rest of the table vacated so fast they made a breeze. Only Cassandra and Beatrix remained behind.

Beatrix pulled the letter from her pouch. "Here's the new verse I told you about."

"Remarkable," Cassandra said after studying it. "I knew the astrolabe had to be a decoder."

"Which makes me think the thimble must be another. The astrolabe needed to be twisted left. Maybe the thimble has a trick too."

Cassandra sipped her drink. "I just can't think what else we could do with it. It's a very simple object. Anything new on the map? Or about Mary?"

"No. William sent over more cartography books, and we split them, so he'll check too." Beatrix caressed the letter with her palm. "I thought we could focus on the words. The last time the little sky did open, so maybe the verse is revealing the mechanism of the decoder."

"Put it away," Cassandra said in an urgent tone.

Beatrix lifted her gaze from the paper with a start. "What? Why?"

"Later," Cass mouthed.

Quickly refolding the message, Beatrix shoved it in her pouch.

"I don't like the attention we're attracting," Cassandra murmured.

Beatrix scanned the room, noticing an inordinate amount of stares settled on them. Some openly hostile. She shrunk inside at the reminder that even here, she wasn't welcome. One seemed friendly though: a boy no older than thirteen winked at her, and she recognized him. Huck Finn still refused to wear shoes.

"Hey, guys," an animated voice said. The newcomer wore a bright patterned shirt. His short hair shone highlighter orange. Everything about him seemed colorful, and when he moved, he swaggered, as if his body thought he was dancing.

"Hi there, Dyøt," Cassandra said, scooting to let the addition sit down. "I guess your exam finished early. How was it?"

Dyøt made a face. "Before I answer, is that tankard full?"

"It's that blue drink you don't like," Cassandra told him. "But you're welcome to it."

"Shudder," Dyøt said. "I hate the stuff. For the record, the test was brutal. Professor Polihistor must have a cruel streak we've all missed."

"No!" Cassandra said. "He's like a grandpa. All nice and slow and caring."

"Until he grades. But anyway..." He turned to Beatrix. "So you're Bea. I'm Dyøt. I work with Cassandra, and she wouldn't stop talking about you. Did you already discuss masks? I'm helping Cass with hers."

Cassandra's face fell. "Oh, Bea. I totally forgot about the Monsters Ball."

"What's the Monsters Ball?"

One day, Beatrix hoped she wouldn't have to ask constant questions. After finishing *Tome III* of the essentials and history of the Zweeshen, she'd managed to get a hold of volumes I and II. But the Zweeshen was still too foreign, and many things others took for granted were new to her. It gave her the feeling of walking on thin ice, each step unsteady.

Dyøt lifted his arms. "What's the Monsters Ball? Only the best party in the worlds."

"Every year, all the guilds come together for a huge bash, and this being the land of stories, it's a masquerade," Cassandra said, a quirk to her lips. "A bit tongue-in-cheek."

"It's the biggest event ever," Dyøt said. "And let me tell you, you can't miss it. The guild of the year is chosen, and celebrities from all over show up. It's lavish. They go totally over-the-top."

"I haven't been invited to any balls." Beatrix's experiences with parties were limited and unpleasant, so popping up uninvited to some big event was not enticing. An image of Evenzaar's twisted lips appeared. Yeah, no.

"Everyone at the University attends," Dyøt said, like that settled the matter. "You're as good as invited."

"I bet Emma will want to pick a costume for you." Cassandra brought forth her holopad and began scribbling on it.

Beatrix smiled at the thought of Emma's obsession with her clothes. "I'm sure she'll be ecstatic. What kind of costume?" Beatrix had never dressed up. Martin wasn't the kind of dad who would take anyone out on Halloween, and being forced into a huge monkey outfit or some such sounded dreadful.

"Taelimns used to wear full-body costumes back in the day," Cassandra said, slipping a carrot into her mouth. "But after a real ogre hid among the guests, they decided to stick to masks."

"They're supposed to represent antagonists from our stories," Dyøt said. "Some are pretty good. Most are impossible to guess."

Maybe this wouldn't be so bad then, Beatrix thought. "What will you be?" Perhaps she'd get some inspiration.

"A deadly disease, of course," Dyøt said with a grin that had a touch of malice.

"Mine has a live serpent," Cassandra said.

"The ball's in less than two weeks." Dyøt grabbed a pickle from Cassandra's plate. She didn't seem to care. "We need to get started on your costume ASAP, Bea. Mine took all of five minutes to prepare, but I've been helping Cass with hers for a month."

"We've just enough time if we get organized," Cassandra said.

Two weeks? Beatrix expected to be gone to the Eisid Naraid by then, but watching Cassandra's and Dyøt's expressions, she opted not to dampen their excitement.

Cassandra began to write on her pad, enumerating tasks. "Dyøt, you know what to do about the invite. Beatrix, we'll need your size for the charmed dancing shoes. I'll take care of ordering those. The chameleon ones, so we can choose the color once we decide on the dress. I know Lucy will want to help with the gown. She can partner with Emma on that. That girl would kill us if we left her out of this. You'll require a good mask, though." Cassandra thought for a few moments, her brow furrowed in concentration. "Magical ones are the best. But all Conjures are probably booked by now. Isn't your friend one?"

"Which friend?"

"William," Cassandra said. "You know, the one who looks worried all the time."

"Oh, he's not really my friend, and I don't think he has any Fantasy magic."

"Are you kidding?" Cassandra's eyebrows shot up. "You can sense his power from a mile away."

"I heard he's a Flush," Dyøt said. "A Royal one."

Beatrix choked on her drink. "A what?" She coughed two more times.

"A Royal Flush is a Conjure who can manage the five elements. It's rare, but I wouldn't be surprised if the rumors were true. He has that look about him."

"Well, he won't be conjuring anything for me," Beatrix said. Even if he was acting friendlier, there was no way she'd ask him.

"No problem." Cassandra put away her holopad. "We'll choose something at the Bazaar. I'm swamped tomorrow, but we can go mask shopping with Lucy and Emma the day after. It will be fun."

Dyøt set a hand on Beatrix's forearm. "She'll find you an awesome one. Cass is great at uncovering treasure anywhere." At the contact with the boy's skin, dizziness gripped Beatrix.

Without warning the Furie climbed up her chest. It clawed like a wild animal while rust flooded her mouth, and the heavy scent of magic pooled around her.

She took a breath. Counted down. But the foreign smell of earth and musk swirled, and a strange touch of cold extended from the floor to reach her. It twined with the part of Beatrix that was wild and violent. And evil, perhaps. She felt herself float away from her seat in the pub—everyone left behind on the other side of a curtain of fog. Rage mixed with want. The Furie rejoiced, eager to be free, while she burned with the wish to grab the world with both hands and mold it to her liking. To force her will upon it without her self-imposed chains.

In a daze of semiconsciousness, she wondered why not let go. Then the edges of the scene blurred, painted by mist, and reduced her vision to a vignette.

The image came as if through rain, grainy but undeniable.

Against the darkness of the sky and the woods, a fire burned, supernatural. A puff of sparks erupted, and dust particles flew up into the air.

The smoke smelled of paper and of singed mold.

In the center of the pyre, a woman begged, her arms extended out offering a tight bundle. The desperation in her shrieks stabbed the night even after the flames engulfed her and her child.

Beyond her, at the edge of the bonfire, stood a man.

His mouth open, his body arched. His heart ecstatic with the power he'd consumed. All of him shook with hunger.

His tongue was coated with rust.

And when his eyes lifted, they speared Beatrix.

"*I see you,*" he mouthed. "*Neither you nor your world can hide.*"

"Beatrix! Beatrix, snap out of it. Come back!" Cassandra was shaking her, and Beatrix's teeth chattered. She blinked, dragging herself back to normalcy.

"Take this. Kelpie water," Dyøt said, pushing a flute into her hands.

Cassandra watched her with concern. "Drink. It will help you recover."

Beatrix sipped on what tasted like cucumber water and shivered. The images were branded in her mind. The horror coursed in her blood.

"You must have some seer in you," Cassandra said. "I recognize a vision trance when I witness one. What was it?"

Beatrix drank more in the hope of ridding herself of the sticky feeling from the vision. She'd never experienced anything like it. Even the Roamer's attacks that by now plagued her nightly didn't have the capacity to frighten her like this. What could have caused it? She wasn't comfortable with the idea of it becoming a common occurrence. She looked at Dyøt, whose eyes were wide with worry.

"Talking about it helps," Cassandra said in a low voice. "Tell me."

"Fire," Beatrix said, her voice hoarse. "Fire everywhere. People dying." And the feeling that it was her fault.

Cassandra took her hand. "You definitely have a bit of the sight in your blood. What you saw is a Charmancer, a corrupted being who burns books to feed on their souls and accumulate power. He's been plaguing my visions too." Cassandra's face was more chalk than cream. Her expression, haunted.

They all fell silent, the merry banter and the plans for the ball forgotten. Replaced with a dread that was both insidious and contagious.

"He can't stop," Beatrix said, the horrible images still vibrant. "He's addicted to burning books."

"Not any books," Cassandra said. "Leebers. The vessels where the souls of books are kept once bound."

Dyøt shuddered before he spoke. "And when a Leeber is destroyed, the world within it dies."

20

SELÐA

Two days later, after a rough night filled with Roamer's attacks, a depleted Beatrix crossed the Market Square with its distinctive guild buildings. She'd agreed to meet Cassandra, Lucy, and Emma at the Union to continue working on the riddle.

As Beatrix walked, she kept an eye out for the slumbering dragon atop the Fantasy Guild. "Watch the tower," Emma had said on a previous visit to the square. "A snore is coming." Sure enough, the buttresses of the Fantasy Guild had rattled, and the whole gothic monstrosity teetered. "Everyone keeps telling the leadership the dragon needs to be rehomed. But do they listen? Oh, no, of course not." Only then had Beatrix spotted the stone creature curling atop the tower. "He hasn't woken in three centuries, caused two fires in the alchemy lab with his restless sleeping."

This time around, the dragon moved not at all, giving the false impression that it was another building feature.

"Don't trust it." Beatrix could almost hear Emma's voice in her head.

The weather had turned for the worse, and even in the midmorning, everything was grey. A perfect match for Beatrix's mood, which had been ruined the previous eve after she had gotten into a shouting match with the Librarian.

Since she'd landed in the Zweeshen, Evenzaar had been a hovering presence, not only watching her throughout dinner every day but always aware of her movements in a manner that felt both creepy and uncalled for. Beatrix had hoped her daily access to him might serve in her search for Mary. She'd tested this theory yesterday.

It hadn't worked.

"I will consider putting your name on the waiting list," the Librarian had told her when she'd requested to read her mother's Leeber. "Maybe."

"But there are no other copies available," Beatrix had said, outrage heating her. "You cannot refuse my request. It's my book."

"And the vessel of a story that's *alive*. You can't expect to borrow it as if it were a regular paperback you can spill coffee on without consequences."

They had gone back and forth for twenty minutes, their voices growing louder and attracting the attention of everyone else in the Great Hall.

"We're at an impasse," Evenzaar had said finally. Then with a sneer, he'd added, "It figures of all her qualities, you'd inherit the worst of her stubbornness." With that shot about Beatrix's mom, he'd swirled his robe and stomped away. Beatrix had almost punched the table full of flabbergasted professors.

But today, none of that anger had survived. She felt too weak after a night in pain to even muster up a rage. She just wanted to find Mary. To make some progress. Any headway at all.

Beatrix had reached the huge fountain in the middle of the Market Square and turned onto the road to the Union to meet her friends, when a crowd obstructed her way. At least eighty people congregated there.

"What's going on?" someone asked, echoing her thoughts.

"A detectives and spies checkpoint," another said, his voice charged with suspicion. "They won't let anyone through without a face scan."

She craned her neck and recognized at least two of the fake detectives she'd seen at the Bureau. The phony Sherlock stood next to one of two Poirots, surrounded by a contingent of uniformed officers. They had cordoned off the side alleys and were funneling everyone through a single street.

"Order," one of the detectives called. "Stand for checks."

The officers herded everyone, and Beatrix was swept along to a line that ended at what looked like a gilded version of a metal detector.

"Step in and look straight at the bot," the officer manning the apparatus said. And one by one, as each person did, a scanner swiped over their faces. "No. No. No." The machine whirred.

Pushed forward, Beatrix stood inside the box while crisscrossing lasers scanned her up and down. "No," the bot said, and the officer ushered her on. Despite her curiosity, she hurried away, eager to get far from this scene. There was something deeply unsettling about it. But a few steps later, one of the detectives detached himself from the rest and intercepted her.

The fake Sherlock. He pinned her with a narrowed gaze.

"Eisidian, aren't you?" Before she could confirm or deny it, he shoved a paper in her hand. "If you know anything, report it. You would not want to be an accomplice." After a quick pat to the weapon strapped to his side, he turned around and left.

She raced to the shade of the Union gallery.

"That sounds a bit extreme," Emma said, reading the events off of her mind when they met up a few minutes later.

Cassandra's face was pale with shock at hearing about them. "Things are getting too forceful."

"It's because of this Charmancer," Lucy said. "Everyone's on edge."

"It's an excuse." Cassandra's voice had an uncharacteristic violence.

Beatrix just wanted to leave the episode behind. "Let's get to work."

Everyone nodded.

"We should find a study salle." Cassandra thumbed her chin. "They're private and comfortable."

The study salles were small rooms dotted around the perimeter of the Union building. Each was outfitted with two doors, one that opened to the Union hall and the other, typically a French door, leading to the wrap-around galleries that characterized most University buildings.

The first salle revealed a minimalist white-grey decor with four chairs, a sofa, and two worktables. Plus, three students deep in their texts.

"Sorry," Beatrix and her friends said, clicking the door closed.

"They should have turned on the Occupied sign." Cassandra tsked, pointing to the little sconce on the doorframe that beamed green.

Three more salles with green lights proved equally occupied. One with a purple sconce was reserved. And everything else shone red.

"I guess we can go back to Beatrix's bedroom." Emma twirled a strand of her raven-black hair. Lucy agreed.

"What about that one?" Beatrix pointed to a smaller doorway that sported a blue light at the end of the corridor.

"I don't know," Lucy said.

Cassandra hesitated too. "The Caladrius salle is technically available. I mean, we could use it but—"

"But?"

"Nobody does." Emma drew a smoky air rune. "Because it's haunted."

"Really?" Beatrix smiled. "That makes it more interesting. Are you telling me taelimns are scared of ghosts? I'm friends with one."

"Not those kinds of ghosts," Cassandra said. "It's hard to explain. See for yourself."

Lucy marched to the door and pushed it in.

Inside, a fireplace warmed a welcoming room papered with bold, organic designs. It was decorated in blues, oranges, and emerald greens with an abundance of feathered details, plenty of plush seating, thick rugs, and an assortment of odd-shaped mirrors on the walls.

To Beatrix the salle seemed lovely. Cozy in the way of things that have had time to settle, and instead of looking old have turned patinated, filled with experience and histories.

"Come look," Cassandra said.

Beatrix walked toward a mirror no larger than a dessert plate. It had an intricate frame with a shells-and-mermaids motif.

She looked into the glass and stepped back.

"You see." Cassandra wore a knowing smile on her face. "Nobody likes this salle because of the mirrors and what they show. And because it's impossible not to look into them."

"Our worst mistakes."

"Or our worst fears. Or our regrets." Cassandra's gaze gained a faraway look. "There are different interpretations. Not happy things, that's for certain."

Beatrix saw a bird in the mirror. Large and stork-like. With a gleaming beak and a golden chest, and a gigantic hole on its side. It lay dead on a bed of leaves in her backyard, the brown highlighting his white feathers. Once again, she felt the horror, the understanding that her power killed. That this was her doing. That being seven years old didn't make one good.

Martin had picked up the bird and thrown it in the trash. Beatrix had hated him for it. She'd wanted the bird buried and mourned. Now, something different struck her. Her father hadn't asked her anything. With the distance of the Zweeshen, a new set of questions emerged. Why? Who was Martin? She knew so little about him. He kept himself far away, ready to pounce with a nasty comment. But even he wasn't all bad. Not all the time. He had allowed a grandfather who had arrived out of nowhere to stay. That must have been strange too. And Martin was generous with his resources. Years ago, he'd given her a credit card, so Beatrix could buy "whatever stuff you want," as he'd put it. "*Esas pavadas de chicas.*" She'd assumed he'd meant clothes or toiletries, and that he was annoyed to have to take her to the store. Now she wondered. She had become so used to seeing the worst about him, she'd almost forgotten about those instances. Not that they excused everything else.

The dead bird remained in the mirror, its blood so bright it seemed to glow. "We should stay," Beatrix said and pulled herself away from the image. Killing the bird was her worst regret. But also a reminder. A mistake that had served to keep her in check, so she didn't accidentally murder again.

She had kept one of the bird's feathers for that reason, so why bother escaping the mirror now?

Emma had already chosen a spot. Lucy dropped the books she was carrying on a table, and Cassandra settled on a deep armchair.

"Let's start with the *D* clue again," Beatrix said, pulling out the journal where she kept the letter. But as she did, the detective's flyer fluttered out as well. She shuddered at the memory of his dark eyes and insidious scrutiny. He'd said *Eisidian* with a disgusted tone.

Cassandra picked up the paper and frowned. "I'd heard of the raid in the Dust, but I didn't know anyone had escaped."

"What happened?" Beatrix asked, grabbing the flyer and looking at it for the first time.

"The spies found an illegal bridge, a rudimentary pageturner similar to the one Evenzaar opened in your room, Beatrix," Emma said.

"They arrested two people, Pioneers apparently." Lucy read over Cassandra's shoulder.

"And it seems one other managed to get away." Cassandra pointed to the notice. "It explains the scans at the checkpoint."

Beatrix inspected the poster she held. Styled like an old Western Wanted notice, it beamed in full color. The words *Dead or Alive* flashed red every so often, giving the sign a horror-movie feel. Below, the picture of the fugitive was pixelated. It showed a middle-aged woman in a cowl, her face roundish and her eyes hard. A scar cut the side of her nose, and a green mark marred the left cheek.

Beatrix flinched. She brought the paper closer to her eyes.

"Need magnification?" Cassandra asked, offering her holofilm. Under the enhancing tool, the blemish on the woman's cheek showed in high definition.

"The rune from the map," Beatrix whispered, recognizing the symbol from Mom's letter. The snake eating its tail. "I have to talk to this woman."

How did one find a fugitive?

Beatrix posed that question to Trelius and Jane when she met them for lunch an hour later.

Trelius scratched his temple. "I might know someone…"

"I'll ask around," Jane promised. "Elizabeth is well connected too. Is it okay if I check with her?"

Beatrix nodded. All the help she could get, she kept repeating to herself.

So after checking with everyone who could assist, she requested a visit with the fugitive's allies. The unlucky ones who hadn't escaped. The chances they would tell her where the woman hid were low, but they might be willing to share other things. Like what the symbol on her cheek meant. Or why the fugitive wore it.

But Beatrix was denied.

"Are they not allowed visitors?

"They are," the jail's admittance officer said. "One each—and no one has come. But you can't enter official premises without a band."

"I have a waiver signed by the Librarian," Beatrix said, showing her Zweeshen card.

"Is it a band?"

"It says I don't need a band."

It didn't matter how she tried to explain. The man set his mouth and refused to listen.

"I can request a visit on your behalf," Cassandra suggested. "I'll ask them what you want to know."

It wouldn't be the same, Beatrix knew. And by now, she didn't want common-sense solutions anyway. She was too angry for that. Ever since her arrival in the Zweeshen, she'd dealt with a million insulting pinpricks, and the pent-up frustration burst out of the seams of her body, yelling for release. Beatrix felt one provocation away from unleashing her Furie without a hint of remorse. One slight short from roasting the Librarian and the whole council into a potato chip.

To complicate things, she'd had two more seizures. In the middle of the day. Until now, her Roamer's attacks had hit her the worst at night. These last instances were harder to ignore.

She told Neradola about it. The ghost had made a point of checking on Beatrix every day since the apothecary visit.

"William overestimates my gift," Neradola had told her that first day. She'd pressed an insubstantial hand against Beatrix's nape, then watched as the arrow under Neradola's skin turned in a dramatic swirl. "Roamer's is a notoriously stubborn syndrome. All we have are potions to relieve the symptoms. But the side effects are often worse than the disease."

Beatrix had frowned. "Then why do you insist I come see you?"

"Because we have to monitor how fast your Inaechar drops. In case we must request emergency transport."

Now the symptoms were getting worse fast.

And Beatrix felt like a failure. After eleven days in the Zweeshen, she still hadn't found Mary. No matter what she tried, she couldn't reveal the next clue—and her body kept betraying her.

"Emma told me you'd be here," William said.

The sculpture garden in Navarsing had become Beatrix's favorite place to think, or in this case brood. She'd grown attached to this abstract art bench, in the shade of an unidentifiable magenta tree. The sculptures had learned to walk around her, and the inkthreads that twined up her legs released her as soon as she stood. Today, the sounds of the cicadas filled the air, and two giant torches kept the cold at bay.

"I warn you. I'm in a bad mood," Beatrix told him.

"I think I can brave it." William sat beside her, a box the size of a large book in his hands. "Maybe I can even help you there. I've good news. Found your fugitive. She goes by Selda—not that it's her real name. Pioneers always use aliases."

Beatrix glanced up. *He found her? So soon?*

"Who is she?"

"Rebel for certain. With a rough reputation. She's in hiding but has agreed to meet us at the Elephant & Castle in Olde Town."

"Now?"

"In an hour. After dusk."

Beatrix hopped to her feet. "Let's go. I want to try the fridge this time."

William looked amused by her eagerness. "We'll have to go the boring way. There was an explosion at the theatre with several casualties, so the alley is closed. Let's copy the map first." He opened the box he held, which contained paper, pens, and a few charcoal pieces. "I'd rather not show Selda the whole letter. If she's Pioneer, we can't trust her."

"How did you find her?"

"I have my ways."

"Oh, please. I bet you checked some Læsting directory or some such."

"You caught me," William said, biting into a slice of peach from a brown bag. He extended it her way, and Beatrix took a piece.

And no matter how much she eye-rolled to hide it, she was impressed.

The West Navarsing Station sat on lower ground than the University, and Beatrix and William had to descend a steep set of stairs on their way to the pods.

"It's a shorter connection to the Elephant & Castle," William explained.

"And less in view of the Librarian's watchers and spies," Beatrix said.

He smiled in his crooked way. "That too."

It was dark down this path, the sky curling in waves above them, swirls worthy of Van Gogh's starry night. *I don't recognize them,* she thought, assessing the unfamiliar constellations.

They didn't speak for some time. The quiet rolled out, placid.

"I hope she can help us," Beatrix said. "This search. It feels circular."

"Do you know the Zweeshen was designed like a labyrinth? No surprise you feel that way. But we'll figure out this Craxtan and find Mary Brandt. We're making progress, even if it seems minimal."

Beatrix had harbored high expectations, but the woman who met them in a corner booth of the pub did not seem loquacious. Large-boned and in her fifties, she kept her face under her hood for the duration of their meeting, which, to Beatrix's disappointment, was brief.

When William showed Selda the copy of the map, the woman snatched the paper away. "That's the Eisid's east coast. Surrounded by mountains is the sacred valley, and the hill of the Goddess rises in the middle. Here." She pointed to the place with the circle of the snake eating itself. "Whatever the purpose of this map, the rune marks a destination—the Temple of Rephait."

Beatrix and William looked at each other. Whoever Mary was, it appeared Mom wanted Beatrix to take her to the Temple of Rephait.

"What's the rune?" Beatrix asked, thinking of Selda's cheek.

"The Evermoon is the symbol of the Goddess Rephait. Of infinity and the eternal cycle. It's the most sacred glyph in the Eisid Naraid. It's power beyond what many understand."

Beatrix brightened. The Evermoon. As in Mom's title. She beamed at William. Finally, answers. "What's the temple for?"

"It's not used for anything," the woman said, her tone so caustic it could strip paint. "It was abandoned after the tragedy. The desert surrounds it and gains ground every day."

William inclined his head, perhaps trying to see Selda better in the dim light. "What about before the...tragedy?"

"Why do you care?" Her stance defensive, Selda's eyes squished into slits. Beatrix had no trouble imagining her in a fight. Neither the cowl nor her whispering hid the fierceness of her heart.

"We wish no harm," William said.

"Good intentions have failed us before. I've nothing more to share about the temple. If you really want my help, show me the original."

After exchanging glances with William, Beatrix pulled out the letter.

Her head bent, Selda softened as she perused it, betraying a hint of glee when she spoke. "These two symbols atop the map. They're archaic magic runes. The one to the left stands for spellwork. The other is the hidden side of the moon." She paused, readjusted her cloak. "The setup is evident. A Craxtan followed by a location. If I were to guess, I'd say what you have here are the instructions and the site for a spell. An obscuring spell perhaps. Or a spell of revelation."

She flipped the missive around, folding it along the worn creases to shape the envelope, and her expression grew grim. "This note in pencil. Don't ever repeat this aloud. Never." The edge in her voice was so ominous a chill stood up the hair in Beatrix's forearm. "Never. Ever. You hear me?"

"What is it?" Beatrix asked, and Selda scanned the shadows before she responded. "It's the Pioneers' telepathic charm for help. It connects you with an agreed-upon person or group, tied through a blood vow. Who knows who might be on the other side of this call."

"I've heard people say it before." Beatrix thought of the weird incident with the vines in her bedroom and the sorcerer arrested at the Bureau. "I thought it was a common phrase."

Selda snorted. "The ignorant say many things. They do not understand the power of voice. Said in passing, once, by someone of little power, it might be inconsequential. A three times incantation from your lips..." Selda's hand lifted to pull down her hood, and Beatrix caught a greenish flash. "It's a dangerous saying you shouldn't repeat."

"I won't," Beatrix said. "Why is it dangerous?"

"Because it invokes the Fogges to pass the message, and once they have their tendrils in you, they won't let you go."

The air seemed to cool several degrees, and Beatrix shivered. The monster stirred while the whispers debated in dire tones.

"What about Mary Brandt?" William said, either unaware of the change in the atmosphere or to dispel the tension. "Do you know her?"

The woman scoffed. "There's no Mary in the Eisid stories other than the Blue Geese's wife. She died at the beginning of the war."

"Was she a rebel?" Beatrix asked.

Selda chuckled, sarcasm twisting her mouth. "She was a tavern maiden, served the beer. What do you think?"

"I think there were many Pioneers not born in the Eisid," William said. "They came from far and wide. Yet the Eisid Naraid was the only book quarantined."

"You're treading a dangerous path." With short-nailed, pudgy fingers, Selda pulled her hood forward, shrinking into it, so that most of her head became hidden. "The rebels' inner circle wasn't revealed in its totality, but I've never heard of anyone of consequence called Mary Brandt. I cannot help you further. I came to confirm the rumors that the Unwritten Beatrix Yoru was in the bookworld."

"Alba," Beatrix corrected without thinking.

"Over Leyna's dead body." Selda sneered. "Names matter."

"You knew my mother?"

A sudden movement exposed part of her face, and Beatrix saw the left cheek in the faint light. The green mark over the Evermoon covered most of it. When Selda spoke, no malice tainted her words. It made her message all the more menacing. "I did know her. Probably better than you."

Beatrix flinched. Even if it was true, it hurt to accept it. Who was her mother? Her few memories were through the gaze of a child. And so much about Leyna remained a mystery. What would it be like to meet her now, to see her through grown eyes?

"I cannot help you anymore," Selda said. "Stay away from the Eisid Naraid if you care for your life. Revenge is on everyone's mind, and Leyna's daughter won't be welcome in that land."

Before they could ask anything else, Selda stood up and left. Her cloaked figure disappeared so fast that only a magical exit could explain it.

21

HATS

The directive Beatrix received a couple of days later didn't come as a surprise. In an envelope embellished with gold, the subpoena was prompt. The council had decided to hear her Bounding case that same afternoon.

"Come on in. Do not be frightened," the Librarian said, his voice echoing off the marble floors of the rotunda.

The words had the opposite effect on Beatrix. Dread squeezed her heart.

"Be careful inside the council rotunda," Jane had warned when Beatrix had shown her the summons during breakfast. "Say as little as possible, because once within the colonnade, you'll be compelled to tell the truth no matter what."

Beatrix stood at the edge of a circular room with thirteen columns around the perimeter. The Librarian strode to meet her with a smirk. His hat towered on his head, more adorned and taller than usual.

"We're eager to start," he said, pushing on her back. "Don't make them wait."

Perched on their high thrones, the council members watched her advance, and like an animal in an exhibit, she shrank under their scrutiny. Gathering her courage, she craned her neck to make out their faces, but they sat too far up, their chairs hanging from the top balcony like window boxes, their feet dangling and disproportionate from her perspective.

A man swiveled forward. His head dove through the air and folded the distance between them so that Beatrix saw him far away, and his breath grazed her cheek at the same time. That's when she noticed a black hood with eye slits covered his head. An elegant top hat sat over it.

"I'm the Chairman," the hovering head said. "Do not dally!"

Leaving her side, the Librarian levitated to his seat between the others, and Beatrix edged toward the center of the room, onto an elevated base of polished black.

As soon as her feet were inside, a glass cylinder enclosed her. A murky, grey-silver liquid rose to her ankles, immobilizing her. She pressed her hands against the crystal. "Let me out!"

"I protest," a familiar voice said from the second level gallery. "Beatrix's not a danger. This is extreme."

She recognized William. He didn't look good. Dressed in long purple robes, dark circles stained the skin under his eyes. She wondered what had caused them. She hadn't seen him yesterday, and he hadn't come to breakfast with Trelius and Jane.

"Quiet, Threshborne," the top hat said. "I will remind you that your presence is barely tolerated, as a special favor to your mentor." He bowed his head in the direction of another masked man with a contraption on his head resembling a tree. "Do not speak again unless asked, or, as a matter of fact—"

Two uniformed figures flanked William while his mouth closed in an unnatural, unmoving line. Beatrix didn't need to feel the magic to know he was gagged.

"Why am I trapped? I haven't done anything," she said, anger boiling. Her Furie woke up with a start. The monster growled, pawing at her stomach.

The Chairman cleared his throat, and his voice glided out like a slithering animal. "As Chairman of the Zweeshen Council and Chief Justice of the Highest Court, I now call this hearing into session." Using a large gavel, he banged a gong suspended from the ceiling by two thick ropes.

"Beatrix Alba, you have been brought in front of this tribunal to assess your guilt on two separate counts. Number one, that you're the unnatural, Unwritten daughter of a fugitive, Leyna Yoru, who in her cowardice deserted the Zweeshen, breaking her vow to the Universe of Words and stealing the Soul of Rephait. And two, that you have on several occasions misused your untamed powers, and as a result represent a threat to our world."

"That's ridiculous," Beatrix said. "A fugitive? What about the Soul? I thought this hearing was a formality so I could be bounded."

"Quiet," the Chairman ordered. "We will vote on the sentence for the accused."

"This is unnecessary," said the hooded man wearing the tree. As he moved, some leaves fluttered away.

Opposite him, another masked council member rose. He wore something on his head as well but sat too far in the shadows to discern what. "I urge the council to take a moderate view. These accusations are feeble and can be corrected by training."

"Containment," said a young voice to his left. "Nothing else will do. Literature must be preserved."

"This is crazy. You have me confused with someone else." Beatrix pushed against the glass once more, her outrage bubbling. She glanced at William and read the warning in his eyes—as clear as if he were begging her to stop with his adamant baritone. She couldn't help herself. "Who are you to bring me here? To trap me? Who gave you the power to judge me?"

"Stop talking," the Chairman said, and the inkwell filled up to Beatrix's waist, paralyzing her further.

"Let me go now, or I'll—" Unhinged, the Furie sprang, reaching her throat and filling her mouth with rust. Electricity coursed up her immobile arms, popping sparks. Her hair stood on end.

"Like we feared," said another hooded man. "Wild."

"Indeed," his neighbor echoed.

"She's not done a thing." A cultured woman's voice; Beatrix could not tell where it came from.

Like Jane and Trelius had warned, she'd lost track of the individual council members by now. "It's on purpose. Don't bother telling them apart."

Beatrix gave up trying. In their balconies, they were hooded, looming figures, their pronouncements disembodied. Except for the Chairman.

His voice sounded louder and more solemn, reaching every hiding place in the hall. "She is her mother's daughter and the core of evil lives within her. She even has a Furie, like Leyna Yoru. Like her mother, she delves in the darkness of the Fogges."

"I protest," a man said, rising and floating in place. "This has gone far enough. The Fantasy Guild will defend this girl and take responsibility for her destiny."

"She did not pass your test of kin. You cannot," said a female voice.

The standing man grew in size while his words acquired a magical resonance. "You will not witch-hunt a Daughter of the Evermoon. Not while I breathe."

"Perhaps we should give the Librarian the chance..."

"Yes," the Librarian said, gliding forward. "My friends, let us calm down. This is not a criminal inquiry but an assessment of our options given that no guild has chosen the Unwritten. A Bounding waiver must be dispensed, and a pass approved to allow her passage to her biblioworld."

The Chairman steepled his fingers with studied slowness. "The crimes have been outlined, Evenzaar. In question is whether she can be trusted, and her history speaks for itself on that account."

"She's no threat," the Librarian said.

"So you say. Yet no guild can guarantee her compliance. She's an aberration at worst and a free agent at best."

"Perhaps she could be bound," someone said.

"That cannot happen. Because as a taelimn, she does not exist. She's not one of us but an abomination who deserves death."

"She passed the Test of Character. Have the Oracle confirm her intentions."

"Or the detectives and spies interrogate her and report their results."

The Chairman lifted his hand. "There's no time for a long process, my colleagues. A terrible danger is upon us, and the question remains, what shall be our response? Will we let bureaucracy and inaction leave us vulnerable?" He paused to let his words sink in and continued with deliberation.

"In the past, we've looked the other way to high-spirited taelimns and rebellious behavior. We've been tolerant." He pointed to William, and Beatrix imagined a sneer curved his lips in disgust. "Our enemies will not show the same restraint. In these times, civility is no longer a path we can take.

"This girl, as unimportant as she is, represents an example. She does not live by the laws of the Zweeshen, or as a taelimn, and so she cannot be allowed to live."

"She's but a child!" For the first time since Beatrix had known him, the Librarian sounded sincere—and insecure.

"Is she?" the Chairman's voice rose, honeyed. "Or is she a cleverly played pawn in the hands of our enemies?" He shook his head, and his top hat teetered. "How do we know she isn't Pioneer-trained? Days ago, the theater exploded with one of their bombs. The rebels run unrecognized in our midst. Perhaps she's in league with this Charmancer, the evil that strikes at us from the dark."

Everyone nodded, concern a breathing presence in the hall.

"How can we be certain it wasn't her doing?" the Chairman continued. "We cannot know."

"You're lying!" Beatrix screamed, unable to control herself any longer. "You're inventing lies about me. Is this what the world of stories is like? A hateful tyranny? Does truth not matter at all?" The Furie welled up, begging to be let out. Her chest burned, her skin stuck with a million pins.

William fixed his gaze on her, imploring. *Stop,* she heard him say, even though he never moved his lips.

"Beatrix, be still." Lids half-closed, the Librarian spoke flatly, and his strange rhythm had the insulating quality of foam. Even before she recognized his effort to enchant her, she realized it wouldn't work. The calming charm rolled over her with no effect. Power roiled inside her and around her, and it smelled of earth and moss. She couldn't see them but felt sure inkthreads crawled up her legs.

After the failure of his enchantment, the Librarian appealed to logic. "Despite the differing views in the council, the Zweeshen is a refuge of justice. Do the clever thing. Wait."

But like a wildfire that once started has to consume itself, Beatrix's brain and heart wouldn't respond to rational thought.

"No, it's not," she shouted. "This is a terrible place. It's nothing like stories. There's no fairness. No goodness or anything to look up to, no heroism. It's all superficial and petty. You're all intolerant liars."

Tears of frustration pooling, she lifted her hand. But the crystal pushed closer, squeezing her until she couldn't move at all. When the viscous liquid rose to her neck, Beatrix's windpipe closed up, and the room spun. Terror and a familiar helplessness cinched her heart. "Let me go. Now! You have no right."

"Let us vote," the Chairman said. "Death or imprisonment."

"Death, death, death." The chanting rose, snaking around the columns and reaching even the darkest crevices of the rotunda.

"This is wrong!" Beatrix yelled, the Furie in her voice.

So fast she caught only a blur, William leapt down from the balcony and landed at her side. Their gazes met for a moment before he pulled out a baton-like weapon and shattered the glass of the inkwell. The cloudy grey liquid spilled like slime, and Beatrix skated on the slippery marble to grab his hand.

The guards were already there. Three of them launched themselves at William, who fought them off with an efficiency that both amazed and scared her, until one by one, they rolled unconscious to the floor.

"Let's go," he said, free from the spell that had kept him mute, and they darted to the door. A sliver of sun was visible through the jamb when a red spurt of sparks exploded from the upper gallery, setting the exit on fire.

William pivoted, pushing Beatrix behind him before a second charge reached them. It knocked him in the middle of the chest. His torso arched forward, and his arm dropped dead, letting go of her. Another flash, this one dark green and from a different throne across the colonnade, hit him in the back. William's eyes rolled in his head as the force of the strike flipped his body in the air. He crashed onto the stone with a loud crack. He didn't move.

"No!" Beatrix cried. Terror ripping the muscles in her heart, she ran to his side.

More guards burst in through the front gate. She was seized by the shoulders and pulled away. Heavy hands shoved her down to her knees, squeezing her chin into her chest while shimmery threads tied themselves around her. The magical rope dug into her skin, bright and hot, and ignited her with helpless rage.

From everywhere at once, a cacophony of shouts resonated.

"Quiet," the Chairman said. "We will vote now."

"No." The Librarian's order rang, cavernous. "Death is not an option."

"I second death," a female voice said.

"Death for me too," a man backed her.

"You sadist fool." This from the one who'd stood up earlier from the Fantasy Guild. "I call for exoneration in place of prison."

"I second," the man with the tree on his head said.

"And I" came a soft whisper.

The Chairman stared at them with distaste. "Three voices each way reverse the options. Death or exoneration. We vote. All death rise."

He lifted his twisted wooden gavel, and a beam of light emerged from the ceiling. It bathed Beatrix in white while the rest of the bottom level receded into shadows. She heard the swish of fabric as the robed figures rose to their feet.

This can't be happening. Someone, please, help me. Grandpa, Mom, she begged soundlessly, desperation constricting her breath.

Help me.

Someone.

Anyone.

But there was no one.

Except the unthinkable.

Furie...

With an eagerness that dizzied her, the Furie swelled all the way to her ears. *"Let me out."* It hissed, *"Set me free."*

The violence inside Beatrix caught fire, so volatile it threatened to erupt out of her. It engulfed her, all-consuming, mightier than ever.

She knew things had gone too far for her to harness the monster in any meaningful way. Without a handle on it, if she gave in, anything could happen. Chaos, destruction, people getting hurt. Maybe worse.

Once before had that happened, and she'd killed an innocent creature midflight. That night she'd promised herself not to let go like that again.

But...

But William lay splayed on the floor. And the Hats were voting for her death.

Squeezing her lids shut, Beatrix sighed out her choice.

"Help me, Furie," she whispered to the monster.

Then, her heart hammering like a war drum, she brought down every defense she'd spent years building and, relinquishing all control, she let it out.

She expected an outburst and the scorching feeling in her mouth to intensify while showers of lightning blasted out of her hands like fireworks. Instead, the power receded. It burrowed back into the depths of her lower stomach and churned there like a witch's brew.

With a deliberation she'd never experienced in all the years since it had first awakened, the Furie responded to her calling. Rather than an angry avalanche of lava, a gentle ooze of power flowed up her arteries. It was warm and steady and rich like chocolate. It didn't come from her belly, rather from lower down, from underneath her feet.

As if traveling through a system of roots, currents of magic coursed through her ankles and legs. They climbed up, speeding the pumping of her heart. The air around her quickened and heated up until, in a shimmering aura, it fused to her body.

She expanded; her presence grew more brilliant, larger than the physical body the magic rope could contain. And when the Furie reached her arms, the newly strengthened muscles tore the ties like paper strings.

The Librarian, who'd been advancing in Beatrix's direction, stepped back. As she held her right hand high to release the power, he ducked.

A cross between molasses and stardust, the Furie poured out. The stream had a fluid, golden-orange radiance and floated in the air as if weightless. Pliable, eager even, it allowed itself to be shaped, and Beatrix shook with amazement as, at the shift of her fingers, tendrils of gold and white began intertwining and twisting into a scintillating globe.

She couldn't believe it was happening, what her fingers were creating with less effort than it took to flip a light switch. Because above her palm, perfectly shaped and mesmerizingly beautiful, shone the Taming Sphere Grandpa had trained her for.

"She's got control!" the Librarian said, his tone awe-filled and breathless.

"Her Furie's not a threat inside a Taming Sphere," someone said.

Beatrix heard them from afar. She was too engrossed in the Sphere that had now started to glow and spin, cooling into a twinkling blue.

"Turn it off!" Evenzaar shouted. "You'll waste your whole life on it. You've made your point."

But Beatrix couldn't listen, hypnotized by the waves of light that accelerated, faster and faster. Letters and symbols appeared on the surface of the Sphere, a gleaming alphabet of curves.

Until the globe burst, shattering into a million blue embers that fell to the floor and died off.

"Always protect your Inaechar," the tree Hat said. One of the branches on his head was burnt to the core. "What's the sense in saving you today if you run out of ink tomorrow?"

"This changes nothing," the Chairman spouted. "We vote now."

Standing by the Librarian, who'd grabbed her arm with a grip of steel, Beatrix froze in disappointment.

"All those for death stand," the Chairman said, unwavering.

One by one the council members rose, and Beatrix counted.

"Five against seven." The Chairman didn't hide his displeasure. "Librarian, we won't need your tie-breaking vote today." He trained his gaze on her. "It appears you will live to betray us, Beatrix Alba. Know that when you do, I'll be there."

22

REPHAİT

"I'm sorry you had to go through that," the Librarian said.

Beatrix trembled. Her body, still paralyzed with shock, refused to obey her. The guards had freed her in the council's training court, a fighting arena at the back of the rotunda.

"Where's William? Is he okay?" she managed to ask.

The Librarian sneered. "I wouldn't waste my concern on him. He walked away five minutes after you left. A bad penny always turns up."

Reality leaking in as if through a drip, Beatrix scowled. Her stale panic reawakened in shudders, like the aftershocks of an earthquake. "That was the most pitiful mockery of justice I've ever seen."

"Now, now," Evenzaar said, his voice plush. "The council has voted to protect you. All is well."

His flippancy enraged Beatrix enough to burn away her fear. From the ashes, the Furie sputtered. "They almost sentenced me to death!"

"The Chairman tries that often." The Librarian fondled his long beard. "A scare tactic. He hardly ever gets away with it."

"Hardly ever? That makes me feel so much better." Her arms hurt and her mouth felt sandy dry. The Furie was depleted. It didn't matter. She'd survived. Beatrix began a mental list of what she still had to do. "I want access to my mother's Leeber." If Cassandra had the right of it, decoder information might hide in it. Or clues about Mary. With Beatrix's limited time left in the Zweeshen, she had to go to the source.

Evenzaar caressed his hat. "The council hasn't authorized that."

"Make it happen," Beatrix said. She was done with games and delay tactics. The memories from the inkwell circled in her head like crows, eating at her. *Abomination, pest, cannot be tolerated.* Maybe the Librarian sensed her determination.

"Very well. I will push you to the front of the line."

"When?"

"Before you leave the Zweeshen." He lifted his palm. "Don't argue. The council has allowed you seven more days here. After that, you'll either return to Pangea or travel on to the Eisid Naraid. Your preference is noted, so I'll expedite your passage to your biblioworld."

Seven days. Beatrix's breath hitched. The sense of failure at her struggles to decipher the letter warred with longing. In another week, she would see the Eisid. A place she might belong to. A land that hid not only her mother but Leyna's secrets. The thought tugged along another. "Are they true? The accusations against my mother?"

For once, the Librarian appeared uncomfortable. "It happened long ago. She was a High Priestess of the Evermoon, chosen Keeper of the Soul, and the Soul disappeared."

"What exactly is the Soul?"

Evenzaar's skin cracked when he smiled.

"A sacred and powerful tool. The Goddess's power preserved in a dagger crafted in a magical crucible, long before the Zweeshen was even a thought. The Soul is the magical heart of the Eisid Naraid. It maintains the balance of the land. Without it, that world cannot survive. And yes, most believe your mother stole it."

"There she is!" Emma said, running to reach Beatrix and bury her in a hug.

After Evenzaar had guided Beatrix out of the training court, she'd struggled to locate the guesthouse in the ever-changing Navarsing landscape. The sun had sunk into the horizon when she found a landmark she recognized.

"We've been looking for you forever," Emma said as soon as Beatrix reached the Union patio. "I'm so glad they didn't kill you."

Beatrix shrank at the girl's bluntness.

"Emma!" Cassandra set an arm on Beatrix's shoulder. "We're just happy all went well."

As delighted as Beatrix was to see them, she didn't have the energy to recap everything. From the Hats' deadly contempt to the startling discovery about Mom, it all seemed unreal and overwhelming.

Mom.

How could it be true? They had to be wrong. Her lovely, sepia-remembered mother couldn't be a criminal and a thief.

Beatrix's friends, intuitive as they were, didn't ask her to recount anything.

"You're pale as rice paper," Cassandra said. "Let's get you something to eat."

"She'll need to rest." Warm relief washed over Beatrix at hearing William. He still wore his robe, a big scorch mark marring the front, but other than that, he appeared unharmed. He held her gaze hostage with something she refused to believe could be respect. And once more that something, that strange string, tightened in the space between them. "You've lost a lot of Inaechar," he said.

Beatrix shivered. Why were dark thoughts scarier when spoken aloud?

Less Inaechar meant less time. She'd suffered enough signs of Roamer's post-magic expenditure to realize her Inaechar had been depleted during the trial. She straightened up. No matter. That would be fixed soon too. By this time in seven days, she'd be in the Eisid Naraid—and she'd hear her mother's side of the story about this dagger, this Soul of Rephait.

"I couldn't sleep now. I would end up staring at the ceiling," Beatrix said, and this time William didn't argue. "I'd love to eat something."

"You're in for a treat then. The Bookends has a new special." Cassandra intertwined her right arm with Beatrix's left.

"I will send Neradola to see you when you're back." The set of William's jaw allowed for no discussion.

"Fine." He didn't know Beatrix had already gone to the ghost today, after her latest episode.

"I'll prepare a potion," Neradola had said. "We're getting to the point where the side effects are worth it."

Now William stared at Beatrix, unspoken words hovering between them. "Well done in the council hall," he said finally, almost through his teeth, and after a curt nod, he walked away. The upper back of his robe was ripped into tatters too.

She watched him in confusion. At his praise and his obvious anger. She was too overwhelmed and too tired to figure it out, though.

"Come on." Cassandra pulled Beatrix into the Union Commons hall, Emma following. "The Bookends shouldn't be too crowded at this time, and afterward, if you want—" But Cassandra never finished the sentence. A thunderous sound, as loud as the relocation of a mountain, rattled the building. The hanging lamps swayed, the pictures on the walls shook, and puffs of sawdust escaped from the wooden beams.

"What was that?"

Emma and Cassandra's faces mirrored the same horror.

"The alarm bells. An Original biblioworld has been attacked."

Cassandra's eyes rolled in her head, turning all white. "The Charmancer's war is upon us," she said in a voice not her own. "May the words save us all."

23

MARY

The next day and night rolled in and out, silent and blurry like the Fogges. Perhaps the whole Zweeshen had gone into shock, because people walked around treading softer than usual, lost in their thoughts.

Jane and Neradola had met Beatrix at the Bookends, but the conversation sagged, their minds far away. Even Emma had been quieter, Lucy, pensive, and Cassandra appeared dazed. Everyone's sense of security had been shaken to the core.

Someone had attacked a famous biblioworld in broad daylight, setting the land on fire with a weapon akin to a nuclear bomb. And no one had seen it coming. People talked of this Charmancer, a being capable of consuming Inaechar to feed his power. Of taking Leebers from the safest place in the Zweeshen, a library protected by the strongest methods both magical and not. How? And where had he come from? Could he get to every biblioworld, taelimns wondered? Were all defenses useless?

Soon they had an answer.

The bells sounded again. And again. They kept tolling. More and more worlds snuffed out. Hundreds. Thousands. Millions of taelimns gone. The metallic sound rent the air, startling everyone at first. People stopped walking. Tears flowed. Some screamed and ripped their clothes. Over time, though, the bells became a sad background, every so often reminding them of a tragedy elsewhere.

But it wasn't just things around Beatrix that had transformed. Something important had changed inside her after the council hearing. Her Roamer's seizures were growing closer together. Now they plagued her day and night. That very morning she'd convulsed on the floor of the guesthouse parlor, hugging her midriff while waves of pain ran her over like a steamroller.

Emma acted terrified, her frenzied shopping and furious packing a measure of her anxiety. Beatrix, on the other hand, resisted panic. If the hearing had accomplished anything, it was to rekindle her sense of purpose.

That afternoon Beatrix found William in an animated discussion with Trelius by the purple-graveled path to the greenhouses. Judging by the pair of scowls they wore, it wasn't a happy debate.

"Hey, there," she said. "Have you guys seen Jane? I have a Prologey question for her."

Trelius smiled at her attempt to lighten the mood. William didn't.

"Jane's stuck on a project for Elizabeth," William said. "Maybe I can help."

Beatrix considered waiting. But time wasn't on her side. "I found a reference in a History book about name-purging as a punishment. Taelimns taken out of all records, the morphlines with their true names burnt, and even their Leebers modified. I thought if that happened to Mary, it might explain why we can't find her in the Codex."

"It didn't," William said with such vehemence that Beatrix flinched.

Trelius lost his grin. "This is too heavy a subject. I will see you later."

Only Beatrix returned his wave.

"What's wrong? What were you arguing about?"

"Nothing. A small disagreement on what constitutes safety." William's face softened a bit. "Your Mary wasn't erased. The last instance of that punishment happened after the Rebellion War, and only the High Leader and his right hand were purged. Her name wasn't Mary."

Beatrix's hopes shut down, she sighed. "I don't know where else to search. And the trip's so close."

"If you don't find her now, you can come back." William looked at her with a new ease. Even after their truce, she had often sensed a wall hiding him. Maybe not magical, but real, nonetheless. But today it had been partially brought down—or its sentry gone on vacation. It made her both warm and shivery, tying her in a knot of want.

"The world won't end if you have to come back to finish the job," William insisted, unaware of where her thoughts had taken her. She stared at his lips as he spoke. "You may search from the Eisid too. Mary might be originally from there. Who knows, people might recognize the name. It isn't that big a place, which made it hard for the Pioneers to hide over there."

And because Beatrix was only half listening, it took her an extra moment before William's words sank in, sparking an avalanche of meaning. "That's it! That's the answer. Mary must be a Pioneer. We discarded that option because Selda didn't know her. But they all use aliases. It explains why she's not in the Codex."

William's face closed up, any warmth frozen to oblivion. "If so, you don't want to find her. It was reckless enough to meet with Selda. The Pioneers are dangerous. Some think they're now in league with the Charmancer. I'm serious, Beatrix."

She gave him a noncommittal nod.

And when Beatrix left him, William's scowl was even worse than when she'd found him.

"What would it mean if Mary was a Pioneer?" Beatrix asked Cassandra and Emma a while later.

Beatrix had called them to her turret room to share her suspicions about Mary Brandt. And to test the thimble yet again. Because she had to keep trying.

"That would make her a criminal for certain," Cassandra said, sitting cross-legged on the bed. "All Pioneers are."

"I know." The notion carried sadness with it. Beatrix had created the image of Mary as an aging woman who'd aid in deciphering the riddle in gentle tones. The kind of old lady who gardened and baked bread.

"What happened to them?" Beatrix asked. Selda had not known Mary, but another Pioneer might.

"They were convicted en masse at the end of the war for almost destroying the Zweeshen and for abusing Fantasy magic."

"All?"

"Every single one." Emma's matter-of-fact look appeared out of place on her childish face, especially underneath the Ascot hat with an ostrich feather that Beatrix had discovered in the wardrobe.

"What about after their sentencing? Where did they go? Did—" But Beatrix paused as a fragment of a previous conversation slipped into her mind. *Everything in the Zweeshen is written somewhere.* "Wait. If Mary's a Pioneer, and they're criminals, wouldn't she show up in—"

"The Criminal Rolls!" Emma's hair recolored a glittery purple and curled up in perfect swirls. "You're a genius. Mary's name and last known location would be recorded there. Her Pioneer one and aliases included." Emma smiled, releasing a kaleidoscope of silvery-blue butterflies. She'd been practicing the magicless mirage Jane had taught her, and the room buzzed with their fluttering.

"We must check," Cassandra said, sliding off the bed.

On the mantel, the strange hourglass marked the hour with its usual racket. They all covered their ears until the exploding sand and glass re-configured itself.

Cassandra sighed. "How I hate that I have to leave just as things get interesting." She twisted her mouth in a rueful smile. "I'm to oversee an exam in Polihistor's stead. But you both should use my faculty access to check the Rolls—and don't mind the Sphinx. She's throwing a tantrum this week but is strictly ornamental."

Ten minutes later, armed with Cassandra's faculty permit, Emma and Beatrix stepped into the Main Library.

"Let me do the talking," Emma said. "The Criminal Rolls are kept in the catacombs. A famous pro-deportation Library Master rules there, and he might not react well to you."

Beatrix agreed, staying close to the entrance where the cool, paper-in-fused air surrounded her in an old embrace. Because she was always aware of them, she noticed how pervasive the inkthreads were here. Marbling the gleaming floor and entwining themselves around columns, bookshelves, and banisters, as if they were more a part of the building than an intrusion. Not belonging but determined to make a space for themselves.

Like Beatrix.

She looked to where Emma debated with the Library Master and frowned. For all her attempts at charm and demurely styled hair, Emma wasn't successful.

The young girl returned to Beatrix's side soon after. "Despite being public, the Criminal Rolls require guild authorization to inspect." Emma's lips lifted, showing all her teeth in a growl. "How convenient they're closing for the day and that tomorrow's a holiday. We'll have to send Cassandra in. Unless you want to ask Evenzaar for special permission."

The mention of the Librarian's name alone made Beatrix recoil. Just yesterday, he had informed her she wouldn't be allowed access to Mom's Leeber after all.

"It might be the last available copy of her book. It's my right to read it," she'd argued.

"That might be, but there are protocols involved. A Leeber is sacred. The world would die if something happened to it. I've tried, but the council will not be swayed."

Beatrix had growled, the Furie so close to the surface it made the air flicker.

"I'm not asking the Librarian," she said now.

"It will have to be Cassandra then." Emma left the building with the air of a dispossessed queen, her mental insults ringing inside Beatrix's mind all the way back to the Market Square.

That avenue of inquiry closed for now, they attempted to speak to members of the Historical Guild next. The college, which kept the records from the war, was both unhelpful and rude. By midafternoon, experts skirted away at their sight.

"They act as if we've arrived from *The Journal from the Plague Year* biblioworld," Emma said.

Curing diseases seemed easier than finding information in the Zweeshen.

It was Dyøt who intercepted Beatrix on the way to dinner and saved the day from being a waste.

She had agreed to meet Cassandra and the rest of the group at the Elephant & Castle. It didn't take much to convince Beatrix to go. Her time in the Zweeshen was dwindling, and she found that she would miss it. She thought of the Bounding issues, the Bureau officers, and the council hearing and had to amend that. Most of it, at least.

"I was just on my way to meet you guys," Beatrix told Dyøt.

True to his style, Dyøt wore a bright kaftan and a sleeveless vest over it. "I know. I came to catch you before so we could speak alone. Cass said you're looking for information about the Pioneers." The strain in his voice had Beatrix doing a double take.

Despite the colorful clothing, Dyøt looked different today. Darker.

"Yes, I'm looking for a Pioneer. Mary Brandt."

"Don't," Dyøt said, the word clipped. "They're criminals. Terrorists. Really, Bea. It's a bad idea."

"I've read about them. They tried to overthrow the council, right?" Visions of the condemning Hats during the hearing shaped in Beatrix's mind. "I can't say I don't relate to a certain point."

"Don't you dare say that!" Dyøt's face redrew itself so that she barely recognized him. He spat his next words with violence, a sheen in his eyes. "You know nothing about them! The Pioneers are traitors. They were supposed to protect the Soul of Rephait in the Eisid Naraid. Instead, they exploited it to kill."

"Look. I'm sorry. I didn't—"

"They're murderers. Did you know they set bombs everywhere? Public parks, cafés, Zweeshen palaces, schools. All fair game."

As if his words weighed their meaning in tons, Beatrix shrank. Until now, she'd imagined the rebels as a sort of indignant resistance, an underdog movement of the discontented. Even their blanket indictments supported that. She'd made them into an antihero akin to Batman: idealistic, misunderstood—questionable, but not truly evil.

"You have to stop," Dyøt said. "Do you get that? You're attracting the wrong attention. Enough people have died because of the Pioneers. Or trying to stop them."

She gaped, looking past Dyøt's outside to the pain she realized was personal. "What did they do to you?"

He turned silent, tried for a brittle nonchalance and failed. "They killed my parents. While they were out on date night at a movie theatre."

Beatrix's chest squeezed the air from her lungs, leaving her heart aching. She knew what losing someone felt like. The hole with their shape that would forever stay vacant. How missing became a part of everything. A flavor of ice cream and a particular brand of cereal. She understood. But she didn't know what to say. Not when sorrow was bigger than words. "I'm sorry, I—"

"Don't," Dyøt stopped her. "I don't need you to console me or feel sorry for me. Just stop searching for dangerous people. The Pioneers are ruthless. Do you understand? They'd use you and whoever else to get power. Just like they destroyed the Eisid Naraid. A whole world, hundreds of thousands of taelimns condemned to die 'cause of them. And many more killed in even worse ways. Please, promise me you will let it go."

The words escaped before Beatrix realized. "How did they destroy the Eisid?"

Dyøt looked away. "Nobody knows the details. I have been researching them for years. I came to the Zweeshen and studied history just to get access to the right information."

"For what?"

Dyøt, the bright, joking Dyøt, sneered. "At some point, I dreamt of revenge. I know better now. I want to protect the Zweeshen from them."

His statement touched her with frost. Cold with the revelation that Dyøt was nothing like he seemed. "You said they used the Soul of Rephait to kill. How?"

"There are theories," Dyøt said, frustration vibrating in his voice. "The Pioneers found a way to exploit the winged dagger to unleash high magic somehow. And it went wrong. No one in that world's uncorrupted. No taelimn who crosses in remains untouched by the evil the Pioneers released. It's like a poison. Or something in the air." He shook his head. "That's why the council sealed the place."

Beatrix shivered, as if an iced hand had pressed a fingertip to her temple. Everyone who crosses in...

And then she watched Dyøt. She narrowed her eyes.

"You know how to contact them, don't you?"

Dyøt shook his head. "Let it go."

But Beatrix couldn't. Not when she had less than a week left in the Zweeshen. "Dyøt, I understand what you're saying. But I need to find Mary Brandt. You saw the letter. If you could reunite with your mom, wouldn't you risk it?"

Dyøt's face lost some of its belligerence, and a different kind of determination set his jaw. "You have to be cleverer about it if you really want to reach them. You can't stomp around and advertise what you're doing." He paused as if weighing a choice. "Back when I craved revenge, I found a way to get messages to them. I dreamt of confronting them. You have to be very sure. Once you open this Pandora's box, it's their game. You'll have no way of controlling or even guessing what they'll do."

"Thank you," Beatrix said, and following an impulse, she hugged him.

Dyøt's eyes shone a bit when he stepped back. "Kargev's Tavern in the Dust. Leave a note with the bartender."

24

PİONEERS

Early the next morning, Beatrix and Emma skipped breakfast to hurry to Kargev's Tavern in the Dust, apparently one of the shadiest parts of Læsting.

Beatrix hadn't planned to share with anyone, aware that her friends might try to stop her. But Emma picked the information off her brain much in the same way a little sister might plunder secrets.

The young girl was spooked by the conversation with Dyøt.

"Are you sure we should reach out to them if they're so dangerous?" she said, her hair tight in a black chignon.

"I have no choice," Beatrix said. "I'm running out of time in the Zweeshen. I've got the travel summons. Five days left. Even Cassandra agrees it's a bad idea to show up in the Eisid Naraid without Mary Brandt. We're almost sure she's a Pioneer, so this might be the best chance to find her."

And so, determined to create a message enticing enough to raise the curiosity of the Pioneers, they spent an hour agonizing about the wording. Eventually, they settled on something simple.

Looking for Mary Brandt.
Reward for information.

The one-armed man behind the tavern's bar snatched the folded napkin without a word, set two drinks in front of them, charged them five dekums—the lowest coin denomination available—and ignored them. The ease of the transaction stunned them.

They left on high spirits, chatting about the options for dresses Emma and Lucy had suggested for the Monsters Ball—so far all too frilly—and until the tip of a knife pushed against her throat, Beatrix didn't see the three figures that surrounded them.

They had Emma by the hair, and as the girl fought and kicked, one of the assailants squeezed a piece of cloth against her face. Soon limp, she dropped to the pavement.

"Emma!" Beatrix shouted. "Let her be. She didn't do anything."

"*You* did," said the man who held the knife. A bead of blood dripped down Beatrix's neck, its warmth waking her nerve endings, and his arm snaked around her, constricting her stomach. "You made it easy to catch you, coming here," her captor said into her ear. "If only you'd release her, we'd let you be. But you won't."

Dragging Beatrix at knifepoint, they began to make their way to a vehicle that looked like an old phaeton with helicopter blades.

This time, she didn't hesitate.

The Furie rose to her hands with confidence, and when she let it go, the release was tinged with joy. A first since the monster had awakened, she felt eager and looked forward to the lesson it would teach these men who'd dared to hurt Emma and take Beatrix.

What came was unexpected and unknown. An explosive tornado, a turbulent wave. Blurred by smoke and mist, the Furie like never before. No red tongues, no lashing whip, but a maelstrom that slashed and tore and crashed as it turned with the speed of a tsunami—with Beatrix in the eye of the storm. It lifted each of the attackers, throwing them a hundred feet down the road. It devoured façades and hoisted vehicles. It uprooted signs and lanterns. It demolished and cracked stone.

And when it calmed down, and Beatrix collapsed, it left behind scorch marks shaped like black vines.

Beatrix swore Emma to secrecy about the episode in the Dust. The girl hadn't seen much, unconscious during most of the altercation. She awoke when Beatrix tried to carry her away, desperate to get out of this place of dilapidated houses and sewage smell. Curious that Beatrix hadn't noticed either before.

William found them ten minutes later.

"What happened?" he said, and while Beatrix searched for a believable explanation, he added, "Don't lie to me. I felt a huge sword stuck between my shoulder blades. That's the oath telling me you were in mortal danger."

"Nothing happened," Beatrix said, too depleted to be annoyed. Or linger on the idea that this oath might connect them in some magical way. "We were attacked."

"What did they look like?" William scanned his surroundings, as if just then realizing their location. "What were you doing here anyway? Did no one warn you about the Dust?"

"I'm tired. I'm struggling to find my way to the pods. If you won't direct me, I will ask someone else."

"Dammit, Beatrix," William said. "You keep using magic and draining your Inaechar. You won't last long enough to get to the Eisid if you don't stop."

"What did you want me to do? Let them take me?"

"They wanted to kidnap you?" The gears inside William's head were almost loud enough to be heard.

She nodded. "It makes no sense. Do you think they were Pioneers?"

"Most definitely," he said. "From the way you described their choice of transportation, there's no other conclusion. But I don't have any clue why they would abduct you." He turned to her, studying every angle and curve of her face with that gaze of his that missed little. "Do you?"

"I'm tired," Beatrix said.

And, probably noticing the way she swayed, he dropped it. "Let's get out of here."

Beatrix gritted her teeth and called on every drop of willpower to endure the trip back to the guesthouse. Once there, she collapsed on the bed and slept for five hours.

Only after she'd bathed and changed did she confront the damage. Beatrix didn't need William's reminder to know she'd lost too much Inaechar. She struggled to stand. Her stomach hurt, and her head was stuck in a vise. Black marks stained her legs all the way to her knees.

They had yet to fade by dinnertime.

25

ÐYØT

The sound froze Beatrix's blood. Part growl, part scream, it was the howl of a beast in pain. Impossible to ignore.

She found him on her way back from the library, in the middle of the courtyard. Dyøt.

Even with his head bent, she recognized him, at first from his clothes, his orange and electric-blue scarf—which lay crumpled on the ground like a garbage bag—and his boldly patterned jacket stained with dirt.

Dyøt knelt. His shirt hung torn, and his cheeks were marred with streaks of mud. Chunks of hair and dried-up blood clung to his semibare chest.

The agony in his screams was so disturbing everyone in the courtyard stood frozen. So it took Beatrix a lifetime to react. An eternity passed before she ran to his side. Before she unearthed her voice.

"What is it? Dyøt, what's wrong?" Anguish closed her airways, a fist in her throat, and the Furie paced in her cage, tearing long scratches across her stomach. "What can I do? Tell me!"

Dyøt focused on her huge eyes. His dried lips parted in his contorted face. "It burns."

The words smelled of char. When he lifted his hands, Beatrix yelped too at the sight of the boils and blisters. Desperate, useless tears sprang out. The edge of Dyøt's wrist was exposed, the remnants of his wristband fused into what was left of his skin. Knots of muscle rubbed against the fabric of his sleeve. His legs were scorched. And in between the tears in his pants, seared tissue and white bone showed.

"It's him," a voice said. "The Charmancer. He's burning his book."

Someone else gasped. Beatrix didn't know who. Didn't care. Because in front of her, after turning silent, Dyøt's face began to melt. Like runny wax, the skin pulled away from his cheekbones, an invisible fire eating him away.

"We have to do something," Beatrix cried. "Someone help him. Please!"

Like never before, she wished she had a different power. Because there was nothing her Furie could do. It only knew how to destroy, not to heal.

By now, a small group had congregated around them, and she looked up at them, pleading. But everyone stood there, helpless, their combined presence oppressive with the fear of death. Her heart attacked her ribcage, her mind raced, searching for an answer.

"I'll go get help," she said, frantic. "Neradola. I'll be back."

"No, Bea. There's no helping me," Dyøt said through his raspy throat; he tugged on her forearm. "Stay with me. My world's almost gone." His eyes began to hollow, the edges of his skull protruding.

Beatrix's soul collapsed onto the cobblestone. For a second, her lids hid the terrifying sight. Then she leaned in and pulled Dyøt into her arms, holding him like a child.

"I was wrong," he whispered, the words thin like smoke. "To obsess about the Pioneers. Only my parents mattered." Dyøt shifted, reached out. His fingers were as brittle as twigs and his voice so hoarse it gurgled. "I see him now. He wants you. Find your mom, Bea."

Dyøt inhaled deeply, perhaps to fight the pain or perhaps to sigh.

But he never exhaled. He turned to dust.

In her bedroom, Beatrix cried as if someone had exploded all pipes in her body and collected every tear she'd ever refused to shed.

The horror wouldn't leave her mind.

She lay on her fully made bed, shaking and sobbing. Wishing to disappear, she squeezed into a ball, scrunched in, curled up, the smallest she could make herself. Her clothes shed dust onto her chinoiserie comforter. She knew it wasn't dirt; it was the remains of a friend who'd been alive and well just yesterday.

"Beatrix," she heard him say, the whining of the door betraying his entrance.

"Why?" she asked in a strangled voice.

William padded in, as if intruding wore on him. She imagined the agony in his features reflected hers.

"The council's known for a while this Charmancer's gaining strength. You've heard the rumors. The bells... I'm sorry you had to—"

"Dyøt hadn't done anything! He was good." Beatrix screamed because the senselessness left no other options.

William sat on the edge of her bed. "Death is rarely fair."

"It was murder," she said. "And you're not very good at comfort." Although her tears began to ease.

"I'm not. Sorry." With a gesture that in any other moment would have meant something else, William caressed her messed-up hair. "Worth was the one who always made me feel better about it. He's dead too. Elizabeth's contacts have confirmed it. The Charmancer killed him as well. Not like Dyøt, but after being taken prisoner and tortured."

Her tear-stained face looked up, her puffy eyes meeting his and holding them. "My uncle?"

"I wish you'd known him," he said, sadness swamping his features.

"I was hoping to. But why?"

"I don't know. We have no clue what he wants."

He wants you. Dyøt's words were a litany.

"What was my uncle like?"

William let out a bitter laugh. "Unstoppable. Brave. A liar in the end. But he was my friend."

"I'm so sorry." Beatrix must not be great at consoling either because she couldn't fathom what else to offer. Then an idea pushed through to the forefront of her mind. "Does that mean you're free of your oath?"

William shook his head. "It means the Charmancer is closer than we thought. And no, the oath is intact. This kind transcends death."

"You should have never promised."

"I don't regret it," he said and dropped his hand away from her head. Beatrix wished she could say something meaningful but nothing came to mind.

So they sat in silence, sharing the pain that hung in the air like an oppressive shroud.

"Do you want me to light your Fogges candle?" he asked. "For Dyøt?"

She watched him, puzzled through her still blurry vision. "Why would—?"

"That's where some believe taelimns go, back to the Fogges of Unformed Thoughts where we came from. They think the candle can light our passage." He offered her a tired half smile. "Or maybe it just makes the ones left behind feel better."

William stood, and after collecting the candle, he placed it in her hand. The tiny spot where he brushed her skin became seared with longing. William pulled his lighter from his pocket, and Beatrix had a feeling of déjà vu, certain the flame to pop out would be bright green.

Her sense of place and time teetered as the wick burst into flame. A swaying that brought along a wisp of vertigo. *May the words light your journey, Dyøt*, she thought, unclear where the phrase had come from. But it felt right. The only thing about all this that did. With care, she set the candle in the silver holder, placed it on the side table. Watched it burn.

The memory of Dyøt melting away clenched her heart in a fist, a bitter, poisonous tightness in her chest. When her voice came out, it sounded a lot lower and more violent than she'd planned. "I don't even know this Charmancer, and I've never hated anyone so much in my life."

William stared at her with an expression she couldn't decipher. "That makes me sad. He's not worth it."

He hugged her then, and she held on, new tears cascading down her cheeks. Unreliable Zweeshen minutes stretched and folded, leaving them suspended, perhaps outside of time, so that she lost all track of anything but William and her tears.

Eventually, she quieted. Maybe no one could cry forever, no matter how deep the horror.

26

NERADOLA

That night, Beatrix went to bed early. Like many others in the Zweeshen, she struggled to shut off her mind. She tossed, kicked, and fought her bedsheets, until she managed to trick her body into a light sleep. Only to be startled awake what seemed like five minutes later.

A blue haze bathed her room, a brighter spotlight pooling over her dresser table, where *Tome V on the Essential Knowledge & History of the Zweeshen* lay wide open, its pages gleaming in the dark.

Her lids slow to unglue, she rubbed her eyes, wondering if she slept still. But the blue didn't dim, and the air smelled like wild sage. *Aestrer*, she thought, untangling her legs and tossing the blanket aside.

Beatrix hadn't forgotten about the unicorn, had wondered why she'd heard nothing from him. In stories, guides and mentors were a constant presence, providing a steady direction. But it seemed now Aestrer had decided to send her a message of sorts. She could use the help. Dyøt's death had brought forth a sense of finality. Of fragility. This wasn't a novel, Beatrix realized, where things would turn out well in the end no matter what. This was life. Unfair, unpredictable, and heartbreaking. And nothing felt guaranteed.

Time scurried away from her, capricious as always. In four more days, she'd be forced to leave the Zweeshen for the Eisid Naraid. Whether she'd be able to find Mom without Mary Brandt was a question that haunted her.

Dragging the blanket with her, Beatrix padded toward the dresser. The mirror above it reflected her face, distorted in the eerie shadows.

She looked down at the book page and the paragraph the blue beam highlighted.

A most precious of gifts, the Alicorn is as rare as it is powerful. It will glow in the presence of danger. Drinking from the hollowed horn will open one's eyes to magic. And its shavings heal many ailments, even those for which a cure is unavailable.

The light shone brighter around the last words. *Aestrer must have little faith in my deductive abilities,* Beatrix thought with a smile.

"I got it, Aestrer," she said aloud.

The blue light dimmed. Then died.

"Thank you," Beatrix whispered before it disappeared altogether.

She felt grateful the unicorn had come to her aid. Just in time too, because on the next breath, her stomach and her chest contracted in pain—and she collapsed.

"How hard will it be to make a potion using the Alicorn?" Beatrix asked Neradola around midmorning the following day. She struggled to get the words out. The attack last night—longer and worse than any so far—had left her sapped and discouraged. And marked. The black lines on her calves hadn't faded this time.

So despite the freezing cold that had taken everyone by surprise, Beatrix had ventured to the greenhouses. Huge glass buildings reminiscent of birdhouses, inside them the air sagged, thick and humid, with traces of rot, and for a moment she was transported to the jungle in her room the day of Emma's arrival.

Beatrix found the ghost working to repot a strange plant with succulent black flowers.

Neradola took off her gloves and glided to her, grasping the horn with reverence. "You should have told me you had something this powerful. I can mix a regular healing potion for Roamer's and add a few shavings. Or we can have the apothecary distill an oil for you." Her husky voice faded. Neradola surveyed Beatrix, touched her nape, then assessed the shining arrow under her own skin. "I will try both. The dose will need adjusting."

"Thank you," Beatrix said with feeling. After such a painful night, she was willing to try anything. These Roamer's episodes had turned debilitating. She hated the way they punctuated her days, stealing whole chunks of them in which she could do nothing but writhe.

Neradola nodded softly. "I will prepare a vial today. Look for the oil tomorrow."

But the ghost proved more efficient than her predictions. Later that same afternoon, after working with Cassandra and Lucy in the Caladrius salle, Beatrix returned to her bedroom to find a small package tied with string.

Inside was a tiny vial with a cork stopper and a note from Neradola with dosage instructions.

"Wonderful," Emma said, who'd joined Beatrix in her room to deliver the required spring water for the potion. "You can already take your first dose."

Beatrix didn't lose a moment.

After filling the horn with water, she measured three drops from the vial and drank the draught. It tasted bitter but not disgusting. Like liquid licorice.

She assessed herself but didn't feel different in the least. The room did of course, but she'd expected that, given the horn's abilities to reveal magic. The crispness, the bright colors, the superimposed illusions in her bedroom didn't surprise her. But as her eyes settled on the desk where the letter lay atop the notes she'd been making in the Caladrius salle, an idea formed.

The Alicorn showed magic. She had tested it on the message once before—and it had worked. But the letter wasn't the only enchanted object about.

Beatrix hadn't tried the horn on the decoders themselves.

"So you have news," William said that evening.

Beatrix lifted her eyes from the book she'd been reading. The guesthouse lounge was deserted but for an old lady dozing in a corner and a strange dog with triangular markings sleeping by the fireplace.

"Did Jane tell you?"

"I had a feeling you were looking for me." He wore regular clothes today, in dark colors. Only his coat looked odd, a cross between a trench and a many-caped cloak of old.

"Not really," Beatrix said. She had wanted to share her discovery but hadn't known how to locate him. And she wasn't going to ask Jane to reach out. "Where are you staying anyway? If I did want to find you?"

"So you *were* searching for me." He smiled, wide, teeth and all, and she rolled her eyes.

"The Fantasy Guild. The dorms." William looked around the room. "I want to show you something. But it's cold. Outside."

Beatrix pushed her book aside. "Too much longer, and I would've fallen asleep too. I have a thermal suit Emma got for me when we went mask shopping for the ball. Akos-Stellaris tech. I'll be right back."

They left less than ten minutes later and walked in a silence that felt not uncomfortable but expectant, as if the night too were waiting for something.

"Let's sit here," he said, setting the blanket he'd insisted on bringing over the top step of the staircase leading to the docks.

This late in the evening, the marina was almost completely dark. A few amber globes floated along the boardwalk, leaving the rest the realm of the Fogges.

William sat, his legs stretched out, and she settled next to him, her back against the right post of the staircase. The ocean purred around them, and she lifted her face, tilted it up to the sky dominated by an orange, crayon moon.

"I thought you might want to see it," he said. "Since you asked me about the moons."

She had. Because the strange-colored moons of the Zweeshen had her wondering about the reality of this whole world.

Maybe it was the sickness that had forced her to stop and think. To reassess. And to realize that everything had shifted. Beatrix couldn't be sure about Grandpa or Mom anymore. Increasingly she doubted what she knew anything about Martin. About her Furie. About herself. With two more days in the Zweeshen, even her successes felt tainted by her lack of understanding and by the layers of secrets that she failed to reveal.

"Is it changing?" she asked, watching the edges of the orange moon.

"A lunar metamorphosis, yes." His breath fluttered over her ear. "Some consider this one of the most magnificent spells to ever be cast, the one that rules the wheel of the Zweeshen moons."

Despite the warming suit that kept her at a cozy temperature, Beatrix shivered. Her hand hovered next to his and when two of his fingers grazed hers, then entwined, she stilled, unwilling to move and break this different kind of spell.

"Now," he said a few minutes later, gazing up to the sky.

In awe, she watched the clouds part like a mythical sea, dissolving around the edges in fraying tassels. In the space they opened, the moon swooped in, beaming shadowy and cratered, and then as she blinked, it exploded in an eruption of flames that lit the ocean. Hidden by the blazing burst, the stars faded away.

One, two, she counted three seconds while the darkness blanketed everything. Three more and the moon flashed back, neon-lit, full and round. And royal purple.

Beatrix beheld it, mesmerized. Then she looked at William. His face was relaxed, no hint of a scowl in sight, and it drew her in, everything in her thrumming with need.

"Do you want to show me now?" he asked, studying her expression.

His intensity sank underneath her skin.

She looked away. Sighed. Of course he knew. "Not that I'm trying to hide anything, but my friends would make horrible spies."

He laughed, tried to stop himself, and the sound turned into a chuckle. "They're really excited."

Beatrix scoffed. "I assume they told you we've uncovered a new clue." He'd pulled his hand away, and this time he hid behind the charm of his smile. But the skin he'd touched still throbbed. Beatrix grabbed the feeling and stored it away. She dug into her pouch and retrieved the battered letter.

It was too dark to see, so William took out his hexagonal crystal, tapped it to produce a soft light, and set it on the paper. Like he'd done the very first time at the Bookends Café, he inspected the writing with care, his eyebrows knitting together. "How?"

"The thimble. I used the Alicorn for my potion today and that got me thinking about its ability to expose magic. I guessed it could help me see through the enchantment on the decoder."

"And it worked."

She bit her lip. "It did."

"How?"

She laughed. "Let me show you. It's my favorite so far." Beatrix retrieved the thimble from her pouch. She'd been drinking off the alicorn all day long, so her eyes were already attuned to magic. Besides, she knew what to search for. "First, I put it on, and then, do you see the thistle? That's what the Alicorn showed me." Beatrix pushed on the tiny flower with her thumb and on the opposite side with her index finger. The thimble glowed red, and the swirls and curves on it began reorganizing themselves to create a crown. The moment the last scroll shifted into place, with a click, a thin blade pushed out through the top of the thimble.

William laughed. "A lancet!"

"Quite sharp. And then..."

Then she'd done the only thing anyone who knew stories would and stabbed her finger. Only, instead of blood, a single drop of black-blue ink dropped out of the wound and onto the letter. It spread into a runny stain that covered all the verses, and for a second, Beatrix feared she'd undone everything. But soon the ink retreated, leaving behind brand-new writing.

"Then?" William asked again.

"I played Sleeping Beauty and the next clue appeared. Wanna see?"

William took the paper and read,

"Enter through the Gate Untold.
At its darkest the veil is naught.
The Goddess Rephait the question begs.
For the answer search your strength."

"I think the key here is the Gate Untold," Beatrix said. "If we can figure out what that is, the rest might become clearer."

When William didn't respond, she pivoted to him. "What is it? Don't you agree?"

"About this Gate? Yes, of course. I was just considering you've run out of decoders. Unless there was something else in your grandfather's box."

"Nothing. Other than the chest itself. And I checked that with Alicorn sight—no enchantment there." Beatrix sighed. "We've deciphered so much, and I still understand so little. The Gate Untold rings a bell too. Like I should know what it is. Does the veil part tell you anything?"

"Never heard of either. A veil in the sense of the separation of the realms, perhaps. Not sure how that would be relevant here." He stared straight at her, and in the orange shadows, she couldn't read his expression. "You should be proud of yourself. Do you realize how far you've come with this?"

"Not far enough." Beatrix unhooked her new hair clip and redid her bun, the humidity from the ocean exacerbating her hair's natural frizz. She huffed in frustration. "I'll be leaving soon, and I still haven't found Mary. I haven't figured out what the riddle is about. We suspect it's a spell, but what kind and what for is a mystery."

William shook his head. "You're terrible at accepting praise and taking compliments, do you know that?" He moved toward her and for a moment Beatrix thought he would pull her into his arms. He didn't. He shifted back and remained sitting just far away enough that their bodies didn't touch. But so close she felt the warmth emanating from it. His scent mixed with hers and the ones from the night and the sea around them.

"Don't worry," William said. "We'll figure out the riddle. Maybe someone in the Eisid will recognize the Gate Untold. We're almost there." The way he said the last words, with both vehemence and hidden fear, made her wonder.

"Do you know something I don't?"

William stared at her with that intensity of his that unsettled her. "I would tell you if I did."

"I wasn't doubting you."

"It's just—this feeling." He looked to the ocean. The ever-moving water tore the reflection of the sky apart, decomposing it in glinting shards. "My teacher used to say our fears feed our curses. So no, there's nothing. I'm eager to get out of here and see you safe in the Eisid Naraid. That's all."

He smiled. A lovely, open grin as bright as the moon above.

But for some reason, Beatrix couldn't smile back.

27

LEYNA

"Nothing," Cassandra said the next afternoon, dropping herself onto an overstuffed chair in the Caladrius salle. "They all clam up. I checked with the bardic experts, the cartographers, and even the pageturner masters."

"No luck either," Lucy said.

"How about you, Emma?" Beatrix asked.

"Nobody has ever heard of this Untold Gate." Emma pulled her satchel over her head and set it on a dainty side table. "Did you ask Jane? She seems familiar with lore."

Beatrix grimaced. "She had no idea. Suggested I speak to the historical experts. Which worked about as well as the last time we tried."

"It's so frustrating." With a huff, Emma plopped onto a green settee in front of the fire. "Not a single mention in the library geographical records either."

Beatrix sat next to her, stretching her legs onto a threadbare ottoman. She glanced casually at the multitude of mirrors, all of which showed the gruesome picture of the dead bird, albeit from a different angle today. She turned away.

"My life's doomed to disappointment." Emma's hair fell in droopy burgundy strands. "I thought we were getting somewhere."

"We are." Cassandra sifted through the stack of papers on the table and forced a smile. "Let's not be pessimistic. We've deciphered clues *A* through *E*. So this one is the last one."

"True." Beatrix pulled on one of the settee's many loose threads. A Cheshire cat's favorite, or so went the explanation.

"But we haven't found Mary." Emma pouted, her shoulders hunched.

"We have new information," Lucy said. "We should count our wins."

"It's true. We've made progress." Beatrix realized she might be trying to convince herself as much as them.

Leaving her seat, Cassandra walked to a large mirror and began writing on it with a glowing marker.

"Let's approach this scientifically." Under the title "Known data," she began to write a list of numbered bullets. "In recap, we know: One, that Beatrix's mom gave her a map to the Sacred Valley region in the Eisid Naraid. Two, that the letter contains a Craxtan-encoded set of instructions, likely for a spell, of which we've decoded four."

Beatrix straightened in her seat, logic beginning to dispel the sense of helplessness. "Three, that the destination for Mary Brandt is the temple of Rephait, marked by the Evermoon rune."

Cassandra nodded and took that down.

"Four," Lucy said, "that we can assume the Pioneers are involved because 'May the Words' is their telepathic call for help, and Mary must be one of them."

Beatrix looked down at her journal, skimming through her own notes. "Five, that the whole letter is either a spell of disguise or one of revelation. Selda was quite convinced of that."

"I agree," Cassandra said and wrote that additional point on the board.

Emma pulled on her cameo. "Don't forget what Beatrix learned during the hearing. That her mom was the keeper of the Soul of Rephait."

"And that according to the council she stole it." Beatrix's voice trembled toward the end. Her chest tightened. She still couldn't accept that of Mom. She wasn't convinced she could rely on the council's allegations. Their accusations of Beatrix had been bogus. Why would their statements regarding her mother be trustworthy? So much about the Zweeshen was contradictory. Dyøt had explained that the loss of the Soul would kill the Eisid. It wasn't a secret. So how could Mom have stolen the winged dagger? Taken the most sacred artifact and condemned her land? After being entrusted to protect it? It made no sense. Beatrix refused to believe it.

She needed to know more... The thought snuck in that Grandpa would have been able to help. She cast it aside.

"If only we could find Mary Brandt." Emma's tone dragged with defeat. "Maybe she'd be able to explain how it all fits together."

Beatrix massaged her temples, the action repeated in the idiosyncratic mirrors on the walls, which chose what to reflect at their whim and now showed her alone in the garden practicing the Taming Sphere. "Our search for Mary has been so unsuccessful I wonder if we were wrong about the Pioneer connection. Maybe that path was a dud."

"Maybe," Lucy said.

Across from them, Cassandra dropped her head with something akin to guilt. She opened her mouth and hesitated. "I'm sorry, Bea. I should have told you earlier."

Cassandra shifted in place with uncharacteristic hesitation.

"There's no doubt the Pioneers are involved," she said after an intake of breath. "At the time, I didn't deem it worth sharing, no point in hurting you, Beatrix. When I checked the Criminal Rolls, Mary Brandt didn't appear on them. But Leyna Yoru did. She was a Pioneer. Inner circle, high leadership. The records show the nuclear attempt on the council hall as her last known sighting."

Leaving the guesthouse through the back door, Beatrix followed a green gravel road into the woods. The freshness of pine and firs was a welcome reprieve. She needed air. And quiet. And the chance to readjust her memories to the reality of who Mom and Grandpa truly were. To mourn them anew, this time as the strangers they'd become.

She let herself in through the gate to the sculpture garden and navigated around the familiar marbles to the always-in-spring corner where a swinging bench was nestled among bluebells and delphiniums.

That's where William discovered her half an hour later, as the last remnants of dusk faded and the sprite lanterns lit up. Emma must have told him where to find her. Again. But he didn't seem to be wearing the sympathetic, bordering on pitying expression of everyone else. Instead, his stride was purposeful.

"I wanted you to be the first to know," he said as soon as he reached the tree that held up the swing. "Your trip's notice has been posted on the outgoing trips board at the Bureau. Six a.m., two days from now."

He seemed to expect a reaction, but she just nodded.

William leaned against the trunk. The leaves that rustled around them sounded like murmurs. Like stories-to-be. "I saw you all hard at work in the Caladrius salle on my way to meet Jane. Did you guys discover anything else?"

Beatrix rubbed her hands on her pants, a chill suddenly flowing through her. "I wish I could stay a little longer. Maybe with a few more days we could locate Mary, and I wouldn't have to show up in the Eisid empty-handed."

William tilted his head, a newborn frown bisecting his brow, and slid both hands in the pockets of what she'd learned were high-tech all-weather pants. "You collapsed twice in two days. It's time to go." His voice had gained that annoying edge, the one he used when he was about to turn bossy and tell her what to do.

"You don't need to become all pushy. I get it." Frustration spilled into Beatrix's tone. She massaged her brow. "I just wish I were further before I left."

He sat on the grass in front of her, one leg stretched out and the other bent in at the knee. "There's something else I wanted to share. I've been working to gather a few folks to accompany us to the Eisid Naraid. A bit of a security detail. It's not the safest of places."

"You have?" While her first reaction was to admire the idea, her next thought had edges and thorns. "On your own? And you didn't think to tell me." Beatrix's Furie stirred. Began to climb. "We agreed to partner on this. Not that you would take over."

"You're right." William said. "I'm not used to working with others. But it's no excuse. I should have told you. I'm sorry."

His apology took the wind out of her anger. "Promise me this is the last time you don't share. This isn't your show."

"Won't happen again." William bowed his head. "Am I forgiven? Or is there a penance?"

She glanced up, scanning the intent face that had become so very familiar. "I assume Emma told you?"

"Only that you might need a friend. What's wrong?"

A part of her wanted to tell him. The rest of her had no desire to delve into the odd mix of disappointment and hurt and shame. Into the conviction that she was a fool for trusting. For believing in anyone.

The moon was a red sliver, its light too dim to do more than stretch shadows around the garden. The sky beamed so heavy with stars it seemed in danger of buckling.

"Why don't I recognize the constellations? I've wondered since the beginning and always forget to ask."

William narrowed his eyes at the obvious deflection but answered anyway. "This is an invented sky, not your standard universe. Those..." He waved to the polka-dotted cover above them. "They're charmed luminaries tied to stories."

"Like the fake-colored moons?"

"Just like that. They're all part of the enchantment that created the Zweeshen. It's how the council can tell when biblioworlds are destroyed. Their stars go out."

"I've always liked stars," she said.

"That's the Ellisius Quill constellation." William pointed to a group loosely depicting a feather. "It's made up of some of the most famous Pangean Originals, like Quixote, some Shakespeare, and *The Story of the Stone*. Over there, the Scroll. The very first world to be bound is in it, *The Fall of J*. And that one's called the Wordrider, in honor of the long-extinct taelimns who didn't need pageturners to travel. Much like Navarsing, the sky configuration changes all the time."

"Wait a second. Emma swore it's impossible to jump into a story. That a pageturner is always needed."

"For normal taelimns. Wordriders were special. Capable of moving across stories freely, traveling through ink, across the Fogges."

"If they could, then—"

Both William's back and tone stiffened. "Don't get any ideas. Riders were the only ones who could see a path. They connected sentences that repeat across tales and flew on them to the next story. Their kind disappeared thousands of years ago, long before the Zweeshen."

"Why?"

"They were killed. There was another Charmancer once. He's the reason the Zweeshen was created, to prevent such power from accumulating again. He murdered all wordriders but one, kept a single survivor to use her magic for himself. It allowed him to travel unchallenged from book to book. That magic gift died with him when he was defeated."

Beatrix rubbed her forehead. The beginnings of a headache were lurking. She hooked her fingers under her hair tie and shook her hair out of her tight ponytail, letting it fall free.

"I like it better that way," William said next to her.

"What? My hair? I don't. It's all messy and full of flyaways."

"I think it has personality—refuses to do what you want. You should stop fighting it and wear it loose."

"Not a chance." Beatrix went quiet, her gaze searching the distance. Hair issues were the least of her problems. "My mother was a Pioneer." She hadn't planned on it, but the words blurted out of their own volition.

His face showed more concern than surprise. "Yeah."

The acknowledgment both stung and enraged her. Of course he knew. Of course he'd figured it out long ago and said nothing. It had been staring her in the face too.

And now, as if unstoppered, her anger pushed out, free-flowing—a warm, familiar current that fueled itself, heating up her core like magma. Darkening at the edges as if accumulating pieces of night from around them.

"How could she? Why? I just don't understand. Why would Mom want to bring down the Zweeshen? She stole something that would destroy her world. Knowingly. She sentenced them to death! What kind of person does that? No. What type of monster kills a whole land? And then Grandpa. All my life, I thought he was good. That he cared about people. About me. But he knew. At the very least about the Zweeshen. And he didn't say anything. He didn't bother to tell me the truth." Beatrix kept going, words pouring, spilling over and piling up until she stood, shaken and depleted, all emptied out. "Everything about them was a lie."

"They loved you."

"You don't know that."

"They tried to protect you. Actions count."

Beatrix stared at him, and the vehemence in his eyes held her there, glued in place.

"You're not her," he said softly, and she flinched because until that moment she hadn't known what scared her the most.

Because her mother was evil. A criminal. Leyna had a Furie. Her eyes looked like Beatrix's. And now Beatrix recognized that underneath the pain of betrayal breathed fear. The terror that the Chairman might be right, and she was no better than her monster.

"Did you ever meet her?"

His hesitation was almost imperceptible, but he didn't ask who. "We crossed paths. You have eyes like hers. They're a rare and revered trait among Eisidians, a sign of the Goddess's favor."

Looking away, Beatrix hid her hands in her jacket pockets. She discovered a tiny ball of lint inside the right one and played with it. "I can't remember her face anymore."

Around them, ghostly birches swayed and climbing vines shimmered.

An eternity passed before he spoke. When he did, his voice breezed out like a caress. "I had a little sister. I cannot remember her either."

Beatrix's eyes lifted, and the air between them crackled. "What was her name?"

For a millisecond, it seemed as if he would reach up to touch her cheek. The air hung, taut. His fingers arched so close she felt the warmth on her skin. But he lowered his hand.

"Allaisin," he said. "Means 'drop of the sea,' and that's what most Inter'Es called her. They were forever messing up, so she embraced it as a nickname."

Beatrix smiled. Then gasped, a current of excitement shocking her as, like puzzle pieces, disparate facts rearranged themselves in her mind. "Names matter..."

"Excuse me?"

"That's what the Selda told us. My grandfather used to say the same thing. Oh, my God. I have to find the girls."

It was a testimony to William's loyalty that he didn't question her. "I saw Emma in the guesthouse lounge, and we can message Cassandra and Lucy. Where?"

She took a moment to consider. "The Caladrius salle. We seem to do our best thinking there."

When they all gathered in the mirror-heavy Caladrius room twenty minutes later, Beatrix didn't bother with introductory explanations.

"Cass, do you still have that book we were using to look for synonyms of the Gate Untold? The one that gave all the alternative meanings of words and their famous uses in literature?"

"I do. Lucy's still stuck in class, by the way. She was going to return it to the library tomorrow."

"Great. Can you look up the meaning of Mary?"

Both William and Cassandra appeared startled, as if they suspected Beatrix had snapped under the pressure of the last few days. But Emma sprang up to her feet, her hair up in tufts of bright green. "Of course! It's elementary! Beatrix, you're brilliant!"

"Would you mind explaining for the rest of us slow-wits?" Cassandra asked while she paged through the book in question.

Beatrix began to pace. Sometimes movement helped her think. "I'm not sure I'm right, but when William and I met Selda, she mentioned something that reminded me of Grandfather. That names matter. Grandpa liked to name things. We had two Jude wrenches. And he always called things according to the country of origin, because names change in different languages. You, William, would be Guillermo in Spain, for example."

He grimaced. "Not thrilled."

"Are you following?" Cassandra asked William, and he shook his head.

Beatrix paced around the room, gesticulating. "We know that Mom's letter contains writing in code. So what if Mary Brandt wasn't a literal name but an encryption, as well? Another kind of riddle. The meanings of names matter. Get it?"

Cassandra looked down to the book in her hands, and her face lit up with understanding. "I can't believe we didn't think of it! One of the meanings of Mary is rebellion."

"Yes!" Emma's body seemed too small to contain her excitement. She twirled and clapped her hands together. "And what does Brandt stand for in the old Germanic language?"

Cassandra grinned. "I don't need the book for that. I did enough studying of linguistics. It means a sword or a blade."

"Get it now?" Emma said to William. "Mary is not a person. It's a thing. If we substitute the correct meaning for Mary Brandt, Leyna's message reads, 'Take the rebellion blade to the Eisid Naraid.'"

"The winged dagger," William said, his gaze finding Beatrix's. "The Soul of Rephait's physical artifact. That's what your mother wants you to take back to the temple."

"But I don't have it."

Emma shrugged, her satchel slipping to the floor. "Maybe she thought you did."

"Or maybe you do," said an unfamiliar voice. It came out of Cassandra's mouth, and when Beatrix faced her friend, the redhead's eyes were whited out.

28

FARÍSAÐ

No matter what she tried, Cassandra could not remember her vision, or further explain the words she'd uttered while out of herself. Such a cryptic, non-actionable snippet only compounded Beatrix's frustration at another dead end. But the trip was finally here—one day away—and with the packing completed, and the legal hurdles cleared, Beatrix found herself with time on her hands. The day had dawned white, with snow piling unevenly all throughout Navarsing University.

But the blizzard that raged around them, depositing snow in white heaps without rhyme or reason—two feet high by the marketplace and the coast, interring most docks, five inches around the volleyball courts, but a mere dusting on the skybridges and none on the roof of the Peist clock tower—fit Beatrix's mood. She was torn between dismay about what she was leaving undone and a deep bitterness at all she'd discovered.

Mostly lies. Lies from the people she had trusted.

Liar.

Martin had accused Beatrix of that many a time. Now she heard a pain he'd packed in the word that she hadn't noticed at the time. And she wondered if perhaps he too had been taken for a fool. Had Mom hidden this world like Grandpa had from Beatrix? Had Leyna lied about her death to him? The whispers, who had been unusually quiet of late, gave her a memory. Martin smiling. Once. At a barbecue next to Mom. Picking Beatrix up, in some place with dunes and briny air. She couldn't tell if they were real. Or if the whispers had pulled images from books Beatrix had forgotten she'd read or some she hadn't yet opened.

Tired of her own thoughts, she had headed to the Bookends, hoping to progress on her newly acquired *Tome VI on the Essential Knowledge & History of the Zweeshen* while enjoying a cup of hot chocolate. She'd found a whole section about bardic worlds, and some basic knowledge could serve her as she explored the Eisid Naraid. Because despite everything, the thrill of discovering her world overpowered the other, less positive feelings about the trip.

The Bookends was crowded, but Beatrix found a table in a corner and burrowed down to read. Five chapters into descriptions of the different landscapes that predominated in bardic world literature, she found it. Right in between a note about the ancient, sacred trees and the most effective ways to defend against wraiths and their brethren was a brief mention of the Gate Untold.

The Gate Untold continues to be one of the great mysteries. Some question its very existence. But this author, who has had the honor to visit it, can attest not only to its being real but to its awesome power.

Beatrix looked up from the page, straight into a black crow. Today's theme was Rue Morgue.

She reread the passage.

The Gate Untold. Someone had seen it. Someone knew what it was. Where. Flipping the pages to the beginning of the book, Beatrix searched for the author of this particular volume.

There were three listed. But only one boasted of having visited three hundred bardic worlds and counting.

"Can she do it?" Beatrix asked William a few hours later, as they walked through an almost unrecognizable white Market Square.

William skimmed the small note that had just been delivered by a raggedy kid with a newsies cap and smiled as he passed it to her.

Beatrix grinned as well. "Jane's right. Elizabeth is really well connected if she could arrange a meeting this fast. Midnight tonight. Why so late?"

"Did you forget about the Monsters Ball? That's the reason we can meet the author of the History & Essentials on such short notice. Everyone who's anyone will be there."

Ah, yes, the ball. She watched the crowded scene around them. Pretty much all of the tourists ambling the square could be blamed on the Monsters Ball.

"I haven't forgotten. Cass keeps insisting I should go, but we're due at the pageturner a few hours after. At four-thirty."

"It's cutting it close, I agree. But it should work out. And if you go, you'd have a chance to ask this author your questions. He's considered quite the expert. But it's up to you."

Beatrix shook her head. She couldn't pass up the chance to learn something that might help her decipher the last clue. "Emma will be delighted. She was upset I considered skipping the party. I even got a mask."

"Emma's right. It won't hurt to enjoy yourself for a little bit. Fun is fine."

She lifted her eyebrows. "Really? Are *you* going?"

He looked a bit abashed. "I wasn't planning on it. Maybe I will now. Perhaps I'll even get a dance." Was it her imagination or had he just looked at her with invitation?

"Okay. I'll meet him," Beatrix said, not in the least swayed by the idea of dancing with William. No. Of course it was just the prospect of learning about the Gate Untold that made her insides flip with excitement.

"Great." William scribbled a quick answer on the note and gave it back to the kid, who ran away as if galloping.

In a gesture that struck her as curious, William clasped his hands behind his back. It gave him a martial stance. "On a different subject—logistics. Once we get to the Eisid, you'll be housed in the official buildings at the port of entry. You might need to stay in the Eisid for a while, and because of the Charmancer, the council's raised the alert level to red, so most pageturners will be on lockdown. I think—"

But she had stopped listening, because over by the chocolatier's cottage—one of the many street shops that had sprouted everywhere in preparation for the onslaught of tourism for the Monsters Ball—she recognized the signs. The familiar muttering and awkward side-glances. A few older men and women had congregated by a carved bench, their fingers like claws around steaming mugs of spiced wine. Their murmurs were loud enough for Beatrix to overhear the insults.

"Don't mind them," William said, guiding her toward a group of singing children dressed in fur-trimmed capes. "When ignorant people feel threatened, they act badly."

Beatrix glared, the Furie pacing. "Is that excusable? I'd like to know how 'badly' is tolerable." Badly as in spreading rumors and talking behind her back? Or badly as in sneaking to kill her in the middle of the night? She hadn't forgotten the Codex's message either. Nor had the episode in the Dust faded from her mind. Beatrix checked the locks on her windows and door every eve.

William watched her with a gentle, almost tender expression. "I don't have all the answers. I'm convinced the best we can do is live our way. It denies everyone else power over us."

"Did your mentor teach you that one?"

He smiled. "You'd like him."

Her mouth curved up. "Maybe."

Soon after, William stopped at a stand festooned in green, black, and white and bought a bag of chestnuts.

"I wanted to ask you something." The question had been nagging her and now felt as good a time as any.

He straightened his back as if preparing for a barrage. "Shoot."

"What did you promise my uncle?"

William's shoulders relaxed, betraying that he'd expected worse. "The oath I made is a blood binding. I swore to keep you safe until you're reunited with your family. Worth being a relation, the plan was for me to take you to my adoptive home where he would wait for us. I would have been free as soon as you met him."

Understanding the full meaning of that admission, Beatrix flinched. "He's dead. How will you fulfill it now?"

"Don't worry about it. I suspect we can track a relative or two of yours once in the Eisid." He seemed genuinely unconcerned and soon switched subjects.

"She's late," Beatrix said as they reached the knotted lantern where they were supposed to meet Emma. The girl had begged to be included in the last few errands before the trip, and no one felt capable of denying her.

William pointed down the street. "There she is."

"Oh, chestnuts," Emma said when she joined them a minute later. "Can I have one?"

William offered her the bag.

"I'm so relieved you're okay, Bea." Emma resettled her ever-present satchel over her shoulder. "Something exploded in the Caladrius salle. They don't know if the mirrors will survive."

William grimaced. "Would that be such a loss?"

"Of course it would be," Beatrix said. There was nothing wrong with the mirrors. "I love the Caladrius. Why would anyone destroy a study salle?"

Emma lifted her arms. "I don't know, but they can't figure out what it was either. A bomb of some kind. The explosion was heard all the way to the marina. If anyone had been there..."

He looked at Beatrix, and she knew what he was thinking. She might have been. If instead of the Bookends she'd decided to read in the Caladrius...

"I won't miss the mirrors," Emma said. "They're blank for me, a horrible reminder of my lack of story. What do you see, Beatrix?"

She considered deflecting but changed her mind last minute. "A white bird. With blue-dotted wings and a golden chest."

Emma looked at her in awe. "You're friends with Farisad too! Why didn't you say so?"

"Farisad?" Beatrix sifted through the multitude of strange names she'd memorized in the past weeks.

"The bird you just described," Emma said in a self-evident tone. "How did you meet him? Farisad's the one the Librarian called on to track you. He chased your magic-print and marked your room to set up the pageturner—and he dropped me off."

Beatrix's eyes widened. Farisad was *her* bird? "You were there? But I was seven." The night the monster awoke was seared in her brain. Together with the horror of striking the animal midflight with a blast out of her childish hands.

"I killed him." She'd never said it aloud before.

"Don't be silly. It'd be like thinking you've killed the sun." Emma shook her head in that know-it-all way Beatrix had grown fond of. "And time doesn't matter to us. You might have been a child when Farisad followed the trail and set the beacon, but we triggered a trap in the process, and I got stuck until much later in your timeline. Don't even remind me of those doves."

"So he's alive and well?" Disbelief made her almost shrill. A boulder that had been hanging around Beatrix's neck, threatening to cut off her airway, released, crashing to the ground. "I hit him. I know I did. I picked up his dead body."

Emma shrugged daintily. "He can't die on Earth. Probably left his shell and regenerated back home. Farisad can travel anywhere. Last I heard, he was enjoying the Nile. He's the happiest bird in the Egyptian *Book of the Dead*."

29

MANY MONSTERS

The night of the Monsters Ball was memorable.

It had been a strange rest of the day for Beatrix. She was torn between the desire to use every minute in the Zweeshen to find Mary or decode the letter, and the temptation to be dragged along by the excitement of the ball.

The discovery about Farisad's well-being had only added to her sense of lightness, a buoyancy that felt foreign and welcome. Cassandra and Lucy had been ecstatic about her change of heart about attending. Emma kept twirling and humming, and even Jane had agreed to join them.

At the last hour, Beatrix had received a formal invitation to the Gala Dinner, an exclusive event attended by the most famous and decorated of taelimns. She questioned the political motivation of the charity that hosted her. After all, her case had been well-publicized and highly contentious. But Evenzaar had expressed his strong disapproval, which had only reinforced her wish to accept the invitation.

Whatever the charity's agenda, Beatrix's wondering was forgotten as soon as she stepped into the Gala, and the glitz and glamour of the dining salon dizzied her.

Liveried footmen took her invitation with gloved hands and passed it on to a herald who announced her name in a voice with a built-in megaphone. Several people pivoted in Beatrix's direction as she walked the red carpet, the flashes of cameras blinding her.

"We will see your pictures in *CH* magazine," Lucy had raved earlier. "I hope you make the best dressed."

"I prefer *BoldPrint* myself." Matt adjusted his perfectly tailored vest. "It has a higher level of journalistic rigor."

"It's a party!" Cassandra said. "Not a war exposé."

Emma beamed. "Just watch out for celebrities. I won't forgive you if you don't describe everything in detail afterward."

But in the end, the Gala turned out to be a stuffy affair, and seated in a corner, far away from the stage, Beatrix had enjoyed limited exposure.

"All the famous taelimns are at the VIP tables, I'm afraid," a tiny old lady with a turban and giant opal earrings bent to tell her. "Nevertheless, the setting is mighty lovely, isn't it? Mrs. Dalloway outdid herself again."

So Beatrix had to disappoint her friends when she joined them after the dinner had been adjourned, and donning their masks, the VIPs poured into the ballroom for the dancing part of the evening.

"Don't sweat it." Paul shrugged, loosening his necktie. By how uncomfortable he appeared in it, Beatrix guessed he didn't wear black-tie attire often. "All celebrities will take their seats at the awards ceremony, and we'll get to gawk."

"I've recognized a few already," Cassandra said. "I spotted Margaret Thornton chatting with the young Abelard by the refreshment table earlier. And Muhe Lin was on the arm of one of the White Queens. Mary Lennox is here somewhere. We should play guessing, see who finds the most famous taelimns."

"Phileas Fogg at eight o'clock," Matt said.

Paul squinted in that direction. "Scheherazade by the golden column."

Lucy waved her tiny Spanish fan. Her red and black gown was reminiscent of a flamenco dancer's. "Oh, I adore her dress. She always has impeccable taste. But this is too easy. We should do it blind."

"Good idea," Cassandra said. "After all, 'It is only with the heart that one can see rightly. What is essential—'"

"Is invisible to the eye," Beatrix finished, recognizing the quote.

Cassandra smiled. "The fox is around here somewhere."

"Who am I?" The girl wore a dark green dress with cream gloves that reached above her elbows. Her mask, gold and peacock-feathered, reminded Beatrix of one she'd admired at the bazaar but considered too expensive.

"You're aware it's a demimask, right, Jane? It's as good a disguise as Clark Kent's glasses," Emma said.

"Who's your monster?" Becca's envy colored her inflection, and Jane's wide mouth stretched.

"I don't need a monster."

"True." Lucy gave Jane an appreciative stare. "Your outfit's fabulous."

Beatrix agreed. The draped taffeta enhanced the figure Jane's regular clothes hid, and a special glow surrounded her. Actually. Not only her. Everyone in their group seemed to be enveloped in the same brilliant aura. It was perhaps a little dimmer around Paul and Becca.

"The music's starting." Matt extended a hand toward Lucy.

"Wanna dance?" Paul asked Beatrix.

She didn't need to catch Becca's silent growl to feel the flaming arrows. Good thing the girl's form-fitting dress couldn't conceal a machete. "I can't waltz. I'm pretty sure people go to classes for that."

"We'll manage. The floor's coated with ease-of-steps to help us out. Did I tell you how great you look?"

"I can't take credit. All Emma and Lucy." And Dyøt's ideas. Beatrix understood now why he'd raved about the ball—and a bit of sadness snuck in.

"Well, you look amazing," Paul said.

Beatrix had never worn a gown like the one Lucy had found for her, grey-silver fabric that flowed like water, silky, smooth, and ever-changing in hue. "To bring out your eyes," Lucy had said. Cassandra had helped arrange her hair in a cascading updo and shared her makeup, while Emma shouted contradictory color suggestions. And in the midst of their excitement, the gloom of the past days died, unable to survive the exhilaration of the Monsters Ball.

Maybe she did fit in here.

Because on this night, Beatrix felt grateful to be part taelimn. Tonight, she could forget about the council and the Librarian, the Charmancer, the Soul, the dying Eisid, and even her mom's letter. She could dismiss her failing Inaechar and the trip later on. Because, for once, under the glittering of crystal and the shine of satin, the Zweeshen was better than she could have imagined.

"It's my favorite event too," Paul said, watching her flushed cheeks. "Wait till the awards ceremony. The Librarian likes to go over the top. Last year they smashed a huge crystal Kraken onstage, and the pieces became award statuettes right in front of us. The nonmagical guilds choked on their wine. It was awesome."

"May I?" The tap on Paul's shoulder belonged to William, who took the other boy's place before he could protest. It figured that William's tuxedo would reduce Paul's finery to a tablecloth.

"Good evening, Beatrix. You look extremely beautiful tonight," he said in a formal tone.

"Why is it okay to interrupt? I always thought that custom rude."

"Invented by the Americans. They're an impatient lot." William smiled in a way that was both teasing and unsettling. "You should learn to take compliments. No deflection. A simple thanks would do."

Young and handsome, he appeared more relaxed than usual. The haze she'd noticed surrounding Paul shone brighter around William.

But he misunderstood her gaze as she compared them. "Don't worry. I'm sure puppy love will still be there when we're done."

"He's not— Why do you do that? Make comments like that? You start out fine, and then you ruin it."

His lips curved, a roguish glint in his eyes. He glanced back at Paul, who'd stayed close by. "You do know he has a sequel coming, don't you?"

"So?"

"So? You'll get hurt. The writer always trumps. His artisan will give him some random love interest with a rare illness, and he'll forget all about you."

"It's not like that! He's my friend. He's nice. And considerate and positive, unlike you." *And so important, I know almost nothing about him.*

William didn't comment, just kept smiling as he twirled her around so easily, she felt graceful. They were right, those silly novels people mocked: it was all in the leading. Dancing with William was effortless, a mixture of walking and floating, and something about the moment made all the pieces fall into place.

Under the light of a million candles and fake amber suns, Beatrix's story blood woke up.

I'm a taelimn.

This time the meaning sank into her soul. Somewhere deep, a thread of paper, a drop of ink stirred. Her heart leapt and dared to dream, because in a story anything was possible, and because for the first time, she felt happy to be who she was. She shivered, amazed and humbled by the sense of belonging, of connectedness with everything. She saw herself, a speck staring at the whole galaxy, and at the same time powerful, the atom that precipitates the reaction to create the stars themselves.

A taelimn.

The words grew out with meaning, expanding like a hot air balloon. Now she was bigger than her own body. She grew as large as the ballroom, breathed with it, beat together with it, turning in sync with every other couple, becoming at once their voices and their feet, the music and the light.

"Forshaltness." William's accent made the sounds whoosh. "There's one thread. That's what you're feeling. We all do. Occasions like the ball, this many taelimns together, compound it. We're the same, all part of the tapestry. All stories are connected."

The question almost tumbled out, but she didn't need to ask. Beatrix knew how. "Stories inspire readers. Readers become writers."

"And writers inspire more writers. Take one out, a single story, a single writer, or a single reader, and the whole piece unravels."

A new waltz began, and Beatrix noticed Paul glancing in her direction. But she didn't want to stop dancing with William yet. Without thinking, her hand rose to touch his mask. Black velvet covered half of his face.

"What's your monster?"

His voice came out hoarse and low, and when his lips moved, the air caressed her cheek. "The curse of my family."

"You're cursed." She wasn't shocked. Or afraid. Somehow it made total sense.

Those moments, the ones of perfect happiness... They were fleeting.

"I should have told you before. It was cowardly not to. The curse is why I left my world. It's believed to be ineffective while in exile."

"Is it?"

"I've never dared test it. It's why I had Jane help you, and I tried to keep my distance when we first met."

This time, a shiver traced a trail along the nape of her neck. Fidgety, she trained a strand of hair behind her ear, unwilling to think too hard about bad scenarios. "I'm sure it isn't a big deal. Do you turn into an owl at night? Or do you look like Shrek?"

He took a deep breath, let the words slip out like wisps. They grazed her with a touch of cold. "People around me die—if they love me back."

She held his stare, unblinking. "I'm not scared."

"I am not sure if that's brave or reckless."

"If you want to know what I fear..."

"One has to do evil to be evil, Beatrix. You have the strength to handle your Furie."

It sounded like praise, and when she gazed away to escape the compliment, a multitude of masked figures assailed her. She wasn't one with the room anymore, but very much by herself.

"Is it me or does this light do strange things to people?"

"Strange how?" His scowl was visible behind his mask.

"I don't know. They have this weird, foggy cloud around them."

There were many couples on the floor, many more, and closer than before. Almost claustrophobia-inducing.

"I don't see anything," he said.

It must be Beatrix then.

She craned her neck, trying to keep the dancers in view. While some were surrounded by a white aura, many were enveloped in dark smoke.

The waltz finished; the music sped up into a twist, and as they spun faster, mist and white, crystal and candlelight melded in a blur.

"William," she began—and never finished the thought.

Fear unlike anything Beatrix had known turned her blood to slush. She tightened her grip on him while ice ran through her veins, paralyzing her for what seemed like an eternity.

She saw *him* across the room. The one from the vision. Only here he looked like a skeletal figure, and out of his sunken-in skull, his stare drilled into her. Malevolent, powerful, and focused. A monster like she'd envisioned her Furie as, before she knew better.

The rest faded. The room evaporated, as if the Fogges had taken over and whisked the party away. She stood in a graveyard of horrors, surrounded by nothing but dead bodies and broken limbs, and as much as she wished to look elsewhere, his eyes held her prisoner. Fear mixed with moss and earth and the cold of black vines.

The entire dance floor between them, his whisper reached her nonetheless like a blown kiss. "I know you, Beatrix Yoru. We're the same."

The scream that brought her back belonged to her, and in that split second, the figure disappeared.

"What is it? Are you all right?" William scanned her face, searching for clues.

"Yeah. I just—I thought I saw something." Scouring the ballroom, she searched for the monster, even knowing from instinct that he had vanished.

And yet everywhere she glanced, Beatrix discovered his black, nebulous trail. It crept from all corners, congregating in clouds that looped around a dozen silhouettes, circling the crowd like vultures, weaving in and out.

"What's—? I'm seeing... There's something wrong with me."

William reached for the silk string and tugged her mask off. "Where did you get this?"

"It's a regular mask from the Bazaar." And she knew it wasn't to blame.

The scene around her had turned back to normal. Guests enjoyed themselves, and the creatures threading darkness like grim reapers had disappeared.

"Are you sure you're fine?"

Beatrix massaged her temples. "Yes, but I'm done dancing."

"Let's get some fresh air. Keep that thing off."

The ballroom opened to a terrace overlooking the formal gardens, which connoisseurs praised as a topiary marvel. To Beatrix, they looked too manicured. They were too geometrical and artificial to inspire much emotion.

William guided her out and stood to her side, not saying much. She glanced up at the sky searching in vain for story stars. She found none.

It wasn't a pretty night, presided over by a moon greenish and sick, with ominous clouds chasing it as if to engulf it.

"We need to talk about the curse." William's body rippled with contained strain.

"Why? Are you in danger?"

His scoff could cut steel. "I'm not the one at risk."

It took her a moment to realize. Then she beamed, her smile expanding beyond her mouth to take over her whole face. A new, thrilling current coursed through her. It spread warmth and clenched her chest until her thoughts disintegrated into unconnected parts. "I thought I'd made it up."

"You didn't," he said, but his expression showed no happiness, just a tired dejection too fragile to tread on, and she watched him, confused, her heart dangling from a line, wondering whether it would get to fly or crash on the floor.

"It doesn't change anything." He stared at her, his eyes full of words that refused to spill out. "I knew it when I first met you. That the possibility was there. We immediately connected and then—"

Beatrix's brow furrowed. "We despised each other when we first met."

"No, we didn't. Not the real first time." And then, William told Beatrix of a conversation, of a hex, of a memory erased.

"Why did you undo it?"

"Because the hex your uncle cast pushed me to act in a way I never would have. I wouldn't have bantered, risked liking you, getting close to you. I've spent years avoiding this. I exiled myself and refuse to use magic on the chance that the researchers are right and that might make the curse ineffective—so it ends with me and no one else. I've been living in an almost tundra to prevent this. I didn't want to get here. To have to tell you that you will die because of me." She'd heard many of his voices, but not this one. This was pain made sound. And he wasn't done. He stared at her, and even when it hurt, she held his eyes.

"I vowed to keep away, Beatrix, and then my damn shoulder blades kept warning me you were in danger, and I had to get involved." He said it with such anger, she flinched. Then he deflated, and his resignation was much worse. William looked away. "I tried to avoid this."

Beatrix tilted her head to assess him, trying to decide how best to reach him. "It didn't work. Maybe there's a reason for it. We're here anyway, you and I." And no part of Beatrix was sad for it. "I don't care about this curse. I'm happy you feel the same."

His eyes were tortured when he looked up. "How I feel changes nothing."

He was wrong. He was crazy. "It changes everything." She stepped forward, breathless, with the desperation of a lawyer whose case is slipping away. "Every curse has a counter-curse. Cass said—"

"Not this one, Be'ah." The way he pronounced it turned her name into something intimate. "I've searched everywhere. My mother and my sister died because of it. Don't you think I tried? I'll take you to the pageturner but no farther. I can't go into the Eisid with you. I can't stay close and not— After you cross, I won't see you again."

Truth snipping the fishline, her heart fell and shattered. The Furie howled. The whispers were mute for once. "But the curse might not even work on me. I'm not a real taelimn."

"Are you sure about that?" His eyebrow rose in the slightest of arches.

"No artisan would write this ending."

William came close and traced her cheek with one of his long fingers. She didn't move at all, held in place by a caress that tensed her body with a power akin to her Furie, only much stronger. Hot and cold spread through her.

"I'm sorry," he whispered.

"Please, don't do this. I don't care about a stupid curse."

He inched closer still, and they both drew the same breath. She saw him fight with the thought, playing with the idea of giving in.

His hand dropped and he moved away. "We have to go inside."

"Why?"

There was no softness, no warmth left in his tone. "For once in your life, Beatrix, follow a direction without questioning. I just got Jane's message. Find her. It's time for your meeting."

As he pulled away, the chilly night air filled the distance between them, and her skin broke out in goosebumps. A part of her felt frozen in place, the hurt of his rejection multiplied like a mirror in front of a mirror by all the other similar times. By Mom's and Grandpa's. By Martin's. By every single snigger behind her back. But the other part, the one the Furie ruled, boiled her tears into a sizzling cauldron and pushed her on. A whisper came, comforting and wise.

She didn't heed it.

"Coward," she spat.

Spinning around, she took a step toward the ballroom, then another. The brightness of the party repelled her, urged her to escape to the quiet of her room and disappear beneath the bed covers. Or inside a pit. Deep into the ground and forever out of sight. So much had changed so fast about this night.

Head held high, she strutted toward the French doors, lifting her dress a bit to avoid tripping. It wouldn't do to ruin her walking-away scene by falling over.

Figured that this would be her end. For a minute, while dancing, she had dared to believe she was a part of something. Like everyone else.

More the fool her.

Beatrix quickened her step but never arrived.

Like a piece of night, the creature launched at her from the shadows, just before she crossed the tween, the threshold from obscurity into light.

It landed on top of her like a waving sheet and in one black mouthful ate the silver of her gown.

When darkness gripped her mind, she sighed and curled in, thinking someone had heard her plea, and she'd sunk into the ground.

The silence was haunting. Beatrix couldn't hear her own heart. Not the rushing in her veins, or the sound of her breathing in and out. Nothing responded in her body. She no longer had one.

So this was what it felt like to be dead. To cease to be and have your soul lifted away so you could fly above the clouds unencumbered.

Without attachment, she grew, unending, infinite.

It lasted a few seconds. Soon she was shoved back down into the turmoil of muscle and flesh, of gravity pushing blood through, the mess of churning emotions and murmuring thoughts.

Her eyes opened, and she was no longer blind. While the setting seemed familiar, the body didn't belong to her.

With a sixth sense, Beatrix knew whose life this was. She didn't only see what the other saw but also felt what the other felt.

And she felt all of it.

The breeze from the open window on the skin of the cheeks, the pull of a crooked bobby pin where it dug in the scalp, the soft cotton of the shirt cuffs on the wrists. And the sadness.

A pain so absolute it pulled apart the muscles of her chest until they were stretched and torn, clamped away as if a surgeon were about to transplant a new organ.

Beatrix's tears welled up, tsunami-high.

Leyna didn't permit herself to cry. She didn't think about consequences or allow herself to look at the sleeping child and consider all she would miss. She barely glanced at the pool of ink around the girl's legs and ignored the dark blotches that colored the arms like morbid tattoos.

Her focus was unyielding. Watching the scene through her mom, breathing through her mother's lungs and listening to the cranking of her mind, Beatrix grew astounded. Respect and fear mixed into confusion. Love twisted her own memories and tugged at her soul.

She didn't recognize this mother.

With a grace Beatrix hadn't inherited, Leyna breezed through the preparations, partly guided by her will, partly by adrenaline.

Her urgency acted like an infectious disease.

Because time wouldn't wait for her.

The moon hung high but hidden when Leyna finished. And now the priestess she'd been took over. Without wavering once, she traced a cut along her forearm and walked toward the sleeping shape in the twin bed. The magic spilled out with a faint iridescence.

"*Rephait, na Alh, Nairid yl Barj,*" Leyna said, singing the sacred words that caused the blood in both their veins to dance along. "Goddess, come to my aid. Goddess, lend me your strength. *Ay vu leiden dearita alia.*" *May the words serve the light.*

A hymn. A litany.

The recitation required to work the spell Beatrix possessed.

And now, out of her mother's lips, Beatrix understood what it meant.

30

INKSOMNER

"She's not breathing," Emma said.

"It's the Inksomner's poison. Give me your shawl."

The words ripped Beatrix out of her unnatural slumber. The cocoon around her shredded to pieces, she fought back. Someone insisted on stealing her blanket in the middle of the night. Icy air slapped her cheeks, and her ears popped. A hand tore her mouth open and invaded it. She twisted. Vomited.

It hurt to be awake.

"Keep your eyes closed," he said.

William? I want to sleep. Let me sleep.

She remained semiconscious while he carried her to the guesthouse. No one got in their way. Maybe everyone stayed at the party, or perhaps his expression sent the curious hiding, to burrow deep inside the folds of the earth.

"Emma, stop fretting. Find Neradola and bring her here." He laid Beatrix on the bed with care.

"Will she—?" Emma hesitated. "Will Beatrix be okay?"

"Fetch Nera."

Beatrix drifted. She came back. Cold liquid ran down her forehead now. Her body was trapped in a wetsuit inside a kiln.

"Get it off me," she tried to say. An indiscernible mumble escaped her mouth.

"Don't try to speak yet," William said.

She felt blazes and knives, her innards melting, her organs withering from anoxia. *I'm choking*, she thought, lifting her hands to her throat.

William grabbed her wrists and gently pulled them down. He dipped a washcloth in a bowl and began to clean the black, tarry residue off. He kept talking to her while he did, forcing calm as he worked on her face, cleaning her closed lids, her cheekbones, and her neck.

She couldn't see him. Her eyes were glued shut. But she felt his fingers, leaving streaks where the piece of cloth slid on her oiled skin.

"I will take over now." Beatrix recognized the voice as Neradola's.

"Yes," William said, but his presence lingered. He appeared reluctant to move.

Neradola came forward and began cutting the sleeves of the ruined dress. "You did fine for a start, William. Alcohol is good. Salt is better. We will need a full bath and healing salts for the rest. Please get those."

He must have said something else or looked a certain way because the ghost sighed. "We'll know the damage after the poison is cleansed. It will take several tries to wash it off."

"I'll be back with the salts." He hesitated, bent down so close she smelled his hair. "*Le'arat di, Be'ah.*" Then he kissed her forehead and straightened up. "Who else knows, Nera?"

"Evenzaar. A few taelimns from Historical who were standing nearby." Her tone soft, Neradola's hands glided over Beatrix's shoulders. "The news will spread soon."

"We'll manage."

"William—"

"I'll be careful. Just get her well."

"Hey."

William turned from the window and rushed to Beatrix's side. "How are you feeling?"

"Better. Tired."

She sat up with effort. Her head throbbed, trapped in a vise, and her arms were crisscrossed by long, black scars.

"They'll fade," he said. "The ink will be reabsorbed. Neradola doesn't believe there will be long-term paralysis."

"What happened?"

"You were attacked by an Inksomner, a black magic creature."

"I couldn't breathe." Beatrix relived the numbness and the lethargy. She'd been so helpless. And magic-less. She hadn't realized how much she relied on her gift. "It was him." Her memories were foggy, elusive and insubstantial like water vapor. *What happened exactly?* "My Furie didn't work."

"Inksomners use your ink to choke you. Your talent comes from the same source, so it's ineffective against them."

Ink... Inaechar! She looked up to eyes that reflected her own conclusion.

Even less time left now.

And she had to travel!

"The trip."

"Postponed," William said. "We'll leave as soon as you're better."

She wondered if it was a slip that he'd said *we*.

"How did you help me? Against that thing." It was coming back to her. The warmth of foreign magic. Something bright and stable, and stronger than anything she'd ever possessed, pushing the darkness out of her. The smell of him, waking her, pulling her, dragging her out. "How come your power worked?"

She expected him to smile and act smug. But the wrinkles on his brow didn't release.

"I used mirrored light. They're beings of the dark and cannot survive outside of it. No magic involved."

Beatrix shrank, confused.

She knew she'd felt it. Shivered with the wonder of the pulsating, comforting energy hoisting her up. As if she'd been cradled by the branches of a tree, its muscular support had given her solace. True and pure and uplifting. A magic so beautiful it made her ache with yearning.

Yet William said it wasn't his.

Her mouth felt dry, coated with a rotten-eggs taste. He guessed and handed her a drink. Beatrix sipped the kelpie water, her throat too tight for more than a few drops, and soon pushed it aside. Had it been a dream?

"How long was I unconscious?"

William's expression became inscrutable. "You've been in and out for two days. But during the attack? About fifteen minutes."

It had seemed a lot longer than that to Beatrix. The nagging feeling of runaway memories wouldn't release her. Her legs, which she hadn't been able to move before, tingled. The paralysis was lifting. And with the receding effects of the Inksomner's poison, the threads of her recollection escaped like sand through her fingers. "It's so frustrating. I just can't remember."

A different memory intruded instead. William's face over hers. "What did you call me the night of the ball? You said my name weirdly."

"You chose not to translate me?" He seemed both surprised and thoughtful.

"I've always liked the way you speak."

"I called you Be'ah." He pronounced the sounds in a whisper, the vowels open, so that it rhymed with flare and with the emphasis on the last syllable. "It's how your name sounds in the language of my world. Translates to voyager through life."

Be'ah... Yeah. "I like it." It felt right. Not stuffy like Beatrix or a joke like Bea.

"What about the rest of what you said?"

William's face closed up. "It doesn't matter. Rest now. You've been through enough." William seemed snippy. He left her side and walked toward the dressing table covered with an assortment of medicinal bottles with a determined, angry stride. Discarded blackened towels lay on a pile on the floor beside it.

Wait.

Beatrix studied him, attempting to read his thoughts as he often did with hers. "You're wrong," she said when she realized what he must have concluded.

"You have no idea how this works."

"I know this attack had nothing to do with your curse."

"And how can you be sure of that? You don't recall what happened."

"I just know. I can feel it. It was him, the Charmancer. I saw him at the party. He was the monster in that ballroom, William."

"The Zweeshen is full of monsters," he said, looking away.

"And this one's after me. I know what I felt. You want to think this is about the curse because that way you're justified in pushing me away. But we would be stronger, and I would be safer, if you accepted who the real enemy is."

His eyes burned with anger and something wild and volatile when he faced her again. "You understand nothing about the curse."

"And you're underestimating both of us."

As if her statement had severed the strings that kept him upright, William sank into the nook by the window, a place she'd love to read in. "Sleep now. Please. You need to recover."

He didn't speak again, just sat there observing the movements of the guards in the yard.

Beatrix sighed. "I'm right about this," she muttered to herself. *If only I could prove it.*

31

THE LIBRARIAN

It was much later that the door hinges whined, and Evenzaar entered the room.

"Nice to see you're recovering." He glanced at Beatrix with anything but well-wishing. "The healer Neradola tells me the Inksomner poison washed satisfactorily. Agh, Threshborne—" he sent William a look full of loathing, "—you're still here. I hope you'll give us some time alone. Head to the council rotunda. The court's awaiting your statement."

William stood with nonchalance. "I'd rather not."

"It was not a suggestion."

"Would you like me to leave?" William asked Beatrix.

What was going on? The animosity between William and the Librarian had gained a new edge, a violent quality. "I'd rather he stayed."

Evenzaar's face twitched into an unhappy sneer. "It won't aid your case to associate with the likes of him, especially under the circumstances."

With a swoosh of his robes, the Librarian slid closer to the bed where Beatrix lay. His demeanor had returned to the blandness he wore on solemn occasions.

"I'm here in an official capacity. The council has issued a warrant for your arrest. I've reasoned with them, and in consideration of your delicate condition, they'll allow you to remain in this tower until you've recovered enough to stand trial."

Beatrix flinched. "Arrest. Why? I didn't do anything."

With whiplash-inducing speed, William sprang to her side, attack-ready. And as the muscles in his back tightened, her Furie's rust mixed with a new magic that wafted in the air, sultry and thick like incense smoke.

"Why, you ask?" The Librarian's outrage was painted onto his pasty face. "A Charmancer is rising, with a power stronger and more vicious than anyone alive has faced." His fingers moved in an undulating motion while he spoke, as if he were the conductor of an invisible orchestra. "Once again, it's the land of the Eisid Naraid that's the cradle to this evil. That forsaken place has grown and fed the monster who threatens us."

Beatrix gasped, fear icing her veins.

The Charmancer came from the Eisid!

Her mind sped up, imagining the implications. She glanced at William. His shared shock was comforting. "But the Eisid Naraid has been sealed for years."

"You understand nothing! Have you any idea how many books the Charmancer has destroyed? Yet, one star still shines. Yours. He's stolen his own story to protect himself."

As if a grenade had detonated in her head, Beatrix's mind shut down. Her ears became muffled, and her eyes stared without seeing. "My mother's book is gone?"

The Librarian sighed in a studied way. "Stolen, along with many others that have disappeared in recent times."

Around Beatrix, the room swayed. He had to be mistaken. It couldn't be.

The warmth of a hand steadied her, reminding her to breathe, and with each inhale, the fog in her brain receded a bit. But the whispers screamed in her ears. The Furie growled and showed teeth.

Mom's story kidnapped. By a maniac who burned worlds. Who'd melted Dyøt to ash. Mom! Was that her destiny too? What of the home Beatrix had yet to see? Because despite all her doubts and misgivings about Leyna, Beatrix had been counting on reuniting with her.

"She's still there," William said, and as Beatrix focused on him, his strength bolstered her. "If it's his own book, the Charmancer won't burn it."

True. The Leeber might be gone, but both Mom and her world were alive. Beatrix's resolve returned. "We should go to the Eisid. Maybe we can warn the people that he has the Leeber. If we—"

The Librarian stopped her, his palm in the air. "Your ignorance disgraces us all. The book is gone, stupid child. Do you not realize Leebers anchor the pageturners? Without the book, there can't be a bridge. There's no way to travel into the Eisid Naraid now."

Like a flash flood, cold dread rushed back into Beatrix. Her heart gasped. Skipped a beat. Sped up again.

"Then make another bridge! You can't do nothing. Are you not even going to try to save her world?"

At her side, William brushed her arm, an imperceptible graze that could be a warning or a sign of allegiance.

"Beatrix has a point," he said. "Perhaps another pageturner could be established. Through a different installment in the series, maybe."

Evenzaar growled, his teeth visible as his lip curled up. "Stop concocting wild fantasies! The fate of the missing books is sealed. Accept it and enjoy the time you have left, Beatrix. Without a bridge, synching can't happen, so either way..."

Synching.

Beatrix had forgotten about that. She couldn't get cured either.

Like a too-tight choker, desperation closed her airways.

What would she do now?

She didn't want to die.

But this all made little sense. The Librarian's sneer didn't fit. There was a self-satisfaction about him. She studied him, and then quick as a whip, fear metamorphosed into rage. "You conniving, cheating, lying little man! How long have you known of this?"

The Librarian observed her with apparent calm, but his beard quivered slightly.

"You are a disgusting, sad excuse for a human being. When was the Leeber stolen?"

Evenzaar let out a long groan. "Since I'm a taelimn, that's hardly an insult. I don't need your approval. The book disappeared long before you arrived. I did what I had to."

"Which is? What did you gain from bringing me here on false pretenses?"

Unconcerned, Evenzaar stalked off to the nearby table with the assortment of medicines, vials, and herbs. He dabbed something on his finger and rubbed his index and thumb together, then smelled it. "Your Neradola has made interesting choices. Some might say questionable ones." He turned to Beatrix, and for a split second his face showed true sorrow. "I don't care for any world to be destroyed. It's a tragedy. Millions of taelimns are gone. But I'm trying to save the rest of the worlds. And things are in motion. It won't be much longer now."

"What is this really about?" Beatrix asked, and when Evenzaar ignored her again, her defiance gave way to pure monstrous anger. The part of her she didn't trust took over, while her good side was too tired to stop it. "You will explain," she said, and the air rippled as her voice echoed, charged with her Furie's rage.

The Librarian either didn't feel it or didn't care about the danger. He lifted *Tome VI* of the Essentials from her bedside table and skimmed through the first pages. Closing it with a snap, he scowled.

"Strange choice of reading material." He looked up, stared at her with piercing eyes. "The council is out for blood. Anyone from the Eisid Naraid is an enemy of the Zweeshen. And a suspect."

"The Charmancer attacked me!"

"Oh, I believe you. Not everyone in the council is as easy to convince. And people need someone to blame. Who knows what you'd confess to under the right inducement?"

Beatrix shrank. "You mean torture."

Evenzaar shrugged. "Call it what you will. This is war. But you have an option. Help me, and I'll ensure you don't suffer. I will plead for your life. We might even find your Leeber once the Charmancer is caught."

William's hand caressed her forearm. She didn't need his warning. She understood all too well how the Librarian lied to her.

"You'd never let me live. If I survived, which without synching is doubtful, and you found the story, you'll destroy it, won't you? If he's from the Eisid, that's the easiest way to defeat the Charmancer. To eliminate the Leeber."

She could almost hear the chess pieces rearrange in Evenzaar's head, move and countermove, with calculating coldness. "Do not be foolish. The whole Zweeshen is at the mercy of this madman. Sacrifices are required. The fight that's coming will touch us all, no choice in that. But we can decide how we go. So here's my offer. I'll see to it you avoid torture if you put your magic to my service in this fight."

"My magic? I've barely got any Inaechar left."

"You should be happy to use the last of it for a good cause."

"Don't listen to him." William stepped forward, and the Librarian flipped his staff to push him back.

"Stay out of it, Threshborne," Evenzaar said with a caustic growl. He caressed his hat, composing himself. "This isn't a game, young lady. The Charmancer is after the Soul of Rephait."

Beatrix flinched; her eyes narrowed. What did the Soul have to do with the Charmancer? She didn't ask. Evenzaar seldom answered her questions, and she'd learned letting him talk served her best. So it was this time.

"I see I've surprised you." Evenzaar smirked. "The Soul isn't what you think. It's not merely a sacred artifact to balance the Eisid like you've been told. It's a weapon. Ancient, fathomless power that can be twisted in deeply dark ways." He saw her blanch and slowed down. The next words were enunciated carefully, to scare her.

"With a single cut, the dagger can steal Fantasy magic, killing the owner while transferring the gift to another. It can call forth power from the earth. Compel beasts. Some say play with time. The Pioneers suspected many more uses. That's the real reason the Eisid Naraid's dying. Their experiments to exploit the Soul unleashed destruction, and the land had to be sealed." The Librarian shook his head in a theatrical gesture. "Despite their efforts, the Pioneers never managed their main ambition—to uncover the secret that activates the Soul's full power, high magic violent enough to obliterate our universe in an instant. Thankfully, the winged dagger can be wielded thus by few taelimns. Your mother was rumored to have that capacity. If you've inherited it, that makes you dangerous."

"I'd never use magic like that. I'd—" Beatrix began.

"You wouldn't have to. The Charmancer could abduct you and force his will on you. Or trick you. He's mightier and cleverer than you imagine."

Evenzaar paused to let the words sink in. "All I'm asking is that you be vigilant. If the Charmancer acquired the Soul, it would empower him beyond what our world can survive. Nothing would prevent him from annihilating stories everywhere."

Within Beatrix, the Furie recoiled. Evenzaar might have been lying to her earlier, but this part rang true.

The Librarian bowed his head, as if his hat were too heavy. "Words connect us all. The Fogges of unformed thoughts extend not only through the Zweeshen and the biblioworlds, but farther, into the artisan worlds as well. Forshaltness. We're all united. Everything's part of the tapestry. If the Charmancer succeeded in activating the Soul, every story would be silenced and the sky would go black, all stars extinguished. But stories are weaved into life everywhere, so beyond, the artisan worlds—your Pangea too—would succumb."

In a room now emptied of warmth, Beatrix trembled. Although she did not doubt the Librarian's veracity, some intuition sent Grandpa's alerts flashing, and the whispers agreed with a stream of cautious verses. Her mind squirmed, caught in the silk of a web she could not see.

"You don't need Beatrix." William held on to her elbow, his touch anchoring her to the present. "If it's so dangerous, find the Soul and destroy it."

Evenzaar's gaze could petrify when he turned to William with a swirl of his turbaned head. "What do you take us for? Fools? It's impossible to be rid of the weapon. Our leaders tried to obliterate it before. It cannot be done." He fixed his beady stare on Beatrix. "The Charmancer is on the trail of the Soul. He will come for you soon, and when he does, we have to defeat him."

"I don't have the dagger. And I couldn't possibly defeat the Charmancer." Was Evenzaar crazy?

"Your mother was the last person to know the whereabouts of the Soul of Rephait. Whether you have it or not is of little import. The Charmancer believes you do."

"Why would he?" Suspicion coated Beatrix's mouth with acid.

William must have read the truth in the man crow's feet too. "You bastard! You fed him that intel, didn't you? You endangered her. That's why you lured her to the Zweeshen. She won't be cannon fodder!"

"You're tedious, Threshborne. I'm done with you." The Librarian clicked his cane against the floor. "Beatrix, the council is sure to sentence you to a painful death. My offer is a chance at mercy with them. I suggest you take it."

The door swung open, and two men in the uniform of the Bureau's officers barged in.

"What are you doing?" she asked, ready to jump off the bed.

"I've warned Threshborne his questioning wasn't optional."

"You're overstepping the office of the Librarian," William said.

"We're at war. I'm fighting to protect the Zweeshen. Take him."

The men marched toward William and began to bind his hands. For some reason she didn't understand, he didn't fight them.

"No!" Beatrix shouted, her huge eyes on the Librarian. "Stop it!" Maybe too much had happened and her control was frayed beyond repair, but the monster snapped. Whatever safeties she'd built were torn and flimsy, so the Furie burst out of her unimpeded. Weirdly, it hovered. Magic tails of red and white poured out of her hands like tentacles.

"Don't, Beatrix!" William said before his mouth flattened into an artificial straight line.

"He's a traitor." Old rot curled the edges of Evenzaar's words. "Inktrash scraps. Don't waste the last of your Inaechar on him."

"Let him go." Her tone became dangerous, the Furie lurking behind each syllable. Ready to pounce like a furious beast.

She met William's imploring eyes. She could feel her Inaechar draining and considered that perhaps this might be her final act. *May it be worth it*, she thought, and from nowhere, *May the words save him*. Lightning lit the tower, and from every crevice, smoke poured in. In giant tendrils, the shadows crept over Beatrix's body, enveloping her and lifting her off the bed. Her neck snapped back while the black vapor pushed into her open mouth and out of her hands, wrapping her in a net of smog and twisting into the currents of her power, strengthening them like fire tempers steel. Rust and earth and moss enveloped her.

"Enough!" The Librarian's nostrils flared as he gave a signal, and the guards released William. "He's free. Stop that. I need you alive."

His voice trickled in from afar. Of course he wanted Beatrix to live. She was the bait for his trap.

"Beatrix, please!" William begged. He turned to the Librarian, fists up. "Get out! Now!"

William's tone more than his words permeated through. With a jolt, Beatrix clamped the Furie down, using every thread of strength she had left.

As suddenly as it had come, the smoke vanished. The candles that had been blown out reignited and the window crashed closed. The tails of her power receded into her now cracked skin. She plopped down onto the mattress.

"Reckless. Wasteful show." The Librarian pulled away from William's reach and straightened his robe where William had grabbed him.

Evenzaar was almost at the door when, derision creasing his paper-thin skin, he raised his arms. He clacked his staff, and two black manacles appeared on Beatrix's wrists. "You're too impetuous for your own good. We'll see to preparations in the morning."

Part Four

THEOLSEA

32

CASSANÐRA

"I'm fine. I'm fine," Beatrix told William as he rubbed her arms to get them to stop shaking after the Librarian left. "I got it." From shoulder to wrist, she was covered in new black marks, rivers and estuaries spreading out.

William pulled back, his face a mask. "Why would you do that! I would've been fine. You have very limited Inaechar left. Don't you understand?" The edge in his voice was forged in terror. "You cannot afford to use any at all."

She pressed her eyes closed and nodded, using all dregs of will to calm the monster down the final degree.

"Did you know? About the book?" she asked a few minutes later when her skin no longer burned.

"No." His word was clipped and forceful. "Jane and I suspected all along the Librarian had ulterior motives, but I never guessed something like this. I wouldn't have allowed you to cross into the Zweeshen had I known."

"Allowed?" Beatrix arched her eyebrows in challenge. "I don't see how you think you could have stopped me."

"I know." William cursed, and if she hadn't known better, she would have guessed he was about to punch the table where Neradola kept her bottles and vials. Beatrix had never seen him like this, his shoulders slumped and his clothes disheveled. The sight lowered her already dampened spirits to basement level.

Despite everything, she couldn't imagine having chosen to stay on Earth. "Nothing would have stopped me." *Nadie te quita lo bailado.* True.

Everything that had happened in the Zweeshen was hers to keep. And not all of it bad.

She looked up at him. At least they hadn't taken him.

"You shouldn't have." An unknown softness had snuck into his face, changing it.

"You saved me from the Inksomner. We're even now."

Escaping his gaze, she inspected the metal bands around her wrists.

"They're shackles," he said.

"They look like black Wonder Woman bracelets."

William's lips curled while she pretended to deflect invisible shots. She twisted her wrists back and forth, testing. They weren't uncomfortable, but lifting her right palm, she sensed the restriction. Her hands flopped, squeezed into submission by a force that tightened her muscles and kept her power imprisoned. The Furie growled, a beast tied into an unsolvable knot.

"Jane will get them off," William said with a confidence that could have been for her sake.

Lowering her arms onto the blanket, Beatrix let her head hang. Even if they could take the manacles off, there was no escaping the truth. She couldn't get into the Eisid. She couldn't synch. Couldn't reunite with Mom.

And she was to become a prisoner.

Of Evenzaar and of the council.

With a movement that managed to be both decisive and gentle, William took her face in his hands, locking eyes with her. "No. We will get out of here."

At another moment, she would have loved the warmth of his fingers on her skin. She'd ached for the closeness. Now... "I keep sinking deeper."

"You were trouble from the first minute." He appeared relieved when the hint of a smile hovered on her lips. "We will figure it out."

"How?" Her tone came out harsher than intended. "The Charmancer has the Leeber. I can't go back to the Eisid Naraid. And now I'm wanted. Where could we go?"

"I'm asking Farisad for help," Emma said, barging into the room in a storm of lavender curls. They floated around her like anemone arms.

"Eavesdropping?" Beatrix asked.

"How else is one to find things out?" Emma swept in and sat by the fireplace, spreading the voluminous skirt of her robin-blue dress on the settee. "I really think Farisad is the answer. If only I could get a response." Emma bit her lip.

"He can travel anywhere. But I've been having trouble getting through to him, which is unusual. I will keep trying, though. He could help us."

"Thanks, Emma. That would be great," William said, and Beatrix thought it sweet that he would humor the kid. "In the meantime, we'll search for other ways."

Beatrix looked away to the greyish sky outside the window. She appreciated his effort. But she'd become familiar enough with the workings of the Zweeshen to recognize there weren't any good options.

William walked back to the side of her bed. Without a word, he helped her lift the pillows so she sat higher. Frustration bubbled at how the small action exhausted her. Beatrix was the weakest she'd ever been. And she hated it.

"I will call Nera." After tapping on his crystal, William sat on the chair by her bedside. "Actually, we have options."

How did he always know what she was thinking?

"I believe Elizabeth's contacts can help," he said.

Beatrix's brow furrowed. "Elizabeth? Why?" Yes, she was famous. And she had been able to schedule the meeting with the Essentials & History's author. Beatrix felt a pang. She'd missed that too. Even though it didn't feel as important now. "I get that she's well connected, but how could she help me? The pageturner is down and the Leeber is missing."

"Illegal ways, of course," Emma said. "It's an open secret that biblio-world borders are porous."

William nodded. "The council likes to think the only way to travel is through their pageturners. But there are back alleys. The Pioneers and several other groups have unlicensed networks which don't rely on Leebers. Before, it wasn't necessary because the council had approved your travel. But now… We need to figure out if there's an underground bridge to the Eisid anywhere. The fact that Selda and the other two wanted Pioneers made it here suggests there might be."

Inside Beatrix, hope bloomed.

William ran his hand through his hair. The action made it stick out, standing on end in a way that made her wish to caress it back to normal.

"I'm not saying it's guaranteed," he said. "But not impossible. Either way we won't let the council imprison you."

"I guess any place is better than here now." Beatrix couldn't forget Evenzaar's dark stare as he'd spoken of torture. How the Chairman would love to get the chance.

"Let me talk to Elizabeth," William said. "See what her people can find out. Even before this, we'd been gathering a team in case we ran into issues in the Eisid. We can call on them now."

Beatrix nodded. "I wish I could come with you. I want to do my part." She hated the idea of staying here in bed. Useless. Waiting. But even she could see reality. Lifting an arm consumed so much energy she thought twice before getting a glass of water. There was no way she could go anywhere right now.

William had retreated to the back corner and was kneeling next to the fireplace bucket. He fed a couple logs to the salamander and let out a long breath. "Don't worry," he said, straightening. "I'll ask Jane to summon Elizabeth, and we will go from there."

"I must go too," Emma said. "Neradola needs more kelpie water."

"You okay to stay alone?" William asked Beatrix.

"I don't need watching over. It's bad enough I can't contribute."

William smiled. He seemed about to say something but swallowed the words, and Beatrix wished with annoyance that she could trade powers with Emma.

"I, for my part, will attempt to reach Farisad again," the girl said. "We really could use his help."

Beatrix hadn't wanted to fall asleep. But after both William and Emma left, tiredness overcame her. A thud that reverberated in the hallway outside woke her a couple of hours later.

Flames of hair poked into the room.

"You're awake."

"Cass!"

Cassandra entered, her usual strong presence subdued.

"I've been worried. I heard the Librarian was coming to arrest you and throw you in a dungeon."

Beatrix gritted her teeth as she sat up on the bed. "Not quite. Maybe soon. How did you avoid the guards? Emma said she had to play a trick on them."

"Those children?" Cassandra's smirk was haughty. "The Librarian's sentries aren't a problem. The Council Guard's a different matter. But they're busy raiding the city now. Even *they* can't be in more than one place at once."

"Raids? Are they still looking for Pioneers? I didn't realize there were that many around."

Sitting on the edge of the bed, Cassandra lowered her voice. "It's not just Pioneers or even Eisidians. All dissenters are in the council's sights. And anyone they can declare guilty by association. "They're going after everyone with connections to the Pioneers or past rebellious inclinations, including trade partners and old acquaintances." Cassandra rubbed her hands in an uncharacteristic show of anxiety. "Former exiles and whoever's broken a vow is being taken too. Any taelimn they deem suspicious. Several activist groups have a warrant, as do the Theolsea islands because they've refused to allow the council to search their cities. They're after some charities too."

Exiles. Beatrix glanced toward the door through which William had disappeared. "I can't believe I missed all this."

"You've been unconscious. A lot has changed in the last two days."

"How can they do this?" Beatrix's outrage swarmed out, bitter. "Is it legal?"

Uncrossing her legs, Cassandra hesitated. "They aren't supposed to. But the Chairman has the courts and the guild lawmakers on his side. Some of the news outlets as well. Zweeshen politics are complicated, and too many of us don't get involved, so in the end, it's not the best taelimns who lead us. The Chairman has always wanted to squash dissent."

Beatrix's fingertips dug into the sheets without her noticing. "The majority doesn't agree with him. I've met enough taelimns to know that."

"People are scared. Academics aren't by nature a courageous bunch. However afraid they are of the Chairman, their terror of the Charmancer is stronger, so he's using that." Cassandra shook her red mane with a strange combination of hopelessness and defiance. "He won't get away with it. It's too extreme. They're trapping taelimns suspected of black magic or Fogges manipulation inside their stories and bringing down the pageturners."

With every new fact, Beatrix's indignation grew. Cold dread settled in her stomach. The Zweeshen, at least the place she'd begun to love, was better than this. It had to be. "The council should be looking for the Charmancer, not harassing random taelimns."

"They argue he visited Læsting last week. Some magic evidence came up. Hence the raids."

"The Chairman's lucky day." Foreign and foul-tasting, the cynicism in Beatrix's own tone surprised her.

"Tell me about it." Cassandra stood up and paced. "He's had the old wall of Læsting rebuilt and blocked all roads with security checkpoints. There's one single path into the city. They're using tech and magic to watch it."

Beatrix gasped. "How can the council let this happen?"

"They've declared martial law. To his credit, the Librarian is seeking to oppose the Chairman, but he's considered a failed leader. Logic doesn't hold anymore."

Glancing toward the corner where William had busied himself with a mortar and pestle before leaving, Beatrix now understood why the muscles in his jaw had looked taut enough to snap. She was beginning to conceive the seriousness of their predicament. Getting out would require a full-blown escape plan.

"Before I forget." Cassandra rummaged in her purse and retrieved a glassy object. "I saved you an award statuette."

Beatrix inspected the figure of a unicorn and laughed. Back when they'd met, they'd exchanged test stories. Cassandra had ended up with a questionable tortoise.

"Did you have to steal it?" Beatrix asked.

Cassandra's lips parted into a sly smile. "Something like that. I have to go now. The Guard's moving again, and I'm trying to avoid them. I'll be back tomorrow with Lucy and Matt. Everyone's been asking about you, and they want to cheer you up. I'm so happy I got that strange bluish vision that told me to meet you."

"Me too. See you tomorrow, Cass."

They embraced long enough for Beatrix to realize that neither of them believed those last words. And as she watched Cassandra disappear, she wondered if she'd ever see her friend again.

Less than an hour later, William strode into the room with the confidence of a conqueror and the self-satisfied smile of a bearer of riches.

"You have good news," Beatrix said, straightening up. She tried to sit higher, but her strength failed her. Damn it. When would she feel better?

William came to her side with a grin. He seemed happy enough to break into dance at any moment. "Elizabeth's contacts have agreed to help. One has knowledge of an Eisid bridge. Non-Pioneer."

Beatrix closed her eyes, overwhelmed with relief.

He laughed, then took her hands, and she thought he would kiss her. He did. A quick peck on her brow before he retreated, giving her his back.

"Tell me everything," she said, making sure her tone didn't show her disappointment. "Who are these mysterious contacts of Elizabeth's?"

"Does it matter? They will help us. And there's not much to tell. The bridge's across the ocean, in a well-guarded island in the middle of the Theolsea—off the radar. Elizabeth has arranged for a ship captained by one of Peter Pan's defected pirates. It will wait for us outside the Læsting harbor security line, which the council has set up. All we have to do is get onboard."

Why did she not think it was that easy? She bent her head. Narrowed her eyes. "Out with the complications."

William laughed. Nothing seemed capable of dimming his good humor. "No, it really should be simple. We'll leave this tower and stealthily cross into the south woods. There we'll meet Elizabeth's crew, who have set up a short-range teleport to the ship. Once aboard, the plan's to use a sci-fi engine to timejump and gain a day in distance. And done." Again he smiled.

Beatrix tried to return it, but a wrenching pain cut across her stomach and convulsions took over.

William had promised to wake her, but Beatrix's eyes burst open on their own. It was dark out, must be past midnight.

"It's not time yet," William said. "You've got a bit before you need to be dressed."

"I'm done resting." She pulled the sheets aside, jumped onto her strongest leg, and sprinted to the dresser. She couldn't believe how much better she felt. William had called Neradola after the last Roamer's attack. The ghost had forced several potions down her throat, one of which had made her unconscious. And Beatrix now believed Trelius's words when they'd first met: Neradola was a fabulous healer.

To distract Beatrix while the potions took effect, Trelius had produced a deck, and they'd played cards. She suspected they must be marked, judging by his incredible luck. They'd wagered things that helped her think of the future on the ship, like polishing brass surfaces or mopping the second deck. She was almost eager to pay up because it meant she'd be well enough to do the chores she'd lost.

Both Neradola and Trelius were coming along to the Eisid.

"The Zweeshen's not a good place for any of us right now," Trelius had said, and added with a wink, "You can't pass up my magic help to get out of here either."

"My talents will be required too," Neradola said in her rustling voice. She was too subtle to explain that her presence was critical to keep her alive. But Beatrix knew it.

Jane, who had returned with the last-minute details from Elizabeth's team, had grinned. "Even if you don't need me, I'm coming anyway."

Now, in the dead of the night, Beatrix wondered if she was putting all of them in danger. "I don't want them hurt for my sake," she told William. "Maybe I should go alone."

A new edge reflected off his irises when he stared at her. His smiling demeanor was gone. As if while she napped, the world had grown even darker.

"None of them is safe anymore," William said. "You saw the way the Librarian talked about Nera. Jane's in an even more precarious position because of her connections. They're escaping as much as we are."

It seemed unreal. How could everything change this much in two days? After the Inksomner, Beatrix had woken up in a more sinister world. She mourned the Zweeshen of her imagination, a place of fairness and peace that smelled of Souvenesses and new paper.

After she'd dressed, Beatrix put on her boots and emptied her rucksack onto the bed.

"Don't overthink it," William said, watching out the window. "Emma threw a tantrum, and Jane arranged for your two trunks to be taken on board."

"I don't need all that stuff."

"Beatrix?" said a slim voice from the door.

William's left eyebrow lifted. "Speaking of the devil..."

"What are you doing here, Emma?"

"I'm coming with you."

Beatrix stuffed a scarf into the backpack for good measure. One never knew what to expect of the weather in the Zweeshen. "Emma, I don't think—"

"I know you were planning to leave without telling me." Emma pushed bangs of rebelling fuchsia hair away from her forehead and repositioned her leather satchel across her chest. "You promised to help me find my artisan."

"Sorry, Emma. That can't happen where we're going." Torn by pity, Beatrix glanced up to William for help.

"You should listen to Beatrix," he said with gentleness. "It's safer for you here."

Emma's stare bounced from William to Beatrix and then back.

"Are you friends now?"

Their gazes met. "I guess we are—"

"About time." Emma climbed onto an armchair and retied her ankle boots. "There's a magic moon tonight, purple again. The wheel of the moons is turning," she said in a conversational tone as if about to pour tea. "A perfect night to leave. Please. My thought-reading's useful. I got past the Guard."

William and Beatrix had agreed not to take Emma for her own sake. The council wasn't after her.

"It's too dangerous," William said, kneeling next to Emma. "We'll be fugitives, enemies of this world. There's no guarantee we'll survive, and if we do, you might never see the Zweeshen again. The researchers, your chance to find your artisan, all that would be gone. At the end of the fight that's coming, even if the Zweeshen wins against this Charmancer, we might still be on the losing side."

Truth had a way of sinking to the marrow, and hearing him, Beatrix understood what had escaped her until now. Their mission had transformed. No longer about reaching the Eisid, curing her, or fulfilling Mom's request, this escape had a much deeper meaning.

A war loomed. And the Charmancer wasn't the only enemy. The recent actions of the council proved they were willing to stretch their powers in the name of the protection of the Zweeshen, even if that meant turning against its people and crushing biblioworlds in the process. It wasn't Beatrix alone who had to run now, but many others who didn't fit in or defied the government's views.

"I don't care." Emma stomped her foot in the daintiest way possible. "I've never had my own quest, and I've adopted this one."

Just then, a high-pitched bird cry punctured the night.

"The signal." William grabbed Beatrix's backpack and slung it over his shoulder. "We're out of time."

"Let her come," Beatrix said. "It's her life."

William pivoted to the young girl. "Fine. But let me take your satchel."

Emma looked terrified. "I can't. My world's so small I have to carry it with me."

33

THE CHAIRMAN

They rappelled for so long Beatrix thought this tower must be taller than Babel's. When she'd first arrived in the Zweeshen, she'd been delighted to discover her room at the guesthouse was high up in a real turret, a twirly stone structure ending in a slate roof, pointy like a witch's hat. Tonight, that happiness had evaporated.

The makeshift rope harness dug into her thighs while one of Elizabeth's crew maneuvered the pulley below. Beatrix inched down with deliberate slowness. In the end, she miscalculated the closeness to the ground and tumbled with a thump. Staggering, she glanced around, concerned about the noise. Next to her, William set Emma down, whom he'd insisted on carrying.

Without a word, they flattened themselves against the dead grass, breathing hard. The earth smelled cold, packed and frosty, but they couldn't risk showing themselves. So they elbow-crawled to the edge of the open space between the guesthouse and the next University building.

William armed his weapon. And then they waited, watching the pattern of the patrolling lights. They had three seconds in the bot's blind spot to jump to the protection of the gargoyle gallery, which they were to follow to the other end of the University. They made it as the guard turned the corner to complete his perimeter round with shuffling feet.

Hand in hand, Beatrix and Emma were readying to attempt for the next arch when someone pressed on Beatrix's shoulder. "Change of plans."

Jane had appeared from behind a lionesque gargoyle.

"What's going on?" Beatrix asked.

"A council convoy has been attacked near the Market Square. They've changed the Guard moves and doubled surveillance around this whole area. They're blaming the civil protesters."

"Of course they are," William said cynically.

Beatrix frowned. "Are Elizabeth's people moving the teleport?"

Jane shook her head. "No, it's still deep in the southern woods, but you'll have to approach from the north." Beatrix read her expression like a page from a large print book. This route was much more dangerous.

"All right," William said. "We'll split up, take the long way by the marina, then cut through the gardens, from there to the woods."

"We have to take care of this first." Jane pointed at Beatrix's wrists with clear disgruntlement.

William blocked her. "We agreed to do it later."

"They have a sensor. We might as well be yelling we're breaking out," Jane said. "I got it, William." She offered a pink pill to Beatrix. "Take this."

With a tortured look that didn't inspire confidence, William said, "Scream all you like."

Beatrix didn't get to wonder. The next moment, he stood behind her, holding her shoulders back. Jane, her wide mouth in a line, grabbed Beatrix's hands. And snapped them. The bones crunched like dried branches, the pain so excruciating it sent her body into shock. She let out a cry, high and curdling, that reached no one except for herself. It lasted a second. Like fire deprived of oxygen, the throbbing vanished midscream, and Beatrix breathed in a mouthful of night. The crisp and by now familiar scents of the Zweeshen—pine, jasmine, the sour tinge of magic—comforted her as she assessed her limp fingers. With broken hands, she couldn't clear the sweat from her brow, but the Furie extended its wings, free from the Gordian knot. Still stunned, she watched Jane wriggle the cuffs out, becoming woozy when Jane stretched the skin and maneuvered around the bones.

"Look away," William said, releasing Beatrix's shoulders and walking to her side. He pulled out a cloth and dried her face, and by the time she checked again, the manacles were gone, and her hands taped with dark bandages.

"You should regain your voice in a few minutes and full movement within half an hour." Jane repacked her supplies with her usual efficiency and pushed the brim of her hat down. "Now, the hard part. We'll separate. Elizabeth's allies will provide the fireworks. Meet you all in the woods."

The group divided, Jane taking Emma and her satchel with her. Beatrix and William waited in the shadows until they heard the first explosion. Then they sprinted out, leaving the gallery's safety and traversing the courtyard to cut to the marina.

They were a mere fifty feet from the water when they bumped into her. The figure who intercepted them appeared as startled as they were.

"Where are you going?"

"Becca?" Beatrix identified the voice even when she couldn't make out her features.

"You're running away!" Becca seemed too incredulous to avoid gaping. "No! You can't leave! You're a criminal come to destroy us. They told us."

"Becca." This was William. He used a calm but threatening tone that Beatrix hadn't heard before. "Move aside."

"I won't." Becca gritted her teeth. "They told us everything. That you're a murderer's daughter. The Charmancer's helper. You burn books to get strong. I've signed the petition to put you to death. I never liked you, Beatrix. You're not one of us, and I knew there was something weird about you from the start. You're a freak." And without warning, she yelled.

The beam from the lookout post woke up.

Strong as the sun, the spotlight dawned an artificial day around them, and exposed, William and Beatrix bolted toward the ocean. They were fast. Her feet blurred as her heels skimmed the stone, lungs ablaze. But they never had a chance. They were surrounded before they'd reached the edge of the playing fields.

And when the red and blue clothed officials circled them, William took her hand in his. She saw him press something in his pocket and felt relief. At least the others would be alerted. They could leave without them.

Beatrix had never paid attention to the Guard before. They were ever-present and unobtrusive. Unlike the Librarian's Sentries, who were plain-clothed and easy to distract, the Council Guard gathered around them, uniformed and organized.

There were about fifty of them, positioned in concentric circles, with the last ring atop hovering boards. All their faces were alike: expressionless, homogenous, repetitive.

Clones, she thought, *or androids.*

None of them moved.

They were waiting.

He came on horseback. Maybe because he'd been an inquisitor in a technology-deprived land, and he enjoyed the advantage height gave him. "I predicted you'd betray us, Beatrix Alba. Now you have."

She would have recognized him anywhere, no matter how many conical hoods he wore. "I haven't betrayed anyone."

"Grab her," the Chairman of the council croaked.

The Guard moved as one.

Beatrix could never get straight what happened next. She remembered calling on her Furie, although with her mangled hands, the jets of power poured down in a wasteful puddle.

She heard William's weapon discharge.

"Down," he screamed. As she crouched, red light flashed, followed by the rumbling the earth makes when it cracks. Out of nowhere, the trees that lined the scenic boardwalk lifted and swung forth, convulsing in a violent twister. The earth opened in zigzags, eating up a whole portion of grass and rock into a sinkhole. Around them, the guards struggled for balance. The air became still, charged and expectant.

Fire came next. A huge flamethrower tongue arched over her head and threatened to swallow her. His arm lassoing her waist, William hurled her behind him onto a humming beast, a flying motorcycle-like vehicle trimmed with neon strip lights.

The air sparked red and white from the nearby explosions and scorched Beatrix's eyelashes. Cold salt hit her cheeks as they sped toward the beach. Hugging William's back, she turned to look. Behind them, the Chairman's horse squirmed sideways on the ground, while the guards struggled to regroup, tangled in a giant fishnet. Some were already in pursuit, but William's light-cycle bolted too far ahead.

"Change of plans," he said, and at first, Beatrix thought he was talking to her.

"Copy that. Plan B it is." Jane's response buzzed through his comm device. "See you on the ship."

34

WILLIAM

The projectiles flew so close Beatrix's ears burned with their whooshing. She nearly fell off the light-cycle and into the ocean as William maneuvered to avoid them, their ride listing one way and then the other, while the waves below sprayed them.

From the opposite direction, a new barrage began. The council had sent aircraft. And speedboats. And swarms of weird insects that could be robotic or not.

"Pick one," William said. "We won't be able to outfly them for long."

Beatrix blinked through the water that thrashed her. Rain came down in continuous sheets.

"Weathervanes," Jane had warned. "The top of the line in magical defense at the service of the council."

"Pick a ship. Quick," William insisted.

Straining toward the darkness of the horizon, Beatrix saw them. Five, six, seven. She counted eight vessels. Eight perfect replicas of the pirate ship. All of them too far to make out well. All of them beckoning to safety. Only one telling the truth.

Trelius's decoys.

They were meant to fool the council. On this side of the illusion, they were confusing Beatrix too. Fear dug sharp nails into her heart. But like they had many times before, at the direst moments, stories came to her aid.

From across space and time, the borrowed words guided her. "After all, the true seeing is within," the whispers reminded her, and so she shut her eyes, expecting her heart to see what she could not. Aestrer's blue haze filled her mind, and she opened them with understanding. The bike still swerving, she managed to pull the Alicorn from her pouch and let just enough rainwater fill it to take a sip. Like glasses curing double vision, all ships faded into one.

"There." She pointed in the distance, and William nodded, veering left.

But as they recovered from the turn, a swarm of buzzing scouts caught up with them. Even above the cries of the storm, their electronic, whirring noises unnerved her as they crashed like kamikazes against William's shield and blackened it. She knew more were coming. Now that they'd found them, they would send back their coordinates to the Guard.

"Do you trust me?" William asked close to her ear.

She didn't get to answer yes.

Of course.

Always.

With a crack less theatrical than its significance, William's shield gave out. The insects plunged toward them, weapons firing.

They didn't reach them.

As if a monstrous beast had awoken underneath the ocean, the surface of the water swelled up. It grew into an arch the size of two skyscrapers and curled over them. The swarm scrambled, trying to fly out of its reach, while William urged the cycle up and over the crest of the wave.

"Let go," Beatrix heard him say, grabbing her hand at the same time that the wave collapsed to the ocean, swallowing both the bots and the plummeting vehicle.

Darkness and silence took over as they dropped.

She hit the raft back first, the inflatable rubber dinghy rocking and drenching her. William landed next to her, and when he stretched his arm to pull her close and share a sigh of relief, she hid in the crook of his neck.

The ocean churned around them, the current taking them away fast and at its whim, and soon the momentary quiet evaporated. Around them, the bursts of the council's fire lit the night. Aware they'd lost them, the Guard had doubled down on the attack.

Sitting up, William conjured a flimsy film that enclosed the raft in a transparent dome. "We're farther and farther from the bot's coordinates, so this should help obscure us while they search. It muffles sound but doesn't mute it. So we ought to be quiet." He sucked in a breath, and if it weren't out of character, she would have guessed he felt unsure. "I apologize about the cycle and making you jump like that. I couldn't risk them spotting the real ship once the swarm found us, especially after Jane and Trelius worked so hard on the mirages to create the decoys. You did a great job figuring out the right ship. I messed it up."

"You didn't. Not really." Beatrix smiled, trying despite everything to stay positive. To fight the despair gnawing at the hem of her consciousness that would swallow her whole if she let it. "You saved us and made us a raft."

"I barely conjured it in time." William rubbed his forehead, pressing with three fingers across it as if it ached.

"Who's bad at taking compliments now? Admit it. We're a good team."

He looked at her, stared hard, and she returned his gaze, unflinching.

"Yeah, we are." The barest of curves lifted the corner of his lips and Beatrix relaxed. The lapping of the ocean created a rhythmic sound against the dinghy, like the hand of a clock ticking time.

"We're sort of stuck here," he said. "Have to wait until the council's given up."

"How long?"

"A while."

Beatrix rolled toward the middle of the raft. It was a small rubber float, no larger than a full bed, and yet under their see-through dome, it gave her an unreal sense of safety. William plucked his comm crystal out of his soaked coat and tapped on it. Soon he lay back next to her, exhausted.

The outside world receded, the sounds of the attack becoming white noise, the way busy city streets turn into lullabies. They remained in that version of silence for countless minutes.

"I'm sorry you had to use your power." It hadn't occurred to her until now all he'd put on the line to help them escape. It couldn't have been an easy decision.

William turned to her, his urgent, always too-demanding gaze piercing. Instead of a shiver, a thrill ran through Beatrix. Electricity crackled on her skin, which was no Furie and no trick of the council, but magical nonetheless.

Beyond the conjured dome barrier, the intersecting search beams shaped trestles across the sky.

"I'm not sorry. I couldn't deal if anything happened to you." This voice. This one she'd only dreamt of. "I don't want to fight it."

Of all the moments he could have picked, William chose that one. His palms cradled her face, and Beatrix smelled the mix of his scent and the after-magic on his fingers when he bent his head her way.

Everything in her tensed, both expectant and running at high speed.

When he kissed her, it wasn't foreign, but a rousing current mixed with the familiar, welcome sense of arriving. She felt him shake, his breath coming out as ragged as hers. Her blood boiled and pumped in a frenzy as she held onto him, anchored by his arms.

Time disappeared—with the stubborn unreality of the Zweeshen multiplied a million times. The sounds of war outside their flimsy refuge faded to nothing.

If she were able to see herself from above, like someone might from the sickened moon in the sky, Beatrix might have been tempted to roll her eyes. She would have puffed and wondered why they would have picked this very moment. Why, of all times, they'd be kissing now, in the middle of a fight that wasn't over, on a sticky rubber dinghy that bobbed like a useless peanut shell.

In real life, no one would dare wonder.

"At last!"

Beatrix shook awake and lifted her head to discover Emma. William was maneuvering an outboard motor attached to the raft.

"Thank the muses!" the girl shouted from above, aboard an enormous ship of which Beatrix only saw a barnacled hull. "We thought you were at the bottom of the sea."

The raft bobbed when Trelius dropped a primitive knotted ladder.

"They got our message," William said, anticipating the question at the tip of Beatrix's tongue. "Once they charted our location, they were able to tow us."

"And I was asleep through that?"

"We both were. A slumber spell-bomb found us, I suspect. Come on, I'll give you a leg up."

Fighting the rocking, she hooked her forearm to hang onto the swaying ladder. Her fingers numb, she struggled to climb.

Emma waved, urging her to hurry.

Judging by the sounds in the distance, the battle raged still.

As if to underscore that thought, an explosion reached the ship, driving a cannonball into the hull. Water gushed in while the crew's screams mixed with the whistling from the guided missiles that came next.

The ladder dangling, Beatrix managed to reach the top, where two pairs of hands lifted her over the railing. Jane draped a blanket over her shoulders. Only then did Beatrix realize how frozen she was. The rain the council had conjured earlier had eased, but her hair dripped in long, icy rivers.

They pulled William up next, and her heart leapt when he surveyed the deck looking for her, their eyes meeting for an instant before he joined Trelius on the stern.

"Get ready for the geo-time jump," Jane shouted, and the crew ran to their posts.

Beatrix had forgotten about the rest of the escape plan, that their success depended on creating a space-time fold to get away from the council.

Across the deck, William worked with Trelius to conjure the last of the tethers to keep them safe during the jump.

"How I wish I were like Neradola." Emma pointed to the bow, where the ghost was gliding to her spot. "To be half ghost and half fairy and even know how to navigate. Some taelimns have all the luck." Then she remembered to be kind. "It's a comfort that she'll guide us."

Neradola positioned herself atop the bowsprit, leaning out, the sleeves of her dress waving like wings. Amidst the feverish activity, she stood unmoving, so still she could pass for the figurehead of an old Norse ship.

"Take cover," Jane said, and grabbing Emma, Beatrix settled them into a cramped nook under the captain's cabin. They knelt there, their hands tight around a set of wooden pegs used to hold lanterns.

"Now!" someone yelled, the words followed by a burst of light bright enough to render them blind. Beatrix's stomach twisted from the acceleration as the ship and everyone on it lurched forward. They were tossed ahead into a centrifuge that seemed to tear every particle of them in a different direction.

For a moment, she thought they'd succeeded.

Before the volcano-catapults reached them, and the air caught on fire.

35

PİRATES

After the fact, the pirates argued the ship's stealth tactics had allowed them to escape unscathed.

"We faded into the sky," one bragged.

Based on Beatrix's experience, the assertion was only half-true. If the sky were black, sure, they could disappear in it, but if the Guard called on their wizard weathervanes to fake a sun—as they had—not so much.

They ended up taking a withering attack head-on. Trelius's shield held most of the magic offensive and averted the storm-makers, while William and Jane worked the leap-drive to retry the jump.

It took four attempts.

When it happened, the leap tore Beatrix apart as if her body had been placed in a blender. Every atom hurt, and for a second, after the sense of nausea cleared, everyone looked at each other, flabbergasted. The deck, half-afire and half-crushed by the stones from the trebuchets, resembled the scene of a forgotten wreckage.

Beatrix braced herself for another barrage.

Instead, silence. No sounds from bots or magical missiles, no cannon-balls or laser firethrowers. They were sailing a sea so calm the moon made a round impression on it.

The pirates were the first to erupt in celebration. Joyous, curse-filled yells spiced the night. Beatrix found William's stare across the deck. She thought Zweeshen time might be on her side for once because he cut the distance that separated them in a second and three strides.

Soon after, Jane accompanied Beatrix to the guest quarters, where she'd been assigned a cabin the size of a matchbox. Although Beatrix was wet and cold, adrenaline still rushed through her veins.

"That was some jump." The unnatural shine in Jane's pupils revealed that she, too, was drunk on their victory escaping the Zweeshen.

Some jump indeed.

Beatrix smiled, the sweetness of success on her tongue.

She was still in a good mood when, much later, William came to see her as promised. Beatrix opened her cabin door before he knocked.

"We need to talk," he said, his voice so heavy with tiredness the words mumbled into a drawl.

"You're exhausted." His eyes were sunken into the sockets, the skin around them purple.

"Long day." He tried to smile, but even that seemed too much effort.

"No talk. Just stay."

"Beatrix, I—" He walked in and grabbed her hands. "No, don't try to stop me. I have to say this. I was wrong to push you away during the ball. I know I hurt you, and I'm sorry."

Beatrix didn't want to have this conversation. Not now. He could barely hold himself up. But maybe *he* needed it.

"What changed your mind?" she asked.

"You did. You said that you would be safer, and we would be stronger together—and you were right. I won't make the mistake of doubting us again. For however long you want me, you have me."

He stepped closer, and Beatrix sank into his arms. She looked up at his face where fatigue and magic exertion drew edges and shadows. Her index finger traced a path from his temple, along his cheek, and to his mouth. "I won't stop wanting you."

Their kiss was sweet and slow, and it removed the need for more words.

William had fallen asleep soon after, within moments of lying down, his boots still on his feet. On a bed that smelled of sea and wet wood, aboard a ship stolen from a story awash with adventure, Beatrix watched his chest lift and drop. As she drifted off, her last thought was that for once, her life seemed better than a book.

Staring out to the ocean the morning after the jump, Beatrix's eyes burned, irritated by the brine, and for the briefest of instants she wondered what it would feel like to fall into this water. In the faint light, it looked as uninviting as a tub full of ink.

William strode to her side in silence, and although she sensed his arrival, she didn't acknowledge him. Having caught his expression before leaving the cabin, she could guess what came next. Better not talk about it.

"We need to discuss what I told you during the ball. We can't keep avoiding it."

See? She'd been right. "Not now. Please."

"Beatrix, we have to. I used magic during the escape. Before, there was a possibility. Now, we know the curse is in effect."

"I already explained I don't care. You can't convince me." She placed a hand on his forearm. No longer electricity, the touch felt like hunger.

William didn't move away. His muscles tensed under the skin while he stood, rigid and cold. "I told you I'll stay with you as long as you want me. That doesn't mean we can ignore the curse."

"Can we have today? We don't even know if I'll make it."

His face hardened. So did his voice. "Don't say that. Words birth worlds. They have power. And your eyes are shinier. Did you meet with Neradola?"

Beatrix had. The ghost had doubled the potion and added new ingredients, but the escape had cost Beatrix, and even if the ship cut the ocean at supersonic speed, it wasn't guaranteed she'd last until they reached the island with the pageturner.

And yet Neradola's healing had helped.

"I can't replenish your Inaechar or heal your human body," the ghost had said, her semitransparent fingers pressing on Beatrix's neck with her soft touch. "I can repair some of the damage Roamer's caused on your ink self for the short term. You'll have to come to me four times a day."

"I saw Nera. I'm doing better," Beatrix told William now, happy that she needn't lie. "No more depressive talk now. Please."

He looked about to argue. Then nodded. "How's Emma?"

"Still green. I feel terrible for her. I hope her seasickness clears soon."

"Too bad she's a Draft and Neradola's medicine doesn't work on her. It won't be too long to the island. Less than a day." The forceful words caused her to cock her head.

His palms moved up to cup her face, kissing her with a tenderness that was thrilling and new. When he dropped his hands, she took them in hers. His fingers were lean, and Beatrix thought it odd she hadn't noticed before: he had the hands of a magician, with the X-shaped folds between the knuckles Emma had taught her to recognize.

"If I were a good person..." he said, letting her go.

"Oh, pleeease." Beatrix's tone teased. "Your artisan should have eased up on the self-flagellating tendencies."

A half smile propped up the edge of his lip. "He'd never. My writer would include a page-long description of my selfishness, talk about how weak I'm being, and speculate about how long I can afford to get away with it."

"He sounds lovely."

William took her in his arms and kissed her again.

36

TRELIUS

"What are you girls doing?" Trelius asked.

Beatrix and Emma sat on the main deck, the unrelenting greyness of the sea wafting around them like a mantle.

It was midday. But no one would guess it by looking at the sky. Ominous and flat, it melded together with the ocean. Thanks to the added antimatter boosters William had conjured, they were barely skimming the surface, almost flying over it, so everything around the ship blurred in a shifting palette of lead.

Time felt tight and urgent, and Beatrix couldn't rid herself of the compulsion to work on the letter. To figure out the very last clue. If by a miracle she made it to the Eisid Naraid, she wanted to be as far as possible with the riddle.

"Beatrix's obsessing," Emma said. The seasickness that had plagued her since the jump had abated, and she was back to herself.

"We're reviewing our facts." Beatrix readjusted her body on the wooden folding chair, careful to hide her legs. She preferred not to be confronted with the damage. Everything from the knee down was streaked black.

Trelius leaned forward. "Can I help?"

Emma jumped to her feet, purple-streaked orange hair bouncing, and set up another chair.

"We believe the letter's a spell of revelation," Beatrix said. She and Jane had discarded the idea of it being an obscuring spell. It made little sense considering Mary was the Soul of Rephait. Much more likely that Leyna would have hidden it and wanted it revealed now. But revelation spells must be cast directly on the charmed object, so Beatrix needed to find the dagger first, and on that, they'd made little progress.

The gladiator appeared thoughtful. "That makes sense." Trelius lifted the paper with his strong, tan hands. He had X-folds around his knuckles like William, but Trelius's were deep and thick, raised white scars. He studied the writing with interest, lifting it against the sky and scratching the map with his fingernail. "So you're stuck on the *E*. One more clue? That's impressive."

"We have no idea what the last decoder might be." Beatrix bent to look, and their three heads leaned over the paper.

"Forbidden Lines: 3X May the words," Trelius read.

Apprehension tugged at Beatrix when hearing the call aloud. Selda had warned her against that, and Beatrix remembered her Furie's anger when Julie had screamed the phrase a million years ago, in a life that seemed to belong to someone else. Out of Trelius's mouth, it didn't sound scary but rather playful, like the tease of a tongue twister.

"That's not part of the riddle," Beatrix said.

"Right." Trelius tapped his fingers on the rough wood of the barrel they were using for a table, his forehead rumpled. The muscles of his legs rippled under the broadcloth of his pants as he stretched out. "Let's focus on this E clue. It goes,

Enter through the Gate Untold.
At its thinnest, the veil is naught.
The Goddess Rephait the question begs.
For the answer search your strength."

"I wish I had talked to the author of the Essentials," Beatrix said. "He had seen the Gate Untold, so that would be a path at least. I just have no idea where to search for a decoder. My grandfather left nothing else behind. And we've used all artifacts in the chest already."

"The Goddess Rephait," Emma mused, flipping her cameo back and forth. "What's the question?"

"Or rather, what's the answer." Trelius perked up abruptly. The rings on the leather strips he wore over his shirt glinted, as golden as his hair. "For the answer search your strength. I'm sure you've been considering it, but what does that bring to mind, Beatrix? What's your greatest strength?"

She would have never thought it a month ago, but the idea of the Furie presented itself in her mind. In a way, her power was her strength. Not the violent aspect of her magic, but the existence of it, which forced Beatrix to control herself. To manage her anger. To decide what battles to fight. And sometimes enabled the decision to stand up for herself. "My determination to try to control the monster, I would say. I'm stumped at how that could be a decoder, though."

Trelius looked to the ocean, perhaps searching for ideas there. "Decoders tend to follow a theme. All of yours were things your grandfather gave you or were indirectly associated with him at least. Think. Did he gift you anything connected to this strength? Something that symbolizes it?"

"I see where you're going," Beatrix said. But nothing occurred to her. She hadn't thought of the monster as something to be proud of. Or her control of it as an accomplishment. On the contrary, she was forever failing to master the Taming Sphere and—Beatrix stopped her thoughts in their tracks. "The Sphere. He taught me how to create it for years, and I never could. It was a huge deal for me. It represents the ultimate control of the Furie." She grimaced. "I still wonder if what happened at the council hall wasn't a fluke."

"She's talking about a Taming Sphere," Emma said, because Trelius seemed a bit lost.

The gladiator rubbed his chin. "A Taming Sphere as a decoder would be a novel concept. With a doctored enchantment maybe. Worth trying."

Beatrix's mouth dried. Her Inaechar had become a precious commodity, and a Taming Sphere would be a significant exertion. She recalled the drained feeling after the incident during the hearing and hesitated.

Emma either read her thoughts or came to the same conclusion. "You shouldn't attempt it now. You can test it once we reach the Eisid."

"If this is the last clue, then the spell instructions will be complete," Trelius said, his eyes fixed on Beatrix, "and you'll be able to understand its meaning. There could be valuable information about the Soul in it. Isn't that what you want?"

Yes, Beatrix thought, torn. So far, they'd concluded the letter contained a spell to reveal the winged dagger. Since revelation spells were cast directly on the target artifact, they'd assumed Mom had expected Beatrix to have the Soul before performing the spell. But what if that was incorrect? What if the spell itself was supposed to bring forth the dagger? Or if the last clue contained information about its whereabouts?

Emma yanked on her cameo so hard Beatrix thought she might choke. "Please don't. Wait until you've synched."

But Beatrix had made up her mind. Nobody seemed willing to confront the reality of her situation. She knew they were to reach the pageturner soon, but everyone, more than anyone Neradola, doubted she would survive the actual passage through the bridge. Illegal bridges took more Inaechar from taelimns and were less safe, so her chances of reaching the Eisid were questionable. And if she died without attempting this, she might be the cause of her mother's world never recovering. The reason her mother died. If there was a chance Beatrix could help so many, how could she be so selfish as not to try?

Calling on her power, Beatrix began to spin the energy Sphere into being. Opposite to what she'd feared, it was easier than the last time. Her power had become tamer, less explosive. Foggier.

Weaker.

"Read the words," Trelius said, while the blue orb floated and sparkled in front of them.

"Which ones?"

"The clue." He held the letter up for her.

"Oh, that." Careful not to lose concentration, Beatrix bent forward. "Enter through the Gate Untold..."

The sounds lingered, preserved in the heavy air. Then the transparent ball stopped spinning. It halted, suspended, and began acquiring a solid, metal-like quality and a glassy glow. A tiny door hinged up top.

Emma didn't hesitate. She crumpled the letter and shoved it into the opening.

"It's so exciting," the girl said, delighted despite her earlier misgivings.

"Now twirl it," Trelius instructed.

Beatrix did, feeling the Inaechar drain out of her with every lap and every revolution. The Sphere sped up, accelerating as it had that other time, in front of the council, the alphabet of characters on it jumping around, dancing, and rearranging. A thin ribbon pushed out from the middle. The sash rippled in the air, gold cursive on it. Emma read,

> "Follow the night to your true name spoken,
> that which only a blue moon reveals.
> Let your soul search infinity,
> and find the secret of life within."

"What the hell are you doing?"

William grabbed Beatrix by the shoulders, his face distorted with rage and terror. Startled, her concentration failed, and the Sphere crashed to the floor. Shards of glass and dark blue powder scattered. The ribbon, the words, the shining threads all vanished, swept away to the ocean. Only the letter remained, crumpled on the floor like a piece of trash.

"Are you suicidal?" William screamed.

"We were just trying—" Beatrix began.

"You," William shot at Trelius, "don't ever come close to her again."

"Beatrix?"

Emma snuck her head in through the door of the cabin. On the girl's face, Beatrix read what she already knew. She didn't look good. Black now stained her neck and her collarbone.

"I should never have let it happen," Emma said, enough guilt in her words to hang a man.

"It was my choice." Beatrix breathed wearily. She felt sadder that William was upset than about her actual decision. She'd do it again. "The last clue of the riddle is deciphered. That's what matters."

Emma bit her lip, unconvinced but unwilling to disagree. "Trelius sent me. William has forbidden him to talk to you."

"That's ridiculous!" Outrage burned Beatrix's throat. She coughed, the effort hurting her lungs. "He doesn't get to decide for me."

"Trelius was wrong to incite you." Emma folded her hands on her lap, sitting on a rough wooden chair that caught on her skirt. She pulled the fabric away with annoyance.

"I've been thinking and researching," Beatrix said, sitting on the edge of the bed. "I think I have done it. I figured out what the last clue means."

Emma pushed forward and sat in front of her. "Well? Don't build up suspense. What is it?"

"When we were searching for Mary, remember I found out that the worst criminals are purged? Their names were erased and the morphlines over their hearts burned. Because that is a taelimn's true name."

"Of course. You're brilliant." The girl eyed her with so much admiration that Beatrix had to look away. A perk of big sisters? "I think you've got the hang of this Craxtan business."

True. Beatrix was starting to understand how the mind of the person behind the letter worked. Perhaps that meant she was getting to know Mom, since she had created the riddle after all.

Beatrix redid her bun, uncomfortable under Emma's praise. "I think this will complete the spell instructions."

"I'm certain of it." Emma grinned. "Cassandra said Craxtans are supposed to gain meaning when seen in their totality. So what is it? Do you know your true name?"

At that, Beatrix faded a bit. She was so close. And yet not there. "No. The only time I saw my morphlines was with Aestrer during my Test of Character, and I couldn't read them."

Emma pursed her lips. "Well, the good news is that if William's right about forshaltness, if you embraced your taelimn essence during the ball, then you'll be able to read your morphlines now. The bad news is you'll need a blue moon, of course."

Beatrix sighed. "We don't know when the next will be."

"But the wheel is turning, and once it starts, it cannot stop until a blue one comes."

37

ALLAİSİN

Later that evening, hoping the cover of the dark would obscure the damage done by her latest use of magic, Beatrix ventured out to the deck. She wanted to find William. She hated the distance between them after his outburst earlier. And she felt guilty too.

Wrapping a shawl around her shoulders to hide the worse of the black marks on her neck, she braved the brisk breeze. It was always windy because of the neck-breaking speed of the ship.

"Tomorrow morning," William had said, furious. "We're arriving tomorrow morning and you want to kill yourself a few hours before being cured."

Beatrix had argued. But she didn't know how to explain to him that waiting wasn't an option. That she was compelled to finish deciphering the riddle. That she feared what would happen if she showed up in the Eisid with her task incomplete. Or if she died before it, and the dagger could never be returned to its rightful place.

The Charmancer still possessed Mom's book—but if it was his own, he wouldn't burn it. So hope existed for the Eisid Naraid, regardless of Beatrix's fate.

She didn't want to fall into that dark thinking. With every hour, though, she felt the weakness growing, and William had been correct that the episode with the Sphere had cost her.

Beatrix advanced shakily, the pounding in her head that was now ever-present dizzying her. The fresh air was worth it. It felt nice on her damp skin.

"She should be dead by now." Carried by the salty air, the overheard words deflated her like a week-old birthday balloon.

Neradola stood by the helm, surrounded by key members of the crew, her winged cloak floating. "After the Sphere, she should have perished. I have to agree it's not natural. I've never seen anyone recover like she does."

Beatrix's heart pummeled her ribs, her knees rattled, and she struggled to breathe air that had turned rarified.

"It could be magical sea creatures." Jane's tone was cautious and restrained. "We're in dangerous seas. Who knows what power is around us?"

"It can't be that!" This came from a member of the crew, whom Beatrix had seen at the helm earlier. "Trelius's trap would've caught cursed beings like that." He crossed himself, then drew a rune for good measure.

"I don't believe it," Trelius said. "It has to be something else draining our magical reserves."

"It's not anything else." The sleeves of Neradola's cape flapped, an eerie glow surrounding her body. "It's black magic. I felt it when I tried to heal her. Her marks are from Inaechar loss, but some have a touch of Fogges in them. Dark magic is floating on this ship, and we all know who it is. Look at you." Her ghostly hand waved to William. "You're depleted, hollowed out as if you'd been through Death's valley. Making another set of magic propellers took you three tries. You should've been done with those hours ago. Trelius, I believe we need to cage her. It's not just her life at risk but all of ours. We can't arrive on the secret island with a black magician. It would mean all our deaths."

"Maybe it's unconscious. A Furie could easily go dark." Jane rocked on her heels, her hands in her pockets.

"Enough," William said, the muscles in his jaw so tight they seemed to engage one by one when he spoke. "Leave her out of this. She isn't to blame. I am."

And abandoning them to gape in shock, he left the deck.

"Is it true?" Beatrix asked.

She'd followed William to the bottom of the ship, the hold, where the rations, pelts, and an assortment of loot the pirates hoped to trade were stored.

He sat sideways on an upside-down wooden crate that until that morning had contained ruby red oranges, his gaze lost.

"Is it true?" she repeated when he didn't respond.

"Mostly." William was easy to read this time, pure sadness, and a vulnerability so raw it made her heart scream. No fight remained in his slouched figure, like an engine all out of steam. "Yeah, it's true."

She didn't need to ask why. Her whole face had transformed into a question mark.

"After the Inksomner, you were so weak. Neradola didn't think you'd make it." Tiredness—blended with a touch of defiance—coated the ebbs and flows of his vowels.

"But black magic!"

"I don't regret it. I'd do it again. I would do anything."

His words curled around Beatrix, both warm—and violent and desperate.

"But black magic takes life!"

He gave her a sly smile. "The spellcaster doesn't have to be the taker. Like with everything, the reverse can happen too. Someone can give out Inaechar willingly."

"You could have died! I know that much. Dark magic kills the giver. Only the taker survives." Her voice rose, shrill and deranged, her heart out of control.

He stared at her, with such determination it scared her.

"You thought you *would* die," she said.

"Most of the times the giver dies. It's almost impossible to stem the flow. I would have. But it didn't work that way with you. I could never open it. All I did was force a bit of Inaechar through. It's a small drip. Once done, I couldn't cut it off—I've remained tethered since."

Like a frozen gust, the revelation made Beatrix shudder. Her windpipe closed up, forcing her words to trickle out. "So they're right! I'm sucking the life out of you."

With a swift motion, William scooped her up and sat her on his lap. She could feel the warmth of his skin through the rough cotton shirt while he held her so tight and so close, she thought she'd meld in.

"Listen to me. Listen to no one but me," he said, forcing her eyes to meet his. "This is my choice. You aren't doing anything. If I can keep you alive until the Eisid, then it's my gift and not for a moment something you should feel guilty about."

Tears rolling, Beatrix hid her head in his chest, letting his hands caress her hair. "This is all wrong. What if the flow opens, and I end up killing you. You should never have done it."

"Would you have?"

She couldn't answer. William knew her response anyway.

They sat together for a while, not needing to talk.

"I didn't even realize you could do black magic," she said.

"The fuel of Fantasy magic is a choice." William pulled away a bit, so she could sit next to him on the crate, and offered her a drink from a leather canteen. She drank it, realizing she was parched and aching.

"I showed the first signs of talent when I turned three. My mother and sister helped me hide it, so my father didn't discover it until five years later." His eyes emptied, as if he'd traveled back in time and the distance had unfocused them. "When he found out, he sent me to live with a hermit, one of the last great sages. The Mage taught me the ways of the dark and the light because both can be used for good and evil."

His shoulders bent with unmistakable shame. His gaze drifted to her, pain distorting his features. "I've—I'm not what you think, Beatrix. I was my father's personal weapon. I conjured for him in many battles, and people died to lend me the strength to keep going. That's what black magic does. It uses others' life force to extend the wizard's power. I still hear them drop to the ground, discarded like emptied batteries."

"I'm so sorry."

He seemed taken aback by that. "Why would you be sorry for me?"

"Because I know you. You couldn't have wanted to do it."

"I didn't." William studied his fingers, the cuticle of his thumb of sudden interest. "Which is a poor excuse. Our actions are still ours. We have more control than we realize. At the time, I thought I was trapped. That if I didn't protect my father, his curse would pass on to me, and my mother and sister would die. In the end, it made no difference. During a battle, I got distracted by an orc and didn't see the arrow coming. Skewered his heart in one swift, clean hit."

William became silent, so drawn Beatrix feared a stranger had taken his place. She grieved for him.

He didn't need to add anything else.

She knew the end of the story. That his mother had long been buried. And that by now, he couldn't remember his sister Allaisin's face.

38

FOGGED MOON

Beatrix sat up on her bed with a start. Her T-shirt clung to her body, soaked under the heavy bedcovers.

She was alone.

After her conversation with William in the hold, they had retreated to the cabin, but now he was gone. Must have run to his midnight meeting with the crew to prepare for tomorrow's early arrival. The emptiness his absence left behind was so thick she could touch it, a phantom hovering over the pillow to her side.

With his leaving, a tundra had taken over her little cabin, freezing her exposed face. Shivering, Beatrix pulled the blanket up. The wool smelled stale, and she cringed at the thought of the years of accumulated dirt that made it stiff.

Careful not to expose too much skin, she checked the watch on her wrist, a recent gift from Emma, who'd grown tired of her asking the time. It had four arrows instead of three. The fourth measured "story time," whatever that might be. Two a.m. regular time.

She surveyed the room. The dream had been so vivid she still couldn't detangle from it. Her lids drooped, curtained.

Urged by the images fresh in her mind, Beatrix braced herself. She snuck her legs out. The frosty air teased her hair in goosebumps while chills tiptoed up her back. Even in this semidarkness, she could see it. The spot on her side had expanded during the night, stretching all the way to her chest. In this light, it gleamed mercury, as though her skin had been inlaid in hematite.

Draping the blanket around herself like a cape, she sprinted across the wooden floor to reach the mirror. It was round and pitted, but she could still see herself.

She looked into her huge eyes. Eyes she'd seen repeated in her dream, only in another's face. Moss and earth and rust and ink reached her, churned around her, and as Beatrix stared into the Goddess-touched eyes of her mother, she fell in.

Except it didn't feel like falling.

She flew, gliding out of herself and into a gauzy mist where images drew in and out of focus and sounds lengthened. Nothingness trapped her again, the same emptiness from the night of the Inksomner, which she had somehow, incomprehensibly, blanked out. It all came back to her now, with the full clarity of the original vision and equal intensity.

When the experience ended, she returned to her body with a jerk. Her heart squeezed with longing. How could she have forgotten meeting Mom?

Ignoring the cold that made her shiver, Beatrix released the blanket and looked at her reflection in the mirror again. Like a spiderweb of blue, morphlines were calligraphed on her skin.

That's why Aestrer had woken her up. The wheel had turned.

The moon shone blue.

Out on the deck, the air hung, calm. With no wind, the sails lay deflated and saggy. Had they stopped moving?

It was a frigid, humid night. The prospect of rain lurked, the drops-to-be not yet heavy enough to fall.

Beatrix glanced up and cursed.

In the short time it had taken her to get dressed, the sky had changed. An inscrutable grey-black, it arched over her so covered in clouds that not a glimpse of starlight could escape. The only glow came from the amber lanterns that swayed at regular intervals, some from sanded posts and others attached to crude hooks.

The whole area was deserted except for a sailor who dozed on the stern deck and another one asleep atop the crow's nest.

Neradola's arrow led the ship. Trelius had cast an obscuring shield, and William's latest iteration of a sweep engine should be propelling them forward. With magic in charge, people rested.

Beatrix set up in a corner of the main deck, careful to position the objects like she'd watched her mother do in the vision.

Hands stretched out, she faced the west, knowing without reason but also without a doubt where it was.

The words of the spell that she'd learned from her mother slipped off of her tongue and narrowed her lips in shushes and esses. Unusual contortions for the muscles of her jaw. Half aware, half in a trance, she thought her mother's language sounded throaty, a tongue of secrets.

"*Va sa sho'h*," she intoned, and while the last sound rang, her fingers turned alight with a purple flame. She lifted her arms, letting the magic flow all the way to the sky.

Above her, the clouds opened up, and the moon beamed down on her with its gigantic, bluish face, making her morphlines pop.

"*Pes Vu me Alk Rephait na lasaan.*"

The cumulus gathered in, shaping with their wispy threads what first looked like a tongue, then a whip, and finally a huge winged serpent that slithered across the sky and down, all the way to the place where Beatrix stood.

Like a cobalt specter, the serpent landed at her side, its shimmery scales burning grooves into the wood as it glided forth. Tail to mouth, mouth to tail, it closed in around her, and Beatrix recognized it for what it was. The Evermoon, the self-eating snake. Its head navigated the circle around her, with eyes that were not reptilian but akin to her own. Eyes touched by the Goddess Rephait.

"Speak your true name and heed its meaning," it hissed. "Speak what you are and cannot change." And in the circle of the Evermoon, Beatrix thought of the morphline on her chest, over her heart, the meaning of which she still didn't understand. "I am...one."

"And I am the Evermoon," the snake said, its voice setting Beatrix's blood to thrumming. "I am infinity. And together we become the Fogged Moon. The All in One. The finite thing that contains all infinity. We're the truth that everything is connected, and in our differences, we are all the same. What we are, what we seek, what we lose, what we give, who we love. What we sacrifice. You and I, we are forshaltness, the reminder that a single soul beats through us all and into eternity."

While the snake explained, Beatrix's mind expanded with understanding. The revelation flashed full-fledged and awe-inducing, its wonder engraving itself in her soul. But a second later she'd lost it, the concept too unfathomable for her brain to grasp and hold onto, so that its truth remained forever fogged, almost in reach but never in hand.

And then the snake stopped talking and began to circle faster around her. The planks of the floor smoked, and flames of purple grew into a wall of fire, until, trapping her inside the ring it had created, the Evermoon engulfed her.

When Beatrix came to, she lay on the hard wood of the deck, her hands bleeding and her shirt torn. The weather had transformed again. A fierce rain swept the ship, and she was drenched.

Between her fingers, the metal of the dagger called to her.

"Give it to me," a violent, greedy voice said.

Lifting to her elbows, she blinked, trying to identify who'd spoken through the curtain of water. She clasped the Soul with force, the hilt of the winged dagger fitting in her palm with magical warmth.

"Who's there?" Standing up and steadying herself as the boat listed, she scanned the deck. She located him on the bow, where the mizzenmast with the folded sails swung in the newborn storm. His arms were lifted high, in the pose of a magician about to strike.

"Give me the Soul."

The air breathed icicles. Arching her stiff neck, Beatrix strained to discern his identity. "Show yourself."

He flew down like a wraith, his short cape waving, and landed a mere ten feet away from her. There, he pivoted and grinned with pride. "There are more than chores at stake now."

Confusion and shock washed over Beatrix. "Trelius? But—why? I don't understand. What's wrong with you?" An avalanche of thoughts buried her mind. She stepped backward, toward the railing. "What do you want with the Soul? Are you working for the Charmancer? What did he promise you?"

"Always the questions." Trelius smiled, his mouth arching like a shade over his perfect white teeth. "Give me the dagger, and I will answer everything."

"You're crazy. I won't let you hand it to the Charmancer. He's killed millions. Do you realize what he could do with it?"

"Hand it to him?" Trelius's eyes stabbed her. A new light lurked in them, appealing and dangerous at the same time. "Hand the Soul to him?" Mockery played in the crannies of his voice. "Poor Beatrix. A little dense today, aren't you? I won't give him anything. I *am* him."

She gasped. His irises, brilliant and blue, laughed, a million sparks in the dark.

It couldn't be. There had to be a mistake.

"In the name of tradition," he said in a tone that managed to be both pleasant and threatening. "Meet the Charmancer." His magic floated, dense and asbestos-smelling, while a long robe replaced his gladiator clothes, and a hood darkened his sandy hair.

Beatrix was stunned when he towered in front of her, every bit the black sorcerer who'd decimated thousands of books and massacred without guilt. The one who wanted to silence all stories.

He was real. Not a distant, disembodied evil, but a familiar person. A good-looking, charming, kind-speaking friend, who'd played cards and joked with her, the same one who had taught her how to hold up a sword, teased her, and helped her fill out paperwork, who'd aided her in deciphering the riddle of Mom's letter. "The spell. You knew!"

"I've known for a long time how the revelation spell worked. Only you could perform it to unmask the dagger—and you couldn't be coerced. Your mother and your grandfather made sure of that. So I had to help you along. Especially when you were getting so easily stuck. Thanks to you, I will soon acquire many new and exciting talents. That's the Soul's most basic feature, to pass a magic gift from one to another. Imagine what a collection I will amass!

"Wordrider's my first goal. Difficult to snatch one. No, don't look at me like that. They're not extinct, merely hard to find."

"You're insane!" She had to run, needed to warn the others. But Beatrix couldn't move. She'd been bolted in place. Looking down, she discovered her feet immersed in the sticky substance whose smell still populated her nightmares. A black, tarry poison. "You sent the Inksomner."

"Apologies about that. My good-for-nothing helper miscalculated your strength. He didn't realize with as little Inaechar as you had left, you wouldn't have woken up from the dark sleep. All is good. Your guard dog was there to save you." His nose wrinkled in repulsion, as if he'd eaten a piece of rotten fish. "Don't know what you see in him."

"Don't you dare!"

"Come on, Beatrix. You're not a hot-headed taelimn from a cheap book. I've seen you control yourself. You have it in you, the will that fuels all great magic. Stop pretending to be like everyone else and join me."

He lifted her, ungluing her from the tar and hoisting her several feet off the ground with a twist of his hand. A wide metal band appeared around her waist, trapping her arms to her body like a medieval torture device, complete with hexagonal bots and butterfly clasps.

As Beatrix hovered above the ship, the wet wind slapped her cheeks, the salt searing her. Rage grew to consume her.

"Furie," she called, and the weakened answer warmed her belly. She eyed the alarm bell above the foretop. A well-placed hit should alert the others, but unable to move her arms, she'd have to aim from the wrist and achieve an oblique shot from below.

"Don't waste your energy. Your end is inevitable," the Charmancer said, and for a moment she feared he'd figured out her plan. "No point fighting me, dying for nothing. You're different. You don't belong on Earth. Or in the Zweeshen. You're an Unwritten. Bigger than the prison of one story. You're like me."

"I'm nothing like you."

He watched her with such calm that, around him, the storm seemed to quiet too.

"You won't win." She wiggled, attempting to better position herself for a strike for which she'd have a single chance. "You're a thief and a murderer."

A swollen sail stood between her and the bell, and while the ship bobbed, she struggled to find a clear line of sight. Wet strands of hair clung to her forehead, obscuring her vision, and she couldn't wipe them off.

Just keep him talking. That's what characters do.

"Buy time. Wait for your chance," the whispers said.

"I'm as guilty of thievery as your mother was," Trelius continued, self-involved. "There's irony in it, isn't it? To take from the one who has stolen."

Beatrix wriggled. If she could free at least one arm... But the metal belt around her was too tight and too wide.

"Poor Beatrix. Watching you squirm is entertaining. So stubborn. I sort of like it. It's the flip side to your persistence—it should serve you well at my side." He shook his head and strands of yellow poked out of the hood. "We got along so well. It's natural. We want the same things."

"You're deranged."

He laughed then. And his laughter managed to be more frightening than anything else. It wasn't the cackling of a witch or the stentorian, raucous sound of a villain. It was a clean-shaven laugh, open and honest.

"I'm not like you at all. You want to destroy. To kill." The waves broke against the hull, stealing away Beatrix's voice and returning it muffled and weak.

"So naïve. It's adorable. Yes, we want the same things. Justice. Freedom. The end of limitations. Of unfair rules. Of the politics and the power-grabbing. The end of the Zweeshen. So did your mother."

Beatrix flinched at that. "Who are you really?"

"Someone who knows more about you than you do yourself. Stop fighting your destiny. You're meant to enable my victory. That's why your mother kept you alive. Why she used the Soul to pass on her magic and gave her life to you."

The revelation stabbed her heart, her head rattling in disbelief. Yet she didn't doubt his words. They rang with irrevocable truth.

Mom.

Mom was dead.

She'd killed herself. For her daughter.

Beatrix had known it; she'd seen it in the vision. She'd realized what her mother was doing as she sliced her arm with the dagger.

And still. A part of Beatrix had hoped.

The letter…

Why would Mom say they'd reunite if she was truly dead?

Beatrix's brain swam in confusion.

"She's dead. Because of you." Trelius tilted his head, amused. "Interesting that he didn't tell you. How did you think you survived all that time outside of your biblioworld? How did you believe you came to possess her Furie? No. You're no regular taelimn. Your fate is to destroy. You were bred for it. You're the master plan. Join me now, and we'll achieve greatness."

Beatrix's tears flowed with the force of rapids now. Pouring out without any control. They mixed with the rain that froze her skin to stone.

She'd never give in. What she hadn't expected was the fear. Not so much of dying—but of him being right.

"You already know I'll say no." She had to yell to overpower the drill of the ocean. The waves were growing taller, shaking the ship as they crested and crashed onto the deck.

He shrugged. "Perhaps. Although saying and doing are two different things. And something magnificent will happen tonight. I win anyway, even if you decide to oppose me. Because tonight you die either way. Tonight, you stop being who you are, and you become like me."

"Never. You hear me? Never!"

"Dangerous word, that. I avoid it altogether. Now I must stop, or I'll spoil the surprise. I've spoken too much already, and I'm getting bored. Don't want to go on like a common villain in a tale."

Trelius raised his arms. The wind picked up and fist-sized hail showered down, bouncing on every surface. Violent gusts ravaged her, scraping her skin with the abrasiveness of sandpaper.

Heavy and numb, her legs dangled below the ring that kept her trapped. The air around her changed, twisting to encircle her in a tube of calm, a cylindrical vise that began constricting her.

Stealing her breath.

Blood drummed inside her ears as the pressure mounted. Her whole body ached with a dull pain, deep and persistent, that warped her spine. From below, Trelius crunched his fingers into a fist in slow motion.

Beatrix heard a rib crack, and she wheezed, coughing for air. Her hand began to shrink, the bones contracting.

"This is it, Beatrix. This is your choice."

Trelius flexed his knuckles in an undulating motion, and a huge pyre appeared before him. At first, she thought he planned to throw her in it. Then she identified what he pulled from underneath his robe.

"The Librarian's wrong. I didn't steal the tale to save myself. I took it because it's yours. Choose me, and you won't just save the Eisid Naraid. I will ensure you see her again." With glee in his eyes, he caressed the cover of a book Beatrix didn't doubt was her mother's. "Say no, and they all die. Your chance to ever see her dies." He held the book over the fire, so close the edges started to smoke. "Pick. Know I'll get the Soul either way."

39

THE SOUL

"No," Beatrix screamed, holding onto the dagger with everything she had. Trelius twisted his wrist, applying pressure until one by one her fingers broke, rendering her grip useless. Horrified, she felt the Soul slip into the Charmancer's waiting hands.

"It won't work." She sounded a lot less victorious than she'd hoped. "I failed to complete the revelation spell. The Soul's outer shroud has fallen, but you can't use it as a weapon."

He scowled, her words the first thing to reach him tonight. And as he dragged her through the air toward him, Beatrix got an unencumbered shot at the bell. Tickled by her Furie, the warning alarm resonated with abandon.

"Hopeless girl! I was going to be gentle!" With a sudden jerk, the Charmancer raised his arms, lifting her into the sky before slamming her down.

She crashed onto the deck with such force the wooden boards cracked open, a piece harpooning her hip. The band around her waist snapped and her leg twisted at an unnatural angle. Her head bounced off the floor, exploding white inside her skull. Pain obscured everything, and she curled into it.

Trelius's arms hinged up again. "Do you need me to wait for you to grow up? To stop being weak and afraid of your strength? Or will you fight like you were meant to? With the power of Fogges magic that flows in your veins?"

He discharged, aiming for the space above her head, and before Beatrix could straighten up, wood chips and splinters showered her, sinking into her skin.

Trelius grinned and resumed his attack, thrashing the planks in front of her with renewed wrath. A rift opened, the wood trembled and gave, free-falling to the belly of the ship in a swirl of debris. The mast tottered and toppled over, the riggings tangled in a mountain of rope, and right and left, the stairs that connected the quarter deck to the main deck collapsed.

Not once did he aim at her.

He's playing with me, Beatrix thought. And she was trapped, skewered to the floor.

Ignoring the throbbing, she lifted herself to her elbows, towing her broken leg like deadweight as she retreated, blood trailing her. The roof of the captain's cabin closed her way to her left, and the Charmancer advanced, pinning her against the railing, dagger in hand. Under the blue of the moon the enchanted blade glimmered, the strange symbols on it beaming like spangles.

She had nowhere to go.

"You already discovered the secret of the Soul," the Charmancer said. "In the right hands, it's the ultimate weapon. Now you will feel its power."

His next hit came for her. Pointing the dagger her way, he mumbled something and discharged. The blow exploded, magnificent and blinding, an outburst that matched the intensity of his hatred.

"Catch, Beatrix!" As if from outer space, William's voice reached her, and she arched back to grab the shield he tossed her. The Charmancer's death sentence hit it on the edge, transferring just enough of the blast to deflect it. The glass disc rattled, the aftershock traveling up Beatrix's arm to her shoulder.

"I warned you not to use it as a weapon," she said when the suspended ashes began to clear.

Trelius shrieked, holding his hand up like a claw. No longer recognizable as a human appendage, it was gnarled, burnt, and smoking, the skin peeling off. The Charmancer looked startled, his eyes wild, while the Soul of Rephait slid down and, as if oiled, skidded across the floor toward the far corner, where it became lodged between the coiled line and the spare chains.

"Give up, Trelius," William said, from farther up on the poop deck. "You're surrounded."

Trelius didn't flinch. With a wave of his good hand, he pitched the book he still held into the fire.

Beatrix's screech cut the night in half, agony slashing her. In the middle of the pyre, the edges of the paper curled while the cover melted, exposing a fan of pages to the flames. As if the fire were an escape rather than a grave, shadowy figures and lacy phantoms poured out, surrounding her in a hazy embrace. A new power rose in her. Not the Furie. A magic deeper and more trustworthy.

It called to her, seeking a way in, asking her acceptance.

Beatrix wasn't aware of her appearance shifting when her story took her in. Her hair unraveled itself out of her bun, and the wavy strands cascaded down her back to be whirled by the wind. Her fingers shone blue, and so did her forehead, marked with the Evermoon. A raven cloak burst out of the sky and enveloped her.

Her left arm winged up, she ascended, lifting above the ship. And then, her new skirt dripping tar, she plunged to try to salvage the book.

What came next happened all together, as if Zweeshen time had folded into parallel paths that were juxtaposed in slow motion after the fact.

Neradola glided in from the bowsprit with such speed she turned blurry and retrieved Leyna's story from the tongues of the pyre. At the same time, Jane hurled a blinding starshell. It burst in front of Trelius, forcing him to stagger back. He tripped into an electric net that William conjured while surfing down a path of hovering discs of his own making.

From above, Beatrix followed the concerted attack, wanting to applaud each maneuver. But she missed the instant the Charmancer freed himself and delivered his worst hit yet. She caught a glimpse of William as he rolled into a mess of limbs and became immobile.

"No!" Pain tore through her, igniting her. The new magic rose, unleashed and brutal.

With a cruel grimace, Trelius smiled. "He's gone too. You're destined to be alone. Rejected. Do you feel the rage yet? Go ahead. Use your power," he said, renewing his attack.

"You won't get away with it." Avoiding his barrage, Beatrix flew down. Even to her ears, her yelling sounded unhinged. She glanced at William's broken body, splayed on the deck, the inside of his chest showing.

At the very last minute, out of intuition or secret knowledge, she drew together the edges of her new cloak and faded into the dark. For a second, she disappeared, suspended somewhere else. Not invisible.

Gone.

Time in this other place didn't exist. She watched the Charmancer as if through a frosted glass. William bleeding on the floor. Jane's perplexed expression. And Neradola taking the chance to drag William's body away.

Then Beatrix saw the Charmancer aim for the ghost.

Desperation seized her. She needed to go back.

The moment she decided where to land, she was there, swirling behind him.

Trelius saw the attack come from the corner of his eye, too late to react. The first blast of her magic crushed his side, mangling him. His torso tore with a jagged cut. Ink and blood spilled onto the wood, and he twisted, careening back toward the stern.

Crumpled down, he crouched against the railing while Beatrix advanced, cornering him the same way he'd done to her.

But he fought back.

The Charmancer's last desperate charge stabbed a hole in her stomach. No pain registered, just as she didn't feel her broken legs as she floated forward. Death running down the tips of her fingers, she towered over him, while Trelius struggled to stand up. In the last moment, he lifted his good palm, as a shield or a call for mercy, she didn't know.

And she didn't care.

Her second blast met him in the chest. It reached him with a magnificent outburst, an explosion of light more impressive than the birth of a star.

His ribs snapped with a series of pops, the muscles shredded, and his mouth let out a wild screech. Trelius's body tumbled and fell overboard.

And as he disappeared into the black water, his handsome face disfigured and half his body ruined, Beatrix could have sworn, she could have vowed on her mother's life, that his lips formed the words *I win.*

Spent and inert, Beatrix's body swirled to the ground like an autumn leaf.

Out of her body and too removed to care, she saw the scene from above. A hazy inertia held her over her own semiconscious shape.

Neradola and Jane ran to the main deck.

William was already there.

"Get me her string pouch! We need her potion," he said, his desperation a chilling thing. "Neradola, heal her like you helped me."

The ghost's face showed pity. "It won't work on her. Her human body's broken. She's not fully taelimn."

"Try!"

William pushed on Beatrix's wound, attempting to stop the hemorrhaging from the gush in her stomach. Her skirt had wrapped around her legs, exposing the area where a piece of wood had pierced through and stuck out like a stake. Blood and ink spilled, mixing with the rubble from the fight.

From above, Beatrix watched it all. And felt nothing.

Ripping the fabric, William tied a piece around her thigh to create a tourniquet. Ink soiled it deep maroon, proving the inadequacy of a physical barrier.

"Stay with me, Be'ah."

That Beatrix heard. And the words ensnared her heart. But the pull of the dark was too strong.

"I've lost her pulse," Neradola said.

Jane returned with the vial from her pouch, holding onto a kicking Emma, who screamed unintelligibly.

Beatrix saw them through a thick fog now.

"It's over. Her Inaechar's gone," a crew member said.

William fulminated him with his stare. "Keep pressure on her side," he told Neradola while he poured the unicorn's potion between Beatrix's lips. They were already turning blue and cold, as the last drops of life trickled out of her. Her chest didn't heave anymore, but William didn't seem to notice. He kept forcing the liquid down and pumping her heart.

When he stopped, Jane couldn't meet his gaze. Until she saw what he planned.

"Don't!" she shouted as he bared his wrist.

He ignored her, bending to kiss Beatrix on the lips.

The dagger cut his flesh like butter, and then it glowed, eager and hungry, the Eisidian markings beaming blue. Murmured by the sea, the forbidden words came out in a whisper that sounded like the Fogges.

"No!" Emma yelled, releasing herself from Jane's grip and throwing her body against William to push him out of the way.

The Soul slipped off his hands, clanking with a flicker under the blue moon before falling through the hole in the deck to the bowels of the ship.

William looked at the girl with murderous eyes.

Just then, a large bird landed on Beatrix's unmoving form. His golden chest gleaming, he extended his wings, cradling her shape in a transparent mesh that grew larger and larger.

Like a madman, William lunged at it, scraping its blue-dotted wings with savagery.

"Let her go," Emma screamed, her tiny fists hitting William's shoulders. "Please."

And as William collapsed to his knees, palms to his face, the bird took Beatrix away, like a portion of carrion. Or a butterfly in a cocoon.

40

WORÐRIÐER

First there were words.

Then, there was light.

Bright, shining sun rays beaming through muslin curtains that puffed out.

Beatrix's thoughts floated, untethered. "You died."

"Almost." William's mouth curved into a slow smile. "Neradola healed me."

He came to her side and kissed her. He tasted of happiness and relief. "Welcome back."

She tried to lift a hand to touch his face. Her body felt heavy and limp. "You're alive." The wonder refused to wear off. When the Charmancer hit him... "Where are we?"

"In the Eisid Naraid. A small town far from the official ports."

Scanning the room, Beatrix noticed the medieval furnishings. A rough table with two chairs, a washbasin, dusty tapestries on whitewashed walls, and braided rugs covering the stone flooring. The Eisid. So she'd made it. Her lips curled up. "How far are we from the temple? We need to return the winged dagger. I revealed it, William. I did it."

"I know." He smiled and gave her a long kiss, bringing her back the rest of the way and warming her body awake. "The temple is half a day's ride from here. You have to get strong before going."

Beatrix assessed herself and winced.

Again, she was in a bedroom, feeling sick. She grimaced, finding the scene repetitive. Gathering every shred of willpower, she sat up, dizziness overpowering her. He held her up, pushed a cushion behind her back. She felt like rolling her eyes. Been there, done that.

"Give it a bit longer," William said. "Now that you've woken, you'll be back to normal in a couple of hours. Your synching is almost complete."

Out of breath, she laid her head back against the pillow.

"What happened? I thought I was dying." She didn't remember much beyond the cold and the sense of peace on the other side of fear. "I think I *did* die."

"Maybe for a bit. Emma and Farisad saved you."

"Is she all right?"

"Downstairs. Worried sick. Has been a redheaded tomboy all week, shouting insults at an invisible Trelius and holding a grudge because she wasn't allowed to join the fight."

"You're here!" came a squeal from the door.

"Right on cue."

Emma hurled herself at Beatrix's neck. "I'm so happy you're all right."

"Thanks to you, I hear."

The girl glanced down, her cheeks burning, and stretched the suspenders of her old-fashioned pants. "William too. He gave you enough of Aestrer's elixir to sustain you between life and death until Farisad carried you here to the Eisid."

"Isn't Farisad that bird? The one I thought I killed?"

Tucking several furs out of the way, Emma sat on the bed and crossed her legs, yogi-style. Her hair framed her face like the petals of a zinnia.

"He is. I told you we could use his help. Farisad came, picked you up, and flew you here. He saved you. It was amazing to watch. Wordriders can carry huge loads, you know."

"A wordrider!" Beatrix's eyes drifted to William. "How did he find us?"

Emma answered instead.

"I called him, of course. I said I would. I've suspected Farisad was a wordrider for a while. How else could he have crossed into Pangea without a bridge? I'd been reaching out to him since we left the Zweeshen, but the Charmancer had him trapped, so he couldn't reply. The moment you defeated Trelius, his magical prison fell apart, and he was free to help us."

"And the rest of you? How did you get here?"

"Farisad came back for us. He wouldn't leave half the job undone."

"I like him already," Beatrix said.

"He's a wonderful friend. The only one I had before you." Emma smiled. And Beatrix thought that as far as little sisters went, Emma was a wonderful choice.

While the girl chatted on, William gazed at Beatrix. For the first time, she felt shy. The way he looked at her made her wish she didn't have bags under her eyes, sticky hair, and the general feeling that a train had run her over.

He left soon after and returned with a tray loaded with herbal tea in pewter tumblers and an assortment of cookies and biscuits. Emma jumped to grab a treat. Beatrix only half heard her, following William as he assembled a plate and offered it to her. He walked away toward a bookcase, brushing her lips on his way with a kiss that wrestled a drunken smile out of Beatrix.

"Ew," Emma said. "That's revolting."

Beatrix grinned as the girl wrinkled her nose.

"I blame it on that. If you guys hadn't been so self-involved, we might have noticed about Trelius."

"I still can't believe he was the Charmancer," Beatrix said. "And that he targeted us. Is he—?"

She didn't want to say it. Beatrix didn't want to believe it. As much as it might have been necessary, she couldn't deal with the fact that she had killed him. Trelius. She didn't want to face that.

"I don't know," William said. And somehow, the uncertainty was worse.

"The Librarian got us into this mess. No surprise there." Even Emma's eyelashes seemed disgusted. "He knew you had the Soul all along, and what it was. From the moment you crossed into the Zweeshen, he put it out you'd brought the weapon with you. And of course, both the Charmancer and the Pioneers wanted it."

"So that's why they tried to kidnap me in the Dust."

"We think so," William said, and his familiar scowl struck Beatrix as endearing. "I don't believe the Pioneers knew about the Soul's disguise. They thought you knew what you had."

"They asked me to release *her.*"

William nodded. "The Soul is the Goddess to them. It's a 'she'."

Beatrix glanced at her wrist. The absence of her Tiffany bracelet felt strange. It had been a constant, as much a part of her as her weird eyes or the whispers. But inside the Evermoon's circle, it had changed, twisted and stretched to reveal its true nature. The winged dagger, the Soul of Rephait. Hidden in plain sight and protected by the strongest of disguise spells. *So much like a story*, she thought.

Then her hand lifted to her heart. Nothing was visible now, but Beatrix had seen the morphline there transform during the spell. No longer just the glyph for the One, the self-eating snake had drawn itself around it. *Together, the Fogged Moon*. Her new true name. She frowned, wishing she understood what that meant.

"Are you listening?" Emma asked.

"You just told me Evenzaar planned to ambush the Charmancer when he came after me," Beatrix said. "Since we escaped the Zweeshen, we foiled his plan."

"Oh, you were paying attention."

Beatrix laughed, levity finally gripping her. They were alive. She was alive. William was safe. Her mother's book had been recovered, and they would return the dagger to the temple.

The letter had been deciphered.

But Beatrix knew her task wasn't done. Too many questions remained. Some, she suspected, would never be satisfied. But some...

"We need to get to the temple of Rephait," she said. Maybe some of the answers awaited there.

"We will." Reaching her side, William folded her hands in his. "You lost a lot of ink and regular blood, too, and were unconscious for over a week. Give it another day."

Unwilling to agree, Beatrix didn't respond. She would see about that. No way she'd come this far to sit around waiting to feel better. Not when she was this close.

"Is Farisad still around? I'd like to thank him." And ask him to take her to the temple without the need to ride.

"He's gone to take your mother's Leeber back to the Zweeshen." Emma's tone turned biting. "We sent a message to Evenzaar to share what happened. He realizes Trelius wasn't really from the Eisid, so you shouldn't fear they'll destroy the Leeber."

Beatrix felt her old disdain for Evenzaar rise back. "So very generous of him."

William laughed. Emma patted her pocket. "He sends his good wishes. I have his letter here somewhere."

"After attempting to get me killed?" Beatrix bit out. "How nice of him. Keep the message. I don't need it." The nerve. "So that's it? Does he expect to be forgiven after all he did? There should be rules against lying and cheating and using people as bait."

"There are rules." William sat on the armchair by the bed that had the imprint of his head. "The Chairman will be eager to enforce them. But the Librarian has agreed to help us. Because you defeated the Charmancer, the council has pardoned you. They've no excuse to pursue taelimns in general, so for now, the alert level has been lowered."

"No more raids," Emma said. "The pageturners have been reopened. Things can go back to normal."

William nodded. "Right now, the Librarian has recovered his place and influence within the council. If he's indicted, however, the Chairman is the next in line. He would rule to the end of Evenzaar's term."

"Why is it sometimes all choices are bad?" Beatrix's instincts prickled with distrust. "The Librarian helped us with the council? That much generosity makes me uncomfortable."

William's mouth arched in a cynical turn. "Self-interest. We know some of his secrets. He didn't run his plan about you by the council. So he has agreed to maintain a pageturner bridge from the Zweeshen to your home. He'll uphold his end as long as it serves him."

"What about the Eisid Naraid? Will the official pageturner be reopened?"

William shook his head. "The council won't budge on that. The land remains sealed. But there's an illicit bridge to the Zweeshen in this very farmhouse."

"Really? The system is broken," Beatrix said, with a rueful voice.

"Spoken like a true Pioneer." A matronly woman pushed into the room. "Please do not let anyone outside of this bedroom hear you say that."

"Beatrix," William said, "meet again your aunt Selda. This is her house."

"Aunt?" Beatrix eyed the woman with the green-marked cheek with interest. "You didn't tell us during our meeting."

"Beatrix! What are you doing?" William stood up, glaring.

She had rolled down the blankets and pushed her legs to the edge of the bed. "I'm getting up. I have spent enough time in bed to last me a lifetime." And her head didn't spin anymore. That was enough.

"Just like your mother," Selda said. "Nobody could stop her once she made up her mind. I'm sorry I couldn't help you back then. I didn't know your intentions."

"Are you really my aunt?"

"Third or fourth cousin, more like it. But yes, we're related. Which is why that bird brought you here." The woman attempted to smile, but it must have been a rare thing because she wasn't good at it, and the green scar that marred her tightened.

"Your feet must be freezing," she said, "standing on that stone barefoot. Emma had Farisad bring your trunks. Come down once you're dressed. We'll get to know each other better while we eat."

Even with William's help, navigating the staircase was a battle. Beads of sweat coated Beatrix's forehead by the time she crash-landed on a chair that was more of a throne, in front of a hearth so tall she could have stood inside it. The room was simple but large. It smelled of the herbs that hung from the exposed beams. A plank table dominated it, and a second fireplace roared opposite where she sat.

She closed her eyes for a moment, breathing hard to recover from the exertion.

"Take this," Jane said, offering her a mug of foaming liquid. "Nice to see you back among the living."

Within ten minutes of gulping the drink, Beatrix's headache had faded, and she felt almost back to normal. "I need that stuff, whatever it is."

Jane's large mouth stretched. "It's only effective here. The magic's linked to the land. That's why it works well on you. A spring of the Goddess Rephait, or so I'm told. Glad it helped."

The rest of the crew drifted in during the next half hour, called in by the promise of dinner. They sat at the long table with varying degrees of welcome, and the absence of Trelius made her shudder. How could she not have noticed?

A shadow swept across her mind when she recalled him throwing her mother's book into the pyre. This world. This place could have become ashes. Gone.

Then she remembered him. Lifting his palm for protection. His victorious smirk while he went down. "Tonight you become like me."

Beatrix shook her head, hoping the movement would erase the somber thoughts.

Trelius. Grandpa. Mom.

A repeating theme of people who'd lied to her about who they were.

And about who she was.

Oh, and Worth. The mysterious uncle who had sent William her way.

"Was Worth a cousin type of uncle too?" Beatrix asked.

William smiled at the question, watching her struggle to carve meat off the bone on her plate. She hadn't realized how famished she was until she'd smelled the food from Selda's kitchen: a feast worthy of royalty.

Selda's finger drew a smoke symbol in front of her face. "Worth, may he rest in peace, was a distant relation of yours. A Pioneer who knew your mother well. He—" Selda hesitated, and Beatrix had the sense she didn't want to sully the memory of the dead.

"He sent William instead of coming himself. Why? Why did he start everything?"

The woman's gaze wandered to William, across the table, as if asking for permission.

"I will tell her if you don't," he said. "Her story."

"*You* started everything," Selda said. "Worth asked for William's help because you called him. When you repeated the 'May the Words' charm, a group of people bound by blood to it was activated. Worth was being followed, so instead of going himself, he sent William, whose magic-print is undetectable. Worth worried the shield your grandfather cast wouldn't outlive him."

Grandpa's cloak. So it wasn't just about protecting Beatrix from the neighbors. But a suspicion wafted into her brain. She stared at Selda, took in her rugged clothes and shining cheek. "How do you know all that?"

"Because I'm one of the people who got your call. I'm a member of a secret lodge led by Leyna Yoru. I traveled to the Zweeshen to fulfill a vow I wish I'd never given."

"What were you supposed to do?"

"My task was to reveal your destination, the temple of Rephait. And to prevent any danger from befalling you while in the Zweeshen. I followed you consistently. Almost got involved in the Dust. But you handled yourself well." She smiled, the mark of the Evermoon crumpling.

"Who else?" William asked.

"I'm not certain." Selda's face flashed with resentment but recovered. "Leyna did not share the full plan with any one of us, and we weren't aware of all the members either. Worth is the only one I'm certain of. Beyond that, I have a suspicion, but I hope I'm wrong." Selda looked away, out of the single window in the room.

"Trelius," Beatrix guessed.

Selda nodded. "Perhaps. Maybe he learned about the Soul through the false intelligence the Librarian put out. Or through his prisoners. Worth wasn't the only one tortured. But I have this feeling... Either way, if part of the lodge, I ignore Trelius's contribution."

The complexity of the plan her mother had set in motion long ago overwhelmed Beatrix. The level of calculation required...

Selda shrugged. "What I know is the vow is unavoidable. Unless dead, the task must be completed."

Beatrix looked down at her plate. This was nothing like she had imagined when she'd found the letter. Even the riddle had never felt this dark. And her understanding of the why was still fractured. Incomplete. More evidence of how little she knew of her mother.

"Leyna always recruited the most powerful," Selda said. She dried her hands on her skirt. Perhaps she'd been sweating too. "You're not done yet, Beatrix. Not until you return the winged dagger to its vessel in the temple. Leyna said the instructions were in the letter. That by the time you reached it, you would have all the tools you'll need. I didn't realize she'd given you a Craxtan until you showed it to me. Like I told you, none of us knew her full plan." Selda fidgeted on her seat. Then took a gulp of liquid from her tankard. "She was something, your mother. And that revelation spell. Brilliant. Without the right decoder, the dagger would be lost forever, the Eisid Naraid with it. Only you would receive the decoders, and you had to have gained control of your magic to cast it. That way, if you were betrayed, you'd be able to defend yourself." Selda stared at her, but Beatrix had the feeling it was not she who Selda saw. "Really something."

41

GODDESS

Beatrix and William left for the Temple of Rephait at dawn the next day. With Beatrix synched and recovered, there was little reason to delay.

As they rode away, she had the chance to see the landscape. Her first impression proved a surprise.

Selda's homestead was staked on a strip of terrain with water visible on both sides. To the east the sound, to the west the sea. Rather than the haven Beatrix had expected, the place felt raw, wind-beaten and rugged, more pirate hideout than quiet retreat.

So this was the Eisid Naraid.

A land of cliffs and bare rock with an ocean so opalescent it couldn't decide on a color and so became all at once: blue, green, turquoise. Her mom's world, Beatrix decided, had a roughness to it. But oh, was it beautiful. And like a corsair, it took a piece of her soul for ransom to ensure she'd forever long to return.

Thinking of her mother made her ache. She still didn't understand the entirety of Leyna's plan. Only that the one-dimensional mother she remembered was instead a complex figure, the portrait of a stranger she'd just begun to piece together.

It took almost eight hours to reach the temple. Riding ended up being less of a torture than Beatrix had feared, and the conversation with William kept her from focusing on her newfound distrust of horses. Ironic, if she considered her choice of guide. *A unicorn*, she thought. Aestrer, who had been there all along just as he'd promised, even if most of the time she hadn't noticed. It made her wonder what else she'd missed.

"I think in time you'll become a wonderful horsewoman," William said.

Beatrix scoffed, then winced, the uneven terrain maltreating her body in creative ways. She'd discovered a whole set of new muscles and doubted she could stand when they finally arrived. "When I imagined visiting this place, I somehow never thought of the horses." She should have—riding and camping and unending horseback quests featured prominently in stories like her mother's.

"You'll get used to it," William said with a smile that hid a slight taunt.

"Easy for you to say." She grimaced. William rode as if one with his animal. He'd probably learned before he could walk, and Beatrix wanted to kick his artisan for succumbing to that cliché. It would have been so much more fun if he'd been clueless, jumping on the saddle like her, a million aches and pains souring the mood.

"If it makes you feel better, I can't drive," he said. "No cars where I live."

"Maybe."

He laughed, and the sound warmed her.

Talking to William was easy, the strain that had existed between them before, gone. In its place lived a thread of understanding that thrilled her. The certainty that she could say whatever she wanted, that he would listen and accept it, at minimum consider her point.

They spoke of everything and anything. Except what had happened with the Charmancer. Or what lay ahead.

The temple huddled on a hill, so they climbed the rocky side at a slow pace. The air was thin and the sky limpid blue, and when they arrived at the top, the old trees of a nearby wood scented the air with eucalyptus.

Beatrix had expected to be overcome. For power to dizzy her, the whispers to scream, or the monster to roar. Instead, the air hung dead. No power coursed through the veins of this land where the ground slept, spent and fallow.

Selda had shared that the temple was in ruins. Still, the sight of the breached perimeter wall, the crumbling columns, and caved-in roofs hit Beatrix with unexpected sadness.

Weeds grew everywhere. A shy white flower bloomed in between the tiles of the front step, and Beatrix recognized it. An Eisidian thistle, like the one from the thimble. She thought of pulling it, then changed her mind. It belonged where it was.

Thriving against all odds.

They dismounted and inspected the temple, hand in hand. It had been a large structure with three wings, of which the foundations and a few walls remained. The abandoned herb garden spread at the back, and the chapel stood to the side, the only structure that had withstood whatever brought down the rest.

"Selda said the winged dagger was kept in a chamber underneath the vestry," Beatrix said.

William scanned the area. "Must be the room past the chapel's missing entry hall. Want to take a look?"

When she hesitated, overcome with what might happen soon, he came close, took a few strands of the hair she'd worn loose, and looped them between his fingers. "Whatever happens, you did your best. You've come far, and you were always true to yourself. I'm proud of you."

She kissed him, because of what he'd said and what he hadn't.

"*Le'arat di, Be'ah.*"

"I do too," she whispered against his neck.

They found the area they sought in better shape than the rest of the buildings, but when they reached the threshold to the chapel, Beatrix set a hand on William's chest. "I'd like to go in alone."

"Are you sure?" He searched her face with penetrating eyes filled with concern.

"I have to. I know Mom's dead. Trelius confirmed it. I saw it myself through her eyes. How she sacrificed herself. And yet—"

"I understand. Good luck," William said. "I'll be out here by the old well if you need me."

Beatrix stepped into the chapel, expecting an echo that never came. Walls of bare stone welcomed her, porous and smudged with mold. The altar and benches, if there had been any, were long gone, and all that remained were the evenly spaced columns supporting a ceiling of Romanesque arches.

The few windows, narrow like archer slits, had no coverings and let in no light. Half a stained-glass panel clung onto one round skylight encrusted with dirt.

She advanced until she could walk no farther, her path hindered by a broken slab the size of a door. And when she bent to inspect the inscriptions carved on it, an indistinct murmuring reached her. It sounded like muffled voices, perhaps distant chanting that came from everywhere at once. She strained her ears, but instead of sound, she detected movement. A stirring in the shadows.

"Who's there?" she asked, on edge.

In answer, fog engulfed her. Black and slithering, it enveloped her, creeping up her legs and leaving behind a sticky numbness that bent her knees down. Her head started to float, irrelevant thoughts popping up. Like how she wished she had straight hair or the memory of hot apple cider in the fall.

Beneath her, the floor collapsed.

She landed on the narrow ledge of a circular hole, a precipice that went down into darkness. She recognized the structure. *Tome II on the Essential Knowledge & History of the Zweeshen* spoke of initiation wells: upside-down towers carved thousands of feet into the ground.

The ledge turned out to be an alcove, one of many interspersed around the well's walls. A beam of light called Beatrix's attention upward to where a blue moon shone, spilling enough glow to cause her morphlines to gleam. It also revealed a pillar in the center of the well. Atop it, the life-size statue of a woman stood on a round platform.

From there, she ruled, beautiful with the cold attractiveness of diamonds and power. Pure white, multiarmed, and loose-haired, she was clothed in a simple tunic, but her posture spoke of a warrior and her expression pulsated with force.

Magic rose from everywhere, the air alive with it. A power that Beatrix had sensed before, which had lifted her when the Inksomner attacked her during the ball. Deep, pure—potent beyond anything she knew.

"The Goddess Rephait." A figure appeared in an alcove across the well's mouth.

Time seemed to stand still. The whole universe shifted.

"Mom!" Beatrix choked on the word—skipped a breath at the sight of the woman standing a hundred feet away from her. Nine years of longing, of missed events, of tears and lost hugs fell on her, reducing the world to tunnel vision and to the sound of her blood pumping in her ears. Mom.

She was here after all. Alive. Beatrix's dreams, the ones she'd believed and the ones she'd never trusted, swirled inside her, emotion pouring through every pore. Desperate, her eyes searched the well's walls for a way to reach her mother, to cross the emptiness that separated them. But the alcoves were un-connected, and she discovered no ledge wide enough to support walking on it.

"Mom," Beatrix said again. "How do I get to you? I can't believe you're here. I thought you died."

Across the precipice, her mother smiled, the long black-blue dress of a priestess flowing around her and shimmering as if inhabited by stars. Her face superimposed itself on the half-forgotten memories Beatrix held. It gained depth, darkening her hair and thickening her waist, softening the hands that had held Beatrix and turned the pages of books. No longer tied to the vision of a child, she saw the strength, the intelligence, and the eyes, huge and fathomless like her own. Tears formed but didn't spill. Stuck between awe and frustration at this distance, the monster awoke. So close and so far. "Mom, how can I cross? Can you come this way?"

But Mom wasn't staring at her. Her gaze had a flatness that was missing in Beatrix's recollections; it remained trapped by a point in the center, where the Goddess reigned.

"Welcome to the sacred temple of Rephait," Mom said, turning Beatrix's way and still, somehow not seeing her. She spoke in the same voice of the stories of Beatrix's childhood, with a lilt that betrayed her original tongue. "You have come. You have fulfilled your destiny like I knew you would. The vessel of the winged dagger is before the Goddess, and the door to the vault lies beyond. Give Rephait her due, and remember who you are when you venture forth. Know that time is not the same here as everywhere else. In the well of the Fogged Moon, one can see past, future, and present in one, infinity in the finite. If one dares."

The Fogged Moon. The word on her heart. Beatrix's brow furrowed. "I don't understand, Mom. I saw what you did in my bedroom at home. You used the dagger to pass your power. How did you survive? And why did you leave?" She hadn't meant to blurt out the last words, and she winced because they sounded pained, tainted with a note that betrayed tears.

Her mother gave her a bland smile. The impassivity of her face heated Beatrix's insides. Anger and disappointment and hurt all mixed into a cauldron and pushed to the surface. "Look at me!" Beatrix screamed. "Why did you steal the Soul? Did you mean to kill your whole world?"

"I do not have the answers you seek," Mom said, and she seemed more of a stranger now. "I'm trapped in this place. I am a memory of another time. A version from before you were born, kept here for the sole purpose of guiding you through."

Inside Beatrix, a volcano erupted. The Furie crept and with it rose the other, unnamed power that had awoken during the fight with the Charmancer and that she still failed to understand. The whispers screamed, and she wanted to shut them up. Tears rolled down, burning her skin. "So you lied! You said we'd reunite. You used me."

The woman offered her a sad smile. "I cannot explain that which I have not yet done. We never met. I'm trapped here without knowledge of what's to come. I know only the past. I cannot look into the Fogged Moon, or leave, or learn, or change. I keep the knowledge of the Order of Rephait forevermore. Your fate is calling, and the winged dagger must return to its rightful place."

Her words floated, and Beatrix's rage whirled and crashed, uncontrolled. Like once before in the Council Rotunda, the limits of her body expanded, magic leaking and fusing into the air around her. "Then explain the past. Tell me about her. All you know. All you've done! I need to understand what drove her, you, to this."

"Only the Fogged Moon has the answers you seek. Face the Goddess and bring forth The End," her mother, or whoever passed for her, said before disappearing.

Beatrix let out a scream, frustration lighting up her skin. She knew her magic hovered beyond it, that it had breached the boundaries of her body and churned around her like an aura of violence. She didn't care. The letter, the riddle, the quest. All the danger, and the pain and all these promises. And in the end, it came down to this. To another lie.

A warmth on her thigh had her looking down. In the scabbard William had tied, the dagger shone blue, its runes and symbols awake. Beatrix breathed deeply. Whatever trickery her mother had used to bring her here, the task to return the Soul of Rephait was a worthy one. To save this land and keep it balanced until the council agreed to lift the sealed sentence.

She had to finish that at least.

"Face the Goddess," the not-truly-Mom had said. But the statue had her back to Beatrix now, and to meet her eye to eye she'd have to cross the empty expanse.

"The fogged moon has the answers," the whispers offered, and understanding, she rummaged in her pouch to pull out the mirror. She angled it up so that the blue moon's light hit her, and she dragged her shirt over her shoulder. The morphline on her heart glowed, then it tingled, vibrated, burned. Her eyes filled with blue, and around Beatrix everything transformed. She saw the well as it used to be. White and gleaming instead of crumbling and cracked.

Before her was a path not a foot wide that led to the statue of the Goddess Rephait. Beatrix stepped onto it, careful not to lose her balance. With precision, without hurrying, she positioned one foot and the next in a straight line. She didn't look down. Didn't bother to consider how deep the emptiness below went. Her breaths came out slow and shallow. By the time she'd reached the wide pedestal on which the Goddess sat, sweat had plastered her curls to her neck and anger had cauterized her hurt into a scar.

The whispers were quiet now, and the monster slept as if drugged.

Beatrix walked around the pedestal to confront the figure. Like the rest of the Goddess, her eyes were white and cold. The marble mouth shaped an endless Mona Lisa smile.

"Where's my real mom?" she asked. "Is she truly dead?"

"Restore what was taken," the Goddess said, through her unmoving lips, and in front of Beatrix appeared a glass amphora the size of a toddler. It ended in a metal top with a slit five inches wide.

"Answer me first," Beatrix said, no patience left.

"You know the response to that. Perhaps you did all along, and now you've come this far. Return what belongs here."

Beatrix swallowed, the pain and the truth she had feared and tried to ignore stuck in her throat. But even if her anger pushed her to leave and to damn the whole quest, the Eisid Naraid was dying. Beatrix didn't need to do this for Leyna. She'd do it because it was right. Because she could help the people in this land.

Without hesitating, Beatrix slid the dagger in the opening. There were no sounds as the Soul began to turn, developing a slow glow while its wings unfolded from the hilt, bleaching the metal to become iridescent.

"Give to receive," the Goddess urged. And even though her eyes didn't change, Beatrix felt the frigid gaze on her and on the mirror she still held.

A large bowl carved with runes materialized. It hovered before her, waiting.

"Give the Goddess her due," her mother's double had said. So Beatrix placed the mirror in what she assumed must be an offering dish. The surface filled with a silver substance, slick like mercury, and when it emptied again, the mirror had disappeared.

A minimal sense of loss registered. She had liked it.

The basin turned clockwise, and one of the Goddess's six arms moved down until the hand curled around the hilt of the dagger.

Since the bowl remained, she searched her pouch for the astrolabe. Selda had said Beatrix would need all decoders.

This time, an arm on the opposite side shifted down to grab the dagger.

Next was the thimble, and again the hand grabbed the Soul's hilt before fading. Yet the offering plate still floated, and Beatrix had used every artifact. Except.

The Alicorn! But although it had deciphered a clue, Aestrer had given it to her, and her mother couldn't have planned for that. Beatrix hesitated to lose it too. It was her only connection to her guide.

But a world is dying, she thought. The lack of the Soul kept destroying this land, and her mother had stolen the artifact she'd sworn to protect.

Taking a deep breath, Beatrix placed the unicorn's gift in the bowl. Another arm curled down over the dagger and disappeared.

Now that she knew all the decoders were needed, she didn't waste time. With only a bit of trepidation, she created the Sphere, contributing a piece of her magic as offering. The Furie felt different this first time she'd called on it again since the fight. More malleable, yet heavier, imbued with edges and twists and depths it didn't have before. So much more complex that she wondered if it was a Furie at all and not something else. If her connection to this world had transformed Beatrix's magic the way it had reinvented her. Changed even her name.

So in a final sacrifice, she wrote her heart morphline over the bowl with her index finger. She watched the foggy smoke solidify and drop into it, to be consumed. This Goddess not only required her magic, Beatrix thought, but a piece of her very soul. A shiver ran through her—trepidation about giving so much without fully understanding what she was doing.

But she had done as asked, and the Goddess's remaining uplifted arms dove down. They settled upon the dagger's hilt.

With a flash of blue, a third eye opened in Rephait's forehead, pushing out a stream of light that bathed the well. The weapon glimmered, its wings lifting it above the amphora, as shimmering dust began pouring from it into the glass vessel. Beatrix's morphlines beamed, projecting the words from her skin onto the walls, pushing blue-tinged shadows into the empty alcoves.

"Which one begins The End?" the Goddess asked. "Say the word to return the Soul."

"What word?" Beatrix watched the symbols around her, but the morphlines had changed since her fight with the Charmancer, and their meaning eluded her.

"You can't yet read," the Goddess said. "There are no shortcuts."

And everything went black.

42

WRAITHS

Beatrix smelled dust. The dust of closed houses and forgotten manuscripts. Of boxes of books at flea markets. She knelt on the stone floor of the chapel, every muscle aching, her lungs scratched raw and her heart as broken as the stone slab on which she knelt.

She had failed again. The artifacts lay spread around her. The dagger back to metal, wings folded into the hilt, all magic once again hidden.

Why hadn't it worked? What had gone wrong?

She didn't know how long she remained there. Her knees hurt at first, then went numb. The sun moved through the skylight and painted colors on her cheek.

Mom had lied. Not only had she lied, she had manipulated Beatrix and used her hopes and love to bring her here. To do what? To atone for her Leyna's mistake, for her crime of stealing the Soul?

I would have done it anyway, just 'cause you asked, Mom.

Beatrix felt tempted to berate herself about failing. Somehow, she couldn't. As she rehashed the whole encounter, a stubborn streak insisted she stop. Because something niggled at her. The version of Mom had spoken of The End. Bring about The End. What did that mean?

The end of what? Beatrix knew the Soul was a weapon, had felt some of its power firsthand. And both the Librarian and Trelius had spoken of dark uses that could be exploited. In light of that knowledge, Rephait's and the fake Mom's words felt ominous.

The pain of losing her mother again was tainted by the anger at the betrayal. And after the discovery of Leyna's secrets, her lies, and her still unclear goals, Beatrix thought the meaning of The End too seemed worthy of inspection. Of caution at the very least.

With a wobble, Beatrix stood up, unsteady but determined, and began to walk around the chapel. Who had told her about the Soul? Selda. The council. The Librarian. None of them reliable sources. What did Beatrix really know about it?

She looked down at the dagger at her feet and picked it up, tracing her fingers along the strange carvings and the metal wings. She knew very little—and she couldn't be sure any of it was the truth.

Watching the runes on the blade, suspicion arose. She wondered how she'd never questioned the whys. She'd wanted to reunite with her mom, so she hadn't considered the implications of what her mother asked. At the beginning, Beatrix hadn't even been aware of what she searched for.

What would have happened if she'd succeeded in returning the dagger? She didn't have a clue.

Evenzaar had talked of a restoration of balance to the land. That was the ceremonial use of the Soul after all. He and Selda had suggested it would save the Eisid Naraid. Now, Beatrix found herself doubting that too. Maybe it was another lie, and the dagger played a role in a scheme bigger than she understood. Bringing forth The End, whatever that might be. The words were in the letter too. Still cryptic. And the Charmancer had mentioned Leyna—even suggested Beatrix was meant to help him. The idea caused a quiver.

She wanted to be wrong, but the Fogges had lurked everywhere down in the well. Their power entwined in all things. Were they evil or not? Was Mom? What about this Goddess who required offerings but gave nothing back?

Beatrix gathered her things and stuffed them in her pouch.

Perhaps it was a good thing that the dagger hadn't worked. After all, she'd been about to perform a spell with an impact she ignored.

Never again, she promised herself.

"Beatrix!" The shout came from the door, and William burst in. "We have to go. An Eisidian raid party is outside."

"Why?"

"You. The dagger. Revenge. I don't care. We have no time left."

"I don't know if—" With a shove, she moved William aside as a wooden beam crashed where he had stood. "Fire!"

They ran, while the roof of the chapel collapsed around them, the stone groaning and crashing.

When they reached the horses, one was missing, so they mounted together. William spurred the bay into the woods, attempting to lose their pursuers. Beatrix caught sight of them in her peripheral vision. A rough mob, armed with swords and bows and axes. At least no guns—but only because they didn't exist in this world.

"We have to reach the pageturner at the farmhouse," William said. "Selda warned us. We have to leave."

"But what of Selda? She went for supplies to the next town. She won't be there to cross through."

William shook his head. "We can't risk it. Those Eisidians will burn down the farm. We must go."

"But I—"

The wraiths disentangled from the trees, as unexpected as any enemy's gift. The mob must have a wizard among them, because someone had called the monsters of this land and set them on Beatrix's scent.

They gathered like a blanket, turning the air cold and the earth hard, and their screeches filled her mind with an oddly familiar voice. Faceless, the creatures gained on them until they were abreast, ready to launch their attack.

They never had a chance.

Beatrix gathered her power and spread it out in a sheet of light, thin and sharp enough to wield like a giant sword. From atop the horse, she released it. Not the Furie but something deadlier. A turning disk that flashed in the dusk and sliced every one of the magical creatures in half.

This time, she smiled.

43

BEATRIX

William and Beatrix had made it to Selda's farmhouse with less than five minutes' lead on their pursuers. Just enough time to cross through into the Zweeshen with the rest of the crew.

They landed in a bare field north of Navarsing University. Nothing there but a leaning shack weathered grey.

The Zweeshen had welcomed them with both pomp and reluctance. A mix of public recognition and suspicious side-eyes.

No one had seen the fight, after all, and many doubted the retellings. Officially, at least, Beatrix was pardoned and in the council's good graces, for what that was worth.

From a fortress to which she'd retreated, Selda had sent them a message two days later. As expected, the mob had burnt down the homestead, the Eisidian bridge with it. Once again, the Eisid Naraid was unreachable, and Selda stuck in it. She didn't seem sad about it. She'd known how it would be—Beatrix felt certain of that.

"Leyna betrayed the Eisid Naraid," the woman, who Beatrix couldn't yet call aunt, had told her before she'd ridden for the temple. "Hatred is rampant, and reason does not work when emotions run high. You're Leyna's daughter. You share her power, and you're in love with a cursed man. You must leave. Neither the Eisid nor the Zweeshen are safe for you. Head back to Pangea. Go home."

Selda's words had slammed Beatrix in the chest.

"I want to get to know the Eisid—and understand where I come from. Pangea is not my home. I don't belong there."

Selda had eyed her with veiled pity. "Do you want to belong? Do you want to be like everyone else? Is that even possible for you?" Selda glanced away. Her voice had grown soft and slow, as if her message was so important it couldn't be pronounced in haste. "There's no belonging, Beatrix. There is only creating your own world and inviting others in. You invent your homeland. Remember that. You only belong to the words."

Beatrix had flinched. Until that moment, she'd always hoped there was a place where she wouldn't be different, where she wouldn't stand out. She had dreamed of a happy ending like the ugly duckling discovering the swans. All she had to do was find it. And even if it took her a lifetime, there had been hope. But Selda's words stabbed her with a poignancy only truth possessed.

"There is no belonging."

Even now, days later, Beatrix felt the desire to cry at the memory, her dearest wish murdered and dismembered. But Selda's message had carried a freeing quality too.

Beatrix didn't have to try to be normal anymore.

Now she glanced to where William stood, talking to Neradola and Jane, his posture relaxed as they bantered in front of the Union. He met her gaze and smiled.

You're wrong, Aunt Selda, Beatrix thought. *I can belong with him.*

A few minutes later, when William joined her to head back to the guesthouse, she had to reassess.

"You know you cannot stay here, right?" he said, echoing her aunt.

"Why not? I'm synched. I can study at Navarsing." What she didn't say: *I can be with you.*

William's jaw tightened, his body tensing. "You're still half taelimn. Even if the council granted you permission to remain here, which they've so far refused to do, we can't ignore the curse."

"I'm not ignoring it. We will search for a counter-curse. We can find a solution for that together." Beatrix had it all planned, and she liked her bright imaginings.

"*I* will search," William said, emphasizing the first word. "I plan to return to my biblioworld and start there."

Pain crushed her more thoroughly than the Charmancer's grip. In all her scenarios, she'd failed to account for this one. A part of her wanted to argue, but she didn't trust herself to do it without tears.

"I think I will see you later." She pivoted on her heels, so he wouldn't see the impact on her face. She had to get away from here.

William touched her arm from behind. "That's not what I meant, Be'ah." He held onto her and gently turned her around.

She stepped away and back. "No, I get it. I do. I assumed wrong. You did your part, and now that the oath's fulfilled, you're free to return home. Selda's my family. Problem solved."

"Come here." When Beatrix didn't move, William trod forward and drew her to him. Landing against his chest, she curled in. "You're so silly sometimes. I told you I'm not leaving you. Like a million times. But you're safer on Pangea. It won't be forever. Only until we figure out a way to lift the curse."

Beatrix lifted her chin to study him. His eyes showed his turmoil, betrayed that he, too, was torn. He lifted a finger to catch a frizzy flyaway and smiled. When their gazes met, they were equally pained.

"We agreed to do things together."

"And we will. But every minute you spend in the Zweeshen brings you closer to death," he said in a voice that was hoarser than usual. "It took less than a year before my mother and sister died after I inherited the curse. I will not lose you too."

He took her hands in his, turning them over to expose her palms. She studied the X-folds on his fingers as he intertwined them with hers. "You understand that, don't you? I can't live always worried you'll die. And that it's my fault."

She did. Beatrix just didn't agree with his solution.

"Then come with me," she said. "The experts believe the curse is neutralized on Pangea. We can just live there." She stared up at him, pushing all she felt through her huge eyes.

"'*Fairly* certain' is what the experts said. Those aren't odds I like. And I have a lead already, in that high fantasy Selda suggested."

"That is the flimsiest of connections. It's like chasing fog."

"It's something to follow. I will check out every path."

"William, there's nothing for me on Earth." They both heard the desperation in her voice.

"Except safety. Please, Be'ah. Do it for me. For a year or so. If after that I can find nothing, I will join you there, and we will figure out what to do next. But I have to try this first."

Inside Beatrix's chest, her heart fluttered with anxiety. With a fear deeper than even what she'd felt in front of the Charmancer.

Going back to Earth.

How was she expected to do it? To return to school as if nothing had happened. Was she supposed to ignore everything? That the Zweeshen existed, and she was half taelimn? She had friends now and had found the most amazing person in the world. Should Beatrix forget about that? Or that she might be more powerful than even she could understand?

His words were soft but determined. "It will go fast, Be'ah. Finish school and stay safe there. In the meantime, we will work together and share all information. You'll study your power, and I will find a way to defeat the curse." He cupped her face and kissed her, and Beatrix's blood stirred and mixed with the ink in her veins as their story wrote itself.

"I had given up," William said. "That's why I ran away and exiled myself. You gave me back the hope that I can do it. You're my courage to try."

"The pageturner's all set," Jane said, waving Beatrix forward a week later. "Whenever you're ready."

Beatrix carried her Eisidian thistle in its protective glass box. She'd found it on her side table the morning after they'd crossed back, the stem in a thin vial.

"As long as you keep it in water, it should live," William had told her. "You can transplant it when you get to Pangea. Who knows, it might thrive there."

She wondered if it was his way of telling her to forget about the Eisid Naraid. Because Beatrix wished to return there. Now that she'd seen the land, the desire to know more was an aching wound. And things weren't over. The Goddess's words nagged at her. "You cannot read yet." As if the deity had expected that to change one day.

The Librarian had promised to support Beatrix's appeal to have the Eisid's sealed status revoked. She wouldn't hold her breath.

"I will work on it," Cassandra had promised. "I will keep you abreast of any developments."

Smiling to Jane, and slinging her Thriller and Adventure backpack over her shoulder, Beatrix strode to the circle marked on the grass with glowing chalk. Her booted feet made no sounds as she walked, and the whispers chattered happily, the breeze from Læsting's river playing with her loose curls.

The pageturner stood in the middle of the circle, dwarfed by the outdoor setting of the sculpture garden. And just like in her bedroom that first time, it settled to a page empty of writing. Halfway up, there was a colophon. But instead of vines, this one depicted a pupilless eye, and inside it, in the place reserved for the anchor of the bridge, there was—a paperclip.

Beatrix had to laugh. "Really?"

Seconds later, the eye stretched, growing into a foggy, swirling oval large enough to let a person through.

This was it then.

She couldn't believe she was going back to Pangea. Earth. Even in her mind, she'd learned to call it the way taelimns did.

Jane stepped forward. "The pageturner builders managed to set the landing close to your original departure date. I think you've lost four weeks or so."

Four weeks! Martin would be ballistic. Beatrix swallowed. Then she straightened her back. She'd dealt with worse.

"Thank you so much, Jane. For everything." On impulse, she hugged her. Then did the same with Cassandra, who stood a bit farther away.

"Don't thank me so much," Neradola said when Beatrix reached her. Her dark mouth stretched in a shy grin. "I'll carry even more guilt around. I didn't always have faith in you."

Beatrix smiled. "I don't blame you. I sometimes didn't have faith in myself."

"I did." Emma's hair shone sparkly blue in her French chignon. She was ecstatic to follow Beatrix and try to convince her artisan to finish her story.

The pirates had long since sailed away, but Elizabeth—as well as Lucy, Matt, and Paul—had wished Beatrix good luck during a banquet the previous night. Even Becca had shown up, as had several others who used to turn their faces at the sight of her.

"Now you're popular," Emma had said, wrinkling her nose.

"Don't worry. It won't go to my head," Beatrix told her. "I know who my friends are."

"It's time." Jane marched toward the pageturner. "This bridge will become inactive after you close it. It will be 'lost' as agreed with the

Librarian, and we'll carry it to a secret location. Remember, both sides are required to reactivate it. Use your crystal communicator when you need to send a message."

Beatrix nodded. She'd discussed this with William, who'd taught her how to use the odd device. Now she turned to stare at him. "You haven't changed your mind."

His face was troubled but determined. He shook his head.

"Come on, people. Move it," Jane said, ushering everyone away.

William walked forward, and his arms tightened around her. "I'll come to you. I promise."

"You should be careful with promises," Beatrix said, a one-sided curl to her lips.

"I am not scared to promise this."

When he kissed her, they both held on.

"I'll come," William said again.

But what if things changed?

As always, he knew her thoughts.

"We'll change together. Would you rather everything had stayed the same? That you hadn't crossed into the Zweeshen?"

Beatrix looked beyond the garden, to the city of Læsting that spread with its potluck of stories and its kaleidoscope of characters. The sounds and scents of a world that was flawed but striving. Full of conflict and wonder and danger. A place that felt too much and fought too much and erupted in drama and flames on the regular. She might be leaving, but this world was hers, and like Emma, she carried it with her.

Beatrix smiled, the whispers a mellow hum in her mind.

"I wouldn't change a thing."

Beatrix found the message on her window thirteen weeks after her return to Earth, his finger-traced words glowing on the frosty glass. From now on, he would always smell of cold.

She made it outside just in time to watch a shrub bloom thistles of ice.

THE ENĐ...

ACKNOWLEDGMENTS

A book is a baby. Birthing it and raising it takes a village. This story wouldn't exist without Chris, the love of my life, my very first reader, and unconditional supporter. Thanks for making sure I didn't stop at bread pudding. To my own William, my son, the sweetest, most encouraging little guy, I hope you will like this story if you ever read it (even if there are no molecules or neutron stars in it). Your cheerleading and insistence on celebrating each milestone helped me get here.

A special thanks to Ana de Vos and Laura Gerke, whose candid and constructive advice pushed me to be better and subtler, and who were patient to the end. And to Lucy Perez, who is the most talented media and marketing person anyone could wish for. To Fa Murphy, my best friend always and sister of choice, for too many things to count, including both super creative visuals, collaterals, webpage… fun, love, and talks long into the night. And to Devan Armstrong, simply for being there on this journey and for calling me out when I need it.

I'm so grateful for my talented critique partners, Megan Flahive and Zoe Erler, for your input and your support, and for your friendship. And to all the other folks who read and took the time to comment, your input made this book better.

Melissa Frain, you saved me. Thanks for telling me when less is more.

To the talented designers who made this book beautiful, I owe you! Micaela Alcaino, who designed a cover I can be proud of, and Fatima Murphy for the gorgeous interior.

My deepest appreciation goes to Fede Sande, he of the perfect eye, for putting together the fantastic trailer and for the developmental advice. And to the whole trailer team: Barbara Cerro and Sergio Faccinetti, Federico Abuaf and Ignacio Cruz, as well as the lovely voice of Annelies Maltha. You guys all rock!

To Reyse Daniels, the reader with the red hair, who reminds me of Beatrix and sounds like I imagined my character would, as well as all the Instagram folks who helped spread the word about Unwritten and shared their excitement for books: THANKS!

I wouldn't be here without my parents, who taught me that spending Sundays sitting each on a couch reading is not only normal but the best family time ever.

To my agents Caroline George and Cyle Young, thank you for believing in me, in this story—and for responding to my texts within seconds. I'd also like to acknowledge and thank the team at Equinopsys Publishing, who worked tirelessly to get this book out to the world.

Finally, a message to all the writers out there dreaming of seeing their books in print: Keep going. Don't give up. Your day will come.

ABOUT THE AUTHOR

Alicia has a weak spot for happy endings and transformative journeys. She spent her teenage years in Argentina and Europe, speaks several languages and loves to travel. Always an eclectic book lover, she's never been cured of reading a bit of everything and is as likely to geek out about Mr. Darcy as Dr. Who.

A big-city girl, she now lives in the Midwest, where she occasionally picks apples and pretends witches exist.

Learn more about Alicia at alicianovo.com, sign up for her newsletter and follow her on social media for the latest news.

Please Review

A book's success is heavily dependent on reviews. If you liked this work, consider leaving a review on Amazon or Goodreads. The author will be forever grateful.

More at alicianovo.com

Alicia J. Novo (Author profile)   authoralicianovo
@aliciajnovo   /aliciajnovo   /aliciajnovo